ABLAZE

SWATI M.H.

Kismet Publishing

ALSO BY SWATI M.H.

<u>Elements of Rapture Series</u>

Adrift

Ascend

(Marriage of Convenience, single-mom, friends to lovers romance)

<u>Feel the Beat Series</u>

My Perfect Remix

(Single-dad, friends-to lovers romance)

My Beautiful Chaos

(Fake-relationship, second chance romance)

<u>My Darling Neighbor</u>

(Enemies to lovers, surprise pregnancy romance)

<u>Fated Love Series</u>

Kismet in the Sky

(Slightly forbidden, second chance, workplace romance)

Surrender to the Stars

(Enemies to lovers, hospital romance)

AUTHOR'S NOTE

Content warning: This book is intended for mature audiences. It deals with themes related to fire/wildfires, and has a scene with on-page domestic violence that may be triggering for some readers.

This book is dedicated to my laptop. Thank you for not breaking, despite the number of times I slammed your screen.

"To be your friend was all I ever wanted; to be your lover was all I ever dreamed."

— VALERIE LOMBARDO

PROLOGUE

Dean- Present Day

Embers dart up into the breeze as the fire crackles like an old staticky radio. The scent of burning logs entangles with the familiar perfume of towering pines and moss tickles my senses. It's a scent that should relax me. A scent I've known for so long, I'd sometimes pretend I could smell it, only to be able to drift off to sleep.

Today, though, it seems foreign, completely wrong and unwelcome. A scent that's captured me in a chokehold so I can neither inhale it nor heave it out.

It's just stuck.

Taking another sip of my beer and placing the bottle in the sand, I strum her favorite melody on my guitar, *Storms* by Fleetwood Mac. The melody she taught me to play at ten when she gifted me my first guitar.

It's still hard to believe she's gone, the earth settling her in, wrapping her in its embrace for eternity. It's hard to believe I won't be exchanging new recipes and old songs, new expressions and old memories with her ever again. The woman I gave my heart to only minutes out of the womb almost forty years ago—the one who raised me right along with my mother. The grandmother who was so much more than her title.

My brother, Darian, throws a small stick into the fire before leaning back on his Adirondack chair and entangling his hand with his wife, Rani's. He might only be mine and Garrett's half-brother, but I'd caution anyone who said we didn't have the same blood running through our veins. He may not have been Grams' grandson, but she treated him just the same. "I still remember when I spent part of a summer here when I was eight or nine. Every single night, your grand-parents would watch WWE religiously."

Garrett chuckles but my chest tightens with memories of Grams and Grandpa exchanging their picks for who'd win the match. No one loved wrestling more than Grams, and no one could convince her it wasn't real.

I still remember how she'd have dinner prepared extra early on nights when her favorite wrestlers were going to be on. Garrett and I spent so many of our childhood summers at this lake house, sitting knees-crossed on the couch, snuggled on either side of her. We'd cheer and boo right along with Grams, even though we knew the whole match was rigged.

"She was a kooky little thing." I try to chuckle, but it comes out all wrong with a choked inhale. I'm just about to take another swig of my beer to soothe the sand inside my throat when her soft hand grasps mine.

Her. The fucking enigma I've spent nine years of my life trying to crack.

The woman who packed up her things and got ready to leave without so much as a discussion with me—the man she claims to be her best friend. The woman who set my heart ablaze the same day she quelled the pyre. The woman who changed me day-by-fucking-day, just to unravel me in one fucking night.

A night she told me to forget, to chalk it up as a blip in

our history, a moment—or rather, *six fucking hours*—of lowered inhibitions and bad decisions. A night that's replaced the scent of burning logs and pine that used to help me drift off to sleep. Because if I can't have the source, then the memories will have to suffice.

I pull my hand from her grasp, blinking back tears.

Loss. The fucking *loss* of it all.

My two best friends. A woman I just buried, and a woman whose touch I can't bury, no matter how hard I try.

We've shared a room together for the past four days we've been at Grams's lake house, and even though I knew we should talk—something that used to be as natural as blinking or breathing—I shut her down each time.

Because she tried. She tried to talk to me, to tell me whatever her fucked-up reasoning was for not being back home—with me—but I couldn't listen to the same bullshit again. So, aside from the times she held me in her arms, letting me mourn my grandmother while soothing me with her soft whispers well into the morning, we haven't spoken a single word.

Because, really, there's nothing to say, is there?

How could there be when she said it all so clearly that day?

Rani yawns before telling us she'll see us in the morning when we're all ready to head back home, and Darian follows after her like the lovesick puppy he is. Meanwhile, Garrett and Bella whisper God knows what to each other across from me on the other side of the fire. My twin brother might have married the woman sitting in his lap on a drunken whim, but the only thing I've seen him drunk on over the past four years is her.

Mala shifts in her chair before standing, her bare legs covered with goosebumps. No matter what the weather is, the woman has always had a vendetta against pants. She pulls the sleeves of her oversized sweatshirt over her hands and wraps her arms around her chest. "I think I'm going to take a little stroll around the beach."

I watch her leave as the breeze picks up her shiny black hair—hair that looks and feels like spun silk. Her sneakered feet make small indentations in the sand as her hips sway with a lilt of their own.

Garrett and I exchange a glance, a silent message spoken and heard only by us. One that urges me to stop being the idiot he thinks I'm being.

But he has no clue. No one does.

It's not that I can't tell him—hell, he and Darian would be the first ones I'd tell if I committed murder and hid the body—but some fears can't be voiced. Some fears are for you to grapple with all on your own.

I pluck the guitar strings a few more times before the weight of the breeze threatens to snuff the oxygen inside my lungs. Placing my guitar on the sand, I lean it against my chair and give my brother a nod before running after her.

The stars twinkle like a dusting of diamonds in the moonlit sky, the ripples in the lake overpowering the crackles of the fire behind me.

It doesn't take long to find her, sitting on the beach with her bare knees drawn close to her chest, wrapped inside her covered arms like a blanket. I know she's cold, but for as long as I've known her, she's preferred it that way, claiming heat has always felt too suffocating to her.

I suppose I can't blame her, especially not when you've lived through the horror she's experienced.

As if she can feel me, she turns to watch me walk toward her before a wisp of hair gets caught between her lips and she pulls it off to tuck it behind her ear, darting her gaze away from mine.

"You promised you wouldn't run away," I start. "You promised to–"

"No, Dean." She shuffles to her feet quicker than I would have thought possible given how cold she looked. "*You* fucking promised. You promised nothing would change. You promised that night wouldn't affect us. Remember that? But it did, didn't it? It changed *everything*! And all the years prior to that, when you told me you couldn't, *wouldn't* mess up what we have . . . or should I say, what we *had*?" She points between us. "What happened to that promise, huh?" She looks over at the lake with rage in her eyes. "I waited for you. Eight fucking years I stood on the sidelines, waiting for you . . ."

"Yeah?" I yell. "As if I fucking *didn't*? You think you're the only one who had front-row seats to watch a show you never wanted to see?"

She takes a step closer, her nostrils flaring. "So why didn't you say anything when you had the chance? Why wait until I was finally moving on?"

"Moving on? Is that what you call it, *sprinkles*?" I chuckle mirthlessly. "Because the way I see it, you weren't moving on; you were *running*."

Her eyes sharpen on me. "Yeah, okay, I *was* running. But have you taken even one moment to consider why? Or is that too hard for you to do, given your brick of a brain?" She seethes. "I was running because I was fucking tired. Tired of waiting, tired of wanting and wishing–"

I heave in a shaky breath, letting the cold air compress my lungs as I hang on her words for dear life. Words she's cut off, like if she says them, they'll float away with the wind. "Wishing for what?"

She shakes her head, wiping her cheek with the sleeve of her sweatshirt, but the moment she does, another tear falls to replace it. "It doesn't matter." She chuckles hoarsely. "Why would it matter? I'm not the one who can make it matter. I never have been."

I close the distance between us, rounding my palms over her biceps and making her look up at me. "Wishing for what, Mala? *Say it.*"

She sniffles, her tear-stained cheeks shining under the silvery effulgence of the night. Her frown intensifies as she whispers, "For it to be me."

Part One

THE PAST

Theme Song: "You Belong With Me" by Taylor Swift

Chapter One

DEAN

Nine Years Ago

I SWING THE CLAPPER OF THE BELL AGAINST THE LIP, making it ring a few times. "Lunch!" I call up the stairs, alerting my crew. "Come and get your gourmet meal of burgers and fries, ladies and gentlemen."

It was mine and Baron's turn to prep and make lunch today, but with the sheer number of dispatch calls we've had over the past forty-something hours, I'm bone tired. I don't know if it's the unexpected rain over the past week or the alignment of the stars, but it feels like every Tom, Dick, and Henrietta decided to have an emergency.

And while I can hope that the next—I gaze up at the clock on the kitchen wall—four hours of my shift are less exciting than the past forty-four hours have been, I won't hold my breath in my possibly charred lungs.

A stampede of footsteps resounds over the stairs as the rest of the crew at Tahoe Valley Fire Station come barreling down to the kitchen.

"Damn, you both have outdone yourselves today!" Malcolm grins, coming behind me and Baron, giving our shoulders a squeeze. "I love when you make burgers from scratch, Dean. Thanks, brothers!"

I tilt my head toward the salad and array of dressings on the counter, knowing most of the crew, besides Coolidge and Samantha, won't touch it. "Make sure to get your daily quota of roughage in. You know how it goes; put a little roughage in, and it won't be so rough coming out." I wink before grabbing a plate from the cabinet.

Samantha wrinkles her nose before picking out a few olives from her plate and putting them back into the salad bowl. "Anyone know where Rohan is? I thought he was on shift today."

Malcolm and I exchange a glance before I fill my glass from the tap. Samantha joined our fire department two weeks ago, and while she may think she hides it well, it's clear she's developed a crush on one of my best friends.

Malcolm clears his throat. "He took a couple of days off to help his little sister move into her new apartment. He'll be on shift tomorrow."

Samantha nods, but I don't miss the slump in her shoulders.

"She ain't that little anymore from what I could tell." Baron winks at Malcolm. "They were on a video call a few days ago, and *oof!*" Baron blows out some air from between his lips. "She ain't the kid Rohan makes her out to be. The girl's a knockout!"

I shake my head, holding in my response. Telling these guys that Rohan's little sister is so off-limits she should be considered government-classified will just fall on deaf ears. Over the past two weeks he's known Mala was going to move back to Tahoe, Rohan has made it abundantly clear that unless we're ready to part with the appendage between our legs, we are to keep our eyes above her neck.

I've only seen pictures of her over the two years I've known the guy who has become one of my closest friends, and yeah, these other horny assholes aren't wrong—she's adorable as fuck. But I'm entirely too attached to my dick to open my mouth.

I don't blame him for being overprotective. When you've raised your little sister practically on your own since she was ten, I'd assume you'd think of her more like your own child rather than a sibling.

I'm just about to pull out my chair to sit next to the others, half-heartedly nodding to the play-by-play Coolidge is now giving the guys about his kid's recent basketball game, when the alarm sounds and the familiar radio announcement comes through the speakers.

Well, hell. So much for hoping the last four hours of my shift would be action-free.

"Calling Engine One, Engine Two, Battalion One, Ladder One, and Medic Eight. There's a residential fire at four-two Sugarfest Avenue, South Lake Tahoe."

I suppose lunch isn't in the cards today.

As with every emergency, everyone at the table shoots into action. Before anything more is said, we're leaving our meals where they are, hustling back up the stairs and getting our gear. And even though my stomach isn't happy about taking a backseat, this is what we all live for.

It's what we sometimes die for, too.

A truth I'm reminded of every time I visit my eighteen-month-old goddaughter.

Less than two minutes later, we're pulling onto the street, sirens blaring, toward the address of the fire. Additional information coming in through the radio lets us know that the woman who reported the fire has evacuated the house safely, along with a couple of pets.

Within five minutes, my crew and I are pulling up to the older American-craftsman style home with smoke floating out of one of the side windows. A woman is huddled on the front lawn, sitting next to a cage with a few parakeets, and holding a small white dog that looks like it's trying to escape to anywhere but here.

Me and Coolidge grab our equipment while Malcolm and Samantha rush toward the woman to ensure she's okay.

Malcolm shouts over at us, "Kitchen fire. Looks like it originated in the oven."

Me and my team are inside in the next minute. Thankfully, the smoke isn't terrible, but there's an active fire still inside one of the ovens, along with a fire extinguisher sitting on a countertop. The other oven is turned off, but there is smoke inside it as well. From the looks of it, she tried to put out the fire herself, but it relit so she left and called 9-1-1.

After extinguishing the fire, verifying that there are no other people inside the house, and quickly assessing the damage—two ovens and the cabinets near them—we head back outside and take off our breathing apparatus.

Malcolm squeezes the woman's shoulder in a comforting way, but I can't see her face hidden behind him. "You alright?"

"Yeah, I'm fine. But, ugh," she groans, putting the white dog on the ground next to her before rising up. Her hand clasps the end of its leash "Can you not tell my brother about this? He literally just left my apartment a few hours ago after helping me move all day."

Malcolm throws his thumb back toward the house with the oven fire. "So, this isn't your house?"

"No. I came here to pet-sit for my neighbor and thought I'd make some treats . . ."

I pick up one of the said treats from the pan I'm holding. They're a little crispy, but I don't believe in wasting food. If it doesn't have visible mold, it's edible. I walk toward Malcolm and the woman still hidden from my view, examining the design.

It's a unique spin on a rocket, but not exactly how I would have constructed it. She's clearly a novice at the fine art of baking and design. Everyone knows a rocket shouldn't have a bulbous tip. And the protrusions under it don't look like the swirls of fume she was going for. Instead, they just look like a couple of small circles where there should have been billowy-looking smoke.

It would be aerodynamically inaccurate and physically impossible to get something like this off the ground. Clearly, the girl's not an aerospace engineer.

Still, my stomach begs me not to be a snob. Beggars can't be choosers, and right now is not the time to be the latter. I take a bite off the end, crunching it between my molars.

It's an interesting taste—a little bland and flaxy—but again, it beats not eating anything at all. Still, this woman has her work cut out for her. Hopefully, she's not considering opening a bakery anytime soon.

"You mean, *these* rocket ship treats?" I ask Malcolm's back.

He turns and my eyes trail up the woman now in view—tan and toned bare legs under denim shorts, with an oversized Iowa University sweatshirt hiding any curves she might have underneath.

I stop chewing for a moment as recognition flashes inside my irises. Dark eyes—the same color as her brother's—under a thicket of dark lashes and shapely brows observe me. I get the sense she might have put together who I am, too.

She covers her mouth with the tips of her fingers, and her gaze travels from the half-eaten cookie in my hand to the tray of others.

"No," she retorts, visibly containing her giggle. The leashed white dog near her ankles yips as if mocking me alongside her. "Those *penis*-shaped *dog* treats."

Malcolm pinches the bridge of his nose. "Seriously, Dean, only *you* would think a penis was a rocket."

The side of my mouth lifts before I pop the rest of the penis rocket into my mouth. It's still disgusting, but it's better than nothing. "Well, I *do* happen to have a rocket for a penis."

Chapter Two

MALA

"For the record, this is *not* what a penis looks like, nor is it what it should taste like," proclaims the fireman holding my burned tray of penis-shaped dog treats in his hand and his helmet under his arm, popping yet another cookie into his mouth.

Just from his shoulder-length, dirty-blond hair currently lifting in the breeze and his airy blue eyes—reminiscent of skylight—this has to be my brother's best friend, Dean. And though I've never seen a picture, since my brother thinks sending me photographs of old, decrepit buildings is more fascinating than pictures of his friends, I'm pretty confident in my assessment based on Rohan's description of him.

The guy I assume is Dean runs his fingers through his hair, pushing his strands back. A cocky smile plays on his lips, and I'm momentarily distracted before my brows dip and I snatch the tray from his hands.

"Oh, come on." I tilt my head to the side. "You're just jealous because yours is smaller and more unpalatable than these."

His eyes flash and his mouth opens with a response

when the other fireman—the handsome black man named Malcolm, who's been standing with me while the others were inside extinguishing the fire—gives him a subtle shake of his head.

Ah, I see my big brother has already doled out threats like Halloween candy. I'm sure he's let them know they'll be shy of a few digits if they even dare breathe in my direction.

"Mala, this is one of our lieutenant firefighters, Dean," Malcolm says before regarding the Adonis now pulling his hair into a messy half-bun. "Dean, this is Rohan's little sister, Mala."

I jut out my hand, balancing the tray in my other and he takes it in his rather large bear paw. "Mala Sharma, glad to finally meet you. My brother has said a lot about you." Disconnecting our hands, I study the house before looking from Malcolm to Dean. "Thank you for getting here so quickly. I tried to put the fire out myself like Rohan taught me, but it seemed to relight as soon as I did."

I try to blink back the vision of the inside of the oven igniting into flames, but it just mingles with another vision of a much more horrific scene. A scene I can't erase, no matter how hard I try.

I swallow against the nerves caught in my throat, putting on a braver face than I really feel inside before reciting my mantra.

You're fine. You're alive and safe. Just count your blessings and put one foot in front of the other.

Malcolm starts to say something when another firefighter walks over to where we're standing. "Looks like an oven malfunction from what I can tell. We're contacting the owners now."

"I called them after I called 9-1-1 and told them what happened," I offer. "They were going to a relative's house in San Francisco for the weekend, but they're on their way back now. I feel bad for ruining their trip, but I had no idea something like this would happen."

"This seems like a random electrical issue," Malcolm counters. "You couldn't have known."

"So, you were going to stay here while the owners were out of town?" Dean asks, reaching for another cookie from the tray, which I promptly pull away.

For a guy who keeps making faces while eating them, he sure likes them a lot.

"Yeah, just for the weekend. Can I still stay here until the owners get back, or do you need me to take the animals to my place?" The parakeets chirp inside their cage. I look down at Marigold, who seems busy panting and observing all the commotion around us with firemen putting their equipment back in the truck and neighbors coming out onto their front porches to watch.

"You should be able to stay," Malcolm says, getting an agreeable nod from the other fireman who'd joined us. "We've cut the power to the oven. I'm sure the owners will be in touch with their insurance company to get the repairs started."

I nod. "That's good. I didn't think I did anything wrong when I was baking those cookies . . .."

Dean shakes his head. "You didn't. This would have happened even if they'd started that oven." He eyes the tray in my hands. "So, why were you making dog treats, anyway? For that overgrown rat-looking thing right there?"

I gasp, lowering myself down and covering Marigold's ears before glaring at the broad-shouldered and all-too-attractive blond man with zero taste in dogs or cookies.

"Marigold does *not* look like a rat!" I hiss as quietly as possible, getting a snicker from the firemen standing around me. "She is a show dog, and her breeders wanted me to make my gourmet cookies for her next breeding party."

Dean's brows furrow, though I should add that the same look is mimicked by everyone standing around me. "What the fuck is a breeding party?"

I offer a penis cookie to Marigold, who sniffs it with enthusiasm but turns her nose up in the air, rejecting it like it's trash. Even she won't eat a burned cookie, no matter how beautiful the penis shape turned out.

"Her owners are also breeders, and they're trying to make her go into heat. These special cookies were supposed to help her–"

"Wait a damn minute." Dean lifts a hand, stopping me from continuing as his colleagues bowl over, hooting with laughter. "Are you telling me that *those* cookies–the ones I just ate, and that taste like garbage, by the way–"

I get up on my feet, taking a step in his direction and square my shoulders. "Hey! May I remind you that I didn't tell you to eat them? May I also remind you that we all saw you reach for more? How dare you call them–"

"Are you telling me that I ate some shit that's going to make me, I don't know . . . go into *heat*? Oh, God!" He bends at his waist, gagging over the grass. "I think I'm going to be sick. What the fuck, woman? Why didn't you say something?"

"Dude." Malcolm rolls with laughter as a tear comes out the corner of his eye. "I feel like I can see breasts protruding through your gear–"

Dean shoves him, shaking his head. "Shut up, jackass! I'm fucking serious over here."

He gives me a disdainful look, and I can't help the giggle that rushes out of me. My eyes water and even though the man in front of me looks like he's one thought away from strangling me, I can't help but want him to stick around and make me laugh some more.

"You let me eat breeding cookies!? Are humans even

allowed to eat them? What the fuck is going to happen to me?"

I shrug, trying to suppress another giggle, but I can feel my shoulders shake. "I mean, as long as you didn't eat more than two, you should be fine."

Dean's eyes widen, and I have to work hard to ignore the howl of laughter from the other firemen. "*Two?* I ate half that fucking tray by the time I walked out here!"

I pretend to wince. "Jesus. Well, you should be vigilant of the symptoms then, and uh . . . potentially see a veterinarian if you find your genitalia is tingling," the firemen all burst out with renewed laughter, "or your nipples start lactating—"

Dean's jaw clenches as he looks around at all of us. "I'm out of here. You guys are the biggest assholes."

I giggle before realizing we need to discuss a very important point. "Wait!" I stop the guys before they all huddle back into the firetruck, making my eyes as doe-like as possible. "Can you please not tell my brother about this? It's literally my second day back in Tahoe, and he'll flip his lid if he finds out. You know how protective he is. If he finds out I almost burned someone's kitchen down, he's going to insist I move in with him or something."

Dean points his index at me. "Oh, you can bet I'm going to tell him about this. You let me eat goddamn hormone dog treats that will apparently make my nipples milk . . ." He takes a breath, trying to steady his emotions, and I have to suck in my cheeks to keep my face straight. "God, I'm so fucking scared—"

Dean glares at me as I shake with a fit of laughter.

"You think this is funny? I am so going to tell Rohan about this." He shoots another scathing look at me over his shoulder, and even though he thinks he looks menacing, it's all I can do to hold back my laugh.

I chase after them, leaving the tray on the ground next to

the parakeets before pulling Marigold's leash along with me. "Dean, please!" I blink rapidly and make a pouty face. "Please don't tell him. He's going to go all protective bear on me."

"No." He pulls the door to the firetruck open as the other guys jump in.

"Do you—" I try to keep my expression as serious as possible, hoping to stall him. "Do you feel emotionally unbalanced at all? Irritable, sensitive . . . *emotional?* It's just that those are always the first symptoms . . ."

Dean glares at me, but his lips twitch with the smile he's trying to suppress. "I don't like you."

"Duly noted," I say agreeably. Locking my fingers together in a prayer pose, I try again. "Please, can you not tell Rohan about this?"

Dean dashes his gaze away, seeming to think before looking back at me. "Do you know how to make cookies for humans?"

I nod vigorously. "I can make all sorts of stuff. Macadamia nut, snickerdoodle, chocolate-chunk. I even have icing and sprinkles, so just pick your favorite flavor and I'll have you covered."

He lifts his chin. "Sprinkles, huh?"

I shrug. "Who doesn't like sprinkles?"

"Nobody." His eyes stay on me before his teeth drag over his bottom lip. "Fine. We'll keep our mouths shut if you bring over a batch of your favorites to the station tomorrow."

I clap, making Marigold bark. "Deal! I can bake them at my apartment tonight."

"Wait." Dean's shoulders slump. "I don't have a shift until the day after."

"Okay, then I'll bring yours over to your house after I drop some at the station. It's the least I can do for all you guys."

He eyes me suspiciously. "You don't know where I live."

"I'm a resourceful girl." I shrug. "I'll find out."

He squints at me like if he looks hard enough, he'll make all my puzzle pieces fit together. "How do I know you won't lace them with other shit?"

I make a hand sign that's meant to be Scout's honor, but since I was never a scout, I'm pretty sure it just looks like I'm throwing up a gang sign. "You have my word and the honor of a lifetime Girl Scout."

Dean's eyes get narrower before he turns and gets into the fire truck. "See you tomorrow, *sprinkles*."

Chapter Three

MALA

I PULL UP TO A MODEST-SIZED, RANCH-STYLE HOME WITH majestic redwood trees flanking the front corners of a manicured lawn, before sneezing, blessing myself, and rolling up my windows. The idea of driving with the windows down on a lovely spring day is always better than the actual experience since the idea never accounts for pollen.

I don't know how I managed to convince Rohan to give me Dean's address without seeming suspicious, but my story about delivering freshly made cookies to his best friend rather than having him come back to a bunch of crumbs the next day seemed to work.

So, here I am, walking up the paved path toward Dean's door, delivering my end of the bargain.

My attention is diverted when a little girl of maybe eight or nine comes out of the neighboring house, skipping down her patio steps. Her mother's laughter follows behind her as she sits atop a swing on the patio to watch her daughter play in the yard. Her dark eyes connect with mine and she raises a hand to wave, completely oblivious to the constriction in my lungs.

I give her a tight smile and nod before blinking back memories that have never stayed at bay but terrorize me even more whenever I'm back home.

It's one of the reasons I did everything in my power to get an out-of-state scholarship and leave as soon as the first university accepted me. For the first time in eight years since that fateful day, I felt like I could finally breathe. Breathe in different air—one that didn't linger with the scent of burning walls or carry the wails as flesh burned.

There was no Tahoe in that air at all.

And while I filled my lungs with a new source of oxygen for the four years I was in Iowa, there was no denying the pull of home.

There was no denying the fact that I missed my big brother, even if he was the most overbearing and suffocating man on the planet at times. I missed him with a longing I couldn't control because it wasn't fair that he had to be here all alone—spinning inside the same record of memories—while I "took a break," knowing full-well I was just running.

Straightening my back and pulling the neck of my sweatshirt up, I rap my knuckles on the door. I don't know which outcome I want more—for Dean to be home so I can hand-deliver the three different flavors of cookies I made last night, or for the door to go unanswered so I can leave them outside with the excuse that I had tried.

The decision is made for me when the door swings open, and a bare chest with droplets of water sprinkled across it, like dew on a pane of glass, steals my gaze, along with the last of the air in my lungs.

My eyes dip down to the fluffy white towel secured over indecently carved abs and a prominent V pointing toward a nether-region I shall *nether* think about. My eyes crawl back up, and I wish I could count each one of those droplets on his expansive chest, before landing on his lips.

Gotta go a little higher, Mala.

Right. Before landing on his . . . eyes.

Ugh, it's no use. Those blue eyes are just as alluring as those lips.

"H-hi," I stutter, shoving the brown bag I'm holding with three plates of cookies toward his bare chest like they might explode in my hands if I don't. "These are for you."

"Whoa!" Dean quickly catches the bag before it falls. "Uh, hi!"

"Hi." I blink, feeling awkward, before looking to my left and then my right, not finding anything but a large spider web covering a part of the panel window next to his door. I try not to flinch at the sight of a rather large spider perching patiently on its woven home, awaiting an unsuspecting meal. I point at it discreetly with my eyes, hoping the creepy thing doesn't decide to fling itself in my direction. "Um . . . there's a huge spider on your window."

Dean leans out the door, and I swing my shoulder back to give him space. A droplet of water trails down his shoulder, curving around his nipple, and I quickly avert my eyes. There's a small part of me that wants to lean in and take a whiff of the shampoo he used to wash his currently wet locks, but I slap that trampy, ho part of my brain and tell her to get her shit under control. *Jesus.*

"Yeah, that's Cassanova. He's cool, really friendly. He just does his thing and chills most of the day. Sometimes he'll catch a grasshopper, and that's pretty cool to watch."

"He sounds lovely," I deadpan.

Dean watches me scoot over to make more room between me and the gargantuan spider. I swear, the thing has gotten larger in the last five seconds. "Want to hold him?"

"Um, no, thanks. Maybe another time." Or, you know, *never.* "Anyway, I just wanted to drop off those cookies and apologize for letting you eat hormonal dog treats yesterday."

I purse my lips, trying to fend off the image of Dean gagging. "I, uh, hope you didn't–" I wave over his barely covered form. "I hope you didn't have an estrogen surge or anything."

Dean tilts his head, his lips twitching with a need to smile. "Yeah. Thanks for your overwhelming concern."

"I feel like your voice sounds higher today."

Dean narrows his gaze again, but this time there's no mistaking the smile almost in full view. "Shut it, *sprinkles*. I was ninety-nine percent sure there was nothing harmful in those cookies."

I shrug. "But that one percent of doubt makes all the difference, doesn't it?"

He opens the bag in his hands, seeming pleased. "That one percent is why people climb dangerous mountains, jump off cliffs, or hell, even fall in love. For the sheer chance that they might just make it. Most don't live to tell the tale, but I suppose I'll take this small risk."

Interesting.

"You guys take bigger risks every day at work."

He smiles, and I get the feeling he's about to say something else when he changes course. "Do you want to come inside? I don't mind warming a couple of these bad boys up and getting to know my best friend's little sister over milk and cookies." He winks and it causes a strange uptick in my heartbeat.

"Uh . . ." I look to my right again and jump. *Dammit! Why do I keep looking in the direction of the human-sized spider?* I am positive his beady little eyes are scanning me from head to toe. I swear, I saw him lick his lips hungrily, too. I shiver at the thought before turning back to Dean. "I don't know–"

"Oh, come on. We started off on the wrong foot yesterday since you tried to turn me into a woman. It's only fair we start over. Rohan's one of my best buds, and now that you're here, we're bound to run into each other, so we might as well play nice."

I eye the bag in his hands. "I'm pretty sure baking three dozen cookies for you *was* me playing nice."

He raises a brow. "No. *These* were in exchange for my silence."

I sigh, not missing his veiled threat. "Fine. Why the hell not?"

Dean moves out of the way as I step inside. "Who knows? We may even end up braiding each other's hair." He tugs on the end of my hair as if to make the point.

I roll my eyes. "Doubtful. And also, none of that is going to happen if you don't get some clothes on."

He smirks, leaning into my ear and a flurry of goosebumps rush over my skin. "Is my sculpted bod putting you on edge, *sprinkles?*"

I snort. "Don't flatter yourself. The only thing putting me on edge is that hand towel wrapped around your torso. You might want to consider investing in something bigger."

He wiggles his brows. "You're lucky I'm even covering myself at all, considering I usually answer my door in the nude when I'm not expecting company."

I smack his bicep with the back of my hand, questioning how I got so comfortable in the matter of moments with the guy. I get the feeling *this*–his easy flirtatious banter and that crooked smile–isn't out of character for him. "Go put on some real clothes, Sparky."

Dean chuckles and I follow him into his living room before he goes down the hall, disappearing into what I assume is his bedroom. I'm still smiling as I take in my surroundings, breathing in the scent of sandalwood and soap. It's a scent that immediately relaxes me, given my nerves were all over the place just minutes ago when I knocked on his door.

Or maybe it's not the scent at all, but the man who owns this home.

He's refreshingly charismatic. In the little time I've known him, he's managed to make me laugh more than I have in a long time. The guy seems to have a way of making people feel comfortable around him, as if they've known him forever. I can't imagine even the most uptight person staying wound up around him for too long.

I swivel my gaze around his space. Though it's sparsely decorated—with modern gray and white furniture and a few tasteful paintings on the walls—his home is astoundingly bright and airy, with natural light flooding the space through every uncovered window.

I walk over to the console table behind the sofa, picking up a picture frame of Dean with two other men—boys, really. The picture seems to have been taken when they were teenagers, but I can immediately spot Dean based on his longer hair and the ever-present mischievous smirk. The boy standing next to him looks quite like him, with the same blond hair—though shorter—and almost the same shade of blue eyes. They both seem to be teasing the third, younger boy in front of them, with Dean ruffling his dark hair and the other laughing.

Everything about the picture warms me from the inside out—from their thin bare chests, to their colorful swimming trunks, to the affection flowing in their eyes for each other.

"Those are my brothers, Garrett and Darian."

I look up to find Dean now dressed in low-hung jeans and a flannel shirt. He's already a good foot taller than me—maybe more—but he looks even more imposing with the way his waist is tapered and how his jeans outline his long legs. His hair is in a semi-neat half-bun at the top of his head, but a strand is still tucked behind his ear. With it off his face, the focus is stolen by his sharp azure eyes and the scruff outlining his defined jaw.

My gaze snags on his bare and corded forearm, flexing under his rolled-up sleeve as he reaches for the frame next to the one I have in my hand. It has me momentarily forgetting why I'm standing here in the first place.

"And this is the three of us in Vegas last year with your brother." He tilts the frame, and I notice the now much older versions of the three boys in the picture, along with my brother. "We decided we'd try to make it a yearly thing if we could."

"I didn't realize Rohan knew your brothers, too."

Dean puts the frame back down. "This was from their first meeting, actually. They loved him."

I smile, knowing he's likely not exaggerating. My brother has a tendency to be the life of the party—something he and Dean seem to share—and can easily have people hanging on his every word. And, unlike me, Rohan has found ways to make peace with our past. Sure, he's more protective of me, probably because of what happened, but he's found a way to let go. Unfortunately, letting go isn't even an option for me. Probably because I lived it, saw it . . . *felt* it.

How does one let go of a past that stares back at them every day in the mirror? That's not only left its mark on my heart and mind, but on my body as well?

I follow Dean into his kitchen, where I set my purse down on the bar and take a seat.

"So . . ." He clears his throat, opening the microwave and placing a plate of cookies inside it. I get the feeling he's trying to come up with the best way to phrase his next words. "Rohan says it's basically been you and him for the past twelve years?"

I play with the strap of my purse on the countertop. "Yeah, our parents died when I was ten." My eyes collide with

Dean's, but I don't see the same pity in them I'm used to receiving from others. I huff out a mirthless chuckle. "I suppose I was fortunate to have a brother who was ten years older than me, so thankfully, I didn't get put into the foster system and end up living with strangers."

Dean nods. "I'm sorry about what you went through that day, Mala. I can't imagine . . ." The ding of the microwave has him turning back to pull out the warmed cookies, and he shuffles to the fridge for milk.

I press my thumb to my wrist, rubbing the rough patch of skin there. A patch of skin that's both a reminder of the past I lived, as well as the past that died that day. It's a habit I've developed—a coping mechanism—to ground me to the here and now when the dark clouds of soot, dust, and human remains threaten to close in on the little bright spot I create for myself every day. The little bright spot I refuse to give up on, no matter how many dark flecks muddle it.

It's the only spot where the chains of my past don't exist; the only spot I'm completely free.

Dean strolls across the kitchen, placing a cup of milk in front of me, along with the cookies, before he comes back with his own cup and takes a seat across from me. He clears his throat, eyeing my face, and I realize I'm too late in hiding my frown. "I'm sorry I brought it up. I didn't—"

"No. Don't apologize." I shake my head, bringing the cup closer. I exhale, feeling like I need to clear my airways. "I was one of the few lucky ones that day, and that's what I try to hold on to—that I'm here for a reason. I have to believe I'm here for a reason."

Dean's eyes glimmer, reminding me of an ocean under the summer sun. "You are. There's not a doubt in the world about it." He raises the plate in my direction, and I pick up one of the chocolate-chunk cookies. I'm just about to take a bite when he blurts, "Hold up." He takes a cookie off the plate and touches it to the one in my hand. "Cheers to new beginnings."

"To new beginnings," I repeat with a smile.

A moan slips out of Dean's throat as we bite into our cookies, and my skin tingles under its vibration. I lick my lips, chewing slowly, but the only thing I can focus on is the way his mouth moves around his bite. The sound of another soft moan tightens my stomach, but he's so lost in the cookie in his hand, he has no idea I'm struggling to breathe.

"Do you want me to leave you alone with your dessert?" I nod at the tiny piece left between his fingers.

He pops the rest of it into his mouth, keeping his eyes on me. "Nope. I'd rather you watch."

My cheeks heat as I try to figure out how to respond, but instead, I end up just shaking my head. If I don't remind myself not to take him seriously, the guy could end up screwing with my head.

"So," he smirks, after taking a long sip of his milk, "I found out yesterday you're good at setting fires and making terrible dog treats. Any other talents you want to warn me about?"

I raise a brow. "I'm also good at putting cocky firemen in their place."

Dean chuckles. "I'll let my crew know. You won't find anyone like that in this room."

I giggle. "Clearly. Zero arrogant firemen here."

Dean stares at me—something I'm finding he has no problem doing—keeping his gaze locked with mine until I'm practically squirming in my seat. "So, what are you planning on doing now that you're back in Tahoe?"

I take a few sips of my milk and wipe my mouth with the back of my hand. "I got a business degree in Iowa, and to help pay for college tuition, I started a small pet care business—pet sitting, gourmet snacks, and dog walking. I'm hoping to expand it here."

He leans back in his chair. "Oh yeah? Like, by adding more services?"

I shrug, fiddling with my cup. I haven't really vocalized my plans to anyone yet, not even to Rohan, so it feels strange to be discussing it with a virtual stranger. "I saw this empty unit at the corner of Bronco and Fourth Street. I think it used to be a bakery–"

"I know the one. It has a nice outdoor lawn area behind it," Dean chimes in. "There was a donut shop there for some time until the owners moved."

I run my hands over my bare thighs. Now that I'm talking about it, it all feels more real. "I was thinking about calling up the property manager to find out about renting it." I shrug. "I thought maybe I'd go all in on a café for both dogs and people."

Dean's eyes light up. "That's a fucking brilliant idea! A dog-friendly café. You'll even have that great outdoor space for dogs to run around and do their business."

I smile, feeling my ears heat from the rush of excitement running under my skin. "You think there's a market for it?"

"Are you kidding me? Have you seen the number of dogs around here?" Dean booms. His excitement is contagious, making me giggle. "Wasn't there some statistic that said there are more dogs in California than people? Of course, it's a good idea!"

It feels nice to have someone else validate my idea and be excited right along with me. "Yeah, alright. I mean, I need to see if I can afford the rent, then get any necessary permits. I'll need to hire someone to help me with the baking since I'm planning to serve all sorts of pastries, and buy one of those fancy industrial coffee machines . . . But yeah, I think it could work."

Whether Dean is wondering if I have the finances to rent a place like that or not, I can't tell, but the most fortuitous thing my parents did for both Rohan and me as soon as we were born was set us up with a small trust—one that both of us could access as soon as we turned twenty-two. For me, that was this year.

My parents weren't extremely wealthy, but they did manage their money well—with my dad being a financial advisor himself. While neither Rohan nor I have huge amounts in our trust funds, we have enough to help cushion our lives.

Dean wrinkles his nose. "Are you planning to have those god-awful hormone cookies on the menu?"

I stick my tongue out at him. "Not the kind you liked so much, but some fun dog treats, yeah."

He grins, something I'm noticing he does often, and it's both sweet and mischievous. "So, have you always been an animal lover?"

I nod. "I find them to be a million times more tolerable and trustworthy than humans."

Dean lifts his half-filled glass of milk in a toast. "Won't argue that one. I always wanted a dog, but with my schedule, it would just be too hard."

"I get that. I don't know that I can *own* a dog at this point in my life, either. Maybe one day, though. My parents got a golden retriever when I was a little over one and learning to speak. I vaguely remember him, but apparently, I started calling him Orange. You know, because his coat was orangish. Somehow his name stuck."

I smile, recalling the baby album Mom had made. And even though my heart pinches and stalls on certain pictures, I still go through it from time to time, lingering on some of those pictures of me and Orange.

"Wow." Dean's lips twitch. "Even at such an early age, you

showed signs of astounding intellect."

"Shut up." I throw a crumb off my plate at him, which he dodges. "I was a year old!"

Dean's gaze snags on my smile before he averts it back to his glass. "So, is this what you always had in mind for yourself? To run your own business one day?"

I shake my head. "After I started the pet-sitting and gourmet treat business in college, I actually became obsessed with the pet food industry. My absolute dream job would have been to work for *Doggone Happy and Healthy*, maybe in their operations or production department."

"The organic pet food company?" Dean asks. "Aren't they based out of LA?"

I nod. "Yeah, but they're really selective with who they hire. I've applied a few times, but have never gotten an interview."

He's about to respond when his front door opens and the sound of someone's keys jingles through the hall. A woman's high-pitched voice comes through seconds later. "Babe? Pookster? Tell me you're ready to go."

My wide eyes fly to Dean's, watching the tops of his cheeks warm to a deep pink. "*Pookster?*" I whisper before placing my fingers on my mouth to hide my smile.

"Shut it, *sprinkles*!" He mouths back before getting out of his seat to respond to the woman, who sounded more like a squealing chinchilla than a human.

But before he can say anything, her shrill voice resounds again. I swear, I'd rather hear fingernails scraping down a chalkboard. Her heels click on the floor, coming closer to us, and I get off my barstool.

"We promised Becky and Sean we'd meet–" Her words are cut off when she catches my eyes. "Oh, hi!" she squeaks before looking from me to Dean and then back to me. "And who might you be?"

Chapter Four

MALA

"Where do you want this box?"

I look over my shoulder at my brother shuffling into the back room of my bakery with a large box of what I assume are baking goods in his arms. "Actually, could you put them on the island? I'll have Meg sort them out when she gets in."

My brother groans, placing the heavy box on the counter behind me. He's been stopping in on his way to work in the mornings, and since his shifts start early, it gives us time to catch up. "How is she working out?"

I shrug, getting up on my toes to pour butternut squash puree into the mixing bowl and switch on the paddle attachment. "She's okay, just not the most punctual employee." I turn back to face him, wiping my hands on my apron. "Yesterday she was over an hour late because her car broke down, and the day before, she said her phone alarm didn't go off."

Rohan frowns, taking things out of the box and putting them on the island, disregarding what I said earlier about Meg doing it when she gets in. "You need to hire someone reliable, munch."

I groan at his use of the nickname he gave me when I was

a toddler before I turn to add the wheat flour into my wet ingredients. "She lost her mother last month. I'm trying to give her the benefit of the doubt instead of adding on to everything she's already going through. Hopefully, she'll get her shit together in the next few weeks."

Once all the ingredients are combined, I stop the machine and scrape the sides. Pulling up the attachment, I take the dough out of the bowl, wrap it with some plastic, and put the entire thing in the fridge. I have plans to make healthy dog treats later this afternoon.

"You aren't running a charity, munch," my brother huffs, opening the pantry and dragging out the large flour container from the bottom shelf. He empties the new bag of flour he brought inside the container. "Sometimes you go so far with considering everyone else's needs that you forget to consider yours. You're paying her, for crying out loud. Tell her that she either needs to get her ass to work or find another job!"

I sigh, lifting the pan of dog treats I took out of the oven earlier and walking past him toward the doors leading into the bakery. Placing the tray next to the glass pastry shelves with the words "Doggy Dessert" handwritten on a paper cutout above it, I slide the door open and place the bone-shaped biscuits on the other side of the heart-shaped ones.

I officially opened *Doggy Bag Café* about four months ago—six months since I told Dean about my idea—and it's been both the most challenging and most satisfying endeavor I've ever taken on.

In a short amount of time, I've managed to not only purchase all the essential tools and acquire all the necessary licenses, but I've created a space that's exactly how I'd envisioned it—cozy and inviting. With pops of deep orange and fun decals of dog quotes stuck to the walls, a few bone-shaped tables placed strategically around the café, and similar tables and chairs placed around the backyard, the café has become one of my favorite places to be.

I even persuaded Dean, Rohan, and Malcolm to string lights around the large trees last week in exchange for fresh coffee and their favorite pastries, and now it looks incredible all lit up in the evenings.

It's been astounding to see the response from people who walk in not knowing what to expect. They're always amazed that such a concept—a café for both dogs and people—isn't available everywhere.

Rohan follows me out, plucking a blueberry-cream cheese muffin from the large platter on the front bar. "You might actually need two people here. One to handle making the coffee and ringing customers up, and another who can help you bake shit in the back. How long can you do this practically on your own?"

I refill the water tank in the large coffee machine and glance at the clock. I only have twenty minutes before I flip the sign on the front door from *Closed* to *Open*. That's not enough time to have this conversation with my big brother *again*.

I know he's right. I need to hire at least two reliable people, but it's not easy to find someone who has baking skills, good references, doesn't mind cleaning up dog poop, *and* doesn't mind waking up and getting into work by five every morning.

I turn with my hands on my hips and my head tilted. "Well, this is unfortunate."

Rohan's brows pinch as he speaks around the over-sized bite in his mouth. "What is?"

"It's only five-forty-one AM, and my big brother has already fulfilled his overbearing quota for the day." I press my palms against my cheeks in mock horror. "However shall I go on about the rest of my day without his ever-streaming advice and criticism?"

Rohan squints at me before taking a step closer with the cream part of his muffin turned toward me. His smirk gives away his nefarious thoughts.

I back away, giggling. "Ro, don't you dare!" I skirt to my left as he reaches out to try to rub the inside of the muffin on my nose or cheek—wherever he can. "Ro! I have customers coming in just a few minutes. I will kill you if you—" I squeal as I dodge him, only barely registering the bell chiming when the café door opens.

I'd left the doors unlocked after Rohan got here since customers have generally respected not coming in until the Open sign showed.

I'm rushing away from him with a broad smile across my face, looking over my shoulder when I run into a wall—a wall whose arms extend to steady me by the waist. My eyes snap up and get caught in ocean-blue orbs. "Dean!"

"Where are you running off to, *sprinkles*?" He keeps me locked in his hands before looking above my head at my brother, gathering the gist of what was happening. "Need me to hold her so you can make her pay for whatever she said, Ro?"

I wiggle out of his arms and shake my head in faux dismay. "Traitor. Coming into *my* café, drinking *my* free coffee, and eating *my* free pastries every morning, yet now you're taking his side? I should ban you from my respectable establishment."

"He's one of my best friends; of course he's going to take my side," Rohan bellows, popping the rest of the muffin into his mouth. He ruffles my hair while I bat his hand out of the way before he fist bumps Dean. "You done with your shift, brother?"

Dean runs a hand over the back of his neck. By the looks

of it, he's running on low fumes. "Yeah, I figured I'd grab some coffee before I head home."

"Heard there was a nasty fire at the warehouse on Smith and Steeple last night," Rohan says, putting his hands in his jean pockets. "Any serious injuries?"

Dean shakes his head. "Nothing serious. A couple of guys with smoke inhalation and some second-degree burns, but nothing life-threatening."

"Good. You look like you could use some sleep."

Dean shrugs. "I plan on taking a nap this afternoon."

My brother looks from Dean to me. "We still on for dinner at your place tomorrow, munch?"

"Yeah–" I start to say when Dean clears his throat, glancing at me.

"I actually won't be able to make it. Nora wants me to meet her parents tomorrow evening."

"Oh, no shit!" Rohan smiles, leaning back on his heels. "I suppose it's about time. You guys been together, what . . . a year?"

Dean scrapes his teeth across his bottom lip, and I get a strange inkling he's trying to avoid my gaze. I can't be sure though, because why would he? "Something like that."

"I guess I'm just surprised she finally convinced you. You've always been Mr. Commitaphobe. But I suppose you did give her keys to your house, so she was bound to start making long-term plans after that."

Dean runs a hand over his face, releasing a *pfft* through an exhale. "Yeah, I guess so."

Over the past six months, Rohan has made it a point to make sure I'm comfortable around all his friends, going as far as to invite me to their gatherings and letting me hang out at his place whenever I want. I wonder if it all has something to do with him making sure I don't "run off" again like I did for college, but I'm grateful for it.

And though I've hung out with all of them, I feel the closest to Dean. The three of us have spent time together every week—sometimes more, depending on Rohan and Dean's work schedules. Whether it's watching a movie sprawled out on Rohan's couch, kayaking on the lake, or playing pool, we've gotten to know each other well.

In some ways, Rohan transferred some of that protectiveness into his best friend, because even when they have different shifts and Rohan is at work, Dean takes it upon himself to check on me, either by stopping by at the café or texting to make sure I got home safely.

Surprisingly, my big brother hasn't had a problem with just Dean and me hanging out together, either. I gather it has more to do with the fact that not only does Rohan trust Dean like he would a brother, but even he can see that Dean's way out of my league.

In fact, he's so out of my league, I might as well be in another country.

It doesn't take a genius to see the type of woman who keeps Dean's interest—long-legged bombshells, oozing confidence and class, dressed in skin-tight jeans and sky-high stilettos. The types of women who count each calorie and workout like fiends to maintain their perfectly proportioned waistlines.

Me, on the other hand . . .? I'm currently wearing an oversized gray hoodie that says, *'Oh, for dog's sakes!'* in neon pink letters, looking forward to chomping down the last carrot and cream cheese strudel I should have thrown out with yesterday's trash for breakfast. My rounded hips and *severely* less-than-washboard-abs clearly take a backseat to my love for pastries.

In my opinion, life's too short to count anything but blessings—*no one understands that better than me*—so why waste your energy on anything else?

And as far as sky-high heels are concerned . . .? I don't even own a pair of shoes without laces.

"Well, make a good impression on the in-laws." Rohan pats Dean's bicep, and I don't miss the frown that pulls down Dean's mouth. "I'm out of here. Gotta be at the station by six-fifteen."

Ro's almost at the door when he runs back to grab another muffin before I can stop him and chuckles, giving me a wink as he heads out.

I sigh, shaking my head and pulling the neck of my sweatshirt higher. I look back at the clock. Ten minutes to open, and Meg is fifty minutes late. My gaze darts to Dean, who seems to be stuck in the same spot my brother left him, looking dazed.

I wish I could figure out what he was thinking. Though, if I had to venture a guess, it's likely about Nora. The woman he rarely talks about, but the woman who has keys to his house. The woman he's been dating for the past year but never invites to hang out with me and Rohan.

While I don't know Nora much beyond the time we were both invited to Dean's dad and stepmom's house for a barbecue, and the time I ran into her when I dropped off coffee and scones at the fire station, I get the feeling she isn't exactly fond of me.

Call it intuition or a nagging suspicion, but ever since she saw me at Dean's house with that plate of cookies between us, her icy gaze has refused to warm to me, and I honestly don't understand why.

Sure, Dean and I are friends, but it's not like she has anything to worry about. My boring dark hair—currently piled high on my head in a messy bun—and brown eyes are no match for her camera-ready looks. It really astonishes me that I would cause a disturbance in her head at all.

"Hey, *pookster*." I smirk, making Dean's eyes snap up to

mine, like he just realized I was even there. "Want me to make you that white mocha latte you like so much? You look like you need extra whip on it today."

He smiles, but it doesn't reach his eyes like it usually does. He looks around as if just noticing that it's only the two of us here. "Where's Meg?"

Oh, for goodness' sake! Not him, too.

I squelch the need to sigh. "Running late, I suspect." Right when Dean starts to say something else–something I'm sure is much like the unsolicited lecture my brother just gave me–I lift my hand to stop him. "Save it, Barkley; I already heard it from Rohan today. I know I need to talk to her."

Dean shakes his head, glancing at the clock before he rolls up his cuffs and ambles over to the bar. "Alright, go do your thing in the back room. I'm sure you're stressed about what-ever it is you're supposed to be baking instead of standing out here. I'll man the bar until she gets here."

"What?" I pinch my brows. "No, it's okay. I'm sure she'll be in soon. Plus, you worked all night–"

Body heat radiates off him as he closes in on me at the bar. I take a step back, hitting the counter behind me. Pulling the neck of my shirt up, I look up at him. With how short I am–at barely five-feet-one-inch–I'm sure the way he towers over me makes me look like a cartoon character.

And despite all that heat wafting off him, a silent shudder runs down my spine.

"I'm not letting you open this café, knowing you don't have help. I'll head out when she gets here." He taps my nose. "Until then, get out of my way and let me do my job."

"Do you even know how to use the coffee machine?" I ask in a huff.

My brain still feels scrambled with his nearness and all the scent of sandalwood inside my nose. Even though it's just a hint of a scent on him, it completely overpowers the scent of coffee and sugar surrounding me.

His eyes drill holes into mine. "I'm pretty sure you moaned around the last cup I made you using this exact machine. Want me to do it again?" He leans down to my ear. "Make you moan, that is . . ."

I swallow as fire spreads across my cheeks. Squirming, I try to push back on the counter, even though I can't go any further back.

He's just a flirt. He's like this with everyone.

No big deal. Stay cool, stay cool.

I clear my throat. "Have I told you how pushy and bossy you are?"

"I wouldn't mind hearing it again." He smirks.

I press an index finger into his chest and push him back so I can get some distance in between us. "You're also incredibly bullheaded and . . . and annoying."

His lips twitch, his eyes finally getting back their missing twinkle, as he locates a steel frothing cup and pours milk into it. "Looks like I'm meeting my life's goals, then. Anything else?"

"And . . . I don't like it when your smile doesn't light up your face like it usually does. When you don't smile for real."

Whoa, where did that case of verbal diarrhea come from?

Dean freezes in place, blinking a couple of times as if he's completely taken aback by my confession.

Yeah, you and me both, pookster.

And though it's too late to take back my words, my shoulders slump when I study his tight jaw. I probably shouldn't have said that; I probably should have left it alone. Whatever he's going through with Nora is not my business, anyway.

But I guess my overwhelming need to let him know that I care, that he has someone he can talk to, outweighed my better judgment to stay out of his business. It still does, apparently, because a moment later, I hear myself voicing my opinion yet again.

"You know you can talk to me, pooch." I smile, using another dog name to try to give the moment some levity. "You don't have to hold in whatever you're thinking."

He nods, putting the steel cup under the steamer wand.

"What's going on?" I press. "Why don't you want to meet her parents?"

In all the times we've hung out, Dean makes a point to be as vague as possible about Nora. All I know about her is that she's a dermatologist—no surprise there since her skin sparkles like it's covered with diamond dust—and constantly hounds him about the crazy hours he has to work.

For God's sakes, woman! The man risks his life to save everyone else's. Give him a damn break!

Dean's shoulders mimic mine before he looks out the large windows over his shoulder. "I just—" he huffs. "I mean, I *should* want to meet them . . ."

"But you don't," I fill in.

He shrugs, leaving the cup where it is before running a hand through his long, straw-colored hair. "I don't know. It's all too real, I guess." His throat bobs as his eyes find mine again, and I notice an anguish in them I'd never seen before. "I'm not the guy who'll walk down an aisle and tear up at the sight of my bride, *sprinkles*. I'm not the guy who has hopes and dreams of raising a brood of kids or growing old with someone."

An unexpected sorrow climbs into my chest, settling there like a heavy weight.

In the time I've known him, Dean has always been with Nora. Sure, he hasn't ever seemed head-over-heels for her, but I never suspected it was due to his reservations about long-term commitments. It makes me wonder what happened to make him not want those things he just spoke about.

Stepping closer, I latch my palm around his wrist, studying his sullen expression. "Why not?"

Dean's eyes roam over my face, as if he's taking me all in. And even though the time we spend together is generally cloaked in light banter and teasing, this moment seems more significant. More real. Like I'm finally getting a glimpse of the man who shields himself behind a mask of jest. "Because those are someone else's hopes and dreams, not mine."

I lick my lips. "Does she know that? Have you told her how you feel?"

He shakes his head. "I'm no good at feelings."

My eyes bounce between his, and I revel over the thickness of his brows, wondering how any man could have such lush lashes. "But you have plenty of them."

"Yeah? How would you know that?"

"Call it intuition. We haven't been friends for long, but everything about you—from the way you talk to your grams every week to the way you put your whole heart into your work, risking your life for someone else every single day, to the way your eyes light up when you talk about your brothers—says you feel a lot. You feel *big*. So when you don't have those same *big* feelings for someone, I guess I have to wonder . . ."

"Wonder what?" he whispers.

I pause, hoping my words come out right. "The way I see it, if those are someone else's hopes and dreams, then it's time you go after your own."

It's when we're both reeling in the weight of the moment between us that the bell over the door chimes, and we turn to find Meg taking off her thin jacket and placing it on the hook before she turns around to me, wincing. "I'm so sorry, Mala. I had a little emergency this morning. My cat jumped into a tree, and I had to climb it to get her down."

Ugh. I wish I was the type to listen to my gut and call

someone on their bullshit, but I'm not. I'm the type to take someone at their word and give them the benefit of the doubt. Maybe she really did have a cat emergency . . . How can I prove it otherwise?

I straighten my shoulders, glancing at Dean before tracking an older couple walking with their chocolate lab toward the set of stairs leading to the café doors. I smile at Meg. "Looks like we have our first customers for the day. Let's get started."

Meg mumbles something apologetically again before shuffling over to the bar. Dean steps out of her way, allowing her access to the coffee machine, and I follow him before making my way to the back room.

I wave to him, whispering, "See you later," and step inside the back room. I take a long inhale before thinking about everything I have to do. *God, I really do need more reliable help.*

Just as I'm about to open the fridge, the double doors to the back room open and Dean pokes his head inside. "For the record, there's *never* a time when my smile isn't real around you."

The double doors swing when he retreats, leaving me to ruminate on his words. It's when I finally get my bearings and am rolling out the dough I just took out of the fridge that I allow myself to smile.

Smile for real.

Chapter Five

DEAN

I SHUT THE DRIVER'S SIDE DOOR TO MY TRUCK BEFORE traipsing to the back to grab the large box from my truck bed, smiling to myself about what her reaction is going to be when she sees it. She's a shy little thing, but hopefully, this will pry her from her comfort zone.

Carrying the box and placing it on the front porch, I ring the doorbell and wait. Their sweet voices come through the door, and I hear her giggle. Seems my goddaughter had a good nap.

The door swings open, and Jane's soft green eyes turn up at the corners, just like her lips. She looks thinner than the last time I saw her, practically swimming in her clothes. "Hi!"

My smile follows hers before landing on the girl I'm here to see, the one who just turned two last week.

"Hi," I respond to Jane, not taking my eyes off the doe-eyed toddler with the cherub cheeks in her arms. "Hey, kitty-cat! You remember me?"

Jane looks at Catherine, placing a kiss on her temple, while Catherine observes me guardedly. It's only been a month since I visited, but her suspicious gaze says she can't quite place where she's seen me before.

"Babycakes, you remember Uncle Dean, don't you?" Jane asks her, swiping a crumb off Catherine's face. "What do you say we invite him in?"

Jane gestures to me, and I lug the big box inside, winking at Catherine. She studies me even more intently from her mom's arms.

I take off my boots in the foyer, and a twinge of something thorny pricks my chest as I take in the beautiful baby girl in Jane's arms. I swallow, kneeling down, trying not to let my smile waver and focus on unboxing her toy. She looks so much like Zander—the same light brown eyes, the same mix of honey and cinnamon locks—I don't know how Jane doesn't break down at the sight of her every single day.

Maybe she does . . .

I turn the box so Catherine can see the picture of the wooden horse on it and raise my brows. "How about we open your new toy, kitty-cat?"

Catherine points her little index finger at the box before placing it between her gums. Her mom puts her down on her feet, and Catherine slowly waddles over to where I am, pushing through her shyness. "What that?"

My smile widens as I pull out the wooden horse. "A horse. Want to ride it?"

She nods enthusiastically, closing the space between us while I take off the additional wrapping around it. Even her energy—the way she lights up when she sees something she wants, and the way her eyes glitter, her body almost trembling with excitement—is the same as Zander's.

Jane watches us from a distance. "What do you say, babycakes? Can you say thank you?"

"*Tank ooh*," Catherine repeats, flashing me a few of her tiny teeth.

I raise my arm, urging her closer. "Want me to put you on it?"

She waddles to me, her eyes swinging from me to the horse. "Put you *onut*."

I chuckle, lifting her before getting her situated on the horse and sitting at her side to make sure she doesn't fall. Catherine grabs hold of the little handles sticking out from the horse's head and giggles when her toes reach the ground and she realizes it rolls.

"I have a feeling that's going to become her favorite toy," Jane says softly.

I regard Jane's stained T-shirt over ripped black leggings, messy ponytail, and the dark circles under her eyes. Even if I looked closely, I'd be hard-pressed to find the woman who once refused to be seen without makeup, perfectly fitted clothes, and a manicure.

And it's not just the fact that she's now a widowed single mom of a two-year-old; it's the way her voice sounds, her entire demeanor. She's barely a whisper of her former self. Where she once used to be outspoken, outgoing, and cheerful, now I doubt she's even stepped out of her house since the last time I visited.

It's as if even after almost three years, she can't move forward.

She didn't just lose her husband and best friend that day, she lost herself. And though every firefighter's spouse knows the risks of our job, they're rarely ever prepared for the worst.

I stay in the foyer playing with Catherine for another hour before Jane puts her in her high chair with her lunch. Catherine giggles as I pretend to eat her sandwich and talk to her in silly voices. No doubt, the kid has warmed up to me again.

After lunch, when she starts rubbing her eyes, Jane has

her wave bye to me before taking her back to her crib and putting her down for another nap.

I look around the living room while I wait for Jane to come back downstairs. Like the last time I was here, it's still in disarray, with cups, plates, and toys lying about on every surface. A stack of unopened mail lies on the coffee table, along with an open album, showcasing pictures from one of Zander and Jane's trips. From the looks of it, it seems like a trip they took before they got married.

A pit grows in my stomach as my eyes lift from the album, following the light coming off the paused image on the TV screen—a glimpse of Zander and Jane's wedding. Their first dance as a married couple.

I remember it well, watching them from one of the tables around the dance floor. The intensity of the moment flits back through me as I study the picture on the screen. The way Zander's hands wrap around his bride's waist and her enamored gaze on him like they were the only ones in the room.

I remember that whole day clearly, in fact. The way they looked—like nothing could get in the way of spending the rest of their lives together. I'd never seen my buddy cry before that, not in the five years I'd known him. Hell, he was one of the toughest, most resilient men I knew. But one look at his bride as she walked down the aisle, and he almost broke down at the altar.

I remember wondering what it would be like to find someone who could bring you to your knees, turn you inside-out like that. I remember wanting that feeling for myself . . .

"Want me to get you something to drink? Tea, soda?" Jane's voice pulls me to the present. I hadn't even heard her come back.

"No." I shake my head and she takes a seat on the other

side of the couch. "I'm going to be heading out soon, anyway. Just wanted to check on you both."

She smiles, though it does nothing to veil the misery that lines the corners of her eyes. "Thanks for stopping by and for Catherine's gift. She loves it."

"I'm glad."

"How are you? How's everyone at the station?" As if just realizing what her place looks like, Jane starts to collect a few cups and paper plates off the coffee table.

"Everyone's good." I clear my throat. "We still miss seeing you there once in a while."

She shuffles to the kitchen, and I pick up a few magazines off the floor and stack them on her table. "Yeah, well . . . I don't really have a reason to visit anymore, do I?"

I run my thumb over the piped edging on her sofa. "You have us—your friends. We were all like family, J. I know the others have tried to call and check up on you—"

"How's Nora?" Jane busies herself behind the kitchen counter, changing the subject. "You guys still together?"

I take in a breath, not letting her dismissal bother me. I've never been great at expressing my feelings, either, so I get where she's coming from.

Mala's words from yesterday surface to the top of my head. Yeah, maybe I do feel a lot and feel big, but it's putting those feelings into words that has always been my weakness. How the woman has gotten under my skin—figured me out in ways that surprise me consistently—in such a short time is beyond me.

She has this magnetic quality, a charm like I've never seen before, where just being in her presence leaves a smile on my face. The way she always has something to say, the way she can dish it just as much as she can take it—I swear, I've never felt more comfortable around a woman in my whole life.

But it's not just the comfortability I feel around her that

has me rapt . . . it's something else, too. Something I haven't quite gotten my arms around. Something that feels too big to even name.

Or perhaps it's something too dangerous to be named.

"Nora's fine," I respond, internally shaking myself for the path my thoughts just took, reminding myself that those thoughts were for my best friend's little sister and completely inappropriate. "We're okay . . ." I let the comment hang. Jane doesn't need the confusion of my dating life added to the already large pile of shit she has to deal with. "We're good. Everything is good."

Truth is, I don't even know where things stand between Nora and me at this exact moment. Not that she has any indication to think things aren't okay. I haven't told her yet, but I plan to tonight, before I have to meet her parents—who I don't plan to meet at all.

Jane smiles, coming back into the living room and taking a seat on the couch. If she knows I'm being aloof, she doesn't question it.

I sit across from her, picking up one of Catherine's toy alphabet cubes off the floor and rolling it in my hand. "How are you holding up, J? Nightmares still waking you up in the middle of the night?"

Jane shrugs. "Off and on. If it's not the nightmares that wake me up, then it's Catherine being sick or going through a growth spurt." She chuckles. "Sleep is for the weak anyway, isn't it?"

My lips tip up in a quick smile, knowing she's trying to hide behind a veil of humor. I know that veil well—I've used it myself quite a few times. "How are you holding up, though?"

Jane leans back on the couch, running both her hands over her face, seemingly giving up the fight to feign the tough outer shell. "If you're asking if it's gotten any easier after three years, the answer is no. It hasn't." She looks around the living room before her eyes land on the TV. Within an instant, they pool at the sight of her late husband smiling broadly, effortlessly, at her. "I still see him when I close my eyes. I still feel him when I least expect it. I can still hear his booming laugh and that rumble of his voice."

Jane's bottom lip trembles and she runs the back of her hand over her nose. "There are days when I feel like I've got a handle on things, but then I have days—like today—where nothing feels easy." She looks to the side, gazing out through her glass patio doors. "I don't know when it'll get easier, Dean, but it's not easy *now*. It's not easy being Catherine's only caretaker. It's not easy when someone asks where her dad is, or when I have to check off a box that says *widow* on an insurance form. It's not easy when a holiday or a birthday or even Father's Day comes around."

A tear runs down her cheek, and I get on my feet to cross the distance between us and sit down right next to her. I pull her into my side and she lays her head on my shoulder. "Nothing has been easy without him . . . I still miss him with every fiber in my body."

My throat tightens but I try to keep it together, remembering my buddy's words as he lay on his hospital deathbed, taking his last few breaths—days after we'd fought one of the worst forest fires in California history. He knew he was up on his time. Even when the doctors and family tried to keep it from him, he knew.

"Make sure she smiles again, Dean. Don't let her lose her spark. She's too bright to lose her spark."

"I won't," I promised him, though I didn't know how I was going to fulfill that promise. "I'll take care of her." My chin wobbled, making my words come out all choppy. "I'll take care of her, buddy, so you rest assured. Okay? You rest."

Minutes later, he was gone, with Jane wrapped around him, sobbing into his neck.

I cup Jane's face in between my palms and wipe her tears with my thumb. "I miss him, too, J. I always will. He wasn't just one of the best firemen I ever worked with, he was a mentor and a friend to me. But this isn't what he'd want for you. You can't tell me this—not sleeping, not eating, not taking care of yourself, three years later—is what would make him happy."

Jane nods, her face resting in my palms. "I know," she whispers. "I know, Dean. But sometimes I wish I could have just gone with him. Sometimes it all feels like it's too much." Her moss-colored eyes meet mine and pain tears through her features before she speaks again. "Do you remember what I said to you the day he died?"

My breath stalls, my eyes bouncing between hers. I give her a quick nod.

Of course I remember what she'd said to me that day. How could I forget? How does one forget words that shredded their heart and fundamentally changed the course of their life forever?

At the time, I'd chalked it up to her grieving, but her words stirred inside my head for weeks and years afterward. Up until then, I'd thought I was the same as anyone else. Up until then, I thought I deserved what anyone else did—the pursuit of love, a picket fence, and a life with my wife at my side and my children running amok in our backyard.

But it was Jane's words that made me realize how selfish that desire was. How selfish it was for me to think I had a right to take anyone else down with me when this—my life, my career, my decision—was my choice. A choice I made every single day without regret, but a choice I had no right to force on someone else.

"Do you remember how I told you that if I could do it all over again, if I could go back in time to that bar where I met Zander, to that moment when he asked me for my number and it changed my life forever—even knowing the profound love I would have in my life with him in it—that I would turn him down?" She nods as if underscoring her statement. "Knowing what I know now, I would have walked away from him, Dean. I would have walked away."

"You don't mean that—"

"I do." She takes in a shaky breath, but her voice stays resolute. "I do mean it. Because, if I knew what I know now—the anguish I've felt for the past three years, the sheer weight of life without him—I'd tell that naive girl sitting at the bar, looking into those alluring brown eyes and making wishes that should never have been made, that the worst thing she could do for herself would be to fall for a firefighter. Even worse would be to marry one."

I INHALE a large breath and release it slowly before opening the door. It does nothing to calm my racing pulse and the twist that's been in my stomach ever since I left Jane's house this morning. I knew what I had to do. "Hey."

"Hi, Pooks!" Nora walks inside, wrapping her arms around my neck before planting a kiss on my lips. She pulls back with her brows knitted when I don't reciprocate the affection. "Wha—what's wrong?"

I swallow, tilting my head toward the living room. "Can we talk?"

She follows me, her heels clicking more hesitantly than usual. "Sure. Um, is this about meeting my parents tonight?"

I wave a hand toward the couch. "Why don't we sit?"

Nora wraps the unbuttoned red coat around her protectively. "No, I think I'm more comfortable standing." Her features tighten as if she's preparing for battle. "What is it, Dean? I can tell something is wrong."

I slide my hands into my jean pockets, running my tongue against the inside of my lip. "This isn't working."

"You–" Nora looks to her right before her knitted brows find my face again. "This," she points between us, "as in . . . us?"

I close my eyes momentarily before nodding.

"Is this about meeting my parents? Because you think we're going too fast? I can back off, Dean. I didn't mean to pressure–"

"No. This has nothing to do with your parents."

It has to do with the fact that I don't know what I want.

It has to do with the fact that a loss like what Jane feels isn't something I'm willing to put someone else through.

It has to do with the fact that nothing and no one is worth that kind of risk.

It has to do with the fact that I don't love you. And I never will.

Her arms fly up, landing with a *thud* at her sides. "Then, what? Is it because I complain about your crazy work schedule? Because you're sleeping at the damn fire station more nights than you are at home? Okay, fine, I admit it. It's unfair for me to do that because there's nothing you can do about it, and as much as I hate your job, I'm willing to accept it."

And there is that, too. Her truth, as obvious as an elephant hiding behind a stripper pole. But, sadly, it's not as big of a surprise to me as the expression on her face is portraying. As if it's the first time she's verbally admitted it, and she's shocked that the words actually had sound. She may not have voiced it so *articulately* before, but I've known her disdain for my work and my hours.

"I'm . . . I'm sorry, Dean. That's not what I meant. I don't hate–"

I lift my hand, interrupting her from continuing because honestly, her disapproval of my job isn't the reason we're here today. Though, it does help that she confirmed it and therefore, makes my decision resolute. "It's fine, Nora. This has nothing to do with your parents or you. This is about me."

Nora's high-pitched laugh resounds in the silence between us. "Oh, come on, Dean Meyer. You can do better than that. Are you seriously going to pull the *it's-not-you-it's-me* card?" If her eyes could throw actual daggers, they would. "Give me a fucking break and come up with something a little more original."

I push back the long strands of my hair. "I'm not pulling cards, nor am I making excuses, Nora. I just . . . I can't be who you need. I told you that when we met–"

"Yeah, sure, Dean. You told me. You told me that we would never be serious. That you don't do love and attachment. But that's not what your actions said when you met my sister and niece and spent hours baking a cake with her. That's not what your actions said when you threw a surprise birthday party for me and flew my best friend in from Arizona last month. That's not what your actions said when you stayed up to comfort me after my fourteen-year-old cat died six months ago. The fact is, you might say you're not who I need, but you're exactly who I want."

I swallow the lump in my throat. This is exactly why I don't do committed shit. This is why I stay away from attachments and long-term bullshit. Because I can't fucking stand to see the look on someone's face when you know you're pulling their heart out of their chest and cracking it open. "I'm sorry, Nora. I . . . I just can't do this."

She stares at me, her jaw tightening. "Tell me something, Dean. And please, at least have the decency of being honest with me, okay?"

I nod.

"Is this about Rohan's sister?"

I squint at her, even as the beat of my heart kicks up for some unknown reason. "What?"

Nora crosses her arms in front of her chest. "You're always checking in on her, spending time with both of them, helping at her little café. I'm just wondering if there's something more there."

A surge of irritation knicks my insides. "There's nothing more there. Mala is a friend of mine. She's . . ." The words feel acrid even as I say them, but in all honesty, I don't really know why they should. "She's like a sister."

Nora tilts her head, blinking at me like she's waiting for me to get a clue—to realize how simpleminded and ridiculous I sound. "A sister. *Right*." She turns around, rushing back toward the door. "Have a wonderful life living in denial, Dean. It's obvious you're happy there."

I shuffle after her, stopping her before she steps out. "What does that mean?"

Grasping the door, Nora gives me a pitiful smile. "Open your eyes, Dean. Acknowledge what you really want. *Accept* it. Because the way I see it, you seem to purposefully be living in the dark. Goodbye."

Chapter Six

MALA

Eight Years Ago

"WHICH KIND DO YOU WANT? I'VE GOT LEMON-GINGER and pomegranate-lavender." I lift the kettle off its base and pour hot water into my cup with the bag of lemon-ginger tea. I add a spoon of honey to it, too.

"Any chance you have something like 'regular, not-a-weird-ass-flavor' tea?" Dean bellows from his place on my couch.

I roll my eyes. "Yes. It's called hot water."

"Brat. Fine, I'll take the lavender shit." He turns from the couch, giving me one of his ridiculously dazzling smiles, and even in the dimmed lights in my living room, I can see a little blush creep to his cheeks. It's so fucking endearing, I have to force myself to look away so I don't end up staring. "Hey, uh . . . do you have one of those peanut butter cookies from the bakery the other day?"

I purse my lips to hide my smile and turn around to get a bag of the pomegranate-lavender tea. I take out the dog treat jar from the cupboard and place a couple of cookies on the plate under his cup. I always have treats on hand for the rare occasions when I pet sit. "You mean, the peanut butter and pumpkin *dog treats*? The ones I make especially to help with canine digestion and bowel movements?"

"I refuse to be deterred by your disgusting marketing terminology." I hear the clicking of the remote as Dean selects different programs on the TV.

I'm carrying the cups to the couch when something dawns on me. Something that Betty, my new helper at the bakery since I fired Meg, pointed out recently.

"Wait a minute." I set the cups on my coffee table and put my hands on my hips, looking down at where he sits. "How do you know I made peanut butter-pumpkin treats? They were on the other glass shelf." I stare at the man who's exceptionally good at masking his thoughts and feelings with humor or a blank expression, like he's doing now. "Come to think of it, I made at least four dozen of those cookies on Thursday, and Betty told me we were running short, even though we both swore we didn't sell that many. Did you—"

"How about we watch this love experiment show where they blind date three people and marry the one who suits them the best after three dates? It's called *Three After Three*. A dumb name, don't you think?"

"You came to the bakery to do that random smoke detector check the other day, even though I told you Rohan just did it recently." My eyes widen. "Dean Meyer, did you pocket a bunch of—"

"I feel like we'll end up binging this like we did *The Bachelor*."

I shake my head, taking a seat next to him and giving him an appalled look. He is both a terrible liar and a chronic subject-changer. "You're never allowed back inside my bakery. I'm reporting you for theft."

He pops a cookie into his mouth. "Or you could make a dozen of these just for me. Turns out, they're really good for my digestion, too. Really loosens stuff up in here." He rubs his washboard abs.

I wrinkle my nose, scooting so my back presses against the armrest and pull the rounded neck of my sweatshirt a little higher. I'm wearing it over my signature black shorts. No matter the weather, I like my legs bare and my torso covered.

I tuck my feet under his thighs, taking a sip of my tea, and holding back my giggle from the memory of him telling me my body was a fusion of microclimates.

"Seriously, Mala. You're the only one I know who wears fucking sweatshirts and shorts in the middle of sweltering heat and *bone-chilling frost, and who has cold fingers and toes all year long. You've got problems."*

"Yeah, I do have problems," I'd responded. "You."

He'd slow-clapped, his sarcasm at a level ten. "Wow. That was a good one. Buuurn."

My fingers and toes are always ice cold, an affliction I've had ever since I can remember.

My dad used to warm my toes between his palms when he tucked me into bed because I refused to wear socks to sleep. My feet would get too hot, too 'suffocated' in socks, so Dad would massage them before kissing me good night.

I don't know when I got comfortable enough to tuck my feet under Dean's thighs—perhaps the first time he came over, and we watched TV alone together a few months ago. And though neither of us have acknowledged it, nor have we verbalized the rules, Dean and I always keep a safe distance from each other around Rohan.

Not like we're crossing any lines or doing anything illicit now. Not like we're secretly holding hands or making out or . . .

It's just feet . . . under thighs. Really toned, well-sculpted, heavy thighs that fill out jeans, or his current getup, gray sweatpants.

My eyes travel from his enormous thighs—covering most of my feet—down his long legs, splayed out in front of him. He flexes his feet and my eyes quickly dart back up his legs to follow the stretch of his navy-colored Henley over his abs, up to the smooth skin of his neck, right under the soft shadow of his scruff. His hair is up in a half-bun today.

I follow the bob of his Adam's apple and my eyes snap to his when he says my nickname. "*Sprinkles.* You good with this dating show?"

I nod, turning to the TV and hoping that the sounds of strangers on the show ambushes the stray thoughts that shouldn't have a place in my head at all.

He's my *friend* . . . my brother's best friend.

He's also a super likable and easygoing guy. And that's the only reason these stray thoughts are even bouncing around in my head in the first place.

Nothing more, nothing less.

No need to overthink it, Mala.

Even a nun would have these thoughts about him.

Okay, so maybe not a nun, because some of these thoughts are indecent and uncouth and . . .

"She's an idiot," Dean declares, making me jolt back to the present. Thankfully, my tea doesn't slosh over the rim. He points at the TV. "Can you believe she chose that idiot?"

I shake my head, realizing I missed most of the show. "Unbelievable. How could she?"

"That's what I'm saying!" He turns to me. "Hey, did that shit turn my teeth purple?"

He flashes his teeth and I make a horrified face, leaning forward abruptly to get a closer look. "Oh, Jesus. Okay, Dean . . ." I say with an exaggerated wince, "just, don't freak out, okay?"

His eyes narrow on me, but I can see both doubt and fear intermingling beautifully in his blue irises. He pauses our show. "You better not be fucking with me, *sprinkles*. What is it? Tell me the truth. Did that shit really turn my teeth purple?"

I place my hand over my mouth. "Look, I'm sure some whitening toothpaste will—"

Dean launches himself off the couch, rushing to my bathroom. "Jesus Christ, woman! What kind of shit do you keep in your house? Why can't you just have normal stuff like the rest of us?"

I face-plant on my couch cushion, my shoulders shaking with laughter as I hear him grumble and curse before turning on the bathroom lights. I don't have to see him to know he's gotten up-close-and-personal with the mirror, examining his teeth like they're under a microscope.

I'm just wiping the happy tears off my face when Dean saunters back into the living room, his bare feet making a soft *tapping* on the floor. "You're hilarious, you know that? A real comedian."

I shrug, my cheeks trembling from barely-tethered laughter. "It's a gift. Not everyone has it."

He sits back down next to me and presses *Play* again, pretending to look peeved. "It's a pain in my ass, is what it is." He looks at me, his eyes betraying his words. "*You're* a pain in my ass."

I give him a gleaming smile and watch as his eyes pin themselves there. "But you put up with me because I make the best digestive dog treats in the world, and they've done wonders for your bowels."

He pulls his eyes away to look back at the TV screen and mumbles, "It's your only redeeming quality. And even *that* is questionable."

I assume my position again with my feet tucked under his

thigh. "I also open up your mind to different kinds of music. I make you more worldly."

He looks at me pointedly. "*Forcing* me to listen to *Miley Cyrus* and *K-pop* is *not* making me more worldly—"

"We'll agree to disagree."

"I lose brain cells every time you make me listen to them."

I nod, feigning concern. "And you're worried because you don't have very many brain cells left to spare."

He pinches the back of my calf and I squeal, slapping his hand away. "No, smartass, because they suck."

"They do not! They're making iconic music in their own right. Anyway, you agreed with my favorite song. You love *Drive* by Incubus."

Dean rolls his eyes. "Thank God, because otherwise, this," he waves between us, "friendship would have been on the fritz."

I snort, shoving his thigh with my foot.

"Hey so, why do you think she's an idiot?" I ask, tilting my head toward the woman on the show who's about to meet the man she picked for the first time. "He seems like a nice guy."

"He's a cop."

I reel back almost unintentionally. "Yeah. So?"

Dean shrugs. "Nothing. I just think if she understood the magnitude of the risk she was taking by marrying a cop, she probably wouldn't make the choice so lackadaisically."

"Lackadaisically?"

"Yeah." He rolls the remote around in his hands. "You know, so casually."

What the hell? "Hey, look at me for a second."

Dean's eyes find mine again, and that same anguish I've seen in them before has his words coming back to me. *"I'm not the guy who has hopes and dreams of raising a brood of kids or growing old with someone."*

"Do you . . .?" I trail off, trying to unravel my thoughts. "Is that the same thing you feel about being a firefighter?" My mouth opens in a soft gasp as if my mind just found a missing puzzle piece. "Wait, is that why you broke up with Nora all those months ago, and why you haven't been serious with anyone else since?"

My memories take me back to the day months ago, when Dean showed up at my apartment, late one night. I could smell the alcohol on his breath, mingling with the scent of sandalwood that always surrounds him.

I took in the blue of his eyes, washed in torment, and wrapped him against me. "Wh—what's wrong?" My fingers ran through his long blond hair while his head rested on my shoulder.

A shudder passed through him, and I held on tighter. "Nothing. Today's just been . . ." he trailed off without finishing his sentence. "I broke things off with Nora."

I pulled away from him, looking up into his eyes as we stood in my foyer. "Why? Because of what I said to you about going after your own dreams?"

He shook his head. "Not really. It was always supposed to be casual with her, but somewhere along the way, it became exclusive. When she asked me to meet her parents and move forward, I just . . . couldn't." His expression lay in defeat. "I think some people aren't meant to dream the same dreams as everyone else. Sometimes their reality is so powerful, it seeps into their dreams and turns them to vapor."

I narrowed my gaze on him, completely confused. "And what are these dreams you can't go after? What reality is so powerful that you're this invested in it?"

His jaw ticked before he shook his head. "I'd rather not talk about it." His eyes went to the couch behind me. "Can we just sit and watch some TV?"

Dean clears his throat, snapping me back to the present. While he avoids answering my question, I can tell he's mulling over my words.

His eyes drop to the collar of my sweatshirt, and my body tightens instinctively in response. I pull my collar up again, feeling exposed, even though I know he can't see anything below it.

"You, of all people, should know what the risks are," he rasps.

My heart tumbles around in my chest, and I thumb the rough patch of skin on the inside of my wrist, trying to find something to keep me feeling steady. "And yet, I'm not the one who's afraid."

Dean's jaw tightens. "That's not what your actions say."

My voice scrapes against my throat. "And what do my actions say?"

His nostrils flare slightly, right as his eyes dip back to my chest, then to my thumb rubbing circles on my wrist. "That you're adept at hiding. That you can't get rid of the memories, no matter how hard you try." His eyes bounce between mine. "That you don't see yourself the way everyone else sees you . . . the way I see you."

"And how do you see me?" I whisper. My body feels alight under my skin, my breaths shaky, unreliable.

"The word doesn't exist in English."

I hold his gaze, my heart determined to bound out of my chest. And as much as I thought his answer would have me finding my footing around this conversation, it has me feeling more wobbly. "I don't hide myself."

Dean lifts a brow. "Yeah? Then what would you call that?"

I follow his gaze to my hand fisting my collar. I didn't even realize I was doing it. I suppose I've always done it whenever I've felt too exposed, too seen. Ever since I was ten, I took comfort in the fact that I escaped with my life, and that at least my scars weren't out for the world to see.

They were mine to deal with. Mine to love and mine to hate.

I release my collar abruptly and drag my eyes toward the TV, not processing a single thing happening on it.

The wails and screams as flesh burned and people rushed to get out of the two small exits on the other side of the theater roar inside my ears. The fear and confusion as I wondered where my parents were overpowered even the feeling of my skin blistering under the massive beam that pinned me to the ground.

They called it one of the worst theater fires in the city's history. A children's show gone awry when the pyrotechnic performance set the stage on fire.

Dad had gotten us front-row tickets.

From what I was told—days after I woke up—Mom died at the scene, and Dad was so badly injured, he didn't make it past the first night at the hospital.

Dean's index finger hooks under my chin, bringing my watery gaze to meet his. "You're a survivor, Mala. Proclaim it like a triumph. Brandish it for all to see. Don't hide behind oversized sweatshirts. At least not from me."

I shake my head, a knot lodged inside my throat. "I'm not–"

"Yeah?" he rasps, his eyes kindling like blue flames. "Then, show me."

My face heats, my fingers coming back to fist my shirt when Dean grasps my hand, tugging it down. He runs his thumb over the patch of burned skin under my wrist, giving me an account of how much he pays attention.

He so often shows me—and the rest of the world—this flippant and playful side, that I forget how observant and intuitive he can be.

"Don't hide from me, Mala. Never from me."

"I haven't–" My voice wavers. "I've never shown–"

"I don't care who you have or haven't shown it to." His molars grind. "I'm not just anyone."

It's on the tip of my tongue to ask who he is, if not just anyone–or why he thinks he should see what I haven't shown to anyone but doctors–but my senses, my thoughts, my fucking sanity, are being overwhelmed by his nearness.

Dean watches intently as my fingers wrap around the bottom of my sweatshirt and I pull it up. I halt momentarily when my nerves overpower me, but the look in his eyes leaves no room to question the path I've already begun.

Lifting my sweatshirt over my head, I grasp it in my fist as I meet his eyes again. They blaze as he takes in the sight of me. It's too much. It's all too much.

I turn my head to the side, away from his gaze, feeling all too exposed when his finger brushes over my mangled scar. A tremble ghosts down my spine as I feel his finger linger down the middle of my sternum, stopping at the top edge of my bra. It continues down to my stomach, halting at the end of the crater carved over my skin.

A souvenir of my survival.

His finger weaves back over my breast, and my stomach clenches, a want pooling between my thighs.

"You're stunning," he croaks.

I grasp his hand, tightening mine over it, feeling too much, like I've been dropped into the middle of an ocean with nothing to keep me afloat. "Don't."

"Don't what? Don't tell you that this scar doesn't define you, but makes you all the more perfect?"

"It's the disfigured remains of a day that will haunt me for the rest of my life, Dean. There's nothing perfect or awe-inspiring about it," I retort.

Dean shakes his head. "No. It's *proof* you survived. That you endured and thrived. That you're a fucking warrior. And what looks disfigured to you, is the most beautiful thing I've ever seen." His voice drops and the moment ignites. "*You're* the most beautiful thing I've ever seen."

My breath halts on the exhale, my eyes dropping to his lips.

Before I know it, Dean and I are millimeters apart. So close I can see the ends of his thick brown lashes. So close I can feel the soft caress of his breath on my skin. So close I can almost taste the drag of his tongue over his lip, as if he was dragging it over mine.

What are you doing, Mala? Think about what the fuck you're doing right now.

"Dean."

The air stands still while my heart pounds against my chest.

But before either of us can close the millimeter's gap between us, Dean squeezes his eyes shut. His nostrils flare and his hands fist on his lap, as if he's physically restraining himself.

"Mala," he rasps. "I . . . I can't."

And despite my cheeks threatening to catch fire, it's as if a bucket of freezing water has been dumped directly on my head.

I pull back, quickly covering myself up with my sweat-shirt, and nod vigorously. "Yeah. No, I get that. We totally can't."

"Mala–"

"I think . . . I think I just got caught up in . . . Oh, God, I'm so sorry, Dean." I place a hand over my mouth, trying to come to terms with my own audacity. I shake my head in shock. "I didn't mean to. God, Rohan would kill–"

"Mala, stop. Nothing happened." Dean runs his hands over his face before looking at my profile. "But nothing can happen between us, either. *Ever.*"

I blink rapidly, looking anywhere but at him. God, what the hell was I thinking? Of course nothing can happen. How fucking absurd and completely out of line of me . . .

"*Sprinkles*." Dean's warm palm wraps around my wrist. "Mala, fucking look at me."

I swallow down my shame, meeting his eyes.

"I won't risk what we have." He shakes his head, his expression more determined with each word. "I can't risk you or this friendship; it means too much to me. *You* mean too much to me. Yes, Rohan would kill me, but . . ." He takes a breath, not finishing the thought. "Anyone else can come and go, but *this*," he tightens his hand around my wrist, "this is forever. Do you understand that?"

My eyes prick with tears I haven't shed in God knows how long. Forcing my lips to tip up, I urge my face not to give away the fissure that just formed inside my heart. Friendship. It's the only relationship we have room for between us. On and above that, I'm not even his type.

"Of course. I understand."

Relief settles in his features as he releases a breath. "Thank God. Fuck, Mala, please tell me we're good. Please tell me nothing has changed."

I don a wider smile, hoping my eyes don't betray my truth, and tell him what he wants to hear. "Yeah, we're good, Fido." I settle back on the couch with my knees folded up against my chest, hoping they'll veil my fractured heart. "I bet it was an aphrodisiac in that tea I gave you, or maybe it's your purple-stained teeth. I just lost my mind for a second."

And despite him knowing I'm lying through my teeth, he chuckles . . . except, it's as fake as my smile. "Yeah, I have that effect on women."

Chapter Seven

MALA

Seven Years Ago

"Stop avoiding the question," I say, watching Rohan center and hang the wreath over the bakery window. "Also, please stop wearing that hat. It makes you look like a seventy-year-old man."

We've spent the past two hours putting up a Christmas tree and ornaments—mainly in the shapes of various dogs—along with affixing a festive garland to the front of the bar and cashier stand. Rohan also wrapped some lights around the trees in the backyard, and my entire bakery feels transformed for the holiday season. And in classic Rohan form, he went through an entire fire safety checklist to ensure everything I did myself met his approval.

Getting off the step stool, he tilts his hat to the side to be extra annoying. "I've gotten a lot of chicks wearing this hat. And I'm not avoiding any questions."

I roll my eyes. "The only *chick* I'm asking about is Samantha, and clearly, she hasn't seen you in it because she would have changed her mind about you." I giggle when he throws me a dirty look. "Now, are you going to tell me or not? Are you guys getting serious?"

Over the past six months, Rohan has been seeing a fellow firefighter named Samantha. And though he's always tight-lipped about his love life—even with me—Samantha and I have gotten to know each other better. She comes into the café almost as regularly as Rohan and Dean, so we've become good friends over time.

She's a great girl—sweet, supportive, and most importantly, she's absolutely gaga over my brother. She even confessed to me that she's liked him since her first day at the fire station, but my bullheaded big brother refused to make a move on her for almost a year and a half, claiming it would make things too complicated to date a coworker. *Dufus*.

Rohan examines the mess on the floor—open plastic wrap and some glitter that's fallen from a few of the decorations. After grabbing the plastic and throwing it into the trash, he jaunts over to where I keep the vacuum before plugging it in. The man does everything like he's on a mission and following orders.

"You're right; she hasn't seen me wearing this hat." He smirks mischievously. "Lately, she hasn't seen me wearing anything at all . . ."

"Ew." I wrinkle my nose, trying not to vomit inside my mouth at the unwelcomed visual. "That's not what I asked, you monster. I'm going to have to wash my brain with bleach now. Thanks for that."

Rohan points at me accusingly. "Suits you right. It's the only way to get you off my back about my love life. Next time you ask, be ready for a more detailed account."

"Jerk," I mumble, placing the new reindeer dog treats I made inside the glass pastry case.

"I heard that," Rohan bellows over the din from the vacuum.

While the café had an incredible reception when I first opened, it took a little while for me to get the hang of everything from operations and budgets to promotions and advertising. I'm still running a mainly word-of-mouth business, but business has boomed over the past year. Not only do I have regular customers, but I've also had to open a small catering business on the side due to the overwhelming demand.

The extra profits have allowed me to hire reliable staff as well, so I can take some time off when needed. A year and a half ago, I hired Betty, an older lady who is my second-in-command store manager and baker, and Max, my full-time barista and cashier. The extra hands have been a boon for my sanity.

I'm in the back, emptying bags of sugar into a large container when the double doors open and Rohan peeks inside. "Need anything else, munch? I was going to take the trash, then head out."

I narrow my eyes at him. "Oh yeah? Another hot date with Samantha?"

My brother raises a brow. "The hottest. I'm planning on having her get on her knees, and—"

I place my palms on my ears as fast as I can. "No! Ew! Okay, okay! I'll stop asking. Now get out of here and never, ever come back, you lunatic!" I hold back a smile as I drop my hands. My brother gives me a self-satisfied grin. "You're the worst."

"You love me."

I roll my eyes. "Barely." I pause, giving him my doe-eyed look—the one that usually softens him up so he can actually listen. "Is it really so bad to admit you guys are getting serious? I'd only be excited for you. I want you to be happy, Ro."

Rohan gives me an exasperated look, relenting. "Fine. Yes." He takes off that god-awful hat and runs a hand through his hair. "Yes, things are getting serious, but . . . I also don't want to rush anything. I'm okay with taking things slow."

I nod. "Is that why you told her you couldn't spend

Christmas with her and her family in Sacramento? Because you're taking things slow?"

"Jesus." He pinches the bridge of his nose after rubbing his eyes. "Of course, she told you."

"You know we're friends, and besides, I really like her for you. Now, stop dodging. Is that why you aren't spending Christmas with her?"

He scoffs, his gaze a little shifty. "Why else wouldn't I? Plus, I'm only getting a couple of days off." He gives me a lopsided grin. "I'd much rather spend that time with my nosey and annoying-as-fuck little sister."

And there it is.

That glint of guilt in his eyes. The bob of his throat as he swallows through the pain that's always ready to surface, no matter how deep we've both tried to drive it down. Because it wasn't just me who lost two vital parts of my life that day; it was him, too.

My throat tightens, recognizing the lie he's not only telling me, but the lie he's willing to believe himself. He's always been this way.

Maybe it has to do with the fact that we have a ten-year age difference, or that he's had to raise me since I was ten, or that he still feels a sense of guardianship over me. No matter the reason, my brother has always put my needs and wants over his own.

I still remember the night of my eleventh birthday, when I woke up with blood inside my underwear. With my chin wobbling, I padded over to Rohan's door and woke him up. Within minutes, he had me on the phone with his then-girlfriend while he rushed to the nearest pharmacy to pick up an array of feminine products.

The next day, he handed me a book about reproduction and sat with me to "go over the basics."

The thought makes me smile as it pinches my heart. How

fucking hard must that have been? To have had to play the part of both my mom and my dad when he himself was still reeling from their loss.

He was always Mom's favorite—not that Mom didn't love me, because she absolutely did. But while I was Dad's little girl, always doted on by him, Rohan was the glimmer in Mom's eyes. No matter what was happening in his life, Mom was always the first to know, the first person he'd run to.

And though I've told him I'm here, that I'm not the same kid he had to protect all those years ago, and that he can tell me anything . . . I'm not our mom.

At my core, I know it was an accident.

I know I'm not to blame for the loss of our parents. And coming to terms with that, and the fact that though I survived, I was still a victim, took years of therapy.

But no matter how many times I've emerged from under the weight of guilt and despair, it has a way of rearing its ugly head from time to time.

More often than not, though, it's times like these—the holidays when everyone is taking time off to spend with family—that I miss our parents even more.

If they were still alive, perhaps I wouldn't just be planning out the café's pastry menu. Perhaps I'd be chatting with Mom about all the goodies we'd make together in her kitchen during the weekend. Perhaps I'd be talking to Dad about all the movies we'd watch together when Rohan and I visited. Perhaps we'd all snuggle together on the couch while I rested my head on Dad's shoulder and Rohan held Mom's hand.

Sometimes my brother reminds me so much of our dad. The way he styles his hair, his warm and steady gaze, his deep voice, and brisk gait.

The way he puts his life on the back burner to spare me from being alone . . .

I won't stand for it anymore.

"You can totally request more time off, and you know it," I throw back, tilting my head. "And, anyway, I sort of have plans." *I don't, but I plan to make some the minute Ro leaves.*

His brows pinch. "What plans?"

I shrug, pretending to feel offended, but really, I'm just stalling. "What? You don't think people want to hang out with me? They totally do. I'm popular like that." I swipe my tongue over my lips, frantically trying to come up with something believable. "Betty asked me to join her and her granddaughter at her lake house for the break. I was thinking about going."

A tinge of hurt crosses Rohan's features. "We've always spent Christmas together, munch."

I walk over to him, blinking back the tears that seem hellbent on brandishing over my cheeks. Grabbing hold of his biceps, I look up at him. "I love you, big bro, more than anyone else in this entire world. But you cannot stop your life and constantly worry about me. *I want this for you.* I want you to find love. I want you to spend time with your girlfriend. One day, we'll spend holidays all together, but this time, I want you to spend it with her."

He stares at me, jaw popping. "Are you lying to me about Betty?"

I shake my head quickly. "No. Why would I?"

"I don't know, munch . . . Maybe it's because you have this way of putting everyone else's needs ahead of yours or getting it in your head that you're a burden or something."

I huff out a laugh. "Clearly, I'm following in my brother's footsteps that way. But, seriously, no. I'm not lying. I *do* have plans, and once you're back from Sacramento, I want to hear all about how things went with Samantha's family."

He rolls his eyes, but reluctantly agrees, nodding toward the ovens and stovetop behind me. I know what he's going to say before he even says it. He can mask his words behind the guise of being a firefighter, but I know the real reason behind them. *Fear*. Fear of losing me like he lost our parents. "Make sure to double-check that all that shit is turned off before you lock up, you hear me?"

"You know I always do," I respond, suppressing the twinge of guilt that pops up now and then at the fact that he still doesn't know about the oven fire from my first weekend back in Tahoe.

He ruffles my hair and I bat at his hand. "Later, munch. Love you."

"Love you, too, brosky."

He shakes his head. "No. Come up with something different."

"I will when you come up with something besides *munch*. It reminds me of a cow munching grass."

He shakes his head before grabbing the bags of trash and heading toward the exit. "Remember to—"

"Turn off the lights on the Christmas tree and check the doors twice after I lock up," I finish for him, giving him a wide grin.

He gives me another exasperated huff, but finally heads out.

I BEND to give Goldie a treat, hugging her around her neck. She's wearing one of the reindeer antlers I had out in a basket on the bar. "Who's my favorite German shepherd?"

She chomps on the cookie enthusiastically with her tail wagging a mile a minute.

Her owner, Terrance, holds the coffee I just made him in one hand while he keeps his other firmly around Goldie's leash. He's a regular at the bakery and always stops by right before I'm closing up since that's the time he takes her for a walk. "I swear, she is addicted to these dog treats. We can't even be in the vicinity of this café; otherwise, she'll pull me toward it until I relent."

I chuckle, giving Goldie another scratch behind her ears. "Well, you both are welcome here any time, you know that."

Once the last of the customers have left, Betty, Max, and I clean up the kitchen and backyard. We pull the shades down over the windows and turn off the *Open* sign.

It's the day before Christmas Eve, and I've decided to close the bakery until the day after Christmas.

After Max leaves, Betty pulls her coat over her arms, eyeing the steadily falling snow through the window. "I hope you have a wonderful Christmas, Mala. I'll see you bright and early Monday morning."

She's a short and stout woman of about seventy, and one of the finest bakers I've met. In fact, I've learned quite a few tips and tricks from her. But even more than that, she's honest, reliable, and incredibly punctual. All the things Meg—the first assistant I hired and fired all within a few months—was not.

"Have a very merry Christmas, Betty. Stay warm and drive safely. I'll see you on Monday."

After Betty leaves, I'm just re-checking the locks on the back door and lowering the heat on the thermostat when the bell above the door chimes. A familiar set of broad shoulders and shoulder-length blond hair fills the entryway. He's wearing a long dark coat and there's a dusting of snow on his shoulders and black cap. But, as always, he looks ridiculously handsome, like he deserves to be on a magazine cover or a poster.

"Hi!" I smile, giving him a quizzical look. "I thought you were heading over to your dad's and Karine's house tonight?"

Dean gives me a look I can't quite decipher. "And I

thought you told me you were heading to the lake house with Betty."

Dammit. He must have run into her outside. I never told Betty about me using her as my alibi, so she probably gave away the fact that I wasn't joining her for Christmas. Heat floats up to my cheeks, but I know he can't see it, given the distance between us. "Oh, well, I had a bit of the sniffles, so I thought I'd just stay home in case it got worse. I wouldn't want to get anyone else sick."

With his hands inside the pockets of his jeans, he closes the distance between us. "You lying to me, *sprinkles?*"

I shake my head, lying, of course. Then, I cough for effect. "Of course not."

He pulls out his phone, turning on the flashlight. "Open your mouth."

"Wha—what? No!"

He stalks closer, holding my gaze while I take a few steps backward, pressing up against the wall behind me. "Open your mouth. I want to see if your tonsils are inflamed."

I pull up my sweatshirt, feeling my pulse accelerate. "No. I might get you sick." I cough again.

"I'll take my chances."

I grunt. "What are you, a doctor now?"

One of Dean's arms cages me in while he holds the phone up, tilting the flashlight toward my mouth. His eyes trail down my neck to the place where he now knows my scar starts.

"No, but I am a paramedic. I'd know if you were lying." He cages me in with his other arm when I swat at him, trying to get away. "What are you so afraid of? If you're sick, I'll leave you alone."

I give him an exasperated look. "Okay, fine. I'm not sick. Can you go away now?"

He holds my eyes. "I get why you lied to Rohan—you

wanted him to spend Christmas with his girl. But why lie to me?"

"I–I just . . . I didn't want you to feel sorry for me or anything. I'm perfectly capable of having a wonderful and very merry Christmas on my own." *No, I'm not.* My plan was to pop a bag of popcorn, paint my nails, and watch *Bambi* or something.

"Sorry for you?" Dean scoffs. "Mala, the last time I felt sorry for you was when I beat you seven times in a row at darts. I mean, you truly suck. Like," he blows out a breath, feigning disappointment, "you're terrible."

I punch him in the abs, but he doesn't flinch. "You're a jackass. I wasn't warmed up that day. And as you can see, unlike you guys at the fire station, I don't have a dartboard at the bakery where I can just practice whenever I want."

He squints. "Oh, is that what's holding you back from beating me? *Practice?*"

I square my shoulders. "Yes."

"So you're saying you'd win if you have time to warm up?"

"No doubt about it. I won two hundred dollars in college from throwing darts and beating a group of guys who were way more sober than I was."

"Alright." He nods. "I'll take that bet."

"But I didn't make a–"

"You're coming to my dad and Karine's house with me tomorrow morning. I'll give you all the time you need to warm up on their dartboard, and then it's you versus me and my brothers."

My mouth drops open. "Um, no, I'm not–"

He backs away from me, walking toward the exit. "Have your bag packed for a couple of days. I'll pick you up at eleven. Karine's making traditional Armenian food, my favorite."

"Dean–" I rush after him, but he's too fast. Before I can

stop him, he's dashed back to his truck, throwing up a peace sign at me.

Ugh, he's annoying.

"TAKE ONE MORE DOLMA, Mala. You haven't eaten a thing!" Karine doesn't wait for my acceptance before she's putting another dolma on my dish. And as for her comment about not having eaten anything, my currently expanded stomach, seconds from ripping through my jeans, would disagree.

Yes, I wore jeans today. It's not often that I dress in anything but my shorts and sweatshirt, but given that I'm a guest at someone's house—though everyone is dressed casually—I wanted to look a bit more presentable. So, I opted for a black turtleneck and dark-washed denims.

Do I feel a bit suffocated and overdressed in this attire? Yes. But I suppose most people feel that way in formal wear.

Dean smiles at me from across the table, addressing Karine, "She's just being shy."

Karine frowns at me. "Mala *jan*, you don't need to be shy when it comes to food, especially not in my house. No one goes hungry here, and there's plenty of food."

I glare at Dean before kicking him under the table. As usual, the asshole doesn't even flinch. "I literally ate half of what's on this table—at least twice what you ate. I'm definitely *not* shy when it comes to food."

This isn't the first time I'm visiting the Meyer family. In fact, I've been invited to Dean's dad and stepmom's house on a number of occasions. Over the summer, I was even here when they hosted a Fourth of July get-together, and then again when we celebrated Karine's birthday in October.

I've never seen a family quite like theirs, blended in a way you wouldn't even know it. Karine is the quintessential mom—

constantly doting on her boys, two of whom, Garrett and Dean, she didn't even birth but loves like her own. Marvin is the calmest, most even-tempered dad. Like his twins, he's fair-skinned with blond hair and blue eyes, but like his youngest son, Darian, he's sharp and perceptive. While Garrett and Dean tend to be talkative and entertaining, Marvin and Darian sit back and observe, taking everything in with keen awareness.

I'm slowly finishing up another dolma, hoping my stomach will create a bit more room in there for it, when Sonia, Darian's wife, turns to me. She's beautiful in that perfectly put-together way with shaped brows and flawless skin. But there's an iciness to her demeanor that rivals the chill in the Tahoe breeze.

With the way she surveys me, I get the feeling she thinks of me as nothing more than an inexperienced toddler fumbling her way inside a kiddie pool.

"So, Mala, how are things at the café?" she asks, garnering the attention of everyone at the table. She chuckles with an air of condescension. "Still giving away half your cookies for free?"

A few months ago, Sonia and Darian stopped by *Doggy Bag Café* to grab a box of cookies and drinks for their staff at their sports school, and I refused to charge them for it. Darian is Dean's brother, and someone I've come to respect over the time I've interacted with him. I just didn't feel right taking his money.

But instead of thanking me, Sonia proceeded to lecture me about the ins and outs of running a successful business. For five minutes, she went on about how giving things away would become an expectation from my customers, and that I'd quickly find myself having to hike up prices to compensate for my generosity. I suppressed my eye roll, nodding as I thanked her for her advice. Again, out of my respect for Darian.

Over the course of my interactions, I've realized that like me, the Meyer family—not including Darian, of course—isn't a huge fan of Sonia, either. For the most part, they seem to keep their distance, but they love Darian so much that they tolerate her for his sake.

Before I can answer her, Dean chimes in for me, a muscle ticking in his jaw, "You know what's interesting? She *does* give away half the stuff she bakes, but somehow, she still happens to make a killing." His eyes wash over me with a warmth I've come to expect from him. "*Doggy Bag Café* was even named one of the top three small businesses in Tahoe. How many people can claim they've been on that list?"

"Congratulations, Mala!" Garrett says, throwing me a charming smile, rivaling his twin's. Garrett is a pilot and quite the ladies' man, from what I hear. Of course, I'm not surprised, given the charisma that seems to roll off him—and his twin—in spades.

"Thanks!" I respond, quickly covering my plate with my hands when Karine tries to place another piece of *lavash* on it. The woman is relentless about feeding everyone, though I haven't seen her ask Sonia if she wants seconds. "I've been really lucky because of the location."

"That location is amazing, but don't sell yourself short," Darian pipes in, leaning over to look at me from his seat next to his wife. "You've worked hard and it's paying off."

I smile back at him, feeling warm inside my chest. "Thanks. It's been an incredible learning experience, that's for sure."

Garrett leans toward me. "It's a really unique concept, actually. I don't think I know of another café of the sort in our area—one that caters to both dogs and their owners. Did you always know you were going to build a business like it?"

I shake my head. It's a question I've been asked often by both customers and friends. "The café was inspired by my love for both animals and baking, but my dream job in college was to work for *Doggone Happy and Healthy*—the organic dog food company," I clarify. "I'd fallen in love with their mission, and I'd heard great things about their work culture. I'd applied a few times even after graduation, but never heard anything back."

"You should apply again," Sonia adds. "Who knows, you might get something now that you have experience."

An oblivious third person listening in might think Sonia was giving me good advice—telling me not to give up on my dreams. But from the little I've interacted with her, she doesn't seem to be the most well-intentioned.

And while a huge part of me still wonders what it would have been like to work for one of my dream companies, I shrug, giving her a polite smile. "I'm pretty happy with running the café for the time being."

"And she's doing a hell of a job of it," Dean adds, addressing Sonia, before scooting his chair back. "Ready to warm up that dartboard, *sprinkles*?" He tosses me a wink. I get the feeling he also wants to pull me away from any additional conversations with his sister-in-law.

I nod, getting out of my chair before heading to the kitchen to put my plate in the sink. Apparently, Darian and Marvin are on dish duty today, so the rest of us grab drinks and head to the game room, where there's both a pool table and a dartboard set up.

For the next half hour, Dean, Garrett, and I throw darts, laughing and talking shit to each other, while Karine lays back on the couch, cheering us on with a huge smile. I can't help but like her. She's not only the most caring and supportive mother, but completely smitten with her kids. And while I miss my own mother every single day, the pain seems to ebb whenever I'm around Karine.

I'm leaning against Dean on the other sofa, watching Garrett try to perfect his dart throwing skills when Dean's phone chimes with an incoming message. I try not to stiffen at the name *Jane* on the screen. Who he texts and sees is none of my business. Why should it bother me? We're just friends . . . we've established that we're just friends.

He types out a response, `I'll stop by tomorrow,` before turning off his screen and I nudge him with my shoulder.

"So, Jane, huh?" I wiggle my brows but don't quite feel the playfulness I'm going for.

He shakes his head, keeping his expression tight. "It's not what you think."

I shrug. "It doesn't matter what I think."

There's a pause between us while we both watch Garrett throw another dart before Dean flips his phone in his hands.

It almost seems like his comment is directed to his phone with the way his eyes are glued to it, but I know he's speaking to me. "It *always* matters what you think."

As soon as Darian and Marvin finish up in the kitchen, Sonia begs Darian to leave, making up an excuse of needing to be somewhere early in the morning. And though they plan to be back the next day to spend the rest of Christmas with the family, I can't help but notice how the twins eye each other with a frown, hating not being able to spend more time with their brother.

Hours after we've played a thousand rounds of darts, giggled, and eaten copious amounts of dessert, I'm looking through a few selfies of Dean and me from the evening on my phone in bed when it vibrates with an incoming text.

Sparky: You seriously suck at darts.

I smile, rolling my eyes as I turn on my side, sending him a response.

> **Me:** It's fine. I'm better at everything else compared to you, so I can live with that.

His text comes back seconds later, and I imagine him scoffing in the bedroom above mine.

> **Sparky:** You realize darts are supposed to be aimed at the dartboard . . . not the ceiling, right?

> **Me:** That was a one-off! I told you, I was getting ready to throw the dart at the board when that loud bang came from the kitchen and it made me jump.

> **Sparky:** And somehow, the dart ended up in the ceiling? I swear, I had second-hand embarrassment for you.

I laugh, typing back my response. If he were here, he'd get a solid punch to his bicep.

> **Me:** Shuddup. I hate you.

> **Sparky:** Liar.

I bite my lip, reading his last message. I *am* a liar. Because the last thing I feel toward this man—a man who is relentless and bossy, goofy and annoying, perceptive and thoughtful—is hate.

He owed me nothing and could have taken me at my word when I told him I was perfectly fine spending Christmas alone. But he didn't. Instead, he called my bluff and forced me to come hang out with his family—a family that made me feel like I was an extension of them, welcoming me with open arms. For the first time in years, they made me miss the things I've missed just a little less.

For the first time in years, the pain of not having my parents felt duller.

Me: Dean?

Sparky: I know, sprinkles. I'm glad you're here, too.

Chapter Eight

DEAN

Six years ago

OPENING THE DOOR TO MY TRUCK, I PULL THE PHONE closer to my face. "There's something different about you today. I mean, you always look like an angel, but you're even more breathtaking today."

"Oh, you hush," Grams chides, gleaming back at me through my screen. She purses her lips, pretending not to glow under my compliment, but I know she loves it. "Between you and Garrett, I don't know which one of you is the bigger flirt."

"Me. I'm the one with the bigger *everything*." I smirk.

"Dean Emerson Meyer! I am your grandmother, not one of the women you pick up at a bar with innuendos and false representations of yourself. Behave!"

I throw my head back and laugh. "Please, Grams, you know you're way more than our grandma. You're like our second mom and a cool elderly best friend combined in one beautiful package." I tilt my head to address the last few words in her statement. "And what do you mean, false representations? I know it's been a while since you've had to dress us, Grams, but I'm sure even back then you saw the truth . . . that I had the bigger–"

"Don't you dare finish that sentence, young man. And who are you calling *elderly*? Don't think that just because I'm getting older, I won't be able to take a spatula to your rear end."

My smile widens as I shut my car door and start walking up the steps to the little café that's become another home to me. If I'm not at the station or my own house, I'm here. "My mistake, Grams. I've never considered you a day over thirty-five."

Gram's gray bob ruffles in the cool Colorado breeze. She's sitting in her favorite chair on Mom's porch. "That's more like it. Now, where are you off to?"

I linger on the steps, leaning to look through the door but not seeing anyone inside. "Mala closed the bakery for the day."

Grams lifts her brows. "Oh! Why on earth would she do that? It's a Saturday. I imagine she'll lose a good amount of business."

"It's Rohan's birthday, but he's on shift all day, so Mala and I decided to throw him a little surprise party for when he gets off. In fact, we're having a bake-off. We're both going to make our favorite cakes and see which one everyone likes more. We have a few guys from the station coming in later to help decorate the place before Rohan heads over here."

Grams' eyes glitter, and I see the same mischief in them I've found in my own from time to time. "I see . . . A bake-off with your *'friend'*, huh?"

"Yes." I pull on the bakery door, only to find it locked. Mala must still be on her way. "No need to put air-quotes around the word. Whatever you're stewing inside that perfectly coiffed head of yours, stop it."

Grams brings up her white handkerchief—something she

carries inside her purse, no matter the time of day–and wipes the corner of her lip as if her lipstick was smudged. It isn't. "Hmm? I didn't say anything, dear boy. I simply said 'I see,' which is what I'm doing. I'm *seeing*. Observing."

"Right," I scoff. "I don't think you've had a single *simple* thought in your entire life. But for the umpteenth time, it's not like that between her and I."

It can't be. It *won't* be.

There's too much at stake. Not only would it fuck up my relationship with Rohan–a friend who trusts me the same as I trust him–but I won't let Mala get trapped in the whirlpool that is my life. Not like that, and definitely not forever.

Not when I see the devastation it causes to those we leave behind.

"Because if I knew what I know now–the anguish I've felt for the past three years–I'd tell that naive girl sitting at the bar, looking into those alluring brown eyes and making wishes that should never have been made, that the worst thing she could do for herself would be to fall for a firefighter."

'The worst thing she could do for herself would be to fall for a firefighter.'

It doesn't matter that things got a little . . . hairy that one night a couple of years ago in her apartment when we were just supposed to be watching TV and shooting the shit. It also doesn't matter that I've thought about that night more often than I care to admit. It doesn't even matter that that tension and electricity buzzed around us for weeks, if not months, after that. We both needed to move past it, and we did. Eventually.

I shouldn't have asked her to show me her scar in the first place. And even as the words left my mouth, I knew I had crossed a line I'd never come back from.

But enough was fucking enough.

Time and time again, I'd seen her tug on her damn collar,

raising it like she was trying to disappear behind it, and time and time again, all I wanted was to pull it the fuck down. Make her show me. Make her see me as someone different. Someone she never had to hide from.

Of course I'd read the reports of the fire she was in. There's not a firefighter in the state who hasn't heard of it. Not only was it one of the worst fires in the city's history—killing over thirty people and severely injuring several dozen—but it weighed on Rohan day and night. He never wanted to talk much about it, but for years after, he hated himself for not being there with them that day. He kept wondering if things would have been different if he were there. That perhaps he could have saved them somehow. That perhaps he could have prevented his sister from getting hurt.

That's when I'd found out about Mala's scars. I knew she had them, but I put two and two together when I realized that in the time I'd known her—no matter the weather outside—she'd keep everything below her collarbone hidden. Well, everything besides her fucking gazelle-like legs. It was as if she was trying to compensate by showing those off.

All. The. Fucking. Time.

She might be short, but I swear the girl's legs go on for days.

"Whatever it's like," Grams states, bringing my focus back to our conversation, "it's between you and Mala. All I know is what you've told me—that she makes you laugh when all you want to do is just smile. That she doesn't just listen to what you say, but she *hears* what you haven't. And *that*, my charming grandson, is more precious than any gem you'll ever find. *That* is the pot of gold at the end of the rainbow. So, whatever this is—a friendship or a chance for something more—don't let your fears get in the way of your happiness."

I'm trying to come up with a response when Mala's car

pulls into the parking lot. "Grams, can I chat with you a little later? Mala just got here."

"Absolutely! But at least let me say hi to the girl. I haven't seen her in months."

Mala makes her way up the steps, her keys jingling at her side. "Hi! Have you been waiting long?"

I shake my head, a smile finding my face at the sight of her. "Nope. Just chatting with this Chatty Cathy over here." I tilt my phone so Mala can see Grams. They both immediately launch into high-pitched greetings.

Mala grabs the phone from my hand, dismissing me in lieu of my grandma. "Did you get a haircut, Grams?"

"Oh! *That's* what was different about her!" I exclaim in the background. "I knew there was something."

"Just a trim, dear. I don't have the beautiful locks you do, so a simple little trim does the trick for me." Grams is all smiles as she poofs the hair on one side of her head. "So I hear you're doing a bake-off with my grandson."

Mala's silky black strands catch the breeze. Her lips only have a sheen of gloss, but I find it hard to avert my gaze from them. "I am. I hope he's ready to have his ass kicked."

I raise my eyebrows, giving her my *we'll-see-about-that* look.

"Oh, I'm sure you'll give him a run for his money, but I'll warn you, Mala," Grams says cheerily, "Dean is no novice. He and I have been baking together since he was a little boy, so he knows his way around an oven."

"It's how I get all the ladies." I waggle my brows at Mala. "My baking skills combined with my God-given good looks. They can't resist me."

"Clearly," Mala snorts and waves her hand. "Just look at them buzzing all around you as we speak."

"Well, you kids have fun. Send me pictures of the cakes and tell me which one was the crowd-pleaser." Grams smiles back at us from the screen before we say our byes and hang up.

As soon as we get inside the bakery, I follow Mala through the double doors to the back. "We never made a wager," I say, trying to keep my eyes off the way her hips swing in front of me. Even so, my eyes find themselves trailing up the back of her legs and sticking to the curve of her ass. "I should get something for when I kick your ass."

We both wash and dry our hands in the sink before she walks over to where all the dry ingredients sit inside large glass jars. She brings one closer to her before looking over her shoulder at me. "Spotty, the only ass that's going to be kicked–the only ass that will have welts from *my* boots–is yours."

I pull my hair up with a tie to keep it off my face before walking over to where she's standing to get the necessary amount of flour for my cake. "You don't own any boots."

Mala rolls her eyes. "Oh, that's right. I forgot that figures of speech are above your IQ level."

"Oh, you're gonna get sassy, are you? You just can't handle the fact that I might win, so you're being mean and deflecting with sarcasm."

"Ah, *deflecting*!" she volleys back. "Throwing out some big words today, are we?"

I smirk and notice her eyes snag on my lips. "I just had a similar conversation with Grams. You should know by now, everything about me is big. Big words, big heart, big di–"

"I'm not even sure how I should respond to knowing that you talked about your nether region with your grandma, because that is just weird as hell," she cuts me off. "But I'm going to stop you right there, Fido. Because the only thing big about you is the size of your hea–"

But before she can finish her sentence, I dump a cup of

flour over her head, covering her hair, face, and shoulders with white powder.

Mala stiffens before a gasp comes out of her mouth, revealing the pink of her lips underneath a dusting of white. She's so shocked, she doesn't even move for a few seconds, but I get the feeling I should run.

Her outraged eyes have me chuckling before she puts her hand inside the glass jar. "Oh, you little piece of shi–"

Coming behind her, I lift her off her feet before she can get much flour inside her little fist. Still, she manages to get some in my hair and on my forehead while she squeals. I turn her right as my fingers travel down to her stomach, finding that ticklish spot on her side, and Mala squeals.

"Dean! I swear to God." She laughs and wiggles in my hold, trying to catch her breath as more dusting of flour flies off her face and hair. "Dean! Put me down, you big ogre!"

Laughing, I tickle her again, but I don't miss the strange feeling pulling inside my chest. The fucking feeling that's been there since the day I met this woman. The same feeling that has me coming to see her every chance I get and running from her whenever I get too close. There's no name for it–at least none I'm willing to define or discuss–but it's a constant in her presence.

"You ready to take back what you said?" I chuckle in her ear. "You ready to admit you're being a pain in my ass already?"

She giggles, trying to swat me over her shoulder and on my arms to try to get out of my grasp. Her giggles turn into coughs, and all of a sudden, I'm not laughing anymore.

Shit! She probably inhaled some of that flour, and now I feel like a fucking idiot for throwing it on her.

I put her down gently on the counter and rush to get her a glass of water. I come up between her legs with both the glass and a hand towel. She takes a few sips of the water before her coughing subsides, her eyes watering.

I rub some of the flour from her face tenderly, looking at her with a frown on my face. God, what the fuck was I thinking? What if this causes a bigger reaction? I don't think she's asthmatic, but it couldn't have felt good to have all that flour inside her throat and lungs. My pulse hammers in my veins, the paramedic in me already preparing for the worst. But God, I pray she's okay.

Once she's fairly dusted off—save for the amount still in her hair—I cup her face. My frown deepens as my thumb slides over her cheekbone. "I'm sorry, *sprinkles*. I'm so fucking sorry. I shouldn't have—"

Mala starts giggling again and my brows pinch. "Told you. You make it just so easy to mess with you, Rufus."

I freeze in my spot, realizing it was all a joke. *She played me!*

My hand reaches back to her stomach as relief washes over me. Fuck, she totally had me. I start to run the tips of my fingers against her ticklish skin. "Why you little shit!"

She squeals, grabbing a hold of my hand. "No! Truce! Truce. I'm sorry I was being a pain in your ass."

"And for talking shit about my incredibly high IQ."

She holds back her laugh and deadpans, "And for talking shit about your IQ."

My fingers twitch inside her hand and she tightens her hold on them. "My *incredibly high* IQ."

She smiles, her eyes glittering even as tiny specs of powder line her lashes. "Your incredibly high IQ."

My eyes swallow up her face and I inadvertently lick my lips, feeling my heart rate quicken. But that's just from having picked her up and rushed around with her. Right?

I clear my throat, getting my hand out of her grasp. I put both my hands on the counter, caging her in. "Good."

A silence stretches between us, and I realize I'm way too close. I'd originally intended to leave my arms where they were to make sure she didn't fall, but she seems to be steady now that her fake coughing has subsided.

So, why am I still standing here?

Before I can even think about the answer to that question, I lift my hand. My eyes are pinned on her lips. I want to touch them, to feel them under my thumb, but somehow, I have the wherewithal to tuck a strand of her hair around her ear instead.

"Dean . . ."

My hand comes down in a fist at my side, and I take a step back, disconnecting whatever the fuck seemed to be buzzing between us. Jesus Christ. What the fuck is happening?

Mala blinks as if she was stunned back to reality, too, and before she can say anything more, I cover the silence between us.

"So, what's your wager?" I force a grin, winking at her and hoping to deflect whatever the hell this was with a dose of humor—something I've always been good at. "Or do you not even want to make one since you already know you'll lose?"

Mala's shoulders deflate before she collects herself with a smile. "Please. I had a wager ready before we even got here."

"Well, spit it out then. Those cakes aren't making themselves."

"If you lose—which, you will—you have to finally watch *Titanic* with me."

I groan. The girl is hellbent on making me sit through the sappiest shit. A few weeks ago, we watched *Ten Things I Hate About You*. The week after that was *The Notebook,* and I swear, I about shot myself. Like seriously, who the fuck says shit like, *'If you're a bird, I'm a bird'*? No one, that's who.

"Fine. But I refuse to watch the part where Leo dies. You know there was enough room for both of them on that float, but she just hogged up the entire thing herself. It's an injustice I won't stand by."

Mala gives me a solemn nod but her lips twitch, holding back a smile. "No, that makes sense. We'll just skip that part."

"Only if you win, which you won't," I remind her. "But if I win, you have to watch *Scarface* with me. That, or another episode of *Ancient Aliens* on the History Channel."

"Oh, hell no," she responds swiftly. "I will *not* watch another episode of that show."

I raise my hand to shake hers. "Then you better hope you win."

Chapter Nine

DEAN

"You guys completely had me," Rohan shouts over the music, taking a swig of his beer. "I just thought I was picking Mala up to go to dinner with Samantha. Almost had a heart attack when I opened the door and all you guys jumped out screaming."

I pat him on the back before clinking my beer bottle with his. "It's called a successful surprise party. Happy birthday, brother."

"And those cakes were so delicious," Samantha says, giving me a smile. "I knew Mala could bake, but I had no idea you could, too, Dean."

Samantha and Rohan have been dating for well over a year, and things seem to be going rather smoothly for them. She's good for him—someone who's not only supportive of what he does, but being a firefighter herself, she knows the risks and stresses of our job.

"But admit it, you liked my Bacardi piña colada cake better." I wink at Samantha, trying to make her change her mind.

She giggles before Rohan chimes in, "Your cake was

fucking delicious, I'll give you that. But that coffee-toffee crunch cake with the Heath bar crumbled over the icing that my sister made?" Rohan whistles. "That shit was *divine*."

I shake my head, feigning offense, but really, I was happy to lose to her. "Dude, she had an unfair advantage because she bakes all the time, and she's your little sister."

Rohan nods. "I'll give you that, too, brother. That kid will always have an unfair advantage in my book. Even if she'd made the cake with salt instead of sugar, she would have won." Rohan shifts his gaze to the bar where the rest of our friends and co-workers are mingling. Something affectionate swirls in his eyes—affection I've only seen for two people, Mala and now Samantha. He drags his eyes back to me. "Still, thanks for putting the party together."

"It was all Mala. She's been planning it for a while."

After the party, I stayed back to help her clean, and when we were done, I asked her to come out with us to the bar, but she refused, saying she was tired and needed to wake up early to open back up in the morning.

Still, I can't deny her presence, her laugh, her witty come-backs—*her*—aren't being missed. It's like when she's around, things just feel right in the world.

Malcolm buys us all another round of shots, and we raise our glasses in cheers before we slam them back. I've lost count of how many I've had so far, but one thing's for sure, I'm fucking feeling them. While I can hold my alcohol well, I don't drink often, so these shots of pure liquid fire are doing nothing but making my vision blurry.

"I love that kid," Rohan proclaims, setting his shot glass on the table behind him. "Which is why, if any of you fuckers touch her," he swings his gaze around the room, not particu-larly landing on any one of us, "I'll cut your fucking balls off. That girl is way too precious for any of you. She's been through a lot in a very short time, and the last thing she needs is for some asshole to come around to break her heart." Rohan hiccups. "Which is why I went fucking CIA beast-mode when it came to this new guy she just started seeing."

I blink.

What the fuck did he just say?

I blink again, taking in his slightly slurred words. He's had a lot to drink, but so have I. My ears ring, my blood rushing through my veins like it's been electrified.

"Don't get me wrong, I'm not happy about it. No one is good enough for my baby sister, but it's not like I can keep her in a cage, either," he huffs. "He's alright, I guess. A little pretentious and a bit of a pretty-boy if you ask me, but hey, what do I know?"

Everyone around us laughs as if in on some inside joke, but I'm still trying to decipher if he's even speaking English.

"His name's Warren. He was coming around the café a lot. Apparently, he asked her out every chance he got . . ."

The fuck?

". . . she finally said yes a couple of weeks ago, and they've been out a few times–"

"I wasn't aware she was dating someone," I clip, my molars grinding and my nostrils flaring. "You've talked to him?"

Rohan pats me on the shoulder. "I met him. Seems like a decent guy. He's a real estate agent and flips houses on the side. Seems to do well for himself, too." His eyes finally catch mine, and he must see the rage in them. "Fuck, I thought she would have told you. You're like another brother to her . . ."

The rest of Rohan's sentence curls around the din from the bar. I don't hear it or the laughter around us as the conversation continues.

She's fucking dating someone and never told me?

We spent the entire day together, making cakes, laughing,

and catching up . . . and she didn't feel the need to tell me? What the fuck?

I try to ease the anger rising to the surface, thoughts that make me feel unleashed, untethered from the inside.

I know I have no right, *no fucking right,* to feel this incensed, but I swear, the betrayal feels purposeful. I have no right to feel any of this—this fury, this shock . . . this ache, as if my chest is being ripped open.

Why should I feel this way? Where is any of it coming from? It makes no goddamn sense whatsoever.

But seriously, *how the fuck could she?*

I'm just on my way to the bar to close out my tab and get the fuck back home—my good mood completely shot—when I feel a hand on my elbow.

I look over to catch the hazel eyes of a pretty blonde with a sultry smile.

"H-hi," she stutters, falling into me when someone bumps her. The drink in her hand sloshes over the rim of her glass and lands on my shirt. "Oh, shit. I'm so sorry!" She puts her glass down on the bar and grabs a couple of napkins, dabbing at my shirt before looking up at me again. "I'm so sorry. That was not how I saw this going in my head."

I swallow through the million thoughts swirling around in my brain—none of them about her. I barely even register the chill from my wet shirt or this woman dabbing at it like it's her mission.

All my thoughts feel jumbled, like they've been put in a blender, but a couple keep coming back to the forefront. Specifically, the thought of some fucker putting his hands on my . . . Mala. Of someone taking her out and making her laugh.

And she never told me . . .

Why the fuck didn't she tell me?

And why the fuck am I having such a hard time with this?

It's not like I never expected her to find someone. Of course, I did. Didn't I?

It's not like she's mine—not in *that* way. She can't be. Not when I can't promise the forever she deserves. So why? Why does none of this feel right?

"How did you see this going in your head?" I ask the blonde, despite not knowing how I formed the words, despite every internal inkling telling me to leave.

Get the fuck out of here and go the fuck home.

Fume in peace.

She sidles closer to me, leaving mere inches between us. Right behind her, my eyes connect with Rohan's. He raises his bottle in the air, cheersing me, as if to say, *"Good for you, buddy!"*

But he has no clue. No fucking clue.

Just like me.

"I saw this with me introducing myself, you buying me a drink, and us finding a place to be alone."

I lick my lips, disconnecting my gaze from her. I'm still seeing red, but that's not her fault. "Yeah." I hear myself say with a nod. "Yeah, that sounds like a good plan. So, how about we start from the beginning?"

Ten minutes and another drink later, I'm pinned against the front of the building with Taylor—or did she say her name was Sailor?—cupping my flaccid cock over my jeans. We're waiting for an Uber because I'm too fucking tossed to drive my truck back home.

Her mouth moves from my neck, where she's been sucking on the same spot for God knows how long, to my lips, but I turn my face away before she can catch them.

She doesn't seem to take offense, giggling through her words. "I saw you from across the bar and knew I had to talk to you. You're seriously the hottest guy I've ever met."

The dull ache in my chest seems to stab against my heart, then my lungs, traveling to my fucking stomach.

I should take her home, fuck her into oblivion.

I should release this pent-up frustration and rage until neither of us can see straight.

I mean, if *she* didn't have the balls to tell me about this fucker she's dating–could possibly be fucking–then why should I feel guilty about fucking a random chick from the bar?

Because you haven't fucked anyone since you broke up with Nora.

And in my drunken state–or possibly even in a sober state–that thought about *why* I haven't fucked anyone since Nora isn't one I have the brain cells to expend on.

I clear my throat right as our Uber arrives. "Listen, Taylor–"

"It's Megan."

"What?" My brows furrow. How the hell did she become a *Megan* from a Taylor-Sailor?

The self-proclaimed Megan doesn't seem offended that I called her the wrong name. Instead, she just laughs as if it's cute that I forgot her name in the span of fifteen minutes. "My name is Megan, silly."

Sure it is. "Right. *Megan*, listen, you're great–perfect, in fact!–but I'm not sure this is a good idea."

Megan juts out her bottom lip, making a pouty-face. "Aww, are you sure? I've been told I have quite the magic tongue." She winks at me, like if she didn't, I wouldn't know what she meant.

"As tempting as that sounds, I'm going to have to pass."

With another frown, she reaches into my pocket, pulling out my phone before asking me to unlock it. When I do, she punches in her number and hands it back to me. "Fine, but call me if you change your mind and remember," she bops me on the nose, "my name is Megan. Megan with the magic tongue."

With a quick kiss on my cheek and a promised whisper to do very naughty things to me, Megan struts to the awaiting Uber. I'm too busy looking down at my phone to notice her driving away. I open my text messages to see one I missed from Mala a little while ago.

> Sprinkles: Just got home. You owe me Titanic, Rufus. I may not be the best at darts anymore, but I own your ass when it comes to baking. #easiestwinever. <sticking tongue out emoji>

And instead of doing the thing I know I should do–go home and act like a fucking adult or jerk off this rage in the shower–I pull up the Uber app and do the exact opposite.

I KNOCK for the third time, my shoulder leaning against the side of her entryway. "Open up, Mala."

Get out of here.

Call another Uber and leave.

She doesn't need to see your drunk ass here.

I hear the latch on her door before the deadbolt unclicks, and Mala's face appears in her door. Her hair is mussed–cleansed of the flour I'd doused her with earlier–and her eyes are bleary, but I'm glad to see that at least she hasn't covered herself up with her fucking sweatshirt. She's wearing a crop top with thin straps that reveals her burn scar, along with some sleep shorts.

"Dean?" Her voice is groggy, like she just pulled herself out of a heavy sleep. "What are you–"

I fumble inside without her inviting me in, and she opens

the door wider, turning on a small entryway light. The scent of fucking lemon and heaven surrounds me, and I clench my fists to be able to endure it.

I have no idea what time it is—way later than it should be for me to show up like this, and too early for her to be up, given she needs to reopen the bakery soon—but I'm a selfish bastard.

"Dean," she tries again, eyeing me apprehensively as she closes the door. "How much did you drink? Wait," her eyes widen, "you didn't drive here like this, did you?"

My finger lifts before I can tell it to stop, and I glide the tip of it over her scar, making her flinch, before my hand closes in a fist at my side again. My voice pricks the heavy silence between us. "Has he seen this?"

Her eyes glimmer, the sleep swimming inside them earlier having disappeared. "W-what?"

My jaw locks as my unsteady gaze lingers on her lips. Her fucking ridiculously plump lips that seem almost unnaturally pink, even without a lick of anything on them. "*Warren*. Has he had the *privilege* of seeing your scar?"

Her eyes bounce against mine as her shoulders release and she registers what I've said . . . that I know. "I was going to tell y—"

"You were going to tell me," I repeat with a chuckle. "*You were going to tell me?* When, *sprinkles*? Because from what I can tell, you've had plenty of time. Perhaps every morning last week when I came to the café, or the two times I helped you clean up after my shift? Or—"

"Dean—" Mala's hand finds my shoulder and I flick it off, making her eyes instantly pool with my rebuke.

I fucking hate myself for this uncontrolled pyre building inside me, but I can't seem to douse it.

"Or *maybe* you could have told me in one of the several hundred text messages we send to each other in a day, or when you came over and we read together on my damn couch *for four hours* just days ago. Or, oh, I don't know . . ." I lift my arms, letting them drop to my sides. "*Today,* when we spent an entire fucking day baking!"

Mala nods, her chin wobbling. "Yeah, you're right, Dean, I could have told you all those times, but why . . .?" She takes in a shuddering breath. "Tell me why you're so angry. Tell me why I owe you an explanation when *you* were the one who–" Her watery gaze battles with mine, and mine dares her to finish her thought. After a pause, she seems to compose herself marginally. "Tell me why you're here fuming–"

"Because we're friends, Mala!" I boom, making her flinch. "Because you're my goddamn best friend, and I should have known!"

A part of me feels like an asshole for yelling, but fuck! *Does she not get it?* Does she not know what she fucking means to me? Does she not know how this is twisting me up so hard inside that I feel like a damn pretzel?

She nods as a tear drops to her cheek. "Yeah, sparky. We're friends. You've made that abundantly clear. So, in that light, we should tell each other about who we see and who we fuck, right?" Her eyes blaze, landing on my neck, at what I'm sure is the hickey Megan left there. "Clearly, you've divulged all your conquests with me."

My hand finds the damn bruise on my neck, and I feel like a fucking asshole all over again. "It wasn't even like that."

Mala laughs without an ounce of cheer. "It doesn't matter what it was like, Dean. We've known each other for what, three years now? Have you told me about every fucking Jane and Julie you've hooked up with?"

I hold her gaze, knowing the reason she specifically brought up that name. "You're deflecting, and Jane *is* a friend."

"A friend." Her eyes bounce angrily against mine. "A friend

I've never met in the years I've known you. A friend you leave to see randomly during Christmas get-togethers without explaining anything to anyone."

My head hits the wall behind me, and I lose the fight inside me. "You want to know who Jane is? I'll fucking tell you. Jane is my friend Zander's widow. Zander and I were in the fire academy together, and he died when we were called to fight the fucking California fires years ago. He told me to take care of his wife before he died, and that's what I try to do by visiting her and her five-year-old daughter, my goddaughter—a kid Zander didn't even know about when he died. I try to see them when I can." I pause, keeping my eyes on her. "Now you know who Jane is. Happy?"

Mala's throat bobs as her anger wanes. Her warm hands cup my face, and she closes the distance between us. "I . . . I didn't know, Dean. You never told me," she whispers as her sweet breath tickles my lips. "Why didn't you tell me about them?"

I swallow through the dryness building in my throat. "I don't know."

How do I explain any of it? My fears, the constant internal struggle, my fucking nightmares? Watching him take his last few breaths. Seeing his heart break into a thousand pieces, knowing he was leaving her but not being able to do a single thing about it.

How do I explain to her the shit Jane has been through, the years of therapy after having lost the love of her life? Sure, she's doing better now—a lot better—but it doesn't take away the likely fact that she still believes the words she said to me after Zander died.

How do I explain to her how those words thrash around in my head every night like wild beasts in a mosh pit?

What would telling Mala accomplish anyway, except shed more light on a fear she likely already lives with?

So many people in her life, including her brother and me, are firefighters and risk our lives every day. Why immerse her further in the fear of losing any of us?

The only hope I have is that she never faces losing the only family she has left and . . . that she never gets involved with one of us. She's already been through too much, and she doesn't deserve an ounce more of pain.

Mala heaves out a sigh as a silence settles between us. "I'm sorry I didn't tell you about Warren. I should have."

I stare at her, knowing I shouldn't ask but do, anyway. "Why didn't you?"

Mala leans away from me, her head hanging as she struggles to answer. "I don't know. Fear, maybe? I guess I was scared of your reaction, but I knew I'd have to tell you sooner or later, anyway."

I nod, despite the burning sensation between my ribs. "Do you like him?"

Her lips lift into a curve and, as much as I hate that they lift at the thought of him, I love her smile too much to want her to stop. "I think so."

We stare at each other in silence for a moment and a million thoughts race through my head—none of which I can voice, not even to myself.

"For the record, I already fucking hate him."

Her shoulders sag as her smile disappears. "You haven't even met him."

"I don't need to meet him to know he doesn't deserve you. No one does."

"He's a nice guy, Dean. It's important to me that you and Rohan give him a chance."

I hold in the roar that wants to be set free and move toward her door, pulling on the knob with more force than I intended. "Fine."

I'm just about to step out when she grabs my elbow, questions floating in her eyes, surely from my curt response. "Dean—"

"You want me to meet him, pretend I like him, and play nice? *Fine*, I will. I'll do all those things. You know why? Because I'd do anything for you, Mala. *Anything*. But . . ." I give her a hard look, "he gets one, *only one*, chance to fuck this up. And when he does, I'll tear him limb for fucking limb."

Leaving her with her mouth agape behind me, I close the door and clumsily amble down the stairs.

I barely even register my fingers moving as I type out a message. The only thing I can focus on is the ire laced with melancholy thrumming through my bloodstream.

I can't make heads or tails of any of it, but at the edges of that anger is a feeling of mourning, as if I've lost something monumental, but I can't name what or why.

All I want is for this feeling to disappear, for it to stop.

Even if it's just for a night.

So, without further thought into the fact that I haven't sent a message like this to anyone in God knows how long, I hit *Send*.

> Me: So about that magic tongue of yours . . .
> Send me your address.

Chapter Ten

MALA

"MIND IF I TAKE OFF FOR HALF THE DAY TOMORROW?" MAX turns over his shoulder from his spot at the sink, where he's washing some steel frothing pitchers. "Blaire has her first sonogram tomorrow, and I want to make sure I'm there for her."

I nod as enthusiastically as possible, trying to quell my anxiety. "Sure, no problem."

Max handed in his notice earlier this week, telling me he accepted a higher-paying job with the water-treatment facility in town that will also offer him and his girlfriend better healthcare benefits. While I know he needs to be there for her during such a crucial and exciting day tomorrow, it's also the start of our busy spring season, and I'm stressed all around.

I've put up a few *We're Hiring* ads, but I haven't had much luck in terms of finding anyone with experience as a barista and someone who likes animals enough to clean up after them.

I take the cup of coffee Mrs. Carver ordered off the bar, along with an apple-ginger dog treat we just baked a few batches of yesterday, and stroll through the back door to deliver them to her. She's an elderly lady of about eighty, who has been a regular at the café with her shih tzu, Gigi.

"Oh, you are such a dear." She smiles, making the heavy wrinkles around her eyes and mouth crinkle gently. She picks up the dog biscuit and offers it to Gigi, who happily gobbles it down. With a leash around her neck, the dog looks up at me with her tongue hanging out from her spot on the ground next to Mrs. Carver's chair. Soon enough though, she sniffs the air and her attention is diverted toward the black lab on the other side of the yard.

"You're welcome," I reply, smiling at the both of them before I notice Mrs. Carver tug her coat around her again. It might be April, but the temperature in Tahoe is known to fluctuate during the month and can sometimes get pretty darn chilly, like today. "Want me to turn on the heat lamp for you, Mrs. Carver?" I ask her, tilting my head toward one of the lamps behind her.

She waves in a *don't-fuss* gesture after taking a sip of her mocha latte. "We're about to walk back home in a few minutes, anyway. I just love coming here and letting Gigi mingle and play with the other dogs. It's quite a unique café you've created here, Mala."

I bend down to scratch Gigi under her chin. "Thank you. I'm glad to see you both."

Leaving them to enjoy their afternoon, I saunter back toward the café, pulling out my phone from inside my shorts to check my messages.

Though I still get raised brows from out-of-towners when they regard my attire of shorts and a sweatshirt, I no longer receive the same quizzical looks from locals. They seem to have accepted me for the slightly eccentric woman I am.

There's a message from Malcolm in response to my previous message in the group chat I have with him, Rohan,

Samantha, and Dean, asking if everyone was still on for *movie madness* at my place tomorrow night. It's a ritual we started a few months ago, where we get together once a month at one of our homes and watch a classic movie together. This month's movie night is at my house.

Malcolm: I'm in. Which movie?

I pull my bottom lip under my teeth, holding back a grin while typing out my response.

Me: Titanic.

Samantha: I'll be there.

A few seconds later, I get the response I was expecting that has me chuckling.

Malcolm: Oh, fuck no. I'm out.

I open the door to get back into the café before typing out another message.

Me: Stop it, you big faker. You've probably seen it a hundred times already. I saw you watching My Girl on your laptop that one day I visited the station.

Malcolm: How many times do I have to tell you, shorty? It was a Youtube clip Baron sent me.

I smile, not taking offense to the nickname Malcolm and the guys at the station have given me. I'm on the short side, so I own it.

Me: Uh huh. Do you cry during all the
Youtube clips you watch?

Malcolm: Oh, you are going to get it the next
time I see you. I'm going to kick your ass
from here to Nantucket.

I giggle as another message pops in.

Rohan: Careful. No one looks at, touches, or
speaks about my sister's ass.

Me: <rolling eyes emoji>

Malcom: <rolling eyes emoji>

Samantha: <rolling eyes emoji>

Malcolm: I'll be there, but no bets on if I'll
stay awake.

I'm just putting my phone in my back pocket when a familiar baritone voice has me snapping my head up to find it.

My smile is immediate at the sight of my best friend munching a cookie—I'm willing to bet it's one from the dog treats case—while talking animatedly with Betty.

God, I am so fucking glad to see him.

It's been two weeks since he showed up at my apartment drunk and we had that rather awkward conversation about me dating Warren.

And while we have texted here and there, this is the first time I'm seeing him since that night. I even stopped by his apartment on my way home one night, but he wasn't around. I can't be sure, but I get the feeling he's been avoiding me.

And it fucking sucks.

I honestly don't know how much he remembers from the night—given how wasted he was—but I've been thinking about confronting him about it nonetheless, so I'm glad he's here now.

He hasn't noticed me yet, but I take the moment to admire him without interruption—loosely slung jeans on thighs I know are large and toned, broad shoulders and a tapered waist, and hair that's up in his usual half-bun.

My fist clenches around my side as I squash the desire to run my fingers through the hair at his nape. I shouldn't be having desires like that in the first place, but definitely not now with me dating Warren.

Dean's words from that night roll around in my head as I close the distance between us. *"For the record, I already fucking hate him."*

I get it. I really do. Like Rohan, Dean feels protective of me, so he was hurt that he had to hear about my love life from someone else. And I understood where that sentiment came from. Hell, I felt the same way about Jane until he told me who she was.

Still . . . there was something else behind his outrage that night. Something that didn't add up. And unless I was outright misreading it, I would go as far as to say he was jealous.

Perhaps it was the alcohol making him more loose-lipped, or maybe it was the shock of finding out the way he did, but I saw the tentacles of anguish and envy grab hold of him, even if it was for mere moments.

But why?

Wasn't *he* the one who stopped anything from progressing between us that day on the couch? Wasn't *he* the one who said he didn't want to risk our friendship?

"Anyone else can come and go, but this is forever."

So why did it feel like I'd taken a sledgehammer to his

heart when I told him about Warren? Why did I feel like the worst best friend in the world?

Dean's eyes turn to capture me, and for a moment, I freeze, before letting go of any inhibitions and running toward him. His arms open wide, almost on their own accord, as he captures me in a hug, swinging me around.

And for that moment, it's just me and him. There is no café or customers, no Betty giggling behind the counter, or dogs barking in the backyard. For that moment, it's just us.

I inhale his sandalwood scent like it's a drug, filling my nostrils, like if I breathe him in long enough, his scent will never dull.

I look up at him when he puts me down on my feet, and for reasons unbeknownst to me, my eyes fill on their own. I punch his arm and he feigns being hurt. Two weeks is a long time to be absent when you've seen or talked to someone almost daily.

"Jerk," I chide in a wobbly voice.

His smile wavers as his hand comes up as if to cup my face, but he stops himself, putting it back down to his side. "I'm sorry, Mala."

So, I was right. He *was* purposely avoiding me, which is why he's apologizing now.

He looks around the café, likely noting that there aren't many customers at the moment, before gesturing toward the doors to the kitchen in the back with a tilt of his head. "Can we talk?"

Without thinking too much about it, I grab his hand and drag him behind me, through the double doors, before crossing my arms across my chest. "You've been avoiding me."

He lets out a sigh before running his hand over his face. His blue eyes plead guilty. "I just . . . I needed a minute, Mala."

I slant my head. "That was a lot longer than a minute. It's

been two weeks since I saw you. You're usually blowing up my phone because you can't keep your trap shut, but aside from a text here or there, I've honestly wondered if you even remembered me." I stab him with my index finger. "That's not how best friends act. How could you be mad at me for that long?"

He gives me his stupid crooked smile that I both want to slap off and kis— It drops off his face when he grabs my hand and sees the mix of emotion in my eyes. "You missed me."

"Yes, you big dummy! I missed you. Didn't you miss me?"

Letting go of my hand, he encircles my neck with his large palm. His thumb caresses the bottom of my jaw. "You have no idea."

My eyes bounce between his. "Then why did I feel like there was distance between us?"

He closes his eyes before focusing on me again. "I just needed a minute, Mala. That's all. I needed to clear my head. Please . . ." He strokes my jaw with his thumb again. "Don't be mad at me. I can't fucking take it."

I furrow my brows even though I lean into his touch. My mind and heart battling to have it out with him—to ask him why he abandoned me for two weeks, or why he can be mad at me for that long, but I'm not allowed to be—but I let it go. "Are we okay now?"

Dean nods. "Yeah, we're okay. I told you that day, remember? This is forever."

I smile. "You never answered my text about tomorrow. Are you coming for *movie madness*? You still owe me *Titanic*."

His hand drops from my face, and he looks to the side before our gazes tangle again. "Just the same crew . . .?"

I know what he's asking—whether Warren will be there. "Yes, just us."

He responds with, "Yeah, I'll be there," right when the doors to the kitchen swing open.

Warren looks from Dean to me, striding inside with a smile. With his dark hair perfectly combed back, his suit and tie hugging his well-toned physique, he looks out of place in my messy kitchen. "Hey, gorgeous!"

Heat travels to my cheeks and I smile at him, praying that the strange tension twisting my gut will abate. "Hi! What are you doing here? I thought you had that open-house until late afternoon."

His hands wrap around my waist when he gets closer before his lips find my temple. "It ended early." Warren turns to Dean, who's taking him in with a hard gaze and tight jaw. I don't miss the way Dean's eyes flick from where Warren's hands lay on my waist possessively back to his face. "And who might this be?"

Tugging the collar of my sweatshirt up, I clear my throat unnecessarily, feeling the tips of my ears heat. I'm positive they'd be red if I viewed them in the mirror. "Warren, this is my best friend, Dean." I smile wider than required. "Dean, this is Warren."

Warren offers his hand to Dean. "I've heard a lot about you, man. It's good to finally meet in person."

Dean throws a glance at me before taking Warren's hand, and only I can tell how reluctantly he accepts the handshake. "Likewise." Pulling his hand away rather quickly, Dean turns to me. "Uh, I'll see you tomorrow, then, *sprinkles*? Text me if you need me to pick up anything."

He's rushing out so fast, I barely get a chance to call out to him, "I have a box of those pumpkin treats—er, cookies—for you at the front. Make sure to grab it."

Dean pauses at the double doors before he leaves, and my heart feels like it's galloping inside my chest. That was . . . difficult, but I suppose it went better than I expected.

My thoughts are interrupted when Warren turns me so

I'm facing him, pulling my arms around his neck. "So, *sprinkles*, huh?"

I roll my eyes. "Yeah, it's just something he's called me for a while."

Warren nods. "Okay. What's happening tomorrow?"

"Oh." I try to go for a casual tone. "My friends from the fire station and I have these monthly movie nights, and I'm hosting it at my place tomorrow night, so Dean will be coming to that."

Warren smiles knowingly, his warm amber eyes caressing my face. "Ah, I'm assuming I haven't passed muster yet, so I'm not invited, huh?"

I shake my head, giggling awkwardly. "No, of course you're invited! But you told me your dad was going to be in town, so you'd be having dinner with him. I figured you wouldn't be able to make it."

I'm hoping he doesn't call my bluff. While Warren has hung out with my brother and Samantha, he's right—I didn't invite him to movie night. It's been something the others and I have done since before he came into the picture, and I guess I'm not ready to change that dynamic yet.

That, and well . . . I get the feeling there's one person in particular who wouldn't show if Warren was coming.

Warren bends to brush his lips on my cheek. He's tall, dark, and handsome. Very different from the blond, long-haired guys with charmingly crooked smiles I've been attracted to over the past several years, but I don't see any of those in the picture, so . . .

"I'm just giving you a hard time. Anyway, I thought I'd come by on my way home and drop something off."

"Oh?" I ask, raising a brow. "And what would that be?"

Warren and I have been dating for about a month. And while it's still new, I've often felt like I've known him for longer. I suppose that comes from the fact that he's easy to talk to, funny, and incredibly romantic. On more than one occasion, he's pulled out all the stops for our dates.

Last week, Betty was sick and Max had to rush out early because his girlfriend thought she was miscarrying—thankfully, she hadn't—and I was stuck cleaning up the café alone. So, instead of just taking me out to dinner, Warren brought an array of food here. He helped me clean up, turned off all the bright lights, and turned on some LED candles he'd brought with him. We sat at one of the café tables, giggling, catching up, and stuffing our faces.

He pulls my hand and, right when we get to the double doors, he turns to catch me in a kiss. I'm momentarily struck and try to ease into it, but I just can't seem to get out of my own head. I try to hide my nerves with an airy laugh. "The suspense is killing me!"

He places another kiss on my cheek before opening the doors and my eyes land on a long red box with a pretty bow sitting at the bar.

My brows fold as I walk over to it, picking it up before taking it over to an empty table to open it. Warren watches excitedly as I open the box.

"Oh!" I chime with forced glee as I regard the gift in my hand. "Socks!"

Warren gleams at my response. "Do you like them? I just noticed you're always trying to shove your feet under my thigh when we're watching something on TV. Now you don't have to!"

I clear my throat, hoping to veil my disappointment. Not everyone is going to like my feet being tucked under their thigh, and that's an expectation I need to reset in my own head. "Yes! These are fantastic! What a thoughtful gift!"

He places a kiss on the top of my head. "I'm glad you like them, *sprinkles*."

And as much as I try not to let it, my smile drops.

~

MY WATERY EYES glide to where Rohan and Samantha are snuggled together under a blanket on the love seat in my living room. Samantha wipes a stray tear from her cheek and Rohan pulls her closer, laying his lips on her temple.

I'm sitting on the other side of Malcolm on my sofa with a blanket over me, while Dean sits on the ground in between me and Malcolm, his head resting against my knee.

Jack gives his speech to Rose on screen, half-submerged and trembling in the frigid waters of the North Atlantic Ocean, while Rose lies frigid on the floating wooden door.

Even though it's my third time watching this movie, my throat tightens. It's always the love and hate for this scene that has me conflicted. The way Leo's character gives up his own happiness and life for the woman he loves—the woman he should be with, regardless of their obstacles. The selflessness of it and the pure dedication to her. If only they could have had a life together . . . a happily ever after.

My eyes linger on Dean's profile. Strangely, he's not looking at the TV screen. His eyes are fixed somewhere below it, lost in thought. What I would give to be able to read his thoughts right now.

"No," Malcolm whispers into his fist, blinking rapidly. "No. This is some bullshit, right here." He sniffles. "That is some bullshit, Rose! You have enough room on that motherfucking door! Move the hell over and save him, you stupid bitch!"

And just like that, the somber mood evaporates. Samantha and I exchange looks before we both devolve into a fit of giggles, the pools of tears created from the intense scene rolling down our cheeks for completely different reasons.

Malcolm sniffles again, making Dean laugh, and I can

barely get myself to look over at the six-foot-four-inch man who's easily larger than anyone in this room. He might be a fearless firefighter like Dean and Rohan, but he's nothing but a big softy on the inside. I force my eyes to turn to him, and it's the worst thing I could have done. The second Malcolm wipes his eyes, I'm falling apart in another torrent of giggles. My cheeks hurt from the strain on my muscles.

Malcolm looks from Samantha to me to Dean, shaking his head. "You guys are a bunch of assholes." He wipes his nose, blinking away more tears. "That was a display of true love right there. The dude gave up his life and his chance to be on that floaty thingy so she could live. That's fucking true love!"

A sob catches Malcolm's chest, and Rohan joins the rest of us while we're holding our stomachs from laughing. "Floaty thingy!"

God, I love this group so much.

As soon as the credits roll, everyone seems to gather themselves, getting up from their spots. Rohan gives me a squeeze, reminding me to check the locks and to make sure the stove is turned off, before clasping Samantha's hand in his.

Samantha and I exchange a hug before the two of them leave, with Malcolm trailing behind them a minute later. Before he leaves, he tells me I'm never allowed to pick a movie again, and of course, that has me in another fit of giggles.

As soon as they're all out, I find Dean in my kitchen, rinsing the dishes we'd used for popcorn and drinks. "You don't have to do that, you know. I could have just put them in the dishwasher."

He shrugs. "I didn't want you to have to worry about it."

I lean my hip against the counter next to him, studying him. If the short exchange he had with Warren yesterday has played inside my mind a few times, I can only imagine he's thought about it, too. "Dean . . .?"

He clears his throat, his eyes lacking the luster they usually have. He wipes his hands on a kitchen towel. "Yeah?"

"I know that was sort of an awkward meeting with Warren yesterday . . ." I'm stating the obvious, but it's in an attempt to clear the air and feel out what he's thinking.

He shrugs. "It was fine. Nothing either of us couldn't handle." He pauses. "He seems to like you a lot."

I tuck a strand of hair behind my ears, and Dean watches the movement, his eyes lingering on my hand. "Yeah . . ." I nod. "Yeah, I like him, too. It's just really new."

"Good," he agrees, though it sounds forced. "Good. Yeah, I'm happy for you."

Is he, though? It doesn't feel like it.

I play with my fingernails. "Are you sure? It's just that yesterday, I felt like–"

"Yesterday was me being a dick, and I'm sorry about that. I'll try to do better." He takes a long breath. "If you're happy, then I'm happy."

I look down at my feet, nodding, when a whispered question makes its way out of my mouth unbidden. "Are *you* happy?"

Because you don't look happy.

You haven't been acting like yourself.

Why does everything feel forced?

Dean's lips part to answer when a sharp knock at my door jolts us both out of our moment. My brows furrow as I check the clock. Who could it be at this hour?

Walking to the door, I look through the peephole before pulling the door open. "Hey! What are you doing here?"

Warren steps into my foyer, enveloping me in a hug so I almost disappear inside of him. Placing a kiss on my temple, his mouth slides to my ear. "I got done with dinner with my dad and . . . I missed you."

I smile, looking up at him. "I'm glad you're here."

He nuzzles my nose with his. "Good, because I'm planning on staying the ni–"

Dean's throat being cleared behind us has my arms dropping off Warren's back. "I'm, uh . . . going to head out, Mala. Thanks for hosting movie night."

I walk over to him, pulling him into a hug. He's unusually stiff in my arms, but finally relents. "I'll see you soon?"

He nods before looking at Warren. "Take care of her."

And as soon as the door shuts behind him, my mind is a tangle of thoughts and emotions battling against each other. Except, I can't grab hold of any.

The only thing that lingers well into the next few days and months is a dull ache. An ache that developed so long ago and one that refuses to subside.

An ache I'm beginning to believe will just become a permanent part of me . . . like the cracked heart it's a result of.

Chapter Eleven

MALA

"WE'RE RUNNIN' LOW ON CARAMEL SYRUP." JESSIE WIPES down the steam wand on the espresso machine before dumping the used coffee grounds into the trash. After pouring some milk into a frothing pitcher, she places it under the wand before glancing at me as I make my way back from picking up a few stray cups off some tables.

It took me almost three weeks after Max left to find someone who had the experience I was looking for, but instead of one, I ended up hiring two people. One who solely helps on the weekends, and Jessie, who works during the weekdays only. I have to admit, so far she's working out really well.

She's a bit of a gabber and seems to constantly be low on cash—apparently, she's also working at the casino across town in the evenings—but otherwise, she seems sweet. She has a Southern twang, bangs that she's constantly blowing out of her eyes, and a cute little nose ring. Not to mention, she's a complete knockout.

On more than one occasion, I've seen the eyes of my customers—both men and women alike—linger on her longer than necessary, but she doesn't seem to mind. I read somewhere that red hair and green eyes are a rather rare combination, so I suppose that adds to her appeal, along with her ample chest and cinched waist. Either way, she's been keeping the tip jar full, that's for sure.

"I'll add it to the inventory for tonight," I respond with a sigh. "Do we have enough left to make it through today or do I need to run out and grab a couple of bottles from the grocery store immediately?"

She pours the milk into a cup before adding some whipped cream to it, calling out a customer's name before placing it on the counter. "No, I think we can manage until close. Plus, you're busier than a squirrel in a barrel of acorns."

I roll my neck and squeeze my shoulder with the tips of my fingers and thumb, trying to rub out a knot. It's been an unusually crazy day.

This morning a customer's miniature pinscher attacked Gigi, Mrs. Carver's shih tzu, in the backyard. Thankfully Gigi was okay, though both she and Mrs. Carver were visibly perturbed. Poor Gigi was shaking from head to toe for a good five minutes.

After the incident, I hand-delivered a special box of treats, along with Mrs. Carver's favorite latte, to her house. Luckily, she seemed to have calmed down and was grateful I stopped by.

As soon as I got back to the café, I found out the toilet had overflowed before it stopped working all together. And since the handyman I've used in the past couldn't come by in time, I wasted an additional hour finding a new one. By the time he finally came in, I was already on my fourth latte and half-way to a full-blown migraine.

And just when I thought the day couldn't get worse, the entire batch of cookies I was baking for a catering order overcooked because I left them in for a few minutes too long while I was talking to the handyman. Rookie mistake. I would have told Betty to take them out, but she was on her lunch break.

Suffice it to say, I'm praying for this day to end before it has a chance to get any worse.

I'm in the back icing the new batch of cookies when the bell chimes and I hear the familiar rumble of a deep laugh. No matter how many times I've heard it, I never seem to tire of it. Even after all these years, it still creates a buzz inside my veins—the kind of buzz I only feel around him.

Between his long hours at the fire station and my time being split between the café and Warren, I haven't seen Dean all week. We've kept up through texts here and there, but I can tell he's felt a little awkward stopping by my place unannounced like he used to.

Is this what things are going to be like from now on? Different . . . distant?

Is this what growing apart feels like?

He says something, though I can't quite hear what, making Jessie giggle and it creates a strange urgency inside me. I want to barge out there and find out what's so damn funny. I sound childish in my own head, but a part of me wants to go out there and lay claim to him—let her know that he's *my* best friend.

Wiping my hands down my apron, I loosen my hair out of its messy bun, making it tumble down my back like a sleek curtain of chocolate and ebony. As much as I want to, I won't be doing any barging in or claiming, but I am excited to see him.

I push the double doors slightly ajar, watching them. Jessie is leaning over the bar, tucking a strand of her crimson hair behind her ear. She eyes Dean with a flirtatious grin while he pops a treat from the pink box he's holding—a box I left behind the bar for him—into his mouth.

"Lord, love a duck, you're eatin' dog biscuits." She laughs a little too enthusiastically. "You do realize we sell cookies for humans too, don't ya, sugar?"

His brow lifts, all charm and intrigue. "You do realize I'm part wolf, don't you, *sugar*? Part man, but all beast." He throws a wink her way and she practically preens.

I smile, knowing this is just him. He's not even vying for her attention—in fact, he's likely to forget her name the minute she introduces herself—but for the moments she's locked in his spell, nothing else will matter. The look on her face says it all; she's caught and he never even cast a net.

She pulls her bottom lip in between her teeth, twisting on her feet like a shy little girl. "I bet you'd be one hell of a beast to tame."

Oh, for heaven's sake!

I'm still standing in the same spot, mid eye-roll, when I catch Dean's gaze on me. The amused look in his eyes, having caught me eavesdropping, has a dash of heat racing to my cheeks. "Hey, you."

I grin, walking out into the café. "Well, look what the cat dragged in."

Dean looks around. "Do you get many cats in here? As far as I can tell, I've only seen dogs."

Before I can respond, Jessie chimes in, her accent in full-effect, "Not a lot of cats, but someone brought their pet raccoon on a leash this week. It was crazy as all get out, let me tell ya!"

I close the distance between me and him. It's been a weird few weeks between us, and I'm determined to keep things as much the same as they used to be. "Why do I feel like the only time I can get you to come by and see me is when I text you with a bribe?" I eye the box in his hands.

"That's a load of bullshit and you know it." Dean watches me through a half-hooded gaze. "You've been . . ."

He clears his throat. "We've both been busy. But, hey, it's actually one of the reasons I'm here today. I mean, aside from wanting to just see you." His lips pull up on one corner, and I lock my gaze on the little smile line that's recently appeared there. It's something new—something that formed without me even noticing. Like a little outline outside of his smile, it's endearing and . . . perfect. "I wanted to see if you wanted to go kayaking this weekend. I figured we could head over to Darian and Sonia's school and borrow some equipment."

A twinge of panic and guilt stabs my chest, making me wince. "I have plans with Warren, but . . ." I give him a hopeful look.

If Warren is going to be in my life, then I really need my best friend on board. I get that he isn't happy about me dating him—his reasons are his own—but he did say he'd do anything for me, even if he had to pretend to like him. And maybe if they hang out a few times, he won't have to pretend anymore.

I know Warren can feel Dean's unease around him, and though he hasn't asked exactly why my best friend seems to run like his ass is on fire at the sight of him, I can tell it bothers him.

Warren is a nice guy—someone not afraid of opening up about his feelings. And while I don't have the wild and crazy wave of bubbles inside my stomach, or a tortuous need to know what he's doing all the time—whether he's thinking about me or not—I've started to really care for him.

Could I see myself with him forever?

Maybe?

And that *maybe* is a possibility my best friend needs to come to terms with.

I clear my throat softly. "Any chance he could join—"

"Oh." Dean catches himself from rearing back but not

before giving away the fact that he's been caught off guard. "Uh, well—"

"Now, I don't mean to brag, but I'm not a half-bad kayaker myself," Jessie cuts in, getting both our attention. She shrugs. "I mean, I do have the weekend off and well . . ." Her eyes bounce from Dean to me. "I'm not meanin' to intrude, but three is just never a good number. Well, not unless you're intendin' to have a threesome—"

My face heats at the same time as it pales. Is that even possible?

I'm glaring at her in an effort to make her stop speaking, but also in an effort to not look at Dean.

"—in which case it's the perfect number!" Jessie's face picks up color, drowning out the smattering of freckles on her nose. It's as if she realizes she's developed diarrhea of the mouth but can't seem to stop. *Jesus Christ. The woman is a danger to herself.* "Not that I'm suggestin' you're tryin' to have a threesome or anythin'. Goodness me! My mouth is runnin' like a boardin' house toilet today! Just sayin'—"

"Yeah, uh, why don't you join us, uh . . ." Dean saves us all from the epic disaster of having to listen to her finish her thought, giving Jessie a quizzical look. His eyes dip down to the name tag affixed on her bountiful chest. "Jessie?" He turns to me. "Is that okay with you, *sprinkles?*"

I feel like I've been sold something way over the sales price, but I don't know what it is or even how I could return it. "Uh, yeah. That's fine."

Jessie gleams from ear to ear. "Really? I mean, I'll have to check my calendar, but lord willin' and the creek don't rise, I'll be there."

~

"Hey."

I look up from my laptop where I was submitting the inventory to see Jessie standing inside the kitchen with her enormous purse hanging off her shoulder. She's changed into a snug, low-cut black T-shirt with the word *Huxley's Casino* written across it in sparkly red lettering, along with tight-fitted black slacks that look like they might be constricting her blood flow.

"Hey. Heading out?"

"Fixin' to, yeah." She looks out the windows, eyeing the streetlights outside before facing me again. "Hey, um, I didn't mean to invite myself to y'all's kayakin' thing earlier. I . . . I don't know what came over me. I don't usually come off that desperate and brazen, but your friend," she throws a thumb over her shoulder as if Dean was still standing on the same spot out in the café three hours later, "well, he's finer than a frog's hair, is what he is. He sorta just turned me into a blathering idiot, and I overstepped." She looks down at her black sneakers. "I'm real sorry about that. Come to find out, I'm busy this weekend, so–"

"Jessie," I interrupt her, because if I don't, I'm not sure she'll take another breath. "You are welcome to come this weekend. In fact, it might help to have you there." *You know, since my best friend seems to hate my boyfriend and anything to ease that tension would be great.*

I don't explain why, but Jessie seems to have caught on. "Yeah?" She smiles. "Super! I'd really like that."

I go back to looking at my computer screen, feeling a mix of emotions stir in my chest.

She clearly likes Dean–her words said as much–and I'm with Warren. And I plan to continue to be with Warren. So, why is her roundabout admission feeling like dead weight around my ankles? Why do I have this intense need for her to leave–get out of here, so I can breathe? It's like her presence is filling up the entire room.

I want to be the type of friend who could be a wing-woman for my best friend. I want to be able to giggle with Jessie, give her ideas on how to win him over, and bounce on my feet when it all works out.

But the doom and gloom spreading inside me, discoloring the blood in my system, won't let me.

It's as if I can feel what's coming. Like it's written as clear as day.

And why shouldn't it? Dean deserves to be happy. And as much as I wish it could have been with me . . .

No.

I'd made up my mind the day I said yes to dating Warren that the pining needed to stop. I'm not going backward now.

My best friend made it woefully clear that he'd never cross that line with me, and no matter how many times I've felt the confliction of his words—the contradiction in his eyes and his touch—I can only take him at his word.

He won't risk our friendship, and I can't risk another crack to my heart. Once was enough.

"I won't risk what we have . . . I can't risk you or this friendship; it means too much to me. You mean too much to me . . . Anyone else can come and go, but this *is forever. Do you understand that?"*

For the longest time after that excruciatingly embarrassing moment in the history of our friendship, I told myself that yes, I did understand. I understood where he came from. In fact, I made myself believe that he was right and our friendship wasn't worth risking.

But as time passed, I realized that while I'd almost deceived my brain into agreeing with him, I couldn't pull the wool over my heart. Because no matter how much I tried, it refused to accept that this wasn't worth the risk. That *we* weren't worth the risk. No matter how hard I tried, it refused to label him the good Samaritan my brain was more willing to see. Instead, it thrashed inside my chest, calling him a coward.

Months later, when that resentment and melancholy lifted—all while I put on a brave face in front of him, pretending his well-intentioned words hadn't slashed me, and covered up my heartbreak with natural smiles—I finally picked myself up.

I'd been through worse, hadn't I?

I could move forward from this, too.

"Can I ask you somethin'?" Jessie's voice has my head lifting up again. I'd almost forgotten she hadn't left. She takes my eye contact as an affirmation to continue, but her stance is less confident than before. "I get the feeling you and Dean are two peas in a pod. Betty mentioned somethin' about how you always bake him a separate box of treats." She tilts her head and my heart stutters, hoping she doesn't finish her thought. "Have y'all, you know . . . dated in the past?"

A moment later, I shake my head.

Her head tilts the other way, as if my response was the most confounding thing she'd heard all day. "Seriously? I mean, y'all have this intense connection—"

"Friendship," I clarify abruptly. "Dean and I have a deep *friendship*."

She nods, chewing on her bottom lip. "So, you wouldn't mind then, if I try to catch his eye?"

That thrashing heart of mine tries to climb up my throat, but as usual, I put on my best smile. It looks like my day was indeed destined to get worse.

"No. Not at all."

～

I grasp the back of his T-shirt in both fists and press my face to his chest, inhaling his sandalwood scent for a moment longer, before he pulls away from me.

The three of us—Dean, Warren and I—are standing next to our cars in the parking lot of Darian's sports school waiting for Jessie. She needed to run back to the ladies' room since she left her phone there.

She came here with Warren and me this morning since she was having car trouble, but I didn't miss how she casually asked Dean for a ride back home a few minutes ago.

The girl is a smooth operator, weaving in her natural giggles and soft touches on Dean's bicep—even outright tapping his abs at one point—at every opportunity. And though I could tell he was slightly uncomfortable, he didn't stop her, either.

His ocean blues meet my earthy browns before he tugs on a lock of wet hair lying on my shoulder. "I'll see you soon, *sprinkles*. This was fun."

I'm just about to respond when Warren's palms land on my shoulders, pulling me back into his chest. He squeezes my shoulders harder than I was expecting, and I wince.

Unfortunately, Warren doesn't seem to notice. "Thanks for inviting us, Dean. I haven't kayaked in years, but that was a fun time."

Dean's gaze locks on Warren's hands on my shoulders before they slide to my face, assessing my reaction. I know he caught my slight discomfort, so I quickly adjust my expression and offer him a placating smile.

We've had a surprisingly fun afternoon, and though Dean wasn't his loud and chipper self around Warren, he wasn't outright rude to him, either. The last thing I want is for my best friend to go all overprotective caveman at nothing more than a territorial and insecure display by Warren.

My smile seems to have done the trick because a moment later, he tilts his chin up to Warren. "Glad you could make it."

"Thank Darian again for me, will you?" I say to Dean as Warren entangles our fingers together, urging me toward his car with a tad more force than necessary.

Dean studies us with a blank face, but I don't miss the tick in his jaw.

I'm just about to get inside Warren's car when Jessie appears, carrying her phone. "Thanks for waitin', y'all. I'm so glad I remembered where I'd put this thing." She lifts her phone for everyone to see before shortening the distance between me and her. "Thanks again for letting me crash y'all's fun today, Mala."

I smile. "Don't mention it."

She turns to Dean, a smile stretched across her face and her bangs waving over her forehead with a gust of wind. "Ready to take me home, sugar?"

Dean swivels his eyes from her to me, pausing to scan my face and gauge my reaction again. I never told him about how Jessie asked me for permission to pursue him, so he has no idea that I'm not surprised by her forwardness. "Uh, yeah . . . I can drop you home."

We wave a quick bye to each other, and I'm just about to close the door to Warren's car after getting inside when I hear Jessie say, "Well, if you're gonna carry me home, then I insist you come up for a slice of blueberry pie. I dare say I make the best in the whole state of California!"

Chapter Twelve

DEAN

Five Years Ago

I CHECK MY AIR PACK AND MEDICAL SUPPLIES BAG BEFORE making a round around the engine, restocking and taking inventory as needed. I'm just inputting the EMS report from our last call on my tablet when Coolidge calls my name.

"Yo! Your girl's here to see you. I told her to wait for you in the kitchen."

I take a breath, trying not to forget my train of thought so I can finish the report. "I'll head over in a minute."

Coolidge heads back inside the station, and I run a hand over my face. It's not that I don't want to see her; it's just that, lately, it seems like she makes it hard for me to see anyone else but her. In fact, I've seen her every night that I haven't slept at the station and every day that I'm not working—she's made sure of it.

Some nights I actually look forward to spending the night here in the bunk room rather than at my own place because it almost feels like a respite from being around her all the time.

Fuck, I sound like a dick, even in my own head.

It's been a little less than a year since Jessie and I started dating, and while we've had some fun times together, there are times when it feels like we've been together forever.

And not in a good way.

It's not that she's a shitty person, nor is she a shitty girlfriend—I wouldn't be with her if that was the case—but there are times I wish she was . . . someone else.

Christ. I'm clearly not doing a good job of highlighting anything good about her.

The fact is, there are good things about Jessie. Great things, even!

She's thoughtful, fun, and caring. In fact, on more than one occasion, she's come over with dinner she made at home so I'd have something to eat after a long shift. A few months ago, I went through a particularly tough bout of heat exhaustion and a bad respiratory issue, and even though I told her I'd be fine on my own, Jessie refused to leave me alone—doting on me hand and foot for an entire week. And above all else, unlike the women I've dated in the past, she also hasn't ever complained about my crazy work schedule.

In general, she's always just gone with the flow. It's why things have worked out well for us for this long.

Sure, she can be overbearing with how much of my time she demands or the way she wants to spend every waking moment together, but in all fairness, she means well. And despite the fact that she can be chatty and spacey at times, I've come to find those things endearing.

But in spite of all the good things—despite me actually caring about her—there's one thing I've always known.

We're not serious.

Let me rephrase that. *I'm* not serious about her, and I never will be.

Since day one—a couple of weeks after we went kayaking with Mala and *Douchebag*—I've been upfront with her. I'm not the guy she'll walk down the aisle with or the guy she'll take home to her mom. I'm not looking to be attached, plain and simple. And if that was good with her, then we could spend time together. Despite my conditions, she still wanted to come around . . . so I let her.

I guess I hadn't noticed how lonely I'd become . . .

I hadn't touched another woman since the day I broke up with Nora almost four years ago. I almost did the night I found out Mala was dating Warren a year ago with that chick whose name I can never remember. Teagan? No . . .

I pinch the bridge of my nose, wracking my brain. What the fuck was her name? The chick with the long blonde hair . . .

Taylor! Yeah, that was it. Wasn't it?

I texted her that night and had every intention of fucking her, if only to escape my own goddamn thoughts and pent-up anger. But I couldn't go through with it. Half-way to her place, I told the Uber driver to take me home.

Even when Jessie came along, it wasn't like I dove head-first into bed with her. Hell, even now—months later—I barely have my head in the game.

She might scream my name, but it's not her face I'm coming to.

Yeah, I'm definitely a fucking prick.

I sigh, turning off the tablet screen after submitting the report, and jump off my seat in the engine. I take a broom and dustpan off the wall and sweep up the small mess in the corner before taking unhurried steps to the station entrance.

Let's see what she needs now. Fuck, this better not be about Luke again, though my gut says it is.

I pull my phone out and read the text that just came in from Mala. A chuckle rolls out of my lips.

> Sprinkles: What rock group has four men but can't sing?

Over the past few months, we've both been busier–her with her boyfriend, the man I refer to as *Douchebag* in my head, and me with Jessie. I suppose everyone has become more busy lately.

Both Mala and Rohan are now in serious relationships with their significant others, my brother Garrett is doing God knows what with God knows who, and Darian always has his balls in a vice because of Sonia. Thankfully, she isn't completely heartless and allows him to meet up with me and Garrett for our poker nights.

Rohan actually just proposed to Samantha, and it won't be long before he's even busier, given she's pregnant.

And Mala . . .

My smile recedes at the thought of her–*of us*–even when she's usually the reason for it in the first place. Goddamn, I miss her.

She lives only a few miles away and we still message each other often, but . . . I still miss her.

Her laugh, her wit, how she always finds a way to take me down a notch. Her hair, her ice-cold toes, and those goddamn legs . . .

I still visit her at the café from time to time, but even that is different now since Jessie usually happens to be there at the times I can find to swing by.

It's just been challenging to spend time together the way we used to, and I'm jonesing hard.

My fingers work fast as I type back my response to the game we've been playing lately. Every time one of us misses the other, or it's been a while since we've spoken, we text the other with a riddle.

Me: The Jonas Brothers.

I wait for her response, and it comes in a moment later.

Sprinkles: <facepalm emoji> There are only three Jonas Brothers.

Me: There could be ten, and it wouldn't change my opinion.

I chuckle, imagining her shaking her head in exhaustion, as I walk to the kitchen.

Sprinkles: The correct answer is Mount Rushmore.

Me: My answer was better.

"Hey!"

I look up with a smile stretched on my face, still imagining Mala rolling her eyes, to see Jessie standing with her hands on her hips. My smile dwindles. "Hey, what's up?"

She huffs. "You've been standin' there on your phone for God knows how long while I've been here waitin' for ya."

I pocket my phone, resolving to text Mala later. Maybe we can meet up, go hiking or something?

I run a hand over my face, feeling exhausted. "What's going on? I wasn't expecting you."

Jessie contorts her lips into a sultry smile before closing the distance between us. She swings her arms around my neck. "What? I can't just visit my boyfriend at his place of work once in a while?"

I give her a smile before pulling her arms off me gently. I pace over to the fridge to grab a bottle of water. "Not really, Jess. I mean, it's fine right now since I have some downtime, but–"

Her head tilts defiantly. "Mala comes by all the time with cookies and coffee. I know because I've seen her pack them to carry over here. Do you tell *her* she shouldn't be coming over?"

"She comes by to drop the packages off and leaves."

"Well, maybe I oughta bring some baked goods with me next time!" Her Southern twang gets a little sharper with the last word, making it sound more like 'tom' than time. "Might be, I'd get a warmer welcome."

I take a heavy breath, unscrewing the cap to my bottle.

Over the past year, Jessie and I have had our share of ups and downs. We even broke up for a month or two somewhere in the middle.

At first, our tiffs were about things like how much time I would spend with her—not enough, in her opinion—or how I never asked her to spend the night. But once she started coming around more, she decided it didn't matter if I formally asked her to stay the night or not, because she'd do it, anyway. Our arguments then evolved to me not being vocal enough about my feelings.

Let's not forget our arguments about Mala . . .

It's not that I'm unaware of Jessie's complicated feelings about Mala. I get that she feels threatened by her, or rather, my relationship with her. But I've been clear from day one—Mala will stay in my life, no matter what.

I know it's a weird situation for Jessie, given she works for Mala and needs her job too, but she came into this knowing the landscape—that Mala was and would always be my best friend. Nothing in the fucking world will change that, not Jessie and certainly not Douchebag Warren.

"What's going on, Jess? You seem . . ." *Snippy*. "On edge."

Jessie closes her eyes, her shoulders slumping. "I need more money."

I knew it. My gut told me she wouldn't be here unless something was up, and I'm willing to bet I know why she needs more money again.

"It's Luke–"

"For fuck's sake," I cut in, running a hand over my face.

Jessie closes the distance between us again, taking my face in her palms. The scent of her heavy perfume floats around my nose. "Sugar, listen, I know this is the third time I'm askin' you to get him out of a bind, but he's as broke as a stick horse and could use your help. He swore up and down this would be the last–"

I chuckle mirthlessly. "Listen to yourself, Jess. You've been bailing out your older brother for years. *Years!* And he's not even remorseful about it. Instead of having any sort of savings yourself, you've spent it all on him. When are you going to realize this is going to be never-ending for you?"

"Dean, listen–"

I shake my head. "He isn't going to change, Jessie. He tells you he will; he swears on everything holy, but then he goes right back to those shady-ass casinos and gambles more. You know why? Because the man has a problem, and he could give a rat's ass who pays the price for his problem."

"Dean, please." Jessie's brows rise, making her green eyes look like saucers. "Please, just this once more."

I hate being the bad guy here, nor am I heartless. I get that kind of attachment–I'm plenty attached to my brothers–but instead of calling him out on his addiction and making him man up to solve his own problems, she continues to coddle him. And since she doesn't have the money to save his ass because she's spent most of it on his problem, she continues to come to me. And because I've lent the money–over three thousand dollars–twice in the past already, I'm also contributing to this vicious cycle.

When do I say enough is really enough?

I hate myself for even asking the next question. "How much this time?"

Jessie has enough decorum to at least look ashamed. "Thirty-two hundred."

My mouth falls open. Does her brother think I'm fucking made of money? Or maybe it's her. Everyone in their right goddamn mind knows my firefighter salary isn't making me millions, so where does she get off thinking I have spare change like that lying around?

Do I? Yes. You know why? Because I'm damn good at saving, and because I've been smart about making some investments. Since I started receiving a regular paycheck with the fire department, I've dabbled a bit in the market and have done well over the years. I've also simply gotten lucky.

So yes, I *can* afford to have an almost-paid off house in the nice part of Tahoe, own my truck, and still have some spare change to visit my mom and Grams in Colorado when I want. But does that mean I'm living some lavish lifestyle? Hell no.

I close my mouth and shake my head again. "I'm sorry, Jess. I can't help."

Her hands drop to my biceps. "Sugar, please. Once more, and I promise I won't ask again. He's just in deep this time 'round. He borrowed money from men who were like snakes in the grass and lost it all last week. Now, they're threatenin' to trim his tail feathers if he doesn't pay, bless his heart."

I run my hand over the back of my neck before looking up at the ceiling. Fuck. What should I do? If I say yes, I might be stuck in this same situation time and time again, given these are the same promises Jessie made me the last two times. If I say no, I'm being an asshole.

But I can't. Even though I feel like shit taking this stance, I just fucking can't keep spinning in the same hamster wheel.

Leveling my gaze back on her, I go with my gut. "I'm sorry, Jess. Like I said, I can't help this time."

Jessie's reddish-brown brows knit as she realizes how serious I am, her expression changing from hopeful just seconds ago to aggravated and resentful. She lets my arms go and squares her shoulder. "I'm asking for you to help him once more, Dean. And it's sad that despite you livin' in tall cotton, you won't. He's not just anyone; he's my one and only brother."

There's no point to me repeating myself, but I do anyway. "I *have* helped him. *Twice*. And I haven't even asked for the money back because of that. Because he's your brother."

Jessie's gaze sharpens. "He's gonna pay you back, Dean. He's just between a rock and a hard place right now."

I shrug. "You might believe that, Jess, but I don't. Again, I'm sorry, but I can't help him."

Jessie nods, making her large earrings swing, and a resolute look takes over her countenance. "Well, if that's how you're gonna be, Dean . . . If you're gonna act like you're too big for your britches, then I don't know that this," she waves between us, "can work between us anymore."

I try to reason with her, but I can tell she's beyond it at this point. "Jessie—"

"Save it." She lifts her hand, stopping me from continuing before blowing her bangs off her forehead and walking away in a huff. "I heard you loud and clear, Dean Meyer, so you can kiss my grits."

Chapter Thirteen

DEAN

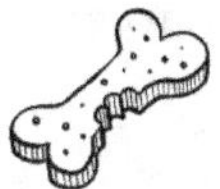

"Alright, I got one for you." I take another swig of my beer. It's my third one and I'm finally starting to feel the day loosen from my bones. That, or because of the girl sitting at the other end of the couch, swimming inside her oversized *Paw Patrol* hoodie—yes, she has one of those—with her back against the armrest and her toes tucked under my thigh. She's a wonderment of various temperatures and climates, all within one small frame. Her fingers and toes are always like ice. "What type of murderer has the most kind of fiber?"

"A cereal killer," Mala scoffs. "Dean, that is the easiest one in the book."

The girl's good at riddles. I learned that when we first started the riddle game through our texts, and she consistently whooped my ass. I often wonder if she sits around memorizing answers to riddles in her spare time. It wouldn't surprise me. She's a peculiar one.

Peculiar and perfect.

I take another swig of my beer as the thought bounces around in my mind. She's perfect. I've always thought that, always known it. Haven't I? So, why does it feel so surprising right now? Like finding your sunglasses on the top of your head when you'd been looking for them everywhere.

I texted her after my shift at the station. After the ordeal with Jessie. All I asked was if she was busy. A half hour later, she was pulling into my driveway. I don't know if there was a tone that she read through my one-line text or just me asking if she was busy was enough to give her an indication, but she said she could tell something was wrong.

But now as I feel the press of her toes under my thigh, the scent of her freshly shampooed hair permeating the space between us, I can't recall what was ever wrong.

I eye the martini glass in her hand. She's a lightweight if I've ever seen one, so the fact that she's on her third one tells me she's likely on her way to passing out on my couch. It wouldn't be the first time. "Alright, smartass, I have one more."

Mala lifts her brows haughtily. "Bring it on, *pookster*."

I groan at her use of the damn nickname Nora gave me all those years ago. Fucking pookster! Who the fuck calls someone that? I should have broken things off the minute she came up with it. And now, this pain in my ass—the one sitting in her short-ass shorts and phenomenal long-ass legs stretched across my sofa—won't let the damn nickname go.

"What month has twenty-eight days?" I take another swig, feeling confident I've got her this time. She can't know all of them. That would be ridiculous.

Mala hiccups, and my eyes roam over her. Yeah, she's not going to make it back home. Fine by me. "All of them."

I balk at her. How the fuck? "You've got problems, you know that? Serious ones." At her giggle and another hiccup, I take the empty glass from her hand and put it on the coffee table in front of us. "No one should be that big of a nerd."

She wiggles her toes under my thigh and I grab the back

of her calf, feeling her smooth skin under my palm. "You're just jealous that, as usual, I'm better at everything."

I shake my head but don't argue.

A few moments later, I ask the question that's been lingering in the back of my mind, though truthfully, I hate that it's even there. "How are things with you and Warren?"

I try to blank my expression, to not let my distaste for her boyfriend be so obvious. I can't point out a particular reason as to why I can't stand the guy—it's just a multitude of things. From his flashy shoes, to his slicked-back hair with not a strand out of place, to his overbearingness. There's also something about the way he grabs her that sets my teeth on edge.

Though, it doesn't seem like Mala minds any of it—from all accounts, she looks happy. He does seem to care about her, too. It's just that there's *something* about him. Something I can't quite place my finger on.

Mala hums. "Things are good. He's out of town for the next couple of days to visit his dad."

Ah, so that's why she was able to come over without much preamble.

And as if she can read my thoughts, she wiggles her toes again, getting my attention. "I would've been here even if he *was* in town, Fido. So, turn that frown upside down." She chuckles lazily.

A beat passes between us when she speaks again, bringing back our earlier conversation about how things ended with Jessie. I'd given her the long and short of it. "So, that was it? Jessie just said goodbye to you in her colorful way and left?"

"Pretty much."

She scoots closer to me, pulling her feet under her and grabbing my hand. And as much as she's focusing on my face, I can see her eyelids are heavy. Even her words are slightly slurred. "You didn't do anything wrong, Dean. In fact, you did the right thing by telling her you wouldn't lend her brother more money. It's not cool of her to expect you to bail him out again and again."

I nod, looking at our linked hands. "Yeah. Doesn't mean I don't feel like shit, though."

Mala's soft hand wraps around my jaw. "You feel like that because you're a good guy, Dean. A really good guy." Her breath fans over my lips, and I can practically taste the cherry liquor on my tongue, making my mouth water. Her hand drops to my chest, and she fists my shirt. "You have a beautiful heart and . . . and you deserve more. A lot more."

Mala licks her lips, gearing up to say more of whatever is bouncing around in that hazy brain of hers, but I can't seem to unpin my eyes off them. I don't care that she's not making complete sense or that the edge from the alcohol has her a bit more emotional and a little loose-lipped. I could watch her talk just like this for goddamn forever.

"You're kind and generous." Her fist tightens on my shirt and she pulls me closer. I don't resist. "You're sweet and smart." Her teeth drag over her bottom lip, and I get the feeling the alcohol is doing more than making her loose-lipped. It's making her feel bold. "You're hot."

If she can feel the thudding of my heart under her fist, she doesn't show it. Not until her eyes slowly rise to meet mine, and then I know she can definitely feel it.

I swallow and she languidly tracks the movement in my throat. "You think I'm hot?"

She nods before a smile stretches over her lips. "Go ahead and say it. That it's a blessing and curse to be so good-looking. That you're not even surprised I think you're hot because anyone with functioning eyes can see that you are."

Her smile falters when she sees the look on my face, devoid of humor. "You never told me you thought that."

Her brows knit and even though her eyelids threaten to

close, the slightest kindle ignites behind her mocha-colored gaze. "There's a lot I haven't told you, Sparky."

A sense of déjà vu washes over me as I take in our position on this sofa. Sure, the last time we were this close was three years ago in her apartment, but this feeling, this moment, seems almost identical.

And though so much has changed since then, some things haven't.

"You're not driving home like this," I say, changing the direction of our conversation and shoving the crazy thoughts out of my brain. Thoughts that make me wonder if those ideas—the damn wishes and desires—I've kept locked inside a fucking box for so long can maybe, possibly, *actually* be explored.

Maybe, just fucking maybe, it could all work out—

No.

It fucking couldn't. It wouldn't.

"You can have my bed and drive home in the morning." My molars grind as I try to control the anger flaring up inside me and rise to my feet.

Mala's hand drops to her lap, her expression dazed. She has no fucking clue how this all went sideways. *Neither do I.* One moment, we were throwing out riddles, drinking, and catching up, and the next, I'm all but ready to throw something because I'm confused. Angry.

Who the fuck am I even angry at? *Me? Her?* This fucked-up situation?

I don't even know anymore. All I know is I need this girl out of my sight before I eat my own words and do something we'll both regret for the rest of our lives.

Before the tingling in my fingers gets too strong to resist and I touch her in ways I shouldn't.

Before this yearning, like some living, breathing entity,

takes full control, and I forget that she's the one girl I won't touch. That I can't have. *Won't* have.

Mala nods, looking a little defeated, and I'm seconds away from telling her it's not her. It's never been her. But I don't. "Yeah, okay. But I can just sleep on the couch."

I crouch down, sliding my arms under her knees and back, pulling her to my chest. "You're sleeping in my bed. There's no buts about it."

She doesn't fight me any further, circling her arms around my neck, and I try to ignore the perfect press of her against my chest. Like she belongs there. Like she's always belonged there.

God, what the fuck am I thinking? How did I get here? At this moment where I'm outright considering what I've never considered before. Where I'm outright wanting what I shouldn't.

"If I knew what I know now—the anguish I've felt for the past three years, the sheer weight of life without him—I'd tell that naive girl sitting at the bar, looking into those alluring brown eyes and making wishes that should never have been made, that the worst thing she could do for herself would be to fall for a firefighter."

I force myself to dredge up Jane's words—they're never really far away anyway, but I need to recall them now more than ever—but even they don't seem to be the deterrent they usually are. Even they can't restrain the hunger that seems to be overtaking my every logical thought.

Mala eyes my profile as I traipse us to my bedroom, hoping and praying that by the time I get there, I'll have some control over my internal hysteria, the fucking frenzy building up inside me.

God, what I would give to have the fucking courage, the balls, to meet her gaze right this fucking second. To hell with everything and everyone—Warren, Rohan, my own fucking reservations—I'd like to meet her fucking gaze and just let instinct take over.

And maybe I fucking should.

Maybe it's about goddamn time I did something I've wanted longer than I've actually acknowledged it, and just give in.

Because how long am I going to deny any of this—the fucking chemistry that's always been there, the deep-rooted feelings, the insane connection? Did I really think it would just fizzle away? Or was it that I expected to keep it all buried forever?

In either case, it's not buried now.

It's here, reflecting back at me like a damn mirror.

I pull down the blanket and drop her gently onto my bed. Her arms stay encircled around me as I hover over her, our breaths entangling in the darkness of my bedroom. The veil of darkness trying to cover what it could never.

Fuck, this is happening.

There's no fucking stopping it.

My mind feels overrun with every thought colliding all at once, as if in battle. But only one thought triumphs, beaming so clearly, it's a wonder I ever denied it.

Mala is mine. She always has been and always will be.

I lean down, my lips less than a breath from hers, giving in to what I've always known. Giving in to her. I'm one second away from obliterating every line I've ever created for myself— for *us*—when Mala lets her arms drop to the bed, letting me go.

Her next words make my stomach plummet, creating yet another crack inside the organ that beats only for one.

"I'm moving in with Warren."

Chapter Fourteen

MALA

Four Years Ago

"Do you love it?" Warren pulls my hand off my phone, bringing my wrist up to inspect it closer. "I wanted to get you something special for your birthday."

I plaster on my best smile, trying to get my mind off the text I still haven't received from my best friend while trying to avoid the diamonds flashing like little cameras on my wrist. "I do. I love it."

"I'm glad. I saw it and knew you'd love it. It was just so . . . *you*." He pulls me closer, placing a kiss on my temple before eyeing my sweatshirt with a playful smile. "Now, if I can just get you to change up your wardrobe."

As if on cue, I pull the collar of my sweatshirt up, wishing I could have the leather strap Warren replaced with the several-carat diamond bracelet back. It's not that I don't love what he bought me, because I do . . . But it's so not me.

And even after I begged him to return it, saying it was too expensive for me to wear on a daily basis–something he requested I do–he begged me to keep it, saying it was a small gesture of his love for me and he'd be hurt if I didn't.

Warren and I have been together for a little less than two

years. Sure, he can be a little pushy when it comes to his opinions, wanting me to wear the things he buys for me—like the dress he insisted I wear on our one-year-anniversary dinner, or the heels he's still hoping I'll try on soon—but he means well. From his perspective, he's helping me fit in, expanding my horizons and making me more sophisticated.

From his perspective, I don't look the part of an up-and-coming real estate mogul's arm-candy. What with his designer suits and his three-hundred-dollar haircut, I'm sure I look like a vagrant next to him.

So perhaps I shouldn't blame him for wanting those things. It must get monotonous seeing your girlfriend in her unique self-imposed uniform of shorts and a sweatshirt day in and day out.

I chuckle internally as my brother's often-said words come back to me. *"Sometimes you go so far with considering everyone else's needs, you forget to consider yours."*

Maybe Rohan is right. Maybe I do consider everyone else's needs and feelings. Maybe I don't like to rock the boat. Maybe I don't enjoy conflicts and awkward feelings. But is that so wrong? Is that such a crime?

Going back to the clothes argument with Warren—not that it's a heated argument or anything, but it has definitely come up a few times during our time together—it's not that I don't own other types of clothes. I do. I just don't wear them unless it's a special occasion. And since I haven't explained the real reason behind why I wear what I wear to him fully—because when my body is covered from head to toe, I can still feel the laps of flames around me—I can't fault him for thinking I'm a little . . . eccentric.

There's only one person I've divulged that to, and he's currently still missing from my birthday party.

Even when it's just me and Warren alone at home, for whatever reason, I still don't feel completely comfortable discarding my sweatshirt in front of him. I'm probably just in my own head about it, but ever since the first time I showed him my scar, I haven't felt comfortable being fully unclothed in front of him.

It's not that he said anything to make me feel that way, but sometimes an expression is worth more than a thousand words.

A look of shock, swirled with repulsion and pity, marred his expression in that moment. A moment he tried to cover up by blanking out his face immediately after, but I caught it, nonetheless. Like he couldn't unsee what he'd seen. Like he wanted to run and wash his brain with bleach to rid himself of the image. It's something I've never been able to get out of my head, regardless of the times he's told me he loves my body.

And I suppose I have to believe he does. No matter when he sees me, no matter where we are, he'll shower me with compliments. From the way he dotes over my curves to the way he kisses me, I know he's attracted to me.

Still . . .

I can't help but notice the way he avoids taking off my sleep shirt when he's hovering over me in bed. I can't help but notice the way he reaches under my shirt to play with my unblemished breast, while leaving the other one completely neglected. I can't help but notice the way he kisses my neck, never going below the point where my mangled skin might be exposed.

But I also forget how ugly my scar really is. How jarring.

It not only mars my skin in a way that it looks like there's a reverse trench cascading down to the bottom of my left breast, but the skin around it looks like it's been irreversibly ripped apart and meshed back together in a wrinkled, horrific mess.

It's for that same reason that I keep it hidden. Because no

one wants to see a bloody battleground once the battle has been fought.

And while Warren knows how I got my scars, he's never really wanted me to delve into my feelings about them. In fact, the one time he saw me running my fingers over it in front of the mirror in his bathroom, he brought over my sweatshirt, silently urging me to cover it. *"Some memories aren't worth revisiting, Mala. Leaving them covered is the only way to let yourself heal."*

I'd put on the sweatshirt that day, recalling how different his words were to those of Dean's when he saw my scar. *"What looks disfigured to you is the most beautiful thing I've ever seen. You're the most beautiful thing I've ever seen."*

Where Warren urged me to heal without looking back—by keeping that box closed—Dean implored me to obliterate the box entirely by freeing its contents for the world to see.

And as if the thought alone brings me back to the present, I smile up at Warren. "I'm wearing jeans today, aren't I? Baby steps."

He pulls me closer, his hands gripping my waist a little tighter than I'd like. "Yes, but I thought that laying out a dress on our bed for you was a subtle hint of what I would have liked to see you in."

I feign a giggle. "Well, I suppose it helps that I'm the birthday girl, then. *I* get to decide what I wear for my birthday." I try to wiggle out of his grasp, only for him to tighten his hold on me more. "Warren, I need to check on the other guests. And . . . you're hurting me."

We'd invited a few of my friends from the fire station, including my brother, Samantha, and my new baby nephew, Sage, over to Warren's house—*our* house—for my birthday today. And while everyone generally knows one another, it doesn't look right for both Warren and me to be back here in the kitchen for this long.

"You mean, you need to go call Dean for the tenth time to find out why he's still not here?"

I pull his arms off me, finally getting out of his hold. "I've called him once—"

Warren quirks a brow. "So you weren't just checking for his message on your phone before I distracted you?"

I level him with a look. I get it. He's always felt like the outsider in my relationship with Dean, but it hasn't been easy for Dean, either. It hasn't been easy for any of us. "I'm not going to lie to you. Yes, I was checking to see if he'd messaged me back—"

"Shocker." Warren chuckles sarcastically.

"But only because he's over an hour late. He's never missed my birthday."

Warren's arms raise and drop to his sides. "Mala, when are you going to realize that things changed the moment you got into a serious relationship? When are you going to realize that whether you're best friends with him or not, neither one of you can be each other's priority anymore? He's back with Jessie, and you're with me. Why does it matter that he's an hour late? If he wanted to be here, he would have been. The only person who should be your priority is the man standing in front of you right now. The man who gave you that fucking two-thousand-dollar bracelet on your wrist. The man who challenges you to be a better version of yourself. The only man who pushes you to *level up*. Not a man who eats fucking dog treats like a pea-brained man-child and watches trash TV with you."

A better version of myself?

My mouth opens in response, but nothing comes out. Honestly, I can't even make heads or tails of where all this is coming from. Sure, it's not a complete surprise that Warren has always felt insecure because of Dean, but to actually insult him? To imply that I need to *level up*? This is a first. And to throw the gift he forced on my wrist back in my face?

Where the hell is all this coming from?

Warren runs a frustrated hand through his hair. "Wake up, babe! He's not coming, and even if he does, I guarantee it won't be with a gift half as nice as the one I got you. You know why? Because he doesn't know you like I do. He can't take care of you like I can."

"I didn't ask for a gift from you, Warren, and I wouldn't expect one from Dean, either."

Warren shrugs. "Good. At least you admit your expectations for him are low."

I square my shoulders, touching the patch of rough skin on my other wrist. "That's not what I said–"

The rest of our heated exchange is cut off when the door-bell rings. I watch as Rohan walks over to open the door, while I try to settle my soaring pulse.

What the hell? Why is all this even coming up right now? Of all the times to choose to have this *discussion*, he chooses this one? When I have all my friends over. When I was getting ready to celebrate what was supposed to be a happy occasion?

A moment later, Dean's presence fills the foyer. His mouth turns downward immediately as his eyes rake over my face. They move over to who he assumes is the culprit who put the expression on my face there.

Warren turns to me with a tight sneer. "Looks like you got your birthday wish."

I reach out to run my hand over his bicep. "Warren–"

He pulls away, busying himself in the kitchen. "Just go, Mala. He's who you've been waiting for, so . . . just go."

My shoulders slump. "Can we at least talk about this later?"

"Yeah, sure. Whatever." Warren moves past me, heading back to the living room to join the others.

Trying to mask the emotion and confusion surely written all over my features, I rush over to Dean with a smile. "Hey! What took you so long?"

As soon as I'm in his arms, I feel his nose in my hair. "What's wrong?"

I shake my head. "Nothing."

"Mala."

I pull him tighter to me. "Nothing, I swear." I clear my throat, looking up to meet his sharp stare. "Where's Jessie?"

Seeming to accept that I'm not going to divulge more, he scans the room behind me. His eyes harden for a moment, and I wonder if he's found Warren, before he looks back down at me. "She might come by a little later. She got called into the casino for a shift. I dropped her off there before I headed over. Apparently, they were short-staffed and needed someone." He gives me an apologetic look. "She's still paying stuff off, and—"

I place my hand on his chest to stop him from continuing. Whether he's saving face for Jessie or not, I'm not sure, nor do I want to know. "No need to explain. I get it." I gleam at him from ear to ear. "I'm just glad you're here."

He pulls me into another hug. "Happy birthday, *sprinkles*."

Dean and Jessie have had an interesting on-again, off-again relationship, but they seem to be working it out again. At least that's what I can put together from my conversations with him.

As usual, he hasn't been very vocal about his feelings for her, not with me, at least. And now that she no longer works at the café—she got a better position at the casino that offered more pay—it's been hard to get a better read on them aside from what he tells me.

I will say—though I feel a little guilty for doing so—it's sort of been nice to not have to see Jessie at work every day. She was a good worker—chatty and a bit absentminded at times—but it's hard to deny the strange awkwardness I felt around her at times, especially when she brought up Dean. It was like she would go out of her way to talk about how much they enjoyed their time together and how happy they seemed to make each other.

I got it. Jeez. She'd peed on him, staked her claim, and wanted to make sure I was aware.

After their big breakup last year, because Dean refused to lend more money to help her brother, I thought they were done. Dean actually took a few weeks off work to visit his mom, stepdad, and Grams in Colorado, but when he came back, so did Jessie.

I talked to him a couple of times while he was there. I was worried because he'd left so abruptly, and even on the phone, I could tell he wasn't himself. He wasn't the Dean I knew. Each time we talked, I felt like I was speaking to a different person altogether, someone aloof and standoffish . . . reserved.

I finally gave up trying to get him out of his shell and called Grams, hoping she'd have a clue. She told me to give him time, that he was struggling to figure out how to move forward. *"Wait for the thunderclouds to clear, dear girl. They will. He's just got his head stuck inside them right now, but hopefully, he'll find his way to a beautiful rainbow after it all passes."*

I honestly had no idea how to make sense of her words. What thunderclouds were looming around him? What was he trying to move forward from? *Why wouldn't he just talk to me?*

I'd felt that shift in our friendship the night I told him I was moving in with Warren. I'd definitely had a couple of drinks and wasn't feeling like myself, but I remember enough to know something was different between us. A pull like the night on my couch all those years ago. But I kept thinking I must have been imagining it. That it must have been the haze of alcohol playing with my senses.

Even when he carried me to his room, I remember trailing my eyes down his profile . . . wondering if perhaps there was something there between us. But the way he'd so quickly changed the subject when I told him I found him attractive, I knew I'd mistaken all the signs yet again.

I internally wince, thinking about my admission. On one hand, I don't regret it. It's something I've always thought—he's hopelessly, unquestionably, *devastatingly* good looking. But I wondered what the big deal was? So what if I said it aloud? It's not anything he hadn't heard before based on the throngs of women who threw themselves at him like possessed wildebeests. So why was my vocalizing the same thing so shocking for him?

I surmised it was likely because he still thought of me as just a friend or—and I cringe—a little sister. It was the only explanation for his haphazard reaction. I swear he was purposely trying to give me whiplash.

But . . . had I imagined that moment when he dropped me onto his bed? Was there something different about the way his fingers felt on my waist—the warm press of them under my sweatshirt, sending currents zipping down to my core—or the way his breathing stuttered, as if he was afraid to exhale? Did I imagine the sheer millimeters of space between our lips or the way his usual pools of blue took on something darker altogether?

The room was dark, so I probably did.

But it was after I told him I was moving in with Warren that everything seemed to change. At least, for a while, until he came back and started dating Jessie again. I guess they must have made amends about her situation with her brother, but I haven't pried.

I'm just happy that things finally seem to be normal between us again.

I pull Dean into the living room by his hand. "Look who's finally here, everyone!"

The rest of the group greets him with handshakes and hugs. Even Warren gets up to give Dean a quick handshake before I strategically place myself next to Warren. I know he's still upset, but I'm hoping the rest of the night will distract him.

"That's some serious bling you're sporting there, munch." My brother rocks the baby in his arms, tilting his head toward my wrist. "Which jewelry store did you rob?"

My face heats as everyone's eyes turn toward me. Everyone, including Dean. He quickly averts his gaze when my eyes collide with his, taking a sip of his beer. My smile wobbles slightly when I look from Warren to my brother. "Yeah, thanks. It was a gift from Warren, so you should ask him."

Warren flashes everyone a smile, raising his hands in a surrendering gesture. "If you see news of a masked man—roughly six feet tall and a hundred-eighty-five pounds—it wasn't me."

Everyone laughs, and I'm thankful that, for his few faults, at least being surly in public isn't one of them.

Dean, however . . . he looks like that beer is souring his stomach.

As everyone catches up, sitting around the family room with slices of cake in their hands—or in Malcolm's case, a sleepy Sage since my brother handed him over to go get another beer from the kitchen—I track Dean making his way out the front door. He's left his phone on the fireplace ledge where he was sitting, so I know he won't go too far.

"Yo! This party's gettin' serious now!" Rohan hollers, startling Sage in Malcolm's arms. He winces when Samantha gives him a look, taking the baby from Malcolm. He lowers his voice. "I was just sayin' this party is about to get serious if Dean brings his guitar."

I swing my gaze back over to the foyer where Dean is taking off his shoes. He saunters back through the living room with his guitar and takes the same spot at the ledge of the fireplace. Positioning his fingers on the strings, he plucks them strategically, creating a hush in the room. A shiver runs down my arms and legs as each note travels to the bottoms of my feet.

He rarely plays in public, but I've been lucky enough to hear him practice here and there when I've hung out with him at his place. Still, it's been well over two years since I've even seen him pick up his guitar.

My eyes are affixed to him—the way his long fingers wrap around the neck of his guitar, the way his thick lashes almost kiss his cheeks while he adjusts his fingers, the way his sleeves are rolled up, showing off the sexiest forearms I've ever seen.

It's not until Warren throws his arm over my shoulder on the couch, pulling me to his side, that I even remember I'm not the only one in the room.

Dean clears his throat before tucking a strand of his long hair behind his ear. "Uh, I didn't get you a present." At this, Warren shifts next to me, surely trying to emphasize what he said in the kitchen to me earlier. "But I've been working on something. It's not Miley Cyrus . . ." He smirks when his crystal-clear blue eyes take me in from across the room. They've always looked like faceted diamonds to me. "But hopefully you still like it."

The first notes to *Drive* by Incubus drift from his guitar, making a few of our friends whoop in excitement, and I'm enraptured instantly. Dean's throaty rumble rings out above the melody, and it's as if I've been transported somewhere else entirely while he sings.

It's a song that's always held meaning for me. It became

my favorite in my teenage years when I was looking for something to ground me.

For years after the accident, I let my fears guide me, too—fear of being in enclosed places, fear of smelling something burning, fear of even looking at my charred skin and reliving the horror all over again. But this song became the anthem for my recovery.

My healing.

Yes, I still have a ways to go—I always will—with accepting myself exactly the way I am, but I'm miles from where I used to be.

I'm so submerged in Dean's crooning voice that I don't even realize tears have soaked my cheeks until one drops on my wrist, splashing over the bracelet. Startled, I look at Warren. I think I'd already felt his eyes on my face, gauging, judging. Assuming.

A frown pulls at his mouth, and before I can place my hand over his, he gets up and walks away.

Everyone whoops once Dean stops singing, but I can't seem to move from my spot. A heavy hum floats in the air from the last chord Dean played, overpowering any other noise, including the way my heart beats out of rhythm.

My eyes keep gravitating toward him and it seems his don't stray far from mine, either. We're in a moment of locked connection—speaking a language only we seem to understand—when the front door opens and a slightly nasal Southern accent fills the room.

"Well, I'll be!" Jessie's eyes linger on Dean before moving to meet mine. Her smile falters slightly as she ambles inside, and I rise to my feet, wondering if she saw the way we were both lost in each other. The question in her gaze seems to suggest that perhaps she did.

She pulls me into a hug. "Happy birthday, hon!" She looks

around at everyone, waving to a few people. "Looks like a great shindig!"

"It is. I'm glad you were able to make it." I try to sound convincing.

"Oh, me too! I wouldn't have missed any of it, but I couldn't miss the opportunity to take on another shift. You know how well they pay."

I get the feeling she's trying to make a point with that last statement, comparing the pay she made at the bakery with the one she makes at the casino, but I don't give her the satisfaction of showing her that her comment affects me in any way.

"Hey, sugar!" Jessie gleams, looking at Dean before seating herself on his lap. She places a kiss on his temple, and Dean's eyes immediately find mine again.

I look away, trying to pull my lips into a smile at something my brother just said that I hadn't heard.

It's not like I haven't seen them together before. I've seen her put her lips on his, seen him hold her when she wraps her arms around his neck, seen her whisper in his ear before pulling his earlobe in between her lips.

So why does it make my stomach turn more today than it always has? Why do I feel like there's a stone lodged inside my throat, threatening to cut off my airflow? Why does my chest burn almost as much as it did the day a fiery beam fell on it, affixing me to the ground?

Maybe it's the lingering glances from him today, maybe it's the emotion in the air that still hasn't cleared, or the fact that I miss him—*miss us*.

Whatever it is, it threatens a flood through my eyes and I know I have to get up. I have to get up because I have no right to be feeling the way I do.

Because if there's one thing my best friend made clear in all the time I've known him, it's that he's not mine.

Chapter Fifteen

MALA

"Fuck! I'm coming." His hot breath spreads over the nape of my neck, above my scar–always well above my scar. I turn my head to look at the curtains in his room–*our* room. They're always closed. He likes them that way. "Oh, fuck! Yes! I'm coming so . . . so fucking hard. You feel that?"

I nod.

Warren's face hovers over mine and even in the dark, he catches the lie reflecting back from my eyes. His jaw shifts. "Did you come?"

I nod again, hoping he doesn't catch my lie. "Yeah. It was really good."

He heaves himself off me and I can feel the tension wafting off his pores. Each stride away from me taut with barely concealed irritation.

It's been two weeks since my birthday and every day since seems . . . worse. I tried to bring up his feelings about Dean and my friendship a few times afterward, but Warren would constantly shut me down.

I even made reservations at the fancy restaurant he loves, and wore the dress he bought me, to try to change the mood between us, but after two hours of small talk, the car ride home was silent. And though nothing has changed in terms of his dismissal of the conversation, one thing has, and that's his relentless need to satiate himself with my body.

While we used to have sex once every couple of weeks, since the party, it's as if he can't get enough of me. Every night seems to pass the same way—with him pummeling me like his life is on the line until he finds his release, only to wake me up hours later to do it all over again.

And . . . I let him.

Maybe it's my need to avoid more conflict. Maybe it's my guilt over him seeing whatever it was he saw on my face that night when I let Dean's voice overpower all my emotions. Maybe it's my guilt over the past two years I've spent with him, knowing he isn't the one. Knowing he's only a stand-in for my one true person. The man who knows me to my core but refuses to accept me for what he knows I mean to him.

Maybe it's all those things, but I let him do as he pleases with my body, hoping this strain between us will pass and we'll go back to the way things used to be—easy, fun, enjoyable.

At my core, a part of me believes this is my fault. If I had worked harder to get over my crazy feelings for my best friend, maybe we wouldn't be in this position. Perhaps I'd have the same strong affection for Warren as he does for me.

It's with that guilt coloring my thoughts that I shuffle off the bed and follow Warren into the bathroom.

Maybe I can make him see that he means something to me, too. Something more than any other man I've dated in the past has ever meant.

His bare back tightens and stretches, and I watch his chest rise and fall in the mirror. He grips the edge of the counter with such force, I'm surprised he hasn't broken off a chunk of it.

"Warren . . ." My hand lifts but I waver on whether to touch him or not.

"I didn't think I'd have to explicitly ask for your honesty, Mala." The ire in his tone has my hackles raising. "I never thought you'd lie to me."

"I haven't lied to you—"

Warren spins to face me. His face, his features, are as cold and stony as a lifeless statue. "You've lied for the past two fucking weeks. Every fucking time I've asked if you came, you've said yes, when I know for a fucking *fact* you haven't."

I shake my head, my heart pounding through my chest. Yes, it's true that I haven't climaxed, but it's not necessarily his fault. Things have just been off between us, and my head is not in it. But it's not like he's tried that hard to focus on my needs, either . . .

"It's not like tha—"

"No! Don't tell me what it's like." He takes a step forward, closing the space between us. "What else have you been lying about, Mala?"

"N-nothing!" My eyes bounce between his steel-set ones. What is he talking about? "Warren—"

"Liar!" He booms, making me jump. "Look me in my eyes and tell me you haven't lied about your feelings for the guy you call your *best friend*. Look me in the eye and tell me you don't love him. That you haven't wanted to fuck him. That you haven't imagined him fucking you when I'm the one inside you!"

My breath stalls and I try to reach for him again. "That's . . . that's not—"

"I said, don't fucking lie to me!" Warren roars, shoving his hand into my chest before I can finish my sentence. I'm pushed so hard against the wall behind me that all the air leaves my lungs. A pain shoots up my shoulder and bicep as my groan entangles with the thud of my body against the wall. I swear, it feels like the whole room shakes, or maybe that's just my blurred vision.

As if he's just realized what he's done, Warren's eyes widen with shock. He studies my slumped form against the wall, almost like he doesn't understand how I got there.

He takes in the towel hanger behind me—the one he shoved me into—and scurries forward. "Oh, my God! Fuck! Oh, God. I'm–I'm so fucking sorry, Mala!"

He tries to touch my shoulder and I jerk back, every muscle in my body contracting at his nearness. The throb inside my shoulder and bicep feels connected to my heartbeats, pulsing with every breath. And yet, I feel breathless, like I can't get enough air in to keep me standing, to keep me alert.

"Mala–" he tries again, raising his hand toward my hair, but I turn my head.

My mouth sets in a way I've never felt it do before. *"Don't. Touch. Me."*

A feeling of emptiness threatens to ensnare my insides. How could someone who claims to have cared for me–*loved me*–hurt me in such a vile way? How could I have compromised everything—my self-worth, my dignity, and my body—for him?

How could I have been so blind?

Warren must see the hurt and fury coupling behind my eyes because he raises his hands. "Okay . . . okay." His chin wobbles as the weight of the moment finally takes him under. "Mala . . ." His eyes pool as he takes a step back. "I didn't mean to hurt you. I just . . . I lost control. It's been a lot for me to come to terms with over the past two weeks. Hell, I think I knew you loved him even when we met two years ago. I just didn't want to believe it. Or maybe I thought I could change your mind. But the way he sang for you . . . the love I saw in your eyes for him–"

He stops himself, taking in a ragged breath before swiping a tear from his cheek. "It's not an excuse. Of course, it's not an excuse for what I just did. I'm so fucking sorry, Mala. I'd never mean to hurt you." He sobs, his shoulders shaking. "I'd never hurt you."

But he did.

And even though I'm brimming with anger and loathing for him—and to some degree, myself—I can't completely deny his words. He may not have *meant* to hurt me, but he did.

Call me stupid, but I believe him.

He's always been a little forceful—gripping my hand or my hips tighter than I'd like when he's trying to persuade me on a point—but never violent. I've always let the other things slide, including his need to change me—to dress me up to look good next to him—because I saw the decent man he was. The caring man.

The man who went out of his way to bring me dinner when I had a late night at the café. The man who left me little notes in our kitchen to tell me he missed me, that he was thinking about me. The man who rubbed my feet at the end of a long day.

What happened to that man?

Because the man I saw tonight was anything but. The man I saw tonight made me recoil, like I was staring into the eyes of a complete stranger. A rabid beast.

I pull myself up, holding my arm with my hand and recite my mantra.

You're fine. You're alive and safe. Just count your blessings and put one foot in front of the other.

I'd forgotten to take my bracelet off before I went to bed and seeing it now, wrapped around my wrist, has bile crawling up my throat. I unclasp it quickly, as if not doing so will burn me, throwing it on the ground as far away from me as I can.

I promised myself not to be bound by fear a long time ago.

I may still be a work in progress, but I refuse to be bound by new fears. I refuse to bend to new shame. *Nothing and no one* will ever have that kind of power over me again.

My breathing stutters right along with my words, but they're both as unwavering as they've ever been. "We're over, Warren."

Chapter Sixteen

DEAN

I STARE AT MY PHONE, AT THE TWO UNANSWERED RIDDLES I've sent over the course of two days. They've been read but not answered. *Where the fuck is she?*

I turn my head to look out the side window of my truck, still parked in my driveway, before scanning the clock on my dash. Eleven-twenty-one AM. If I swing by the bakery, I can still make it in time to meet Jessie. She's been wanting to have a picnic at the park near *Heavenly* for the past couple of weeks, so I told her I'd be game for it today since it's my day off.

We still don't live together—not for the lack of her insisting, though. After the way things ended with Nora, and the several times Jessie and I have broken up over the past couple of years, I'm just not ready to have her in my space all the time.

I like where we are now—together but not always together. I have my independence and space, and so does she. Moving in together would change all of that. Plus, the woman already wants all my free time. I'm just not ready to give her all my space, too.

Fuck it. I need to check on Mala. I don't know why, but my gut doesn't feel right. She's never left a message from me unanswered after having read it. Never. I even called her last night on my way home from work, but she sent me to voice-mail after one ring.

Something isn't right. I can feel it inside my ribs as sure as the air I'm breathing.

But I saw Rohan yesterday at work, and he didn't say anything. I know he's been adjusting to having a baby, and now busy with getting ready for his and Samantha's wedding, but surely if something was wrong with Mala, he'd know. He'd tell me.

Making my decision, I reverse the truck out of my driveway.

Twelve minutes later, I'm parking outside *Doggy Bag Café* before running up the steps to the front door. The familiar chime on the door rings, announcing my welcome and getting a couple of yips from the dogs eagerly waiting with their owners in line for their mid-morning snacks.

I scan the indoor space for Mala, but don't see her anywhere.

"She's in the back," Betty hollers over to me, noting me lingering near the front door. She hands over the next customer to Blake, the new barista Mala hired after Jessie had quit. She rushes over to me, her silvery white curls bouncing over her shoulder. "Dean . . . can I speak to you for a moment?" She tilts her head toward the opposite corner, a crease forming between her brows. "Privately."

"Sure." I shuffle behind her, my stomach tightening with each step.

Betty takes a deep breath before regarding the doors to the kitchen in the back, and I wait on labored breaths. "I . . . Well, it's really none of my business, Dean, but I thought I ought to tell someone, and I haven't seen Rohan in a couple of days."

My brows pull together. "What is it? Is it something to do with Mala?"

She nods, her eyes glistening under her glasses. "I can't be sure but, um . . . I think something happened between her and Warren. I think she's slept at the bakery the past two nights."

I stare at Betty, not able to grasp her words completely. A snake-like feeling crawls up my spine and my hands fist at my sides. "She slept *here?*"

Betty purses her lips, blinking back tears. "I've never seen her so . . . sullen. She's such a fun-loving girl, always sharp and witty. It's like . . . like the light inside her—her whole personality—is dimmed. I've asked her if everything is alright, but she won't talk to—"

I'm walking toward the back kitchen where Mala is before Betty even finishes her sentence.

My hands connect with the double doors, and I find Mala on the other side of the island with her back to me. She turns to see who's entered before her teary eyes widen and she quickly turns back to wipe her face.

I'm in front of her in a flash, even though she's trying to dodge me by turning this way and that. "*What. The. Fuck. Happened?*" I grit out.

My hands grasp her shoulders and Mala winces audibly.

It's as if I've been burned. I let her go, knowing inside my gut, inside every fiber of my being, that that bastard did something he'll pay for, even if it means I'll go to jail for the rest of my life because of it.

"Go away, Dean," she whispers, closing her eyes and turning her head to the side. Her wet lashes flutter under her lids. "It's nothing you need to worry about."

I close the gap between us, locking her in place with my arms around her, grasping the edge of the island. "Look at me, *sprinkles*." I try to ease the sheer fury wrapping around my words.

I wait for her to open her eyes and when she does, I make sure she sees exactly who she's talking to. *It's nothing I need to worry about?* Is she fucking kidding me? She must be, because if she only knew . . .

"I don't give a single fuck if you broke up with that asshole. I don't give a single fuck if you spend two years or ten with him. I'm fucking raging because you spent the night *here* instead of calling me. I'll even put that aside for now. But—" I place two fingers under her chin, turning her head to me since she stopped looking at me again. "But if that motherfucker laid one hand on you—"

She shakes her head almost violently. "No. Dean, I . . . I'm fine. Okay?" Her eyes shift and I know—*I fucking know*—she's lying.

Why the fuck is she lying? And on behalf of whom? That douchebag motherfucker with his overpriced car and his stupid-ass grin? The grin he makes sure to flash at me when he knows she isn't watching? That grin that fucking gloats, *"I have what you want, and I'll never let it go."*

She's trying to cover for *that* motherfucker?

Mala heaves in a breath. "It's over now anyway, and I'm fine. I'm just . . ." she clears her throat as her chin wobbles, "I'm just trying to move forward."

My nostrils flare. "Move forward?" I turn my head to the side, catching one of her sweatshirts strewn on a sleeping bag on the floor, along with a rolled-up blanket. That enrages me even further. "Move forward by sleeping at the bakery? Move forward by not telling me or your brother anything—"

She wipes her cheek. "Dean, this isn't something for you or Rohan to worry about, okay? These things happen.

Couples break up. It's not like I'm going to live at the bakery forever. I'm going to find a new place soon."

"But why didn't you call me? Why not come over to my place when–"

"Come on, Dean," she scoffs before her words get a little less assured. A vulnerability floats over her face when she looks down to her feet. "I-I didn't want to bother you, in case . . ." She shrugs. "You know, in case you were with Jessie."

God help me.

When will this woman understand her place in my fucking life?

I grind my molars so hard, I'm surprised she can't hear them. "Mala, look at me." She does reluctantly, slowly raising her head to meet my eyes. They're so fucking deep and rich and brown, I'm lost in them momentarily. Her lips–her fucking beautiful, heart-shaped mouth–twitch as she tries to compose herself, and I tighten my grip on the counter behind her to do the same. "You are my goddamn *best friend*. Do you know that?" When she doesn't say anything, I repeat, "Tell me you fucking know it."

She nods.

"Then you should know that no one, not Jessie, not Rohan, not my brothers . . . *no one* takes your place. When I told you I'd do anything for you, I meant it."

She nods again, whispering, "I know."

"Then you should have come to me. You should have called me." I raise my hand, letting it fall on her shoulder again, momentarily forgetting that she'd winced when I touched her earlier. When she jolts again at my touch, I'm seeing red.

Fucking red everywhere.

What did that piece of shit do to her?

I grit out my next words, "Show me."

She shakes her head. "It was nothing, Dean. An accident—"

"Mala, I swear to God . . . Fucking show me, or I'll head over there and bury the motherfucker with my own hands."

Mala sobs, placing the heels of her hands on her eyes. I let her because that's what she seems to need right now. But I wait.

Her sobs quell and she sniffles, nervously looking back at the double doors to the kitchen.

"No one is coming in here," I assure her. "Now, show me."

She slowly pulls off her sweatshirt and I take in her pine-green bra. My eyes only faintly linger over the scar on her palm-sized breast before they sharpen on her shoulder. I'm positive my lips pull back so I'm baring my teeth as I take in the black and blue bruise forming all around her shoulder, seeping down to her bicep.

That piece of shit motherfucker! I knew—*I fucking knew*—there was something about him. I felt it in my gut, but made myself believe it was all in my head. Made myself believe I was only seeing him that way because I was jealous.

I'm fucking beside myself, trembling in a kind of rage I've never felt before. My growl is barely restrained from becoming an all-out roar. "How the fuck!?"

"It was an accident, Dean. He was angry about . . ." she hesitates, "some things, and I shouldn't have tried to touch him at that time. It's never happened before. *Never*." She emphasizes the last word as if it'll help smooth over his 'pristine' image. "He didn't mean to. Plus, I already broke it off. I'm never going back to—"

"That motherfucker put his hands on you and you're *defending* him?" I ask incredulously.

"I'm not defending him. I just . . . I just want to forget about it."

Well, I don't! I won't!

My ears ring, even as I try to control my voice. "I'm going to get your stuff."

"Wh-what? You . . . you can't. No, I'll go there later—"

"You most certainly will not," I grit out. "I'm going over there right now—"

"Dean." Mala's hands land on my shoulders, the tips of her fingers digging into my shoulder blades. Her eyes bounce between mine. "You can't go there alone, not when you're this angry."

"I'll take Rohan."

Mala's mouth drops in shock. "Are you kidding me?" she hisses. "You can't even *tell* Rohan! He'll . . . he'll murder Warren!"

I'll do worse.

I pull out of her grasp, rolling up my shirt sleeves as I walk toward the exit. Pure venom tears through my veins as I imagine my palm wrapped around his weasley neck. "Then let me do this my way."

She rushes in front of me, holding me back with her hand on my abs. "I'm coming with you—"

"No." I tug her hand off me. "I don't want you anywhere near that piece of shit."

Her glassy eyes plead with me, and for reasons unbeknownst to me, I can see how much she wants this. "Dean, please."

My nostrils flare as I take in her crumpled form in front of me. I want to fucking pull her into me and keep her there for the rest of time.

My instinct is to protect her, to refuse her request again, but as I study the vulnerability in her eyes, I notice something else behind it. Dignity. Fearlessness.

This beautiful, strong girl, who's dealt with everything life has thrown at her. If a fucking fire couldn't extinguish her spirit, then Warren's got no chance.

And that's why she's insisting on coming with me—to show that bastard how resilient she really is.

"Fine."

Her worried gaze stays on me even as she pulls her sweat-shirt over her. "Do you promise not to do anything to him?"

I stare at her for a moment. Does she not know me at all?

"If you're asking if I'll commit homicide tonight, then yes, I promise."

THE FUCKER DOESN'T EVEN KNOW what hit him.

One moment, he's opening the door to let Mala and me in to pick up her stuff, and the next, he's holding his broken nose as blood gushes out of one side.

At least he can't say he wasn't warned. Mala texted him that we were coming to pick up her stuff, and he let her know he was there. He also added—I'm sure for her benefit alone—that he wanted to talk to her privately.

Over my fucking dead body.

I punch him again in the ribs and he groans, sinking to the ground. A second later, I'm above him, one hand squeezing his neck and the other rearing back to throw one more punch to his jaw for good measure. "Motherfucker, that was the last and only time you put your grimy hands on her. You come within a mile of her from here on out, I'll—"

"Dean!" Mala shrieks, rushing to my side and holding my arm in the air. "You promised—"

I turn my raging eyes to her. "I promised you he had one and only one shot to mess up and when he did—" I chuckle darkly, looking back down at the asshole's pitiful face, "—because I fucking *knew* he would—I'd fuck him up."

"Fuck!" Warren groans under me, holding his nose. Some of his blood has seeped into the collar of his ugly-as-fuck expensive shirt. "It's fine, Mala. I fucking deserve it." A tear rolls out the side of his eye as his gaze finds hers, and he heaves out a sputtering sob. "I fucking deserve it. I'm sorry, babe. I'm so fucking sorry."

My hand tightens on his throat and I practically shake with ire. "Don't you fucking *dare* call her that. You hear me?" I grit. "You don't get to call her that. You don't get to call her, period."

He nods the best he can under my grasp, his face turning red.

And even though my rage is only minimally subsided, I heft myself off him, looking down at him with disdain and repulsion. My pulse throbs inside my temples, my eyes feeling like they could burn his whole goddamn house down with the sheer fire behind them.

I turn to Mala, my gaze immediately softening at the sight of her. I tug her toward me, wrapping her in my arms. I run my fingers through her hair right as she lets out a sob into my shoulder.

My lips rest on the top of her head. "I got you. I've *always* got you." At her reluctant nod, I add, "Now go get your stuff."

She pulls herself together, surveying Warren with heartbroken and betrayed watery eyes before squaring her shoulders and heading toward an open room in the back of the house.

My phone vibrates in my pocket for the fifth or sixth time. *Fuck.* It's probably Jessie, wondering where the hell I am. I'm over an hour late.

I pull it out, stepping away from Warren. He hoists himself up, stumbling as he disappears into the bathroom. Goddamn piece of shit.

I read the first message, running a hand over my face. "Shit."

Jessie: Hey, where are you?

There are four more after it. One from just a few seconds ago, along with a picture of the picnic she has set up with various sandwiches and a champagne bottle lying next to a pair of flutes.

Jessie: Seriously, where are you, Dean? I've called you a hundred times. Unless you're in the hospital, at least have the decency to message me back and tell me you can't make it.

I sigh, knowing I'm going to pay for this later, but also knowing there's no other place I'd rather be right now than with Mala.

Me: I'm sorry, Jess. I got tied up with something urgent. Unfortunately, I'm not going to make it today. Any chance I could get a rain check?

I'm not surprised when her response comes in a moment after.

Jessie: <middle finger emoji> Go fuck yourself and your urgent issue, Dean Meyer.

With a sigh, I pad over to the room where Mala is gathering her stuff, clenching my jaw as I try to avoid the bed she likely spent every night in over the last two years with that piece of shit.

I busy myself with pulling some of her clothes from the hangers in the closet—she tells me to leave some fancy dresses and heels that don't seem like they could even be hers —and throwing them into a suitcase.

Forty-five minutes later, we're on our way out. I don't have the slightest intention of acknowledging the jackass standing in the corner with his head hung low, but I can't miss him, either. There's a paper towel stuffed up his nose and he's holding an ice pack on his cheek.

Mala tenses at the sight of him, but I place my hand on the small of her back and guide her forward, giving him another disgusted look.

I need to get her the fuck out of here.

We've just stepped out onto the porch when Warren's voice resounds, making Mala stiffen again. "I was never going to have your heart, was I, Mala? How could I when it always belonged to someone else?"

Part Two

THE RECENT

Theme Song:"Left and Right" by Charlie Puth

Chapter Seventeen

DEAN

Fifteen Months Ago

"Of all the trucks you could have bought, you had to buy the one that feels like taking a hike up Mount Everest?" Mala releases my hand as soon as I help her into the passenger seat of my new truck. In fairness, she really didn't do much work to get in since I pretty much picked her up and put her there, but I know if I say as much, she'll bust my balls.

Plus, I have no reason to tell her that since I like being able to pick her up any chance I get.

I swing around to the driver's side of the truck, shaking off the snow on my leather jacket and my hair before getting inside. Looking at her, I wait until she's buckled. "It's not a hike up Everest for the majority of us who kept growing past third grade."

As expected, she punches my arm. "Jerk. I *did* grow past the third grade. Some of us just don't have the ogre genes you do."

I shake my head somberly. "You're going to regret saying that when I tell Grams you called her an ogre."

Mala's mouth drops. "I wasn't calling her an ogre, I was calling *you* one!"

I shrug, backing out of her driveway. "That's not what I heard. I heard you insulting my genetic makeup and my lineage—a part of which comes from Grams." I look at Mala, reveling in the way I've made her cheeks flush. Getting her worked up is one of the finer joys in life. "Grams the ogre; I'm telling her you said it."

Mala looks out the window, pretending to fume. "You're awful, you know that? I honestly don't know why I still keep you around."

"Because you need me to keep you humble and grounded." I purse my lips, trying to squelch my smile. "Oh wait, I forgot . . . you're pretty close to the ground as it is."

"Oh, ha ha. Someone's quite the comedian today. Must be a full moon or something."

I laugh, getting onto the snow-covered road out of her neighborhood. My wipers work overtime as they clear the incessantly falling snow off my windshield. It's the first week of December and, as expected for this time of year, there's a multi-foot blanket of snow in Tahoe. And even though visibility isn't great right now, at least the roads aren't slick, so driving all the way to South Tahoe doesn't feel like quite the haul.

I texted Jane before I left Mala's house, letting her know we were on our way. Her response lights up my phone sitting in the middle console, and Mala picks it up. "She says 'see you guys soon' and sent you her new address again."

Jane and my almost *ten-going-on-twenty-year-old* goddaughter, Catherine, moved into a new home in South Lake Tahoe recently with Jane's steady boyfriend of three years and his highschool-aged daughter. Jane met Owen—a widower who'd lost his wife to cancer several years ago—through a grief support group, and they seemed to connect right off the bat.

Based on everything I've heard from Jane, everyone seems to be getting along well, but this will be the first time I'll be seeing the four of them together in their new home.

"You think Catherine will like the baking set I got her?" Mala fiddles with the gift bag at her feet. "She seemed to enjoy baking when she helped me at the café last year."

I turn my blinker to get onto the freeway. "I'm sure she will. Jane said she loves to help out in the kitchen."

I introduced Mala to Jane and Catherine a few years ago, and Catherine took an immediate liking to my best friend. I thought over all the years of knowing her that I'd seen all the sides of Mala, but I was proven wrong when I saw the way she was with Catherine. She almost turned into a kid herself. Catherine was only seven or eight at the time, but the way they connected over shows on Disney Channel and played video games, I'd have thought they'd known each other for years.

Catherine even spent a whole weekend with Mala and me last year when Jane and Owen left for a little romantic out-of-town getaway. And even though I had the extra room in my house, Catherine insisted on staying at Mala's small condo—though, I think I have my suspicions as to why. And when I had to work, Mala had Catherine help out at *Doggy Bag Café* and taught her how to get comfortable with baking.

Jane and Catherine have never said it outright to me, but I have a strong suspicion they weren't fans of Jessie. So, when Catherine was supposed to spend the weekend away from Jane, she didn't want to run into Jessie again, even though I told her Jessie wasn't going to be at my house that weekend at all.

For whatever reason, they just never really took a liking to Jessie the first time they met her. It was around the same time they met Mala, but maybe it was the fact that Jessie didn't come across quite as warm that day. We'd had some argument or another, and Jessie was in a sour mood by the time Jane and Catherine showed up at my house.

I wish I could say I remember what we fought about, but truthfully, we've had so many arguments over the years, that particular one is a blur.

Several years ago, our arguments—and one of our major breakups—were around her relentless need to support her brother. Since we got back together after that, Jessie made a conscious effort not to ask me for more money to lend him, though I know she still helps him from time to time.

More recently, our arguments have been about me not wanting to spend time with her pretentious friends from the casino. And I don't know if it's because of their influence or just Jessie changing on her own over time, but she's been rather judgy and high-nosed lately.

In fact, last week when we visited Rohan and Samantha for dinner, Jessie told me afterward that she felt suffocated in their home. That it was small and *'unimaginative'*. Sure, they don't live in a mansion—I don't, either—but where did she get off talking about their house when she didn't own one herself?

Nevertheless, whatever our argument was on the day she met Jane and Catherine, it bled into the way she presented herself. Needless to say, the two women I consider an extension of my own family were not fans of my girlfriend.

Which is likely why they only invited me and Mala over to visit their new home and not my girlfriend.

Mala changes the music playing in my truck, jostling me out of my thoughts. I smile over at her as she mouths the words to her favorite song by Incubus—it's my favorite song, too, but I won't admit it to her. Her voice mingles with the lead singer's, filling me with memories. And if I'm reading the look in her eyes correctly, she's recalling the same night almost three years ago when I sang for her on her birthday.

"Dean?" She plays with the leather strap on her wrist I got for her not too long after she left that douchebag ex of hers. I found matching ones with half-hearts stuck to the straps, so I bought the matching set for myself. She wears one half of the heart, but the truth is, she has my half, too.

Is it cheesy that we wear best friend bracelets? Absolutely. Do I give a shit? Not even a little.

"Mala." I keep my eyes on the dark road ahead.

"Thank you."

I tilt my chin down. "You know I don't like you thanking me."

She pulls my hand from its place on my thigh and brings it to her lips, laying a kiss on the back of it. I feel the tingles all the way up my arm, settling somewhere in between my ribs.

She entangles our fingers together, placing them on her lap. Thankfully, she wore wool tights and boots today, given the freezing temperature outside. As much as I love her phenomenal legs, I would have had a heart attack if she wanted to come along wearing shorts.

"You can't keep shutting me up when I want to, though. I need you to just hear me out one time."

Relenting, I huff, "Go on."

She looks at something out her window before squeezing my hand. "What you did for me after the way things went down with Warren . . . The way you were there for me . . . I can't thank you enough."

I tighten my fingers around the steering wheel, trying to force out the image of the asshole she used to date. Last I heard, he moved somewhere upstate soon after the incident with Mala. Just the thought of him laying his hands on her has my blood boiling to dangerous levels. This fucking perfect girl. Someone he should have never gotten in a million lifetimes. He hurt *her*? He had the fucking *audacity* to touch her?

He's lucky I didn't do more damage to that pretty face of his. I hope he has a crooked-ass nose for the rest of his life.

I clear my throat, hoping to clear away my dark thoughts because once I go back down that road, it'll taint everything through the night. "Do you know how many times you've done the same for me? Every time Jessie and I have a fight, you're the first one at my place with an excuse to watch a movie and keep me company."

She nods thoughtfully, but a smile plays on her lips. "I lost count after your forty-fifth break up, but hey, at least we've watched some good movies together."

My shoulders shake as I laugh. She's always had a way of knowing when to make light of the heavy moments. "Smartass."

She plays with my fingers, running her index finger over each one of mine, causing my pulse to flutter, the hairs on my arm to rise. Fuck, I wish she'd stop, but God, I hope she doesn't.

"Rufus?"

"*Sprinkles.*"

The corners of her mouth twitch like she's trying to hold back her laugh. Without even hearing what she's about to say, I already know she's going to ruin whatever moment we were having with one of her dumb jokes. "Which movie should I pick for your next breakup night?"

I narrow my eyes on her, pulling my hand out of her grasp, while she starts giggling. "You're the biggest pain in my ass."

"So, we have some news." Jane smiles, looking from Owen to me and Mala across the table from us. Both Catherine and Owen's daughter, Maddie, exchange looks with similar smiles on their faces. Jane lifts her manicured hand, showing off a ring I hadn't noticed until now. "Owen and I are getting married!"

"Oh, my gosh!" Mala exclaims, rushing out of her seat. "I thought I saw a ring on your finger, but I didn't want to presume." She moves around the table to wrap Jane in a hug. "I'm so happy for you guys!"

"Thank you." Jane holds Mala's hands between them. "We haven't finalized any dates, but we'd love for you and Dean to be there."

Mala looks at me for confirmation before turning back to Jane. "Of course, we'll be there!"

I shake Owen's hand, congratulating him as well. It's been a hell of a journey watching my old friend's widow find someone who can give her the love she deserves. I see the way Owen looks at her, the way he's always touching her, smiling at her. He loves her with all his heart, and it's because of him that I'm finally seeing her smile, too.

I still remember Zander's last words to me, begging me to make sure Jane never lost her spark, that she found reasons to keep smiling. And while I may not have been able to keep my promise to him, I'm glad she found her spark again, none-theless. So much so that she now looks a hundred times healthier and happier than she did for years after Zander died. She's even been back to visit the old crew at the station a couple of times.

Jane keeps her hold on Mala's hand. "Actually, I wondered if you'd want to be my bridesmaid? I don't have much of a family or any siblings and—"

Mala leans down, hugging Jane again, cutting off her words, "I would be honored."

Just her words alone have me remembering the way Mala looked at Rohan and Samantha's wedding a couple of years ago, where we both came as each other's plus-ones. She was no longer with the douche nozzle, and I was detached from Jessie for reasons I no longer recall.

If I thought Mala looked adorable as hell on a normal basis—wearing shorts and a sweatshirt with her hair thrown up in a bun—then she looked like a fucking goddess that night.

The way the light blue dress hugged her every curve, accentuating her tits and her already plentiful ass. The way her silky hair was pinned to one side, revealing the smooth skin on her shoulder, and the long slit on the side of her dress went far enough up to almost be considered indecent, but not indecent enough.

I swear, I've never had a hard-on last that many hours.

At one point during the reception, after I'd danced with her, after I'd had her tits pressed against me and my hands begging to inch down to the bottom of her ass, I even considered going to the restroom and fucking my hand to give myself some relief.

I'd even waited for my normal bout of guilt to come bounding in, but it never did. In fact, ever since that night several years ago when I almost kissed her—the second time around, the same night she told me she was moving in with Warren—I haven't felt guilty about my feelings for her.

But I also didn't want to do anything about them, either.

Not when she was still recovering from her breakup with that asshole—when she *specifically* told me she wanted a break from men and dating. Not when I still believed what I did about permanently tying someone to me, given my line of work. Not when I still couldn't fathom breaking her heart the way Zander broke Jane's . . .

"Want to see my new room?" Catherine grabs Mala's hand, pulling herself out of her chair. "Owen put a TV in there for me, so me, you, and Maddie can even play a game on my new Nintendo Switch!"

Mala looks back at Jane and Owen for approval as she gets pulled up the stairs behind the two girls.

Jane waves at her to follow with an airy laugh. "Go, go! Have fun."

A few minutes later, Owen gets called up by the girls because they can't get something working on the TV, so I'm left alone with Jane.

She hands me a beer, turning on her fireplace with a remote control, and we both take a seat on some chairs in front of it. "Can I ask you something, Dean?"

I give her the side-eye. "Never stopped you before if I said no."

Jane giggles. "True." She takes a sip of the cider in her hands. "You haven't mentioned Jessie at all tonight. Are you still together?"

I sigh. "We are."

She nods slowly, as if processing something new and interesting. "That sigh says a lot." She lifts a brow. "What's up?"

Jane's always been perceptive, astute. And while we've never had a long conversation about mine and Jessie's relationship, Jane's not a stranger to our ups and downs.

I twirl the bottle in my hands, watching laps of fire surround the charred wood inside the fireplace.

When I look back through the time I've spent with Jessie, yes, our ups and downs, our breakups—generally having to do with me not giving her enough of my time, or my feelings, or my affection—put a dark tarnish over any of the good memories we've made. But I can't deny some of the good memories, either.

Like the time we went off-roading on my day off a couple of years ago and found a hidden warm spring. We floated in it for hours, just enjoying the day. Or the time I helped her paint her bedroom, and we started out flicking paint at each other and ended up getting into an all out paint war. Or even the time I taught her how to snowboard, and we spent an entire day laughing and playing in the snow.

But somewhere along the line, the fun times dwindled and her expectations of me changed. She started wanting more from me and my time, and I started wanting less.

I run my tongue along the front of my teeth. "I suppose things aren't as easy and uncomplicated as they used to be between us."

Jane seems to ponder that for another moment. "Were they easy because it was easy to be with her, or because it was easy to break up with her?"

We both listen as a giggle and squeal rings out from somewhere upstairs, and I can easily pick out Mala's voice. I smile, my chest feeling warm. I've always loved her laugh. Sometimes when I watch her laugh, I hear myself laughing, too.

I know Jane's still awaiting my response. "Both."

Jane turns her body to face me. "Dean, I've never been the type to bullshit, as you know. I was in a bad place, a *really* bad place, years ago. After Zander died, you saw my life flip on its head, and I lost myself."

I nod. "I remember."

"But what I realized when I finally made it out of all that fog is that life isn't just short or fleeting, it's your last chance to live." Her brows pinch. "Do you know what I mean?"

I nod hesitantly. "I think—"

"It's your last fucking chance to have what you've always wanted. It's your last chance to be who you've always wanted to be. Your last chance to love." She takes a breath, and I see a tremble catch her chin. "Don't waste this short life—your last chance—on someone you don't love with every fiber of your being. Don't waste your precious time on someone only because it's easy to break ties with them. Spend it with someone you can't untether your soul from."

Her eyes ping-pong between mine. "What you're doing—

stringing Jessie along, knowing full-well she isn't the one for you—isn't fair to her or you. But you know who else it isn't fair to?"

My heart beats inside my ears and I swallow, waiting for her to finish, knowing in my gut what she's going to say.

"That beautiful woman upstairs. The girl you love, the one who deserves to know how you feel—"

I shake my head, hoping it'll cut off the rest of her words. "I can't. I won't. No matter how much I fucking want to."

"Why?!" Jane's green eyes harden on me. "Why the hell not?"

I jump off my seat, trying to keep my voice low but not having much success with my tone. "Because of everything *he* put you through! Because if she feels the same for me—which, for the record, I don't know if she does—I can't . . . I won't let that happen to her."

Jane rises to her feet, taking a step toward me. "What Zander put me through?" Her eyes widen before they fill, pools of unshed tears threatening to fall. "Oh, Dean. Is this all because of what I said all those years ago? Is . . . is that why you've been holding back from falling in love? Because you think you'll leave her, like Zander left me?"

I clench my jaw. This isn't what I wanted—to make her feel guilty for feeling any of the things she felt before. What she felt was valid. She didn't deserve what she got. She didn't deserve to be left alone like that, pregnant and grieving.

Jane puts her drink down and places her hands on my forearms after wiping a tear from her cheek. "I am so incredibly sorry if I had any part in you holding yourself back, Dean. I was so consumed by my own grief at that time." She takes a long breath. "It took me a long time to come to terms with Zander's death. But once I did, I was finally able to move on from thinking about the way he died or why he died, to thinking about the way he lived and *why* he lived. He lived and loved without restraint. And he gave me the most beautiful gift anyone could ever have before he died." She sniffles. "I've lived each day after him for our beautiful little girl and honestly, she's the reason I'm here today. Because if it wasn't for Catherine," she shakes her head, "I'm not sure I could have gone on. I wasn't strong enough. She saved my life. *He* saved my life."

My jaw tightens at the thought of possibly having lost Jane right along with Zander. It fucking breaks my heart to think how lost she was.

My words feel shaky as I say them, "So, why would I want that for her?"

Jane wipes another streak off her cheek. "Do you remember when the station got called in to help with the California forest fires a couple of years ago?"

I nod.

"Do you remember after you all came home safe, you and I sat out on your porch with a beer and you told me what Mala said to you before you left?"

My thoughts travel back to that day. Mala had shown up at the station right as Rohan, Malcolm, and I were preparing to leave. Samantha had been excused because she still had an infant at home, but most of us—including hundreds of firefighters from across the US—were asked to come help fight another deadly forest fire.

I remember how stoic Mala seemed. I knew she was worried—I could tell based on the dark circles that had formed under her eyes after we all received the news—but she kept herself together. She never let her worry deter her support and determination on our behalf.

Where just the night before, Jessie had held on to me, cried into my shoulder as if I'd already died, begging me to find an excuse not to go—"Say *you're sick! Tell 'em you've had a family emergency!*"–Mala gave me a warm hug, kissed my cheek, and said, *"Go do what you do best. Help however you can. But come back home to me. I'll make you a lifetime supply of dog treats if you come back to me, safe and sound."*

Jane squeezes my forearms, getting my attention again. "Do you remember how strong she was? The girl lost *both* her parents in a fire, her brother and her closest friends risk their lives every day on the job, yet somehow, she still finds a way to smile. Living with that kind of loss and still finding ways to work through her fears? Now that's commendable."

I start to speak, but Jane bulldozes right over me. "And before you tell me that at least she won't have to face losing the love of her life in a fire on top of it all . . . I'd like you to look in a mirror." Her eyes drill into mine. "Because she'd still lose him anyway if, God forbid, something happened to you."

Chapter Eighteen

DEAN

"WELL, DON'T THOSE LOOK LOVELY!" GRAMS EYES THE TWO orange velvet pound cakes on my kitchen counter through my phone screen. She's sitting outside on one of her favorite chairs on my mom's patio. A blanket of snow covers the patio behind her, looking similar to the way my patio looks here in Tahoe. "And you made two! You've had quite the busy day already."

I lick the orange glaze off the tip of my index finger before placing a cover over the second cake. "I used your recipe. The first one is for when the guys come over tonight for poker, and the second one is for Mala. She's been trying to recreate it for the past couple of years, but I won't share the recipe with her." I wink at Grams. "The girl has plenty of recipes, and I like having one she can't recreate so I can make her something from time to time."

Grams coughs into her white handkerchief before wiping the corners of her mouth and adjusting the woolen scarf around her neck. This is the second cough I've heard over the past couple of months, and as much as I want to tell her to go inside where she'll be warm, I know how much she loves the fresh air, even if it is bitterly crisp. Plus, between my mom, my stepdad, Garrett, and me, she's exhausted with everyone trying to fuss over her health—she's said as much. So, I force myself to ease up and keep my concern to myself for now.

"Well, it's only fair to reveal the recipe to her after you officially bring her into the family," Grams states as casually as if she's making some off-handed remark about the damn weather.

I freeze, my hands still on top of the kitchen counter. "Pardon me?"

Grams waves her hand in front of the camera as if to reprimand me for being dramatic. "Oh, for Pete's sake! Dean, I love you more than all my grandsons—"

"You said the exact same thing to Garrett last week!"

"But it is about time you get your head out of your ass, dear boy." She completely ignores my outburst. "How long are *you* going to deny how you feel about her?" Grams coughs into her handkerchief again. "You both deserve more from each other . . . from yourselves!"

This is the second time in a week that someone has said basically the same thing to me. Last weekend at Jane's place, and now with Grams acting as if it's the most obvious thing. Like she's exhausted with having to explain to me that the earth is round.

I cross my arms over my chest. "And how do you know how I feel about her?"

She tilts her head. "You may think you're fooling the world—even yourself—but you're not fooling me, son." She lifts her hand, stopping me when I start to speak. "I've suspected for quite some time, but I was absolutely certain when you came to visit me right after Mala moved in with her then-boyfriend. You were a mess."

It shouldn't surprise me that Grams has known how I feel about Mala, likely before I even admitted it to myself. I've never been able to hide anything from her for long, even if I've blatantly lied to her—and myself—about my feelings.

The thing she *doesn't* know is that I'm not in denial anymore. I haven't been since that night a few years ago when she told me she found me attractive—the same night she told me about moving in with Warren.

It's not that her finding me attractive was some sort of magic key to unlocking my feelings for her or anything; it was just the first time I allowed myself to acknowledge the physical pull between us. It was the first time I realized I wanted more—to touch her, to kiss her.

It was the first time I admitted to myself that I wanted to fuck my best friend.

And while Jane's words last weekend opened my eyes in many ways—from making me realize that I deserve the things I've been withholding from myself for so long to what I need to do, like break things off with Jessie for good—they don't change the fact that I'm still scared to act on my feelings for Mala.

Just the idea of doing it has sweat beading over my brows, my heart thumping like a drum.

What if I tell her, and she looks at me like I've grown two heads? What if the chemistry I've felt between us is one-sided, and I had read it wrong? Or what if, even if she agrees there *is* something between us, she doesn't want to risk our friendship?

Any one of those is a potential outcome, and any one of those has the potential to change everything between us.

Sure, I can tell myself that I won't let anything change between us, even if she doesn't feel the same way, but just the idea of finally putting my heart on the line, only for her to reject it . . .? I don't know that I would recover from that type of disappointment.

How would we chalk up my confession to just an awkward

moment in the history of our friendship? How would we sweep that under the rug?

I sigh, no longer in the mood to argue with Grams. No longer in the mood to deny anything anymore. "It's complicated, Grams. Telling her could change everything."

Grams smiles, as if satisfied with my answer. "And that's what I'm hoping for."

~

"You boys really cleaned up that cake! Looks like it was a fun poker night," Jessie chimes, placing her purse on the kitchen counter. Her eyes find the second cake I have covered on the counter behind me before she steps toward it. "Oh, good! There's another one. I was hopin' to get a slice."

I place my hand on the cover, getting her attention. "Actually, this one is for Mala."

Jessie's face sours. "Oh. And you didn't think to make me one?"

I sigh internally. I swear, if I'd told her the cake was for anyone else, she wouldn't have cared. "I thought you said you were avoiding sweets for a while?"

Jessie snorts, strolling over to my fridge. Her long red hair swings from side to side along with her hips. "Whatever. I don't give a hill of beans either way. Give your precious cake to your precious Mala."

She scans the fridge, finding an open bottle of white wine. Walking over to the cupboard, she gets out a stemmed glass and fills it halfway. She takes a healthy sip, closing her eyes like it's the most rewarding thing she's had all day before looking at me. Her brows pinch when she realizes I'm still standing in the same spot, watching her. "What's with the long face, sugar? Somethin' the matter?"

Yeah, something has always been the matter . . . I was just too stupid to see it until now.

I clear my throat. "I think we should talk."

"Okay," she says slowly, observing my stance. "What's goin' on? Wait, is this about you not wantin' to go out Saturday night with my friends from the casino? It's fine; I already told them you were busy, so–"

"It's not about that."

She steps closer. "Then what is it, Dean? You're makin' me as nervous as a fly in a gluepot."

I run a hand over my scruff, taking a moment to gather my thoughts. "I want to break up."

"What" Jessie blinks, barking out a laugh as her wine sloshes inside the glass. "Why?! Things have been the best they've ever been between us!"

The best they've ever been? She must be watching a different movie or reading a different book.

Sure, we no longer fight about the same things we used to, but we still argue almost every single day about something or another. I'd hardly call either of us happy.

"They haven't been, Jess. We haven't been happy together in a long time. We've grown in different directions, and I've just . . . I've realized things I never had the courage to come to terms with before."

She reels back, crossing her arms and squinting at me like she's preparing to argue. "What things? What have you realized? What did you not have the courage to come to terms with?" Her mouth turns downward. "I've never been good at riddles, Dean, and right now, you seem to be speakin' in 'em."

I take a deep inhale. "Things I should have realized a long time ago."

It's as much as I'm willing to say. Maybe Jessie deserves to know more, but the first time I admit my feelings out loud, the only woman I want hearing them is the woman they're for.

"I'm wasting your time, Jess; and you know it as much as I do. You deserve the things you want–love, marriage, kids–and I've told you from the beginning that I won't be able to give you those–"

"So don't!" She shakes her head. "I've done fine without them things all this time, and I'll do fine goin' forward, too. I . . . I just want you, Dean. I don't need those other things, anyway!"

My chest burns, hating myself for breaking her heart, but knowing I have to.

"Please, Jess," I beg. "Please don't make this harder than it already is. I care about you, I really do. But I know we'll both be happier apart."

"No," she whispers, shaking her head. "Don't you dare try to decide what *I'll* be happier with or without, Dean Meyer. You can decide that for yourself, but not for me. And, from the looks of it, you already have."

I don't respond.

The trench between Jessie's brows deepens before her throat bobs. "Where is this comin' from? Things were *fine*. In fact, things have been great the past coupla weeks."

As much as I want to argue that just because we haven't had a major disagreement over the past couple of weeks doesn't mean we were fine, I don't.

Because the only thing that matters is the fact that for the past almost eight years, I've been walking around with my eyes closed. I wasn't blind–that would imply I couldn't see–I was just simply too scared to open my eyes.

Jessie puts her glass down on the counter and braces her hands on my forearms. "We can work this out. I can work on whatever you need me to." Her voice shakes while her eyes fill. "Please. I know I can make you happy, sugar. Gimme another chance."

My shoulders slump and I clasp her head against my chest. "You don't need to change in any way, Jess. You deserve someone to love you exactly the way you are. And I know you'll make him incredibly happy one day. It just . . . it can't be me."

"Why?" Jessie blubbers, sobbing outright. "Why can't it be you?"

Because I'm in love with someone else.

Because I've been in love with someone else this entire fucking time . . .

I close my eyes as her arms tighten around me. "I'm sorry, Jessie."

After a few minutes, her sobs quell and Jessie looks up at me with so much remorse but so much hope. "Please don't do this. Think about it some more."

I take a step away from her, letting her arms drop to her sides. "I have thought about it . . . a lot. And I hate that I'm hurting you, Jess, but my decision is final."

Jessie's chin wobbles before she wipes a tear off her cheek. "Every time we've broken up in the past, it's been after some big disagreement." She wipes her other cheek when a tear drops over it. "But this . . . this feels different. *You* feel different. Why? What changed?"

I swallow, my eyes finding a spot over her shoulder. "Everything's changed."

Chapter Nineteen

MALA

Thirteen Months Ago

COLLEEN'S TWO SMALL MIXED-BREED DOGS JUMP FROM MY lap, to the ground, and back again. One of them makes an excited circle around me before getting back on my lap, balancing herself on her hind legs with her front paws against my chest.

I'm crouched down in front of them, giggling. "You guys already got five treats each! That's the most I've given anyone else today." I laugh when the brindle-colored floppy-eared one licks every tiny morsel of the apple crumble treat I made earlier from my empty hand. "You're going to make the others jealous!"

Colleen smiles, standing above the three of us on the ground. Her blonde hair is pulled up into a high ponytail, and based on the wet spots around the shoulder and neck of her T-shirt, I can tell she's just finished her daily run. She generally stops by afterward with her two adorable dogs. "You've spoiled them rotten. They won't eat any other treat I give to them at home."

"Well, I have a fresh batch of the apple treats in the back, if you want me to get them for you." I wink at her, getting back up on my feet. The dogs raise up on their hind legs, trying to get me back on the ground again.

Colleen laughs. "Oh, why the hell not? I'll take a few."

I look over at Betty, who gives me a smile as she places the last of the carrot cakes on the glass shelves. "I'll run back and get them now!"

I'm humming in the back kitchen a few minutes later, lost in my own world while washing some mixing bowls, when the double doors open.

I turn to look over my shoulder. "Hey, Betty. What's going on? Has Gus shown up yet?"

I hired Gus after I fired Iris, who was the one I hired after Jessie left. It's been sort of a revolving door of baristas, and while Gus seems to have been working out well the past few months, I'm not holding my breath, given the number of times he's been late.

Betty raises a gray brow, giving me a curious once-over. "There's a gentleman by the name of Jason Bourne waiting for you in the café. He claims he just needs a few minutes of your time."

I smile at her with my eyes narrowed. "*Jason Bourne*? Oh no! Do you think he's figured out my true identity as a powerful drug lord? Is he here to assassinate me on behalf of the CIA?"

Betty blinks at me like there's a leak in my think-tank, clearly unfamiliar with the Bourne films. "Should I let him know you'll be right out, then?"

I giggle at my own joke, and the fact that she didn't find it funny. It's fine. What matters is that I can make myself laugh.

Betty turns to leave, but halts to look back at me. "He's quite the handsome young man, and I didn't see a ring on his left hand."

I roll my eyes, chuckling under my breath. "Thanks, Betty."

You'd think with the way she states it, she's reporting back on some mission to find the marital status of every man who walks into the café.

Ever since Warren and I broke up, Betty has taken it upon herself to find me a boyfriend. She doesn't make it a secret that she really wants that boyfriend to be Dean, but I've always hand-waved over it whenever she tries to start that particular conversation.

Because he's not interested in me like that, and the sooner she comes to terms with that, the better it'll be for the both of us. Because a mirage in the desert never brought anyone to water.

It's for the same reason I haven't told her about Dean and Jessie's breakup. Because the moment I do, Betty will get that mischievous and hopeful look in her eyes and start planning our wedding. I know because I've seen her do it every time they've broken up.

I smile to myself, thinking of how ludicrous the idea even is. I'm not in denial of pining for my best friend, but even I have my limits.

The guy was dating the same woman for *years* and never asked her to move in, he's explicitly stated marriage isn't even in his dictionary, let alone his periphery, and he still thinks of me as nothing more than a good friend.

So, pining? Sure. I don't think I'll ever stop having thoughts about Dean. Dirty, filthy, outright obscene thoughts that have me finding my wet center with my fingers in the middle of the night, wishing they were his.

But marriage? If I don't stop myself, I'll burst out laughing at the sheer absurdity of it.

A few minutes later, I find the man Betty referred to looking out the window to the backyard. With a smile on his face and a coffee cup in his hand, he seems to be in his own thoughts.

As if feeling my presence, he turns toward me a moment later. "Mala Sharma?" He reaches out his hand to take mine. "I'm Jason Bourne."

I try not to giggle at his name, giving him a genuine smile instead. "Glad to meet you. How can I help you, Jason?"

Jason's wide blue gaze assesses me. He's wearing a blue suit without a tie, the top button of his shirt undone. "Glad you asked. I have an offer for you, actually, and wanted to chat."

"Okay . . ." I state hesitantly. I point at an open table and two chairs away from another customer, who is enjoying his coffee alongside his pooch, sitting with his eyes glued to his owner and his tail wagging. "Would you like to sit down?"

"Yes, that would be great." Jason takes a sip of his coffee after we both take a seat. "Mala, I run the gourmet pet treats division for *Doggone Happy and Healthy*."

My brows rise. *Holy shit!* This guy runs the entire pet treats division for one of the most sought-after companies in the nation? The company I applied to so many times after college?

Over the years, I stopped looking into open positions at the company, of course, with everything I had on my plate with the café. But I can't deny a part of me still wonders from time to time what it would have been like to work for them had I gotten a job there.

In fact, when I had an opportunity to fulfill a rather large custom order for our popular pumpkin and sunflower seed dog treats from them recently, I jumped on it, rounding up all the help I could.

"Wow," I stammer, hoping I don't sound like a star-struck schoolgirl. "Welcome to *Doggy Bag Café*! I hope the pumpkin treats worked out for you guys last month."

"Thank you." Jason smiles, putting his cup on the table before leaning back and placing his foot on his knee. "Actually, that's why I'm here. The treats were a huge success for a taste test we conducted, and when my team told me where they were from and how you ran this operation on your own–"

Betty clears her throat notably while cleaning a table near us with a damp rag, getting both mine and Jason's attention. After having worked with her for years, I'm no longer surprised by her perceptive hearing and observation. The woman is as sharp as a tack, even at her age.

I laugh softly. "I haven't done all of this on my own. Betty has been working with me for several years and has been one of the biggest reasons I've been able to take on more."

I don't mention it, but recently Samantha, my sister-in-law, has been helping me as well. With the toll it took to raise my nephew with two busy firefighter schedules, Samantha decided to take some time off from working full-time. She now splits her time volunteering at the station and my café when Rohan is home with Sage. She's been a boon for Betty and me since she's an excellent baker as well.

"Right, of course." Jason chuckles, nodding at Betty before she strolls away. "But it got me thinking . . . We have an opening on my team to head up the operations of our new gourmet dog treats department." He holds my gaze. "And I'd like you to take it."

I reel back, putting a finger on my chest. "Me? You want *me* to head up your multi-gazillion dollar treats department?"

Holy shitballs and milk!

Betty coughs somewhere near the café counter, clearly still eavesdropping.

Jason's eyes twinkle. "It's a few dollars shy of multi-gazillion at the moment, but essentially, yes. You'd get to hire your own team, structure it the way you want–"

I lean forward with my eyes wide. "I'm sorry. You must have the wrong person, Mr. Bourne. As much as it was a dream of mine to work for *Doggone* for many years, I'd only applied for individual contributor roles, not the head of a large division. Plus, I haven't worked in a corporate setting before; I don't know the first thing about town hall meetings and PowerPoint presentations." I look down at my sweatshirt that says, *I like big mutts and I cannot lie.* "Or proper corporate attire."

Jason sits back on his chair, watching me without argument—gauging, assessing, judging. A lot like I'd expect an assassin trained by the CIA to do now that I think about it. His calm demeanor unnerves me, given that my nerves seem to be rattled at the moment.

I'm still processing the fact that the opportunity I waited for—the one I dreamed about so many times—all those years ago is now sitting across from me, awaiting my acceptance. The irony of how the tables have turned has me befuddled.

Jason lets his offer hang between us before he speaks again. "Mala, I'm sorry on behalf of the company that we didn't reach out to you sooner when you'd applied, but perhaps you were destined for something bigger. And though the role seems immense to you at the moment, I assure you, you'll have all my guidance and support to get your arms around it. I've done my research. You have the academic credentials and built this incredibly popular café practically from the ground up. You have what it takes."

I want to ask how. How does he know so assuredly that I have what it takes? Yes, I'm passionate about what I do and have the formal schooling to back up running a business, but how does that make me more qualified than someone who has already led operations like the one Jason is describing?

Jason must see the questions written all over my face. "You're both creative and a risk-taker, Mala. You haven't just worked at a café over the years; you've poured everything you've had in it. You've marketed and advertised correctly;

you've grown and diversified. You have several small business awards and incredible reviews. And from what I understand, you're even taking on more custom orders, like the one *Doggone* placed." He tilts his head. "And I'm willing to bet you have had to hire temporary additional staff to help with orders of that size. Therefore, you've had more experience in managing larger operations than you think."

I chew my lip but don't respond. He's right, and he knows it. I have had to hire temporary staff to meet deadlines for orders of the size *Doggone* had wanted. And though he hasn't said it, I'm sure he can guess that I even had to rent a commercial kitchen to have access to the number of ovens and other tools we needed to complete orders of that caliber.

I regard a couple walking back into the café from the backyard with their two dogs. They wave at me, and I wave back as they head out.

My pulse rises inside my chest. It's not that I'm even considering taking Jason's offer, but just the fact that he's here asking me to join his team has me feeling like a porcupine hiding under balloons. I feel anxious, nervous.

It doesn't even make sense, really, but even though a part of me wants him to leave—let me live my life as I have been—another part of me is intrigued.

I finger the burn scar on the inside of my wrist before adjusting the neck of my sweatshirt. "What about my café? I love my café. What about everything I've built here? How could I leave it all?"

How could I leave him?

Jason shifts in his seat. "My intent isn't to ambush you with my proposition. I understand you'd have a lot to consider should you accept this position, but I assure you, you'd gain the type of experience you could never get anywhere else. The type of experience you could take to build something at an even bigger scale one day."

"I'm happy with my current scale. I'm happy with what I have. It's small, but it's mine."

I can't imagine leaving this adorable bakery I've come to love, even for the sake of something I wanted so badly years ago. It's become a second home for me—in some ways, I've spent more time here than I have my own home. It's also become ingrained in the fabric of our little town. It's the same reason I know almost everyone who stops by. I know their favorite drinks, the names of their pets, even their schedules.

So, Jason is right. I *have* built something unique here—something small and my own—but I've also built a life. I've built friendships.

Can I deny the growing pains or the months I'm barely covering the rising costs of both labor and ingredients? Can I deny the cost of maintaining a place like this? The cost of insuring and updating and remodeling?

No. Those are all constant worries I'm saddled with.

Can I deny the constant stress of not having a reliable barista who shows up for work every day?

I groan, looking at the time on my phone. Gus is late by twenty minutes at least, and I still haven't received a call or text from him telling me why.

Jason takes my quick glance at the time as an indication of our meeting being over. He gets up just as I do, offering me another handshake. "I don't need your answer today. Chew on it for a couple of weeks, figure out logistics for the café if you decide to take my offer, and then call me."

He pulls out his wallet to hand me a card with his direct line. "You have a special gift, and I'm ready to make you an offer you'll be hard-pressed to say no to. Allow me to tell you more about it when you're ready to take the leap. Remember, it was once a dream of yours, and while it took a little time to fruition, it's here for the taking now. But before you decide anything, ask yourself one question." He pauses. "Do you have everything you want here?"

THE NEXT WEEK both Gus and I are in the middle of trying to fix our secondary coffee machine on our own before the afternoon rush starts.

My shoulders slump. "I think I'm just going to have to buy another one. This is the fourth time it's stopped working."

"Maybe just have the repair guy out again to fix it?" Gus suggests, but even from the look on his face, I know he's not convinced.

I sigh, wiping my hands on a towel. "Yeah, maybe. But, for now, we're just going to have to let everyone know we're a little backed up on orders."

He nods, going back to replacing the parts we were examining while I make my way to the back to check on Betty. I'm just about to go through the double doors when the bell chimes and I look over my shoulder to see Jessie walk in.

"Hey, stranger!" I greet her, turning to walk over and give her a hug. "Good to see you!"

Jessie offers me a placatory smile and hug back, but her usual bright green eyes are red-rimmed above dark, puffy circles. Her normally voluminous red hair seems limp and tangled, like it hasn't seen a brush in days.

"Oh, Jess. Are you okay?" Moving past a couple of customers in line, I rush her toward an empty table in the corner of the café. "Is this about Dean?"

It's been a couple of months since Dean called things off with Jessie, and though I knew she was upset based on what he told me the next day, I didn't expect her to be so morose even now. I chide myself internally for not checking in on her.

We may not have been great friends, but we'd gotten to know each other while she worked here. Even though Dean denied it every time I asked, I also knew Jessie didn't love my relationship with him. But I'm grateful she never stopped us from hanging out or created unnecessary drama. And if she did give Dean a hard time about it, at least she never made it obvious to me.

It's more than I can say for the way my ex handled my friendship with Dean . . .

Jessie's chin wobbles before she places the heels of her palms to her eyes, resting her elbows on the table. "I'm still so confused about everything, ya know? I thought we were like two pigs in mud, doin' better than we'd ever done. But it's like he woke up one day and realized things I wasn't privy to." She releases her face, focusing on me. "Ya know, I was thinkin' back to the night y'all came back from visitin' Jane. I felt this change in him . . . He was different. *We* were different."

I try to recall the night at Jane's house. Dean was quieter than usual on the ride back, but I didn't think much of it. He always seems to reflect more and get lost in old memories of Zander whenever he visits Jane, so I figured it was the same that night.

Jessie pulls her hands off her face before blowing her bangs off her forehead. "Did somethin' happen there?"

I shake my head. "No. I was trying to recall, but I don't think so . . ."

Nodding, Jessie sniffles. "Well, then it has to be what I've been suspectin'."

"What?" I shift in my seat.

"He's in love with someone else."

I reel back. "What? No, that can't–"

"I heard him on the phone this mornin', Mala. I was at

the grocery store, and I heard him tellin' someone that he was gonna *tell her* how he felt. That he was *waitin' the past two months out of respect* for me, but that he'd waited long enough and he needed *her to know* he had feelin's for her." She takes a shaky breath. "I don't know who this *her* is, but I definitely heard enough to know he's serious about her."

"What?" I whisper again, all the gears latching and turning inside my head like a watch.

She sniffles again, wiping her nose with a worn tissue she pulls out of her pocket, being careful around her nose ring. "It's just that all this makes about as much sense as tits on a bull, ya know? Not once in all the time we were together did he tell me he loved me or that he thought we had a future. I know most people think I was as blind as a bat for stayin' with a man who couldn't offer me his love or his future, but I was okay with it."

She presses her lips together and her ache pools inside her lids again. "I thought that if I had enough love for the both of us, it would all work out. Sure, I pestered him about future plans—what girl wouldn't?—but I was happy with whatever he could give me. But to hear he all of a sudden has *feelins* for someone else? Like, what the fuck? Excuse my French."

I place a hand over hers. "I'm sorry, Jessie. I had no idea."

I'm as shocked as she is. I've hung out with Dean several times over the past couple of months. I'd gone over there to make sure he was okay the day after they broke up—we even made a snowman out in his backyard—but he never told me anything about having feelings for another woman.

Maybe he was ashamed to, given he'd just broken up with Jessie? Maybe he thought I'd judge him for it?

Who's this girl he's already moving on to, anyway?

Jessie shakes her head, taking her hand out of my grasp. "It's not your fault. I mean, it's not like he was talkin' 'bout *you.*" She chuckles as if the idea is preposterous, oblivious to the constriction she just caused inside my chest. "I mean, we've broken up about as many times as there are Sundays in a year, and you've been here the whole time. If he thought of you as anythin' more than a little sister or a good friend, he's had years to tell ya." She wipes her wet lashes with her tissue. "I just don't know who it could be. I figured maybe I'd come here and see if you knew."

I shake my head, hoping she doesn't see how my heart is lodged inside my throat.

She's right.

Every word out of her mouth, however oblivious to my feelings, is right.

I *have* been here the whole time. Waiting. Pining. Yearning.

And for what?

What the hell has it gotten me? And now, not even two months after he breaks up with her—as he claims, *for good*—he's already moved on to someone else? Someone he's developed *feelings* for?

Wow. Just wow.

She's right that it wouldn't be me. If it was, wouldn't he have told me already? Moreover, I still remember what he said all those years ago. "*Nothing can happen between us. Ever.*"

Jessie continues speaking, but I'm barely listening. "Honest to God, I was doin' better the past month, you know, with everything. I was fixin' to get over him and was done bein' pitiful. And then I saw him at the grocery store this mornin' and just like that, I was back to actin' like a fool, followin' him like a damn stalker. He had no clue, of course. No clue he was breakin' my heart all over again."

I nod absently. It seems the only person Dean has a clue about, is himself.

The dam threatens to break, and I blink away any impending tears, trying to keep myself together.

I've been here the whole time . . . but it doesn't matter because I've never been enough.

Jason's question from last week circles inside my head.

"Do you have everything you want here?"

Chapter Twenty

DEAN

Me: What can break without being held?

SITTING IN MY CAR, I WAIT FOR HER RESPONSE. THE LIGHTS in her room are off, so she's either sleeping or in another room not facing her parking lot.

It's not often I make my way over to her place this late uninvited, especially given her schedule, but it's not often that I have to tell her what I'm ready to, either.

It's not often that the universe seems to be on my side, clearing all the hurdles that held me back until now—self-created or otherwise.

I tap my steering wheel at the same fast beat as my heart, recalling my quick conversation on the phone with Grams a week ago at the grocery store, when I told her I was ready.

Truth be told, I've been ready since the day I broke up with Jessie, but A) I wanted to be respectful of the time we were together, even if it was on and off, and B) I wanted to be sure that when I told Mala, she didn't think of herself as some sort of rebound. Maybe I was overthinking it, but I wanted to get it right, given how much I've gotten wrong over the past eight years.

My mind shifts to the first day we met—the fire that Rohan has no idea about to this day. I still remember the thud my heart made inside my chest when my eyes found her that day, as if it was trying to tell me something. As if it wanted me to stop in my tracks and recognize who I was looking at.

The girl who'd change my whole fucking life.

My conversation with Rohan a couple of days ago at the station floats back to the surface as I wait a little longer for Mala's response to my text.

His arms were folded as he leaned against our gym door, assessing me as if he was seeing me for the first time while my admission lay between us, alive and breathing. He was still wearing his gear from the call he'd just finished when I told him I wanted to chat with him.

At first, his jaw clenched, and I thought he'd pummel me to the ground—his sharpened gaze and flaring nostrils certainly said as much. But the more we stared at each other—me not taking back the fact that I was in love with his sister, and that I wanted him to hear it from me first out of respect for him—the more he seemed to ease up.

"You love her?"

I put my hands inside my pockets and lifted my chin. "I do."

Rohan kept his gaze on me, almost unblinking. "And you want to be with her?"

I nodded. "More than anything."

He shifted, standing up straighter. "What about," he cleared his throat, "your reasons for not wanting to be with someone long-term?"

I should have known that even though I've never voiced my fears aloud to anyone besides Jane, Rohan would be smart enough to put two and two together.

"I won't tell you they've magically disappeared. They're still there, and I still worry about putting someone through the kind of pain Zander put Jane through one day, but . . ." I shrug, "I've let fear run

my life for more than a decade. I've purposely refused myself the chance to be with the one girl who knows me inside out and cares about me still. The girl who's been by my side longer than anyone else, and who has picked me up time and time again. A girl I've been crazy about since the moment I met her." I paused, blinking away Mala's beautiful face for a moment to focus on Rohan. "It's time to let hope run the rest of my life."

Rohan glared at me for another moment, and I was sure he'd boom out his disagreement, start foaming at the mouth, God knows what.

But before I could even process what was happening, his entire face transformed. A laugh cracked his irate facade, and he came charging at me, wrapping his arms around me. "Dude, you're a fucking idiot!"

My brows knit, but my stomach untwisted as I tried once again to figure out what the hell was happening. Was he fucking with me the whole time? "What?"

Rohan shoved me back, smiling. "You think I didn't know you were in love with my sister? Dude, not everyone is as big of a moron as you. I've known for years. I was just waiting to see when you'd get your head out of your ass."

I stared at him, dumbfounded. "You didn't say anything."

He scoffed, "Why the fuck would I? It wasn't my place or my realization to come to terms with. You don't think I see the way you look at her? The way she looks at you?" He shook his head. "Jesus. Neither of you are that good of an actor."

"Does she . . . ?" I swallowed, my heart galloping inside my chest. "Do you know if she . . ." Fuck! I couldn't even get the words out.

Rohan raised his hands. "Listen, that's not something I can tell you. I've never asked her how she's felt about you straight up, and I doubt she'd tell me even if I did. That's something for you to figure out. But if you're here asking for my blessings or some shit, well, all I'll say is this, asshole. You fucking ever hurt my baby sister, you hurt me.

Samantha, Sage, Mala . . . they're mine. Mine until my last breath, you got me? If you break her heart—"

"I won't," I cut him off confidently.

"Good." His jaw ticked. "I don't know what the fuck happened with her and Warren. She never told me, but given the way she found another place in the matter of a weekend and the fact that she hasn't been with anyone since, I know things ended badly. My only regret is not breaking the fucker's nose. I know he fucked something up between them and then skipped town like a weasel."

I tried to keep my sneer to myself, not giving away the fact that I'd done the job for him. I hope the asshole looks at his crooked nose in the mirror every day and sees his self-loathing and cowardice stare back at him, reminding him that he had the fucking audacity to physically hurt a woman.

Rohan gave me a nod before he pulled me in for a one-armed bro-hug. "Glad you finally grew some balls, brother. Now go tell her."

I didn't argue about the balls comment. As much as I hated to admit it, he was right. I'd allowed fear to overrule my heart like a fool, and my head kept me from recognizing what my heart had always known.

And before we went our separate ways, I got one quick promise out of him—to keep my admission to himself until I told her myself.

My phone lights up, glowing with a text from her inside my darkened truck.

Sprinkles: A heart. A promise.

I smile, knowing that was an easy one for the queen of riddles. I'm going to find one she won't be able to solve one of these days. Call it a life goal.

Me: Did I wake you?

My teeth sink into my bottom lip as I imagine what she

might be wearing in bed. Maybe that crop top I've been lucky enough to see a few times. Her tits always look magnificent in that, and without even having seen them before, I know her nipples will be the perfect size.

I groan, palming my hardening dick over my pants at the thought of running my tongue over her pebbled nipples. Would she writhe under my touch? Would her soft pants fill the air along with her scent? Would her pussy drip like an overflowing pot of honey, waiting for me to sink my tongue into it, lapping up every fucking drop.

Jesus Christ. If I don't redirect my damn mind right the fuck now, I'll be walking up to her place with a large wet spot on the front of my jeans.

Sprinkles: Would you be sorry if I said yes?

Me: No. I'd just turn back around and not knock on your door.

A moment passes, and I gather she's realizing what I just said.

Sprinkles: You're at my door?

And before she can get out of bed and get to her door, I run out of my truck and rush up the stairs to her apartment.

She opens the door only a second later, and the reason for the quickened pace of my heart is replaced with something else entirely. My gaze strolls down, snagging on the luscious skin of her neck to her black nightie.

Even with the dim nightlight illuminating her form, I can make out her taut nipples and the bottoms of her breasts under the thinnest material. With thin straps over her shoulders, it barely reaches below her ass.

She follows my predatory gaze down her body, shifting in

place from one gorgeous bare leg to another when she realizes what she's wearing. Her hand finds the old burned flesh on her other wrist, a tell of her nerves. "Uh . . ."

My eyes blaze against hers before I fist my hands at my sides to stop myself from ripping the thin straps off her shoulder.

I don't know why irritation flows through my bloodstream right alongside the adrenaline, but it's probably for that reason that I sound more like a jealous boyfriend than the best friend she knows. "Tell me you don't always answer the door wearing that tiny excuse for pajamas this late in the evening."

Confusion flickers between her sleepy lids before she blinks it away, raising her chin and holding back a smile. "No. My regular callers see me in what I usually wear at this hour." Her brow rises defiantly. "Nothing."

My nostrils flare, and I'm seconds away from throwing her over my knee to give her a not-so-discreet account of what I'd like to do with that smart little mouth of hers. The woman has been hellbent on testing my resolve since the day she strutted those phenomenal legs into my life, and I'm barely holding on for both our sakes.

I tilt my chin toward her entryway instead, my palms sweaty. "Can I come in?"

She must see the lack of humor on my face and tries to lighten the mood as she swings the door open wider. "You know, if you needed a refill on those hormone-balance treats, you could have just texted me. I would have brought them to the station tomorrow."

I run my hand through my hair, turning toward her once inside. "I, uh . . . I needed to talk to you. I'm sorry it's so late but . . . I couldn't wait any longer."

"Ah." She nods and a look of understanding crosses her face, and I almost wonder if maybe she's already spoken to

Rohan. But he promised he wouldn't say anything to her, so perhaps I'm just misreading it. "I think I might already know."

My brows pinch, my heart steadily hammering inside my chest. "You do? How?"

"Jessie." Mala fingers the hem of her nightie, pulling it down. "She came to the café the other day and said she overheard you speaking on the phone with someone at the grocery store. You were telling them about a woman you had feelings for."

What the fuck? That Jessie would follow me around the grocery store and listen to my private conversation is one thing, but for her to tell Mala? That crosses every line.

My mind whirls with questions. Did she hear everything? How much did she tell Mala?

I eye Mala and her reaction to knowing what I was supposed to tell her myself. "So, uh, what . . ." I clear my throat. "What did you think—"

Mala's arms come around my neck, pulling me to her, and I breathe in a sigh of relief. My nose lands inside her freshly washed hair as I grip her hips. God, I just want to raise this little nightie and find out what it would feel like to bury myself inside her.

"I'm so happy for you, Dean. I'm glad you found someone who could make you happy." She pulls back, her arms still loose on me, but her smile doesn't reach her eyes. "Have you told her yet?"

Wait. What?

My brain struggles to catch up with her words, and another wave of relief hits me when I realize she doesn't know. Jessie must not have caught the name during her eavesdropping. Come to think of it, I don't think I even mentioned Mala's name once while I was speaking to Grams. But I didn't have to because her name was already implied.

I suppose this means I can go back to my plan of telling her myself.

"Not yet. It's . . . it's why I'm here," I reply cautiously.

Mala nods before grasping me by the hand and pulling me toward the living room. "Let's sit down and you can tell me all about her. I actually have some news of my own, too."

She turns on a lamp on the side table, illuminating a pile of empty boxes against the walls of the hallway to her room. There is an additional set of boxes in the corner of her living room.

I chuckle. "You planning to start a moving company, *sprinkles*? What's with all the boxes?"

Mala perches next to me on the couch with her knees folded under her. There's a stiffness to her that she tries to hide with a wobbly, forced smile.

Why does it feel like my gut is trying to clue me in on something?

She still hasn't let go of my hand, and while I'm always looking for ways to keep her close, the prickly sensation at the back of my neck makes me feel like I should disconnect our hands and walk right out the door this second.

A faint ringing starts in my ears, and I'm worried I know what she's going to say before she even starts.

"I was actually going to tell you tomorrow." Her smile wobbles again before her eyes fill, and it's everything I can do to not stop her from finishing whatever she's about to say. "Remember that company I told you about a few years ago? The one out of LA that I applied to several times and wanted to work for after I graduated?"

I nod. It's the only movement I can make without triggering the roll of my stomach so that I'm stumbling over to her bathroom.

She blinks, pulling another smile in place. It doesn't look nearly as ecstatic as she would like me to believe. "The head of their pet treats department came into the café the other day. He, um . . ." She swallows and my gaze moves from her face to her neck to the top of her burn scar and back again. "He offered me a position to lead their dog treats operations and . . . and I accepted it. I'm moving next week."

I stare at her as her words finally make it to my ears.

I accepted it . . ..

I'm moving next week.

I accepted it . . ..

Her fingers tighten around mine, but they might as well have tightened around my heart.

"Dean," she whispers, and I meet her watery gaze. She pulls the corner of her lip into her mouth, but I don't miss the shake of her chin. "Did you . . . did you hear what I said?"

I blink, realizing I've been quiet this whole time. Perhaps the buzzing inside my head had me believing I'd spoken. "That's great." I rise to my feet, letting her hands drop on her lap. I suddenly want to be anywhere but here. I plaster on the same fake smile she did as I muster up the courage to congratulate her. "That's great, Mala! It's a huge opportunity for you. Something you've always wanted."

Ever since we met, she spoke about the prospect of working for *Doggone*. It was her dream back in the day. But I guess I never asked if it was something she still wanted to do. I guess I assumed she was content with what she already had.

I guess I assumed she was content with her life here . . . with me.

"What about the café?"

She looks up at me from her spot on the couch, a frown pulling her mouth down. "I talked to Rohan and Samantha this morning. Since I still have a little more than a year left on the lease for the building, Samantha thinks she might be able to manage the café with Betty, and I can supervise and do the paperwork remotely from LA."

I nod, swallowing against the jagged stone lodged in my throat. "Seems like you have it all figured out."

Mala gets to her feet. "Dean–"

I don't let her finish, trying to hide the roughness in my voice. "Congratulations, *sprinkles*! This is great news."

And even though I'm saying exactly what she wants to hear, her teary brown eyes glare back at me as if betrayed. A tear falls to her cheek, and as much as my hand begs to wipe the damn thing off, I don't.

Her husky whisper crawls over my skin before burying inside my ribs. "Is that all you have to say to me? Tell me how you feel, Dean. Tell me what you think."

Tell her what I *think*?

How I feel?

If I wasn't feeling like the earth had just slid from under my feet, I'd actually laugh.

Tell her what I think?

What does she expect me to say here?

Demand that she change her mind, her plans? Tell her that what she and I have here is far better than a dream job she's always wanted? Beg her to stay for me?

Could she want that?

And if I told her what I came here to say, would it change her mind? Would it make her stay?

What if it did? Could I live with that? Could I live with knowing she didn't take a job she's wanted for years because I finally got my shit together to tell her how I felt?

Could I live with possibly being the reason for her resentment years down the line when she realizes that life with me isn't as exciting as she'd hoped?

Or what if she doesn't feel the same way?

Could we save our friendship across the distance, despite my confession? Could we work through the awkwardness through texts and phone calls?

A little voice inside my head says I already know how she feels because if she loved me the way I love her, she wouldn't have chosen to leave in the first place.

It's unfair and such a fucking cop-out on my part, I know. I can hear it even as the thought forms, but I can't find it in me to argue with it, either. Not right this second.

If only I'd gotten my shit together to tell her how I felt sooner—God, even a fucking week ago would have been better than this. If I only told her that she's not just some girl I shoot the shit with when I'm bored or someone I keep around to make me laugh. She's not just my best friend or my closest confidant. She's my fucking world. My home.

But I can't say any of those things to her now. I won't for all the reasons I shouldn't.

My molars grind and I force my voice not to shake. "No, I forgot to say one more thing."

She takes a step closer, placing a tentative hand on my forearm. Her words tumble out with a sob. "Tell me."

I reach out and wipe her tears with my thumb. God, I fucking hate them. Hate them more than anything I've ever hated before. And I won't be the reason for them.

She's crying because she thinks she's letting me down by moving. That she's moving on from our friendship. She's also crying because it's hard to leave a place you've been in for so long. And the last thing she needs right now is for me to beg her to change her mind.

I flash her a quick smile, trying my fucking best to mean what I say, hoping to be the supportive friend she's been to me. "I'm happy for you. When do you start?"

Her shoulders slump as if that's not what she wanted to hear. "In two weeks. The company is moving my stuff. I'm driving there next Friday after I pack up everything and get Samantha set up at the café."

"I'll drive there with you."

Mala's brows pinch. "What? No, it's okay, Dean. I don't want you to change your schedule for me."

I entangle our fingers together, shoving my shattered heart aside. "I'm driving you there, and I'll rent a car back."

"Dean—" she starts, gazing into my eyes. They're saying so much, but I can't seem to read them at all. Or maybe I don't trust myself to read them correctly.

"What did I tell you before, Mala? What have I said time and time again?"

Her frown deepens. "That you'd do anything for me."

I boop her nose. "Don't forget it. I'll be here Friday morning."

I'm just turning around to leave, my smile already dropping, when her hand catches around my wrist. "We never talked about the girl you like. Was there something you needed my help with? Are you planning on telling her how you feel soon?"

I shake my head, staring at her. "Nah. I found out I was too late . . . She's moved on."

Chapter Twenty-One

MALA

THE WEATHER TELEGRAPHS MY SULLEN MOOD AS I ROLL MY suitcase out of my apartment. After locking the door behind me, I look up at the heavy gray clouds, shivering when a cold breeze finds its way through my heavy coat, sending my hair flying across my face.

I pull some strands of it off my lips before handing Rohan my keys, who will be returning them to the management office.

A wobbly smile finds my lips as I regard my nephew watching me from his dad's arms with curiosity.

I know I'm going to see him again. It's not like I'm moving to the Sub-Saharan desert. I'm only going to a different city on the same coast, but I can't stop the twist inside my chest, my stomach. I can't seem to get enough water into my throat to keep it from feeling so dry.

As if Rohan can read my face and knows how much I need a snuggle right about now, he hands over my nephew to me before grabbing the handle of my suitcase. He eyes the stairs with concern. "Careful coming down, munch. Some of the steps are still slippery."

My ever-careful, ever-concerned brother. No matter how many times he's come over during the winter, he's said the same thing while giving the offending stairs the same look.

But as much as he's been my protector and my unsolicited advisor, even he wasn't able to change my mind about taking this job. He didn't understand why I would want to leave when I seemingly had everything I wanted here, but I suppose I can only blame myself for his lack of knowledge.

That the one thing—the one person—I've ever wanted was not available to me here or elsewhere. That I'd rather not bear another eight years of waiting, hoping, praying for that one person to finally see me when I know he won't.

I glance at Dean and Rohan exchanging words outside of my car. Dean's face is still pulled tight, like it was when he left my house last weekend. The same night I told him I was moving. And though we've texted here and there in terms of the logistics of him driving me there—something I once again insisted I could do myself—he hasn't said much more about it. Nor has he come by until now.

I swallow hard, thinking about that night. I had gone to bed trying to prepare myself for how I would give him the news the next day. I knew it wasn't going to be easy, no matter when or how I told him, but I hadn't expected it to be quite so hard, either.

The way his face froze, despite the crack I could see I was making internally somewhere. The withdrawn and dejected look in his eyes, as if I'd told him he'd have to live with half the amount of oxygen he requires for the rest of his life.

And even though I'd signed the employment contract with *Doggone*, started the process of handing over the bakery to Samantha and Betty, and put my request in to break my apartment lease, I still stupidly held out hope that maybe, possibly, he'd beg me to stay. I naively envisioned being the one Jessie overheard him talking about on the phone. I foolishly imagined him placing his palms around my face and telling me that it's always been me. That he'd been an idiot to have not seen it before.

I would have stayed.

But no matter how badly I wanted him to tell me, he didn't. And *that* confirmed my belief even further—that I'd never have what I wanted here.

So as much as this move is my decision, it's also his, too. He may not see it that way, but I do.

Maybe a part of me knows I'm running. A lot like the way I ran to Iowa the minute I got accepted into the university there—to give myself space from the constant barrage of memories that followed me around like a shadow all through my teenage years. But that same part needs the space again, because I can't keep living like this—with unrequited hope and unfulfilled desire.

I press Sage's fist to my lips, making him smile. He's bundled up in so many layers, you'd think he was dressed for a winter in Siberia. "Aunty Mala loves you, pumpkin. I promise to FaceTime you as soon as I can." I tell him, as if he understands the use of electronic devices for any other purpose besides teethers.

I make my way down the steps with Sage, handing him over to Rohan before pulling the two of them into a hug.

"Keep your bedroom door closed while you sleep. Gives you more time to react if the smoke alarm goes off." Rohan tells me the same thing he has for years, but I don't argue with him today. "And make sure you don't have any of those damn candles lit unattended."

"I promise," I respond, still wrapped in his hug.

He pulls out of our embrace, his shiny eyes turning to Dean. "Check each alarm in this new place of hers. Might want to test some of the electrical while you're at it."

Dean nods right before he looks up at the sky. A flurry of new snowflakes make their way down, resting atop the melting slush.

It's going to be snowing all through the weekend and into next week, so delaying the trip wasn't an option. At this point, we're just hoping to get on the road before the snow really starts to come down.

I press a kiss on both my brother's and nephew's faces before waving at them. "Tell Samantha she can call me about anything. I feel like I dumped a lot of information on her."

Rohan nods. "Betty will be able to answer most of her questions, but I'll tell her. Now get out of here before I change my mind and demand you stay."

I smile through the almost-sob that tries to wiggle free, turning toward the door Dean has opened for me. He refused to let me drive, so as soon as I settle into the passenger seat, he shakes Rohan's hand and comes around to the driver's side.

Rohan wiggles Sage's arm in an attempt to have him wave at me, and I wave back once more before Dean pulls my car out of the parking lot.

My heart feels heavy with both a sense of loss and an added anxiety—the nerves right before embarking on something brand-new on my own.

I lean my head back on the headrest and watch as my familiar neighborhood—though covered in snow—passes by slowly.

Along with the packing, it's been a week of goodbyes. It was as if every customer I've ever had any sort of conversation with decided to come to the bakery to tell me how much they'd miss me. And even when I told them they were in good hands with Samantha and Betty, they insisted it wouldn't be the same. It simultaneously broke and warmed my heart.

Malcolm came by after his shift almost every evening to hang out at the bakery. He said he was only there in case I had left-over pastries I was thinking about throwing out, but based on the way he hugged me each time when he came in and when he left, I know it wasn't that.

"Your fingers are blue."

Dean's gruff bark has me bounding out of my thoughts. I follow his side-eye to my fingertips laying on my lap. I hadn't felt them, obviously.

My lips twitch. "That preschool education did wonders for you, Fluffy. Now, let's see if you know all your primary colors." I lift my fingers to touch the ends of my hair. "What color is my hair?"

Dean rolls his eyes, grabbing my hand in his gargantuan one. "Fucking bane of my existence."

I almost moan at the feeling of his fingers rubbing mine, warming them like marshmallows in a bonfire. I can't deny the warmth in the center of my chest, either.

It's been awkward between us ever since he left that night, and a part of me wants to demand he tell me why he signed up to take me—why he reminded me he'd do anything for me—only to show up at my door looking like I'd put a gun to his head to do it today.

But I don't because I see the barely restrained pain and melancholy in his expression even though he's tried hard to cover it with smiles that don't quite reach his eyes. I see the worry for both of us. How will we survive without one another? What will happen to our friendship?

He's dealing with the grief of what he thinks is losing me and the anger that I didn't include him in my decision in his own way. He hasn't said it, but I hear him regardless.

I quickly shift, giving him my other hand. "It's as if you harness all the fires you fight inside you, like some sort of human volcano."

His lips twitch, despite the annoyance he's holding against me, and I'm hoping my dumb jokes will bring back the levity we've always had between us. "That's not how volcanoes get created. They don't fight fires to harness fire."

I suck in my cheeks to hold in my grin. "Is that what you're going to argue with me about? You're going to give me a lesson in earth science because you're too pissed off to voice the real reason you're angry with me."

I try to pull my hands from his grasp, but he holds on tighter. His shoulders slump but he keeps his eyes on the road. "I'm not angry with you, *sprinkles*. I'm . . . I'm . . ." He blows out a breath and I finish his thought for him.

"You're hurt that I didn't discuss it with you before I made my decision."

His thumb rubs a circle on mine and a shudder runs up my arm, despite the fact that I'm now nice and warm all over.

Surprisingly, he shakes his head. "No, that's not it, either. I'm happy you got the opportunity . . ." A muscle moves inside his jaw. "I'm just sad for me."

DEAN GROANS when we stop again for what feels like the hundredth time. It's been like this for the past three hours we've been on the road, driving at a turtle's pace behind a sea of cars. Any time we seem to make even the tiniest bit of progress, we're quickly stalling again only a couple of miles later.

What was supposed to be an eight-hour drive is looking like it will turn into twelve or more.

I lean to my right to see if I can get a clearer picture of what's happening ahead but between the lack of sunlight and the snow now dumping down on us like white confetti shot from a cannon, I can barely make out anything past the two rows of red brake lights from the cars ahead of us. "I think they blocked another lane."

Dean pulls up a traffic app on his phone to see if we can get any more information. "The highway is just highlighted in red for miles ahead." He glances at me. "It might take us through the night to get there."

I groan, watching our wipers push snow this way and that. "We'll need to stop for food soon. I need to pee, too."

Dean sighs. "Can you hold out another hour or so? If I see an exit, I'll pull off and we can look for food."

I smile at him, that same warmth I usually feel around him settling over. "Thanks for being here with me. This would have been a lot scarier and more frustrating if you weren't here."

He purses his lips. "So, you're saying there's something more frustrating than me?"

"Marginally," I deadpan. "You've been beaten by pelting snow and bumper-to-bumper traffic, but believe me, you're still number two on my list of most frustrating things."

He chuckles softly and, as usual, I store the sound away somewhere for me to retrieve later. A tightness pulls at my chest, knowing I won't hear it as readily as I did over the past eight years and now, it'll mainly be through the phone when I do.

I try to shove away the gloom by pressing another smile on my face. "Want to play a game?" At his raised brow, I continue, "We're just sitting here; might as well use the time to get to know each other even better."

Dean puts my car into park with the engine still running, spreading out his long jean-clad thighs. God, why do I find his thighs so sexy? Actually, it's his whole frame that I find irresistible. All six-feet-three of him.

"Alright. What do you have in mind?" His blue eyes, reminiscent of beautiful sunny days unlike today, twinkle back at me.

I tap my lip, pretending to think. Truth is, I'd already settled on the game minutes ago. "What's something I don't know about you? Something you've never shared with me."

I see his eyes snag on my lips before he licks his own. It's such a small movement, the barest of gestures, but it has my breath catching on an exhale.

I amend my previous question, clearing my throat. "And don't give me something dull, like you weren't fully potty-trained until you were six or that you've spit your gum into a church donation box twice—once by accident and the second because you were feeling naughty. I want something juicy. Something embarrassing."

Dean's bewildered and judgmental glance has me lifting my shoulders. "What? It took me a while to get out of my Pull-Ups. Apparently, Aristotle and Einstein didn't get out of their Pull-Ups well into their teens. It's a sign of extremely high intellect."

"Clearly," Dean deadpans. "Think a lot about Aristotle in his Pull-Ups, do you? Is that what does it for you?"

I turn my nose up. "Na-uh. You don't get to turn the tables on me just yet. If you want to ask me my most embarrassing secret, then you'll have to wait your turn. I'll throw you a bone, though." I wink at him. "Thinking about Aristotle in Pull-Ups from time to time isn't the worst one of them."

Dean shakes his head disgustedly at me, as if he's seeing me in a completely new light. "What the hell kinda shit goes on in that head of yours? You've gotta get it checked."

I stab my index into his bicep. "Stop deflecting."

The cars ahead of us inch forward a few feet, and Dean

pulls forward to follow before stopping once again, but I can tell he's taking the time to think.

Meanwhile, I take the time to stroll my eyes over the smooth skin of his neck, the broad stretch of his chest, and what I know are rows upon rows of delectable abs underneath his sweater. I've had the pleasure of seeing them on more than one occasion in the summer when we've gone to the lake and a few times when he didn't know I was being a Peeping Tom while he changed inside his bedroom as I sat on the couch in the living room. The way I see it, if he really didn't want me to see, then he should have closed his door.

I smile thinking about the very first time I went to his house with the treats he demanded as ransom for keeping my secret of burning down someone's oven on my first weekend here. He was bare-chested then too, and subsequently the star of several of my fantasies where he was Tarzan and I was Jane.

He'd pull me up against a tree—bare chest heaving and wet, shoulder-length hair tousled to perfection, cut biceps quivering—before pulling my thighs up around his waist. He'd enter me in one go and pound his fist on his chest like the warrior-beast he was before growling, "You're mine, Jane! Just mine."

Things get weird inside my head from time to time, and I hadn't been laid in a while back then.

Okay, so maybe I do need to make that appointment to get my head checked.

"The first time I jacked off was to the vision of a nun."

I'm just taking a sip of water from my bottle when Dean answers, and I have to quickly put my hand over my mouth so I don't spray it all over my dashboard.

My mouth is hanging on the floor, post-sip, before I quickly make the sign of the cross in front of my chest. "Jesus!" I wince and then look up at the gray sky in apology.

"No pun intended. But seriously, Dean, what the fuck? Did finding porn online not do it for you like the rest of the pimple-faced teen population?"

His smile turns mischievous. "This *was* online. I had a little fetish for nuns at that age. I think it was after Grams made us watch *The Sound of Music* one Christmas." He tilts his head, giving me a *oh-stop-being-so-judgmental* look. "Didn't you just say you spit your gum into a church donation box on purpose?"

"It was merely an example of something one *might* do," I reply haughtily.

"Uh huh," he replies. "It seemed more detailed than a *might-do*. More like a *did-do*. And you must realize I wasn't the only kid in history to jack off to Julie Andrews."

I gasp, now seeing *him* in a completely new light. "You're sick in the head."

He chuckles. "I guess we'll both be going to the same doctor, then."

More movement in front of us has Dean putting the car back into drive. We trail the other cars slowly, but the visibility is still terrible.

I know there's an exit about two miles ahead where we can get food and gas, but at this rate, I'm not sure how long it will take to get there.

I see Dean eyeing my profile, his large hand—the one wearing the matching leather strap I have on mine—still wrapped around the steering wheel.

His teeth scrape across his lip and one of his blondish-brown brows hitches up. "Well? I showed you mine, now show me yours."

Heat rises to my cheeks like a brush fire at the insinuation of his words. In fact, the car turns just a tad warmer, despite the freezing temperatures outside. His piercing gaze makes me squirm, and I try to come up with something quick before he turns me into a puddle. "I accidentally put dog treats inside the human treats glass case and didn't realize it until they were half-gone."

"Most of your dog treats taste better than the human treats, anyway. What's wrong with that? Plus, it's not like you ever use ingredients that either type of customer can't eat."

I punch his arm, but he doesn't budge. "That sort of sounded like an insult to my human treats."

"It wasn't. But also, that wasn't even close to as embarrassing as mine, so I call a do-over. Now give me something real."

I pull my lip into my mouth.

I can't.

I can't give him *that* one.

It would change everything. It's too . . . I press my hands to my face when I see his eyes on me again. Dean can read me like no one else can, so I'm hoping if he can't see the lie written all over my face, he'll just let it go.

"I'm trying to think," I mumble from behind my hands.

His warm hand wraps around my wrist, sending another zing of electricity rushing up my arm. He pulls my hand down, despite me trying to keep it there. "Look at me."

I shake my head, feeling the blush creep into my cheeks again. "I can't."

"Mala. *Look. At. Me.*"

I do reluctantly and immediately wish I hadn't. His eyes are pinned to my lips before they slowly dip down to my neck, the rise and fall of my chest . . . my breasts. I've seen him eye my ass and breasts before, but never like this. I always thought it was an instinctual thing that men just do, even if they were your best friend.

But this . . . This feels different. This feels intentional, not instinctual.

"Tell me," he commands gruffly.

I close my eyes, taking a deep breath. And whether it's his command or his deliberate perusal of me, I'll never know, but something emboldens me to speak.

"The only times I climaxed while I was with Warren was when I thought of you."

Chapter Twenty-Two

MALA

Yup, I've made everything weird. Torched my friendship on my way out of town.

Just fucking fabulous.

My gut kept telling me not to do it. In my heart I knew, *I just knew*, I shouldn't have. But what did I do? The opposite.

And now I've ruined the closest friendship I've ever had.

Dean hasn't said a word in the past fifteen minutes that we've been driving, albeit still slowly, and I haven't had the guts to ask him what he's thinking.

A part of me just wants to open my passenger door and roll into the barren snow. Even the prospect of freezing to death feels better than sitting in this cloud of awkwardness.

All I can think about is the way his face froze when I voiced my words. His nostrils flared like he was pissed–the same way they flared when he showed his dissatisfaction for my nightie last weekend when he came over. The same way they flared when I told him I thought he was hot all those years ago. The same way they flared when we almost kissed years before that, and he realized it was a mistake.

So, basically that's his tell. When he's pissed off or disappointed or disgusted, his nostrils flare. And telling him that I thought of him when I was in bed with Warren pissed him off.

No. It outright disgusted him.

We both see the blinking sign up ahead as we progress and a groan leaves my throat. Fuck!

Roads closed ahead until tomorrow at noon.

My panicky voice breaks the silence inside the car, and I look behind us as if we can turn back somehow. We can't. The roads are packed with cars on both sides, and the snow is still piling down on us in what feels like an avalanche. "What are we going to do? What are all these other people supposed to do?"

Surprisingly, Dean stays calm, clicking the blinker to take the exit behind what feels like a million other cars. "We need to find a place to stay tonight."

I lean forward with my elbows on my knees and my face cupped in my palms. "God, this is such a mess." I'm not talking about just the snowstorm, either.

An hour later, we pull into another motel parking lot, but my gut tells me that like the two others we tried, this one will be without vacancy as well.

"Stay here." Dean's low-spoken command leaves no room for me to argue as he makes his way out of the car toward the entrance of the motel. I'm assuming he's going to check anyway, like he did the others.

He's been texting with someone sporadically too, but with the way things have been over the past hour and a half, I haven't had the courage to ask who it is.

Five minutes later, he's making his way out of the motel, his phone on his ear. Based on the look on his face, I suspect he's going to tell me what I already know—that the motel's all booked. Maybe we can try a few other motels down the street.

But instead of going to the driver's side, he comes to my passenger door, opening it after putting his phone inside his pocket. "Let's go. I'll get your stuff."

"Wh–? They have *room*?" It seems hard to believe given the number of people I watched coming out of the entrance, shielding themselves inside their already wet coats, and going back into their cars.

He helps me out of the car, and I'm immediately met by a gust of freezing wind. Still, I take the chance to look at his face. His eyelashes and brows are sprinkled with a dusting of snowflakes. His nose and unfairly high cheekbones are tinged with pink. Has any man ever been so beautiful?

Without thinking, I reach up to run my thumb across his brow, and Dean takes in a quick breath. My eyes lock with his, and despite the fact that it's bone-chilling cold outside, my insides feel like they're on fire.

I fold my fingers instinctively, as if I've been burned. God, what am I doing? Why do I keep messing up? Am I trying to sabotage my friendship on purpose?

Dean tilts his head toward the motel, his voice gruff. "Go inside. I'll bring our stuff."

"I'll help you." I turn toward the trunk of my car, but his hand comes around to lock on my wrist.

"Get inside," he repeats more firmly. "I don't want your fingers and toes freezing off."

Reluctantly, I do as he says because the last thing I want to do is piss him off even more than I have, but I can't deny the acid souring my stomach and rising to my chest. I can't deny that his gruff tone doesn't hurt.

I wait for him before we both make our way to the reception desk. He pulls my roller bag, along with his own bag hanging over his shoulder.

"There we go," the receptionist says with a smile, handing

over a set of keys to Dean. "You're all set, Mr. Meyer. Please let Mr. Case know he's welcome anytime."

My brows fold as I follow Dean to the elevator. "Who's Mr. Case, and what does he have to do with this?"

Dean and I enter the elevator along with four other guests. We're all wearing heavy coats, our shoulders wet from the snow melting atop them. "Hudson, Garrett's best friend. He's connected to the owner of this motel chain and called in a favor. Somehow, he was able to get us a room."

"Wow, that was really nice of him."

I'd casually been introduced to Hudson a couple of times at Meyer family events. He's a big name in the science and research community and has built a successful multinational business from the ground up in a short time. Not to mention, he's incredibly handsome, albeit a tad bit intimidating if you're into that sort of thing.

The elevator doors open with a ping, and . . .

"Wait . . ." I follow Dean out into the hallway as he turns the corner to find our rooms. "Did you say room or *rooms?*"

His exasperated sigh fills my ears as he comes to a stop in front of a room, taking out the key from its envelope.

"The favor extended to one room." He opens the door and holds out his arm. "Get inside."

I hesitantly step one foot in front of the other, taking in the small but comfortable bedroom as I wiggle out of my coat before my eyes land on the plush king-sized bed.

As in, *one* plush king-sized bed.

It's not that I haven't spent the night at Dean's house before or even passed out next to him while we were watching movies, but actively sharing a single bed? That's something we've never done and today, of all days, it just feels almost all too forbidden.

I turn to him. He hasn't moved except to take off his

jacket, but I notice his eyes are fixed on the same thing. "I can take the couch—"

"No." His glare meets my eyes. "You won't."

My shoulders slump and I suddenly feel exhausted. Perhaps the anxiety of the past couple of hours is wearing me thin. Perhaps it's the twist I've had in my stomach ever since I accepted the job, ever since I told Dean about my move. Or perhaps it's the push and pull between us over the course of the past eight years—the push and pull that only I seem to feel.

Whatever it is, I don't have the energy to argue right now.

I place my purse on the console under the TV before pulling my suitcase onto it. I unzip it to find my toiletry bag, a pair of sleep shorts, and a tank top. If I'm going to be stuck here with a fire-breathing dragon, then I'd rather be stuck wearing comfortable clothes.

Besides, it's not like I have much more than a disgruntled, disgusted, nostril-flaring effect on him when I'm wearing anything besides my normal attire of sweatshirts and shorts. And frankly, it's not my problem what he thinks about what I wear. If he has issues, he can shut his eyes.

I march over to the bathroom. "I'm going to freshen up."

Once I'm in front of the large mirror, I place my face in my palms, barely holding back the tears. *Why did I tell him what I did? It was so stupid.*

"So fucking stupid," I groan softly.

I hear Dean order us room service. He knows me well enough to know what I generally like to eat—burgers, fries, doughnuts, and pastries. Basically . . . the healthy stuff.

I avoid his stare when I get out of the bathroom. I find my phone and my book, and then get into bed.

He ambles into the bathroom a few minutes later, and I finally take a breath. God, this is so awkward. Should I just take back what I said? Can I even do that now?

Room service arrives fifteen minutes later, and both Dean and I eat our burgers quietly while I pretend to be busy on my phone. I try not to notice the way his undershirt spans across his chest or the way his legs look almost infinite and thick inside sweatpants with his station's logo on them.

Gray sweatpants. It's like he's trying to be extra sexy just to rub it in my face that I can't have him. Well, fuck him!

After finishing my meal, I scoot out of bed and shuffle over to the bathroom and brush my teeth, only to have him walk in and do the same. I rush through washing my mouth and get out of his way.

It's still early—seven PM—but I'd rather just turn off my lamp and read on my Kindle. I scoot all the way to one side of the bed so he can take his pick of the other side or the couch. I'm not going to try to convince him of either one. If this is how he wants our last night together to play out, then that's on him. He can take all that nostril-flaring and shove it up his butt . . . or his nose.

I'm just in the middle of staring at the same paragraph I've read for the tenth time when I feel the bed dip. The comforter shifts and I feel his presence at my back. My heart still aches and I just can't do it anymore. I just can't be the reason we ruined everything.

I turn to lay on my back and my voice wobbles as I speak. "I take back what I said in the car, Dean. Please." Oh God, if it wasn't enough that my voice sounds like I've been smoking, my eyes are now ready to flood. "I can't stand it when you pull away from me. I can't stand it when you're mad."

He's quiet for so long, I wonder if he's heard me at all. Could he have fallen asleep that quickly? "You think I'm mad at you?"

I place the heels of my palms on my eyes. "It sure feels like it. You haven't said a word since . . ." I swallow through the thickness in my throat. "Just tell me what you're thinking.

Tell me for once how you feel, Dean. I'm fucking begging you."

The movement is so quick, I honestly have no clue how he did it. One moment he's on that side with a span of the bed between us and the next, he's hovering over me. For a moment, I'm struck at the sight of him.

His golden hair hangs at his jaws. "You want to know how I feel?" He pulls down the comforter at my neck all the way to my torso so fast, I suck in a loud breath. Goosebumps fly across my skin, curling my toes as he makes a lecherous perusal of my body. "This is how I feel."

His large palm spans my hip as his erection lays heavy between my thighs. And then his lips descend to press on mine.

For a second, I'm frozen, wondering if this is even happening. Has my love-starved brain actually made this all up? Am I hallucinating?

But as the synapses in my brain finally start firing, I come to, realizing that indeed, I'm kissing my best friend. Well, he's kissing me at the moment, but that's just semantics.

My hands travel up his chest, securing themselves at the back of his neck, inside his hair and I pull him further into me. My mouth opens at his demand and his tongue slips in— soft and warm. He tastes as good as I thought he always would—minty, delicious.

I'm lost in a haze of sandalwood and soap as his scruff glides over my mouth. He delves in further, tangling our tongues, before a low grown spills out his throat. It travels across my skin, hardening my nipples in its descent to my core, settling there.

My pussy contracts as my hips jut out, trying to find fric- tion against him. And they do. His hard bulge—secured behind nothing but sweatpants—shoves deeper into my center and we both moan.

He runs his nose over my jaw before coming back to my mouth. "Mala."

My name spills from his lips like a plea, and my chest heaves as the moment hits me. I lock gazes with him, his lips glistening from our kiss. But the longer I stare into his eyes, the tighter the knot in my stomach becomes.

How long have I wanted this moment? For him to say my name in that exact way? How many times have I prayed for this?

And only now . . . now when we're on the cusp of separating, he finally gives me what I'd been waiting for all these years?

What happens from here? Where do we go?

How will this even work if I'm in LA and he's still in Tahoe? And for how long?

By his own admission, he's never wanted a commitment, nothing long-term to tie him down. So what will this even mean after tonight? Will he have just gotten me out of his system?

Will our friendship survive this once it's all done? Can we even *be* friends once this is over? Have we already gone too far to turn back?

Panic kicks off inside me, crawling through my veins and increasing the beat of my heart. What if this is all a mistake? What if I lose the best thing that's ever happened to me because we crossed a forbidden line?

"Wh-what are we doing, Dean? We can't. It'll . . . it'll change everything. Our friendship and what we have now. And with me leaving . . ." I search his gaze. "And you not wanting anything long-term . . ."

I wait for him to argue. Silently, I beg for him to ask me to stay, to tell me it would be different for us, but he doesn't.

A moment later, he finally speaks. "Then let this be something just for tonight."

My eyes bounce between his, my heart breaking even while it leaps to latch onto something, anything. "What if it ruins everything?"

He presses another kiss to my lips, my jaw, then the side of my neck. "It won't. We won't let it."

I swallow, my heart racing like it's trying to get to the finish line with everything it's got. "Promise me," I beg, running my fingers through the hair at the back of his neck. "Promise me this won't change anything."

His reply is steady, earnest. If he's lying, it's not just to me. "I promise."

I dig my teeth into my bottom lip, keeping my smile at bay. "Then, please continue showing me how you feel."

He chuckles before his eyes darken and he finds my lips with his again, stoking the fire still alight inside my core.

"Fuck, I've dreamt about this," he mutters, kissing my jaw, my neck. "I've thought about how you'd taste. It's all I've thought about for the past few hours."

Bracing himself on one forearm, his other hand works up under my tank top, gliding over my side. It comes to rest under my breasts before he brushes his thumb over my nipple.

If I was wet before, I'm dripping now. If with only that slight movement from him—that tiny little brush of his finger— he has the power to elicit a full-body shudder from me, what would I do if his mouth dipped lower? If his cock thrusted inside?

Dean watches me intently, rolling my nipple between his index and thumb. His eyes are ablaze like sapphires caught on fire, and I pull my lip into my mouth, trying to hold in my groan while I writhe under his touch.

"Don't." His voice is low and guttural, like he's barely restraining a growl. "Don't hold back on me. I want to hear all your sounds."

His mouth dips down over my shirt to pull my nipple into his mouth, and I release a ragged gasp. God, it feels so good. I love the feeling of my nipple against the wet fabric of my shirt once his mouth releases it. It's obscene and electrifying.

He helps me shed my top a few moments later, and his nostrils flare as his sight lands on my breasts. I'm starting to rethink my previous assessment of his nostril-flaring. I get the sense I may have been wrong and the reason for it is when he's turned-on, not disgusted.

His mouth lands on the top of my scar, kissing and licking until he reaches my nipple. I mewl as his warm tongue laves and strokes it, flicking it back and forth. His other hand slides down to the waistband of my shorts, and I instinctively push my hips up to meet it.

He chuckles. "Someone's eager."

Dean crawls his fingers over the thin center seam of my thong, tracing the entire length with his middle finger. My toes curl as a heady sensation hums beneath my skin. He tugs aside the thin material and finds my swollen wet bud, circling it lazily as if time doesn't exist. I moan outright at his touch, my breaths feeling like they're being pulled through a narrow pipe, escaping in tremulous spurts.

His mouth moves to my other breast as his finger dips below, almost to my back entrance, taking my wetness with it. "Jesus Christ, *sprinkles*. Is this all for me?"

"Mm-hmm," I mumble. I can barely stitch sentences together at this point.

Even the slow, lazy brushes of his fingers feel torturous against my skin. Like I've been doused in kerosene from the inside and each flick of his fingers has the power to light me on fire.

His mouth finds mine again and he pulls me into another heated kiss, biting and licking my bottom lip. Without more preamble, he pushes a finger inside me.

"Oh!" I cry into his mouth, opening up my thighs as white-hot lust zips down my spine, pooling at my center like a lake before a lightning strike.

"So hot. So fucking wet." His gritted murmur, along with the way his finger starts a steady rhythm inside me, has me climbing.

I moan, squeezing my eyes shut. "God, yes!"

The sounds of his fingers driving into my wet center, along with our heavy breaths colliding against each other, have my core so tight, I'm ready to combust.

He continues, adding another finger, and I dig my nails into his bicep. He lowers his head, kissing my neck, his scruff biting at my skin deliciously.

But right as I'm climbing to the zenith, ready to see stars, Dean slows his pace. My eyes open to find a smirk over his delicious mouth, his eyes smoldering. "Wh–?"

And before I can gather my wits about me, he crawls down by body, pulling off my shorts. He licks his lips before running his nose down my center, like he's breathing in my scent. His eyes stay on me. "The first time I let you come, it'll be on my tongue."

Chapter Twenty-Three

DEAN

"I PROMISE."

"*I promise.*"

"*I promise.*"

The words spin inside my head like a tornado ready to demolish everything in its path. That's what this woman does to me. She's demolished my self-restraint, the promises I've made to myself every damn day, and my fucking sobriety. She's like a liquor being pumped directly into my bloodstream through an IV, and I'm the drunkard who'll never get enough.

I want to believe I'll never break a promise to her—I've never broken one before. But fuck, how will we go back to being oblivious and platonic after this?

How will I ever wipe the memory of what she looks like, top to heavenly bottom, bare naked and writhing under me?

How will I erase the wet sounds her pussy makes when I wrench my finger in and out of it?

My mouth is mere centimeters from her dripping center, and I can practically taste her already. Will I be able to enjoy any other meal after I have the taste of her on my tongue?

Fuck!

Why? Why did she have to tell me what she did today? She could have picked any other embarrassing memory. She could have lied for all I care. But no. She had to say the one thing that would break my resolve. The one thing that would betray what she was holding back from me all this time.

That she was mine.

Even when she was with him, she was mine. Every moan, every touch, every fucking orgasm was mine. They might have been wrenched from him because I hadn't had the fucking balls to claim her myself, but they were mine, nonetheless.

And that fact pissed me off.

God, I was angry. Not at her, never at her. That would be akin to being pissed off at the softest gust of wind.

I was angry at myself. Angry that I'd missed the signs. Angry that I'd overlooked what should have been clear to me all these years. Angry that it was only now, when she was days away from starting a new job—one she'd always dreamed about—in a new city, that I finally had the knowledge to do anything about it.

I couldn't wrap my head around everything I'd fucked up.

I wanted to tell her. Even as she pulled out her clothing from her bag and stormed into the bathroom. Even when she came out and we ate in almost-silence while she tried to ignore me by staring at her phone. Even when she turned off her lamp and gave me her back.

I wanted to tell her to leave it all. To come back with me. To be with me.

I wanted to tell her my love, my fucking heart, would be enough. I'd make sure of it.

But how could I guarantee that when I didn't know for sure? How could I ask her to toss away her dream for a life I didn't one hundred percent know she would be happy with?

Sure, she said her every orgasm was mine. But what about her heart?

Was it in a moment of lust that she saw my face, or did she see it like I did hers—with every breath?

And then, not even a couple of minutes into kissing her, she was stuck inside her head, saying the one thing that has me stumbling backward. Knowing I was right to not have asked her to stay.

"It'll change everything. Our friendship and what we have now."

How I wanted to respond was, "Yeah, it fucking might, and that's okay. Isn't it?"

But I couldn't. Because something in her eyes told me that would be where she drew the line—the thought of losing any part of our friendship. She couldn't even fathom the thought. She wouldn't risk it.

So, I couldn't, either.

But I also couldn't see myself going backward from the moment we were in right now. I couldn't see myself not finishing what we started. Not kissing her again like I needed her to keep me conscious. Not tasting her when I'd been starved for so long. Not seeing her tremble under my touch until she exploded like a nuclear bomb.

So, I said the only thing a selfish asshole like me would. I told her it would only be for tonight.

It killed me to say it. Tightening everything inside my chest so I felt like I was suffocating. But as much as I wanted one night with her for myself, I wanted it for her, too. Call it a fucking parting gift, call it self-inflicted torture, but I wanted it to paint every fucking memory she has of me.

I couldn't deny either of us that. Not when she was looking at me with those molten pools of lust and hope.

Not when she's looking at me with them now.

I run my nose along the seam of her thigh before taking my first swipe of her beautiful, swollen pussy. Her body quivers under my touch and satisfaction courses through my veins.

"You smell like heaven and taste like home," I murmur over her skin.

I follow the movement on the other side, running my nose down the seam of her thigh and laying a kiss over her sweet center. Her thighs tense and her hand comes to tangle in my hair. She wants more. So much more.

I chuckle as I take another swipe, my tongue like an arrow inside her seam, making her jump and whimper. I do it again, soft and slow, running the tip of my tongue deep inside her folds before sucking on her little bundle of nerves. It's so small, so fucking perfect.

Grabbing her thighs with my palms, I lift her hips and flatten my tongue against her. I drag it from ass to clit, back to front.

I do it again and again, making her almost clamor out of my hold. She wants more like she's never wanted anything in her life but can't stand it all at once, either.

Burying my face in her heat, I bring my flattened tongue over her entrance and lap her like a cat to milk before I spit on her perfect pussy.

"Oh, God! Dean . . ." Mala moans so loud, the next town over will certainly hear her. One hand tightens around the comforter while her fingers dig into my scalp almost painfully.

Oh, she liked that. My dirty girl. So fucking perfect for me.

My groan mixes with hers as I lick and suck. I bite and feast, working her clit until she's practically trembling in my hold.

"Such a pretty little pussy," I mumble over her skin, lapping up my spit that's now mixed with her juices. I press my finger back inside her. "Wet and messy. So needy for me."

She's practically sobbing when she breathes my name, her

eyes fluttering closed. She bites down on her bottom lip. "Please."

I lift her thighs again so her knees go up and I can get deeper inside her with my tongue. "So fucking delicious."

My brain feels like it's melting in overdrive. A part of me doesn't believe she's real, that this is even happening. But as slow as I want to go with her, as long as I want to prolong every minute, I'm amped up like I've never been before. So fucking hard, my cock might drill a hole in this mattress.

Mala undulates against my tongue, and I flick it back and forth over her clit, keeping in rhythm with my finger and fucking her like it's my calling. I press another finger inside her, lapping at her entrance before biting down on one of her folds and Mala screams.

"Dean!"

Her entire body tightens, and her hips jerk as the first of the many waves I have planned for our night has her exploding like champagne from a shaken bottle. I feel the shudder that rolls over her as she comes down from her release, still in my mouth.

Laying a few more kisses on her pussy, I drag myself up her body, nipping and kissing her hip, her stomach, her breast. I trace the burn scar across her breast with my tongue, watching goosebumps flutter across her skin.

My throaty drawl at the shell of her ear pulls another tiny shudder from her, sending another wave of satisfaction soaring through me. "If we only have one night, then I'd like to be inside you for every minute of it."

I put my forehead to hers, fisting her hair. Our lips are only a breath apart, and all I want to do is devour them.

A tremor of worry passes through her hooded eyes. "Dean," her cinnamony breath wafts over my lips, "say it again."

She wants my reassurance. Her last-ditch attempt to take

all this back, to set us back on square one, as if it's as simple as turning back time.

She knows in her heart that we'd be lying to ourselves, that I'd be lying to her, but I'll do it, anyway. I'd fucking do anything for her, and she knows it.

"I promise."

Her short nails drag up my back and under my shirt, guarded relief settling in her expression. A smile tugs at the corners of her mouth. "Don't waste time, then, Rufus. Give me everything you've got."

My brow lifts. "Giving you everything I've got would mean me coming inside you so hard that your veins flood with my cum." I press my heavy cock between her thighs, getting a soft exhale from her. "You ready for that, sweetheart?"

Her eyes stay locked on mine defiantly in response before her hand snakes down between us. She wiggles it into the waistband of my sweatpants, under my boxers, grasping my cock with her small hand.

I groan, my nostrils flaring, shoving myself into her warm hand. "*Fuuuck.*"

Her hand moves up and down my shaft before it freezes in place with a jerky stop. Her brows pinch as she stares at me, but I keep my eyes locked on her. I don't want to miss even a second of the surprise on her face.

Her thumb hesitantly moves to the head of my cock, sliding over the ridge tentatively, as if what she just felt might have been concocted by her imagination.

She pulls in a breath before her eyes widen. "You're . . . pierced?"

I roll inside her hand, my molars grinding to keep my groan at bay. Fuck, her hand feels so good, I might not last as long as I want to this time around. "It's called a king's crown."

Her lips flatten and the vulnerability in her eyes has my

throat feeling dry. "I hate that I don't know everything about you."

I brush my thumb over her jaw before I find her ear with my mouth again. "Want to know my biggest secret?"

Her thumb rolls over the tip of my dick again, and I guess that's her response for a yes.

"You're the only face I've come to in all the times I remember."

Her brows pinch and a quiver finds her chin. "Dean." Her eyes bounce against mine. "Show me. I want to see."

I rise off the bed and take off my shirt first. Mala's gaze strolls over me, taking me in hungrily. Her eyes darken as I move to the waistband of my sweatpants. I pull them down along with my boxers, and my cock springs free, hard and glistening at the tip.

Mala's shaky breath catches when her eyes freeze on my tip, her tongue snaking out to tap her lips. Her eyes find mine again and that same defiance I've come to love floats inside them. She sits up, reaching out for me. "I want it in my mouth."

I grin, basking in the satisfaction of her response, before I shake my head. "Not yet, baby girl." I crawl over her so she's forced to lie back down. "First, I need to come inside your pussy, and then I'll come inside your mouth. Now open those legs for me again."

She does as I ask, and I reach over to the nightstand where my wallet is, pulling out a condom.

She eyes it. "Dean . . ."

"Yes, baby?"

She clears her throat as a blush creeps up to her cheeks. It makes my lips twitch that voicing her thoughts is what makes her blush—not the fact that I just ate her out less than five minutes ago. "I want to feel everything. All of it." Her teeth sink into her bottom lip. "I'm on birth control."

I hear her unsaid words and throw the condom over my shoulder, making her giggle. Fuck, I'm going to miss hearing that sound every time I want to.

I kiss her to shut her up, swallowing her laugh, followed by a moan. I've never paid too much attention to the way a girl kisses. They've always been sufficient, done the necessary to move things along. But Mala? She kisses like she does everything in her life—with everything she has. So thoroughly, it wipes away the memory of everything before her.

Was there ever anything before her?

Our tongues dance as I line us up, her knees falling to the sides for me. I pull away only slightly to brush the tip of my cock through her wet seam, and Mala's mouth follows to catch mine, as if she can't fathom disconnecting our kiss so quickly. But as soon as I slide my cock against her again, her head falls back on the pillow, her chest lifting into mine as a guttural moan follows.

"God, that feels so good."

"Watch me," I growl. "Look how good you take my cock, baby girl. I want you to remember us like this."

And before the grief of this moment, the knowledge that I only have tonight, and the thought of her moving away can piss me off again, I thrust into her in one go.

Chapter Twenty-Four

MALA

OUR MOANS COLLIDE ALONG WITH OUR BODIES AS DEAN plunges inside me.

I feel *full*. So full, I feel him in my stomach, my lungs.

Dean pulls out and thrusts back inside me, and the graze of the two metal beads at the head of his cock against my G-spot has me sucking in a ragged breath. Light flashes behind my eyes, making my hips jump to meet his. At this rate, I'm going to come again not even five minutes after the last time.

I feel like I'm floating in an ocean of Dean. He's everywhere, overwhelming my senses with his heady sandalwood scent, his throaty groans, and his heated touch.

I always imagined him to be a generous lover, wild and unruly. But that he would be downright filthy with both his words and actions? That he would have me begging and needy for every word of praise, every lascivious touch, like a sunbather soaking up the Hawaiian sun? *That*, I did not expect.

And now, I'm ruined. *Wrecked* and ravaged for anyone besides him.

Dean's arm is braced on the bed next to my head while his

other hand lays possessively around my throat. His gaze bores into mine, like he won't allow himself to blink, lest he miss even a millisecond. There's so much want there, but there's something else, too. Something that always softens his eyes when he looks at me, but it's more marked today.

Affection.

A worship and adoration that's so intense, I can barely stand to keep our gazes connected. It's all too much. An overdose, overstimulation, overindulgence.

My hands cup his jaw and a silent hopelessness passes between us. A pang so strong, I feel the sudden onslaught of tears pricking the backs of my eyes.

One night.

It won't be enough. It'll *never* be enough.

I turn my head, trying to look away as a tear bursts through the dam and spills through a corner, soaking into my pillow. My lips purse to hold in a sob.

God, what the hell am I doing? I'm mourning us before we've even started. I'm mourning us *because* we can never really start. I should have stopped this, but not a goddamn thing in the world could have.

What if I've ruined everything?

He promised we'd go back to being friends, that we wouldn't let tonight change anything, and though in my heart of hearts I know we're not fooling anyone, I want to believe him. He has a history of keeping things casual with others, and while I don't know it for sure, I imagine this isn't his first one-night stand. So, maybe that's how he'll treat us as well.

The thought makes my stomach roll irrationally, and I have to blink past another well of tears.

Dean grabs hold of my jaw and swings my face to him. What he sees has his jaw tightening and his brows furrowed. A sheen envelopes his irises like fog over a lake. If there's ever been a person who could read me, it's him.

Except he hasn't read everything I've wanted to say.

"Come back to me," he croaks.

For a second my heart leaps, wrapping around his words like they're a boon, a shelter from an impending storm. But as I wait for him to follow it up with a, "Don't leave me," or a "Let's go home," and he doesn't, I realize my shortsightedness. My futile hope.

Dean's hand slides down my body, lingering around my breast before he brings his mouth down to suck on my nipple. His entire body glistens as he continues to drive into me, the end of his erection making me feel both elated and insane.

My body tingles from head to toe and a new pool of want collects at my entrance. I'm so close. So, so close.

"Fuck, you're wet." His chest rumbles with his groan. "You look so good sucking my cock into your sweet pussy. Such a good girl for me."

My core contracts in response to his filthy praise and my fingernails dig into his shoulders, telling him without words what he does to me. There's no doubt his dirty words will be on replay inside my mind for the rest of my life. No doubt I won't be able to get off without the memory of them.

His hand drifts down to rub circles around my clit while he plunges in and out. His piercing drives home each time as he seats himself fully inside me before pulling back out and doing it again, and I'm less than ten seconds from the strongest orgasm I've ever had.

Sweat beads over his brow and his chest heaves with each breath. "Ah, fuck. I can't hold on much longer, baby. I need you to come."

Dean pulls my knee up with a hand around the bottom of my thigh, changing our angle and driving in deeper, harder. I only have a chance to see his eyes darken to an abysmal black when my own clench shut and stars explode behind my lids.

I come with a violent start, as if I didn't know I was even holding on. It's both a surprise and a revelation when my teeth chatter and ribbons of electricity zing through my body. My outcry resounds inside the room, overpowering the slick sounds of our bodies connecting.

My pussy pulses around him, spurring on his climax, and Dean bucks. His body tightens from head to toe before the flood of his release bathes my insides. The feeling is so hot, so carnal, I find myself climaxing once more.

We're both an entanglement of limbs and gasps, our chests bumping as we try to gain control of our breaths. Dean collapses on me, and I wrap my arms and legs around him, cocooning him like if I try hard enough, we'll be merged forever.

He's so heavy, so solid, and I relish the weight of him pressing down on me. My safe haven. The man I'm so in love with, I don't even recall the exact moment I fell.

He kisses my neck, lifting his head to study me before dragging a strand of my wet hair off my cheek. I'm still feverish, wet and warm all over, as my heart continues to thunder inside my chest.

"Want to know another secret?" His voice is so low, so hushed, if he wasn't right next to my ear, I might not have heard it. "I've never taken a woman bare."

My eyes volley between his. "Seriously?"

I would have thought with his piercing . . . And the fact that he was with Jessie for so long . . .

He gives me a lopsided grin before he presses another kiss on my nose. "You're my one and only."

～

MY BODY FEELS RAW, like every layer has been stripped away by sandpaper. If I was to see myself in the mirror, I know an unrecognizable reflection would stare back. A reflection exposed all the way to my soul rather than the outer parts.

The truth between us is deafening—*this is it; this one night*—yet we've masked it with hours of sex. Hours of him railing me with punishing thrusts and strokes. Hours where we've explored each other's bodies from top to bottom,

He's taken me twice from behind, once on my side, and God knows how many times hovering over me with that same look in his eyes—like I'm the only thing that keeps him together and loosens him to shreds.

He's a perfect parity of rough and tender, brawn and beauty. He's so far inside my bones, I'll feel him until my last breath.

I'm spent, depleted in a way I've never been, but replenished like I've been transformed and awakened from within.

The little light that was filtering in from the curtains has long since disappeared, and even though we're lying here, face to face, in a veil of darkness, I can see every emotion flitter over him. Just like I'm sure he can see them flitter over me.

Our eyes are fastened and the intimacy of this moment outweighs anything the darkness could ever hide.

We're both heaving from the last round, desperately trying to get a hold of our heartbeats—in more ways than one . . . at least, on my part. His fingers are buried inside my hair, his heated breath wafting over my skin like a blanket.

The emotion between us is so immense, it's like its own entity. A bystander with front-row seats. The lump inside my throat feels like it could break the barrier as my hands curve around his neck and my thumbs trail up his scruffed jaw.

Dean's index finger trails a line down to my chest and gently over my long scar. He caresses it with such affection, I'm tempted to close my eyes to heft some of the weight off the moment.

His mouth turns downward before he looks at me. "I hate that you hide yourself; that you hide this."

"I don't hide it from you."

"I hate that you think you have to hide it from anyone." His eyes come back to connect with mine. "I wish you could see yourself from my eyes. Head to toe, you're the most beautiful woman I've ever seen."

I stare at him, hearing his admission.

The rough pad of his thumb brushes across my cheek. "You might have been a victim once, but you're a survivor now. Resilient, strong, and so damn beautiful. Show them what I see. Give them all of you, *sprinkles*. Don't hide behind a single unnecessary thread." He takes in a strangled breath. "*That's* what I want for you."

My eyes well, knowing he's talking about tomorrow and the week after and the week after that. All the weeks we won't have each other physically.

Dean pulls me in to lay a kiss on my beestung lips, keeping his there and inhaling the scent of my skin. I know he can feel the quiver in my lips and the quake in my chin as he pulls me closer by the waist so my nipples brush against his chest.

Does he feel it, too? The deep melancholy. The loss of everything good.

I've done this to us. First by accepting the job, and then by letting us obliterate the barriers we've always had erected.

The ending to a story written without a beginning.

And I ruined it.

Our kiss turns hotter, more desperate. His tongue thrusts inside me, similar to the way his cock did not long ago. Claiming, taking, consuming. A moan slips through his throat as he cups the back of my head, fisting my hair. His erection digs into my thigh, but we're too engrossed in the kiss to move any other muscle.

"*Sprinkles* . . ." His whispered sigh has me pulling him further in, tangling my fingers with the long strands at his nape. "I'm . . ."

I pull back, disconnecting our locked lips and gaze into his eyes. He blinks but doesn't continue. "You're what?" I coax. I swear a sob is building inside me, and I don't even fucking know why. "You're what, Dean?"

His jaw clenches under my palm before he squeezes his eyes shut, closing the window he'd only briefly opened to give me a glimpse of his soul.

"Please." I tighten my fingers on him. I don't even know what I'm begging for. I don't know what he was going to say, but I'm dying for him to finish. To let me in.

Dean unwraps himself from me and the cool air inside the room floats over my warm, exposed skin, making me shudder. He runs a hand over his face before turning to sit on the bed with his feet on the floor. He places his elbows on his knees and scrubs his face again, pinching the bridge of his nose.

I lay a hand on his back, but it slips when he rises to his feet, turning to face me. Without a word, he scoops me into his arms like I weigh nothing at all and carries me into the bathroom.

Flicking on the light, he puts me down on my feet and turns on the shower without any words. We're already undressed, so as soon as the water is the right temperature, Dean pulls me in with him.

He positions us so I'm under the spray, squirting shampoo on his palm. He massages my scalp so gently, so affectionately, you'd think I was made of porcelain. Getting soap on his hands, he lathers my skin from my neck down, paying special attention to my breasts and between my thighs.

The steam from the shower and Dean's touch has me feeling languid and lithe, like I'm no longer in control of a single muscle. I don't know what time it is at this point, but all I can think about is pressing my head to his chest, having him envelop me with his strong arms, and drifting off to sleep.

Once I've rinsed everything off, I do the same for him, washing him from head to toe. I roll my thumb over his piercing, and Dean's length jerks against my hand. I can feel the heat taking over my skin, my eyes, as my hand wraps around his shaft.

Pressing my fingernail under a bead, I tug on it and Dean groans. His head falls back under the spray, trickles of water rolling down his broad chest and arms. He places a possessive hand on my hip while the other braces against the shower wall, almost like he's trying to keep himself upright.

I work his hard length from base to tip, rubbing my thumb over the metal beads and tugging them a few more times, until he's practically vibrating with need. Pressing his shoulders so he leans against the shower wall, I get down on my knees.

"Fuck, Mala." His throaty groan intermingles with the splash of the water hitting all around us, and he places his dick on my lips like he can't stand not having it in my mouth for even a second longer. "Suck my cock, baby."

My pussy contracts at his words, and as much as I want to relieve the pressure between my thighs using my fingers, I focus on him.

I widen my mouth as far as I can, wrapping my lips around his tip before sucking it over my tongue. I roll my tongue over the beads, playing with them inside my mouth, and making him huff out a strained breath.

Dean gathers my wet hair in his hand while I stroke him from base to tip where my mouth is, before I shimmy down, taking him as far as I can go.

"Oh, Jesus." His nostrils flare as his hand tightens around

my hair, guiding me up and down his shaft. "Fuck! Take that cock, baby. God, you take it so good."

I pump him slow and then fast, sucking in time with the strokes of my hand and rolling my tongue over his piercing, knowing how much he likes it.

"God, this is going to be embarrassingly fast, Mala. I'm about to fill your mouth with my cum. Don't fucking stop."

I have no intentions to. Instead, I hollow out my cheeks and suck, hard and fast, placing my hand on his ridiculously taut ass and pulling him even further so he hits the back of my throat. I can feel my gag reflex kicking in, but I'll be damned if I stop now.

I feel his entire body tremble as his orgasm builds. Within a few seconds, Dean spills into my mouth with a hiss and groan, his hooded eyes watching my throat work as I swallow every drop.

He pulls me up and kisses me raggedly, messily. "Fuck. Any other talents you want to familiarize me with?"

I giggle, swiping my tongue over my lips. "Maybe. But it would take more than one night."

And with the way Dean's smile drops, I realize I've said the wrong thing yet again.

MY EYES FLUTTER open to the stream of light coming in from the curtains. It's a deceptive allure that would have you imagining a warm spring day rather than the freezing temperatures outside.

As I slowly gain a sense for where I am, my senses fill with the scent of sandalwood and soap, and I breathe in as if to flood my every cell with him.

My eyes snag on a long thicket of soft hair underneath a

tight pack of abs, and I make a fist to withhold reaching out and running my hand over the expanse of his delicious skin.

My head is on his chest, my arm tucked around his waist. Overnight, I've even managed to nestle my always-cold toes under his calves.

From the rise and fall of his chest, I get the sense he's still sleeping, so I slowly lift my head to glimpse his face, but instead, I find him looking back at me. There's a distant look in his gaze, and even though I know his eyes are on my face, his mind is nowhere nearby.

My hand trails over the ridges of his abs, the pebbled bump of his nipple, the collarbone I've found myself marveling at more than I should, to the edge of his jaw. His scruff scratches my palm, and my thighs clench at the recollection of how it felt between them.

"Dean . . ." I breathe, trailing off and trying to figure out how to put everything in my head into words. I'm not sure there's been a language created to translate it all. "Maybe we could–"

"We need to get on the road while they're open."

I snap my mouth shut, realizing he cut me off purposely.

He doesn't want to talk about the maybes. He doesn't want a conversation exploring how we could *potentially* work this out. What he wants is to get on the road and get me to my destination as fast as possible.

Shame and embarrassment warm my cheeks. I've never thought of myself as the needy, clingy type, but given what he just saw in my eyes, that's likely what he's thinking about me. In his head, he's thinking, *"Jesus. I need to get away from this woman before she mistakes a night of fucking for wedding vows."*

Burying the ache somewhere deep and plastering a smile on my face, I nod. I scoot off him, avoiding his stare. Thankfully, I'd put on my pajamas again last night after our shower, so I'm not stark naked and exposed in more ways than I need to be at this point.

Dean's sigh resounds in the room that didn't feel quite as small last night, but I continue to my bag, picking out a change of clothes and head to the bathroom.

Dean is dressed and almost ready to go by the time I'm out of the bathroom, and while I'm repacking my toiletries, he goes inside to brush his teeth without any exchange of words.

I hear the bathroom door open and the slide of his feet on the carpet behind me, lingering.

"Mala . . ." His voice is a resignation and a plea. One that feels too little and too late based on what we shared last night.

"We should get on the road." I pull my suitcase off the console and shuffle over to the door, ignoring the acid filling my chest or the prick of more tears at the corners of my eyes.

Dean follows me with another sigh.

Chapter Twenty-Five

MALA

Eleven Months Ago

I walk back to my office, looking down at my phone screen, my heels clicking on the ceramic floor with a *tap, tap, tap*. Even now, after almost two months, the sound is foreign to me, like it's coming from somewhere far away.

My usual attire is one of the many things I've had to change since I started working at *Doggone*. I still change into my sweatshirt and shorts almost as soon as I get home, but there's a part of my closet that looks distinctly different from the rest with skirts, blouses, blazers, and heels.

It's been an adjustment.

Another adjustment? The lack of conversation with my best friend.

It's not like we haven't spoken, because we have, through texts here and there. Twice I heard him in the background when I spoke to Rohan on the phone, too, but it doesn't take a rocket scientist to figure out that he's avoiding me. That he doesn't want to speak on the phone. That he doesn't want to hear my voice.

And that sucks more than anything. More than having to learn something totally new at a job I've never done. More than trying to fit into the corporate life when I can't possibly feel any more out-of-place. More than finding a new show on Netflix, only to watch it alone, without him there to let me warm my feet under his thigh or comment on how stupid the show actually is.

We tried to cover the silence between us on the drive to LA with music and meaningless conversation about the weather, the road conditions, logistics for when I got to my new place, but the elephant sat between us like a solid wall. And no matter how much I knew it was my own doing, my fault, I blamed him, too.

Because he promised me . . . He fucking promised, and not even hours later, everything changed.

"Is this how it's going to be now?" I glared at him from my passenger seat. "You're going to be all weird and distant?"

He'd chuckled. Chuckled! *As if I were delusional. "Not being weird or distant with you, Mala. I'm right fucking here."*

I looked out the window with my arms wrapped around my chest and mumbled, "It definitely doesn't feel like it."

And despite the casual tone he was going for, I couldn't miss the way he white-knuckled the steering wheel. "What would you like me to do?" He glanced at me. "What do you need from me?"

I gritted my teeth and said what I knew I shouldn't. "What I'd love, Dean, is for you to fucking forget last night happened, like you'd promised."

He stayed quiet for a long moment, and I almost took back what I said, but before I could, he nodded, his jaw as hard as his glare on the road. "I must have forgotten what I promised." He placed an index on his temple and blinked animatedly, like a character from some sci-fi movie. "There." He smiled without a lick of amusement. "Forgotten and erased from my memory. You happy?"

I wasn't and he knew it, but the tingles inside my nose from impending tears and my throat feeling clogged just had me turning my head to look out the window again.

Aside from the detached way he helped me get settled into my apartment and the long inhale I took of him when he wrapped his arms around me before he left, those are the last memories I have of being in my best friend's presence.

And while I've replayed our night together more times than I can even count, it always ends with the same despair he left me in the morning after.

God, I miss him. I miss him so badly, sometimes I feel like I'm being pulled underground by quicksand. The more I fight it, the deeper I go in, and now I feel like I just need to succumb to it.

I've asked Rohan and Malcolm about him as much as I can without seeming like a creeper, but my questions are never what I really want to ask, anyway. Sometimes they aren't even what either of them can answer. Like, what has he been up to? Is he seeing someone? God, that makes my stomach twist, but it's the one I think about the most. Does he miss me? Because he doesn't seem to miss me.

Sitting down at my desk, I look at the three dots jumping around on my phone screen with my heart hammering in my chest. Where he used to answer my texts almost instantaneously, he's just now responding to the message I sent to him earlier this morning. His texts always did things to my heart, but I never felt anxious reading them like I do now.

> Me: What starts with a T and ends with a T and has T in it?

> Sparky: No idea. What's up?

I reel back with my mouth turned down. *No idea? What's up?* That's how he responds after hours of me waiting? Not even an attempt at a dumb response to make me laugh? And the *'what's up,'* like I need a reason to text him. Like I'm bothering him with my text . . .

Am I just looking too far into his response? Being overly sensitive?

Getting up to close my office door, I pull back my shoulders and FaceTime him from my desk. I'm tired of holding in my frustration and hurt just to not come across as needy. If I'm needy, then I'm needy. So-fucking-be-it.

Dean's face shows up a moment later, sweat beading above his brow, his cheeks pink. I'm surprised he even picked up, to be honest.

As much as I don't want to recall it at this very moment, the pink in his cheeks, creeping down to his neck, reminds me of the way he looked when he was hovering above me not too long ago.

Still, he looks . . . different. Harder? More distant? For a second, I wonder if I've even called the right guy.

"Hey!" I somehow voice around the stone lodged in my throat. And as much as I want to scream at him, shake him for the way he's being, I school my features. Because despite the way he's being, this is all my fault. I'm the one who couldn't hold back any longer. I'm the one who triggered it all.

I'm the one who ruined everything.

His brows lift, but I don't get the same smile he usually reserves for me. "Sup?"

With a barbell, along with the emblem for their station partially visible behind his head, I know he's at the gym inside the fire station.

"Nothing." I hesitate, feeling awkward. "I . . . I just haven't talked to you properly in a while and . . . I miss you."

I pull the collar of my V-neck sweater, as a force of habit, realizing it does little to cover me up the way my sweatshirt does, and I notice Dean's eyes dip toward the top of my scar. Whether he's happy about what he sees—whether he realizes the changes I'm making are not just due to my new job, but his words to me that night–he doesn't show it.

"You're talking to me now."

"Right." I nod, covering up my vulnerability and the fact that he doesn't tell me he misses me back with a forced laugh. I've never had to force a laugh with him, but as much as I called him initially to chew him out and tell him to get his head out of his ass, I also just want to talk to him since it's been so long. I just want to paint a facade of normalcy–maybe if we pretend enough, it'll feel real again. "Well, in case you were burning up with anticipation, the answer is teapot."

Dean's blank face stares back at me.

"The riddle," I clarify, hoping my smile doesn't wobble. "The answer is a teapot."

"Got it," he responds with a shuttered look.

God, this is so fucking hard. I feel like I'm trying to drain blood from a stone. "So, how are things? What have you been up to?"

He rolls his tongue over his teeth. "Good. All's good." He pauses, and then, as if he just remembered to ask me the same thing back, he adds, "How are you?"

I clench my fist, digging my short nails into the inside of my palm to focus on something other than the way nausea seems to be crawling up my throat. "Good!" I say all too cheerily, like an overdramatic actress. "Things are good! Just busy, but I've been learning a lot and getting to know everyone here."

I don't tell him that, in the two months I've been here, I've had more nights where I've cried myself to sleep because I miss home, I miss my café, and I fucking miss him like I've been ripped from the inside out.

I don't tell him that so far, I haven't quite enjoyed anything about working here besides the couple of friends

I've made. I keep telling myself that it's still too early to make a judgment call, but I already know how I feel in my gut.

I don't tell him that on most nights, I get back to my empty apartment and instead of doing the things I used to love, like watching movies or reading books, I flip through years and years of pictures of him, finding myself back in those memories as if they were just yesterday.

Like all the pictures he's sent me of sprinkles. Sprinkles on a cupcake. Sprinkles of rain on the window at the fire station. The picture of a sweatshirt he bought for me for my birthday a few years ago—a sweatshirt I wear so often, its cuffs are tattered—that says, *Life is better with sprinkles*.

Under each picture is just one word. *Sprinkles*.

Pictures of when we went kayaking and sat on a grassy knoll near the lake afterward, talking about anything and everything. We even silently photographed a family of black bears in the distance, napping atop one another.

And pictures of when Dean taught me to rollerblade. The smile on my face, rollerblading right beside him, once I felt confident enough to do it on my own, rivals the brightest star in the sky.

Dean swings his head front to back in a placatory nod. "Looks like LA life is really suiting you."

I can't mistake the accusatory note in his voice. What does he expect me to do? Wallow in sadness—*Well, newsflash, Fido! I already am!*—or run back home? The way he's acting doesn't make the prospect of being near him any more exciting, either. Though I can't deny it's all I want to do.

Still, I'm exhausted with how he's being. I'm trying. I'm trying so fucking hard to keep things as much the same between us as they used to be, but he doesn't even want to budge.

"Right." I look out the window to the sliver of Santa Monica Beach visible from my high-rise office before coming back to study him on the screen. The Pacific Coast water may still have the winter chill during this time in April, but the number of people bathing would indicate otherwise. "What's wrong, Dean? Why does it feel like we're so far away from each other right now?"

Dean wipes his face with a towel. "I don't know, Mala. Maybe it has something to do with the fact that you're in LA, and I'm still here . . . in Tahoe."

My jaw clenches. "You know I'm not talking about physical distance. Is this what we amount to after eight years of friendship? Is this what you want?"

"No." His eyes sharpen. "This isn't what we amount to after eight years of friendship. This is where we are after you—" He stops himself, looking away. He comes back to the screen, running a frustrated hand through his hair. "Forget it."

I snap my mouth shut, realizing it had dropped open. "Wow. I'm sorry, Dean, but as I recall, *you* were the one who suggested one night between us. *You* kissed me first."

"That's not . . . That's not what I was going to say." He takes a deep inhale, squeezing his eyes shut, as if he's trying not to lose his temper. "You know what? Never mind."

"When, Dean?" I throw a hand up. "When are we going to move past that night? When are we going to go back to what we had?"

I hate that my chin shakes. I hate that my chest burns and my sight blurs. I hate not being there to make him talk to me, to make him listen to me.

And most of all, I hate this limbo where I can't hate him but I can't love him, either. I fucking hate all of it.

I turn in my chair and Dean's eyes look past me—or, at least, I think they do from what I can tell on my small screen. I look over my shoulder to follow his gaze to the vase of pink roses. I'd forgotten they were even there.

"Nice flowers. Did a new boyfriend get them for you?" There's a hint of something in his voice . . . Sarcasm? Irritation? *Jealousy?*

I think about lying to him but can't get myself to, even though from the looks of him, it might be the better option. "I'm not dating anyone. They're from my boss. I just completed two months here, and he got me flowers. They're nothing."

Dean chuckles, his gaze burning. "They seem like *something* to me. Wonder if he gets flowers for all employees on their two-month anniversary. Let me guess. He took you out to dinner, too. You know, on a *non-date*."

I open my mouth and close it again. He's making it sound like something it's not, and he fucking knows it. Yes, Jason and I went to dinner last night. So what? It wasn't anything but a gesture of camaraderie between two coworkers. Bosses and employees go out to dinner all the fucking time. That doesn't mean there's anything going on between them.

I shove away any thoughts of the attached note I read this morning that said, *"These flowers pale in comparison to the company at dinner last night. I'd love to do it again soon."*

It isn't how it sounds, no matter how much a little voice in my head chants the opposite.

A knowing smile plays on Dean's lips at my silence, and I read each emotion as it flutters across his face. Hurt, anger, and betrayal. And all fucking misplaced. Yet I'm still the one left feeling guilty.

"Glad you're doing well, *sprinkles*. Looks like you're moving right on past that night."

"Dean–"

"I've gotta go. Have fun on the *non-dates* with your boss."

DEAN

"Show off," I holler from my seat on the barstool before taking a pull from my beer.

Garrett walks around the table and aligns himself behind the cue ball again. He's brought his A-game today, and I wonder if it has anything to do with frustrations with his *wife*. In my head, I still say wife with quotes around it because, in his situation, it's not really clear if they are or aren't married. Technically, they are. But physically, emotionally, metaphorically? Who the fuck knows.

They accidentally married a few weeks ago when we all went to Vegas, and since then, Garrett has done everything in his power to keep her close.

He's been in love with the woman for the past four years, but never had the balls to tell her. That fact alone had all of us scratching our heads because as much as it kills me to admit it, my twin is nothing short of a pot of honey around bees when it comes to women. So the fact that he has pined for one woman all this time without having it reciprocated by her is mind-boggling.

Garrett grunts, mumbling something about being able to

kick my ass with his eyes closed, and I snort out a laugh, volleying back with my own retort.

This is how it always is between both my brothers and me. I laugh internally because our *baby* brother, Darian, gets it the worst from both me and Garrett. I swear, there's a sick pleasure I get from teasing his broody ass that I get with little else in life.

Garrett lobs the eight-ball against the back wall, making it into the pocket he called and winning the game. Darian and him have some sort of stupidly smug exchange of handshakes since they were playing against me and Hudson before Darian clasps Garrett's shoulder. "Let's get a round of beers and sit for a bit. I'm fucking beat."

That's a surprise since Darian rarely drinks.

Hudson waves down our waitress and orders us another round of beers before we all take a seat around the table. Like Rohan is to me, Hudson is one of Garrett's closest friends, but he and I get along well, too.

He's slightly older than us, in his early forties, but one of the most regimented and disciplined people I know. Though none of us are lightweights when it comes to pushing our bodies in the gym, I doubt any of us could hang with him. The man is a fucking machine and built like one, too.

He's had one hell of an interesting life, making a pretty big name for himself as a world-renowned geologist—or Earth scientist, as he formally calls himself—even after having to raise a daughter practically on his own since the age of seventeen.

"Fuck, if you're asking for a beer, you must have had a rough night. I haven't seen you drink anything but water, ever," Hudson says in astonishment to Darian.

"Or milk," I offer with a smirk. "Preferably in a sippy cup, with chocolate mixed in."

Darian flips me off before we're all laughing. Everyone in

this crew knows the story of how Darian was addicted to chocolate milk as a kid because that's the only way his mom, Karine, could get him to drink it. I still laugh when I see our old family photos where he's holding his sippy cup in one hand and his blanket in the other.

It should make me feel terrible, but some of my favorite childhood memories are of Garrett and me being total jackasses to Darian.

I still remember how Garrett and I would hide his beloved blanket—something he was attached to until he was almost ten—all the fucking time and use it as ransom, making him do stupid shit to get it back.

Like one time he had to respond to *anything* Karine or my dad said with, "I poopied my panties."

"Darian jan, why aren't you eating your lamb kebab? Do you want more lavash?" Karine asked, looking concerned at Darian's pout, mistaking his annoyance with me and Garrett for his disinterest in the food she'd cooked.

Darian gave us another pleading look, and I kicked him under the table to assert the point silently—say you poopied your panties or wave goodbye to your precious blankie.

"I poopied my panties," he gritted out.

Garrett and I turned beet-red, holding in our laughter. I swear, my stomach was cramping because I couldn't breathe.

Karine's face morphed into confusion as she tried to comprehend what her nine-year-old had said. She even looked down at his pants in shock and disgust. This just made holding back our laughs even more difficult.

But it was our dad who spoke up first. "Darian, that is extremely inappropriate, especially at the dinner table. What is going on with you? Please go and get yourself cleaned up."

Darian nodded, turning around to head to his room, when Karine ran after him. "Darian jan, let me help you."

Darian shook his head violently but glanced at us, knowing he couldn't say anything besides what he'd agreed to. "I poopied my panties!"

Karine stared at him like perhaps there was something wrong with her son's head, in addition to the apparent loss of control of his bowels. "Yes. I understand, jan. *You've made that very clear. And stop calling them* panties."

It was then that both Garrett and I bowled over, not being able to hold our laughs any longer, getting an unamused look from our dad, who'd just realized we were the culprits.

I hold back my grin, thinking about that day. As much shit as we gave him, he took it like a champ, but if there was one thing we impressed on him, despite the incessant brotherly ragging, it was that we would be there for him, no matter what.

We loved him not an ounce less than we loved each other. Which is why when his life turned upside down a few years ago, and he lost Sonia abruptly in the most heart-wrenching way, mere hours after she gave birth to his son, we were all there for him.

I took off as much time as I could from the fire station, and Garrett did the same from the airline to be at our brother's side.

His life was in complete shambles until his current wife, Rani, showed up. If Darian is like a quiet night, then Rani is his complete opposite—bubblier than the sun's rays. The way that woman washed his gloomy world with all her sunshiny smiles and kindness is beyond explanation.

The waitress drops off our beers, and Darian tells us a little about how he's been having to get up multiple times through the night because his newborn daughter—my niece—likes to party through the night and sleep during the day, and Hudson gives him some experienced fatherly advice.

The conversation changes to us talking about Garrett's sour mood. He's been unusually irritable lately, like a fucking

bear with a toothache. He tells us about his current predica-
ment with his *wife*, Bella.

"You need to talk to her," I say, seeing the heartbreak on
his face.

Garrett scoffs, "As far as I'm concerned, I've said everything I needed to, everything I could have."

"Well, then you need to be there to hear her response.
Has she even tried to reach out to you since?"

"Yeah, but—"

"So don't be an idiot. That was probably her way of
breaking the ice. Women are complicated like that."

Don't I know it?

They are complicated as hell, but pretend to be all simple
and shit. It's all a ruse.

Garrett chortles, and I know he's trying to dodge any
more attention. "You'd know. Care to tell us about your
current relationship status?"

I run a hand over my neck, twisting it this way and that.
I'm not having this discussion again. "No. This isn't
about me."

Over the past year, everyone from my brothers to Grams
to my mom, and even Rohan, have tried to broach the subject
about Mala in terms of where we both stand.

Of all of them, Grams is the only one who knows that
lines were crossed when I drove her to LA, but even she
doesn't know the extent of it.

Even she doesn't know that a month after dropping her
off, I drove eight straight hours to go back and see her. That I
couldn't stand another fucking moment without her knowing
how I felt. That I was fucking withering away to nothing
without her.

That first month was excruciating, like trying to figure
out how to live without your sense of sight all of a sudden.

But if that first month was brutal, then the next few were worse.

I still remember parking at the corner of her street to avoid having her notice my car. I was going to surprise her. But as soon as I did, she came bounding down the stairs, smiling at someone inside another car.

For a second she didn't look like herself—the woolen black skirt hitting above her knees, the black stockings and heeled booties, the light V-neck sweater. Had I ever seen her wear something that so boldly displayed her scar in all the eight years?

And as happy as I was that she was able to do that—that she was more comfortable in her own skin—there was a part of me that felt left out. Like I was a spectator on the sidelines when I used to be a starting player.

I knew it was my own fault—I wasn't coping well with her leaving. With us having slept together in what was the single hottest night of my life. With knowing the feel of her against me, over me, in every fiber of my being, and yet not being able to do anything to keep her there.

I wasn't coping well with burying my truth—my fucking feelings—for her, knowing I could do nothing about them.

But I was also doing my best to work through it. She might argue with that given how strange the next morning was between us, but in my heart and mind, I swear, I was trying to come to terms with it all. *Failing*, but trying, nevertheless.

But that wasn't even what had my head in a spin. It was her second promise. The one she had me make when we were driving there.

"What I'd love, Dean, is for you to fucking forget last night happened, like you'd promised."

She'd changed the rules. *That* wasn't ever what I'd promised. The first promise was to go back to being friends after sharing the night—words I never should have agreed to in the first place, but did for her sake. But then she threw in another promise—as if I was some fucking genie fulfilling wishes.

She asked me to forget it even happened.

How? How could she expect that? How could she *want* that?

Sitting in my car, I got a glimpse of the man in a suit and tie who'd come to pick her up. I suppose she's always had a thing for men in suits. The guy exited his car and walked around to open the passenger door for her. But it wasn't even that that had caught my eye. It was the look on his face at the sight of her—the familiar soft caress of his eyes over her entire frame, his possessive hand on the base of her spine.

"Oh, shit. Is this about Mala?" Hudson asks, bringing me out of my thoughts. "What's happening on that front?"

I get off the barstool and grin at the cute bartender headed our way to ask her for another round of drinks. I have no intention of giving her anything more than a friendly smile. Even if I did, even if I wanted to—which I don't—Mala made sure my dick doesn't so much as twitch in anyone's presence but hers.

"Shit." Garrett gets up abruptly, looking down at his phone. "I have to go."

"Everything okay, brother?" I ask, studying his face. Based on the excitement swirling in his eyes, it doesn't seem like a bad kind of emergency.

He looks up like he just realized we're still here. "Yeah, uh, sorry to cut this short, but I just got a text from Bella. Everything's fine, but I need to see her."

He gives us all a bro-hug, but when he gets to me, he pulls me in for a little longer. "There's no one I know better than you, brother. And if there's one thing I know right now, it's that you're fucking miserable without her." He pulls back to look at me. "I don't know what the fuck happened because you won't tell anyone, but here's a piece of unsolicited brotherly advice. Sometimes *missing* communication can be more detrimental than miscommunication. So, do yourself a favor and tell her what she doesn't know."

I look down at the phone clutched in his hand. "Is that what you're doing? Going off to get missing information."

He gives me the smirk we're both known for. "I'm going off to get a lot more than just missing information."

Once Garrett leaves, Darian, Hudson, and I start a game of *Cut Throat*. I've just sunk the last of Hudson's balls and only have two more of Darian's left on the table. My own two are on there as well, so it's a guess as to who will win—me or Darian.

"How about we make this game more interesting?" Darian says, holding his cue stick like a mountain climber with a trekking pole.

I eye him over the table as I try to line up the cue ball behind one of his. Darian may come across as quiet and reserved, but the guy can be a shark on the pool and poker table. And right now, he has that same gleam in his smile that I've seen when he's just gotten a bad idea. It's rare, but it's been known to happen.

"How much are we wagering?" I already regret encouraging this conversation.

He rubs his palms together. "Not money. Let's wager something that'll hurt a little more if you lose it."

Hudson smiles. "Oh, this'll be good. I'm going to need another beer for this." He waves to our bartender again.

"Like what?" I ask Darian, ignoring Hudson.

Darian thinks about it. "I'll wager my boat."

I stare at him, dumbfounded. He loves that boat. "Your boat. You're being serious right now?"

He nods, a smug look on his face. "Not forever. I'll let you have it for six months.”

I blow out a breath through my lips. “I’m not betting my truck, if that’s what you’re thinking. It’s the only transportation I have.”

Hudson chimes in, looking at Darian, “Oh! Make him wager something else he loves just as much.” I knit my brows, not knowing what he’s even talking about, but suspecting I’m not going to like it. “Like that man-bun of his!”

I step back as if they’re coming after me with scissors. “Hey, now. Leave my hair out of this.”

Darian shrugs disappointedly. “I’m wagering my fucking boat, and you can’t bet a haircut? Seriously? You can grow that shit back, jackass.”

I look to the side, my jaw clenching as I take a second to process. These guys are serious assholes. I’ve had my hair long like this for as long as I can remember. I’m fucking attached to it!

With a groan and more cursing under my breath, I succumb to their idiotic idea. “Fine. Let’s do it.”

Ten minutes later, I’m slamming my beer bottle down on the bar table, ready to punch something while they’re bent over laughing.

I’m just shoving myself through the exit at the pool hall when Darian bellows at me, “Rani has great recommendations for nearby salons if you need ‘em.”

I think back to the shit Garrett and I pulled on him as kids, knowing this has to be some form of karma. “Jackass.”

Chapter Twenty-Seven

DEAN

Four Days Ago

I LOOK UP AT THE SKY CAMOUFLAGED BY DARK CLOUDS, LIKE ghouls floating over a darkened lake. The weather has been unpredictable this year, but the chill and electricity in the air travels down my spine, raising the hair at the back of my neck.

It's only a little past eight in the morning, but it already feels like a weird day.

I don't know why, but something feels off. Like the strange pit at the bottom of my stomach. Like the bizarre wrench inside my chest. Like the unwanted grate against the walls of my throat.

I wonder what it's about.

Is this some sort of weird twin-telepathy thing? Garrett and I can definitely read each other, but we've never had that unexplainable connection that twins talk about. But then again, we're not identical either, so maybe that's why.

My mind wanders, thinking about what this feeling is and whether I should just call him to see if he's okay. Walking into the station, I'm just pulling up my phone to message him when a familiar voice—one I haven't heard in a few months—floats into my ears.

My molars grind as I try to saunter past Rohan without being seen while he's on a video call with Mala. As if they can't help themselves, my eyes float to his screen and I catch a glimpse of her.

Fuck.

The ache in my chest grows as I take in the way she laughs, her full lips tuning upward like two points on a crescent moon, her nose crinkling on the sides in the way it always does. She looks . . . happy.

Unlike me.

The sounds of her laughter cease abruptly, and I realize her eyes have stalled on me. I also realize I've stopped moving and am staring. *So much for trying to move past them without being seen.*

A pronounced frown replaces the smile that was previously there and her brows bunch together. Rohan turns over his shoulder to find me, and I quickly hasten my pace, directing myself toward our bunk. I'm not changing into my turnout gear or anything . . . I just need a quiet minute to quell the upsurge for everything flitting inside my brain like debris inside a tornado. Thankfully, it's empty.

My breaths are shallow as her face spins inside my head. Her beautiful, perfect, sweet face.

"Fuck!" I pound my fist against one of the bunk lockers before taking a seat on a mattress. I've spent quite a few nights inside this room. I lower my head into my open palms and focus on my breathing instead of the twinge inside my chest.

It's been four months since we spoke. Four months since I've heard her voice.

The last time we spoke it felt like we were both trying to pull out each other's teeth and not having much success—

neither of us used the damn tools at our disposal to just say what was on our mind. We kept walking on eggshells and pretending they weren't slicing our feet.

She asked me about my day and what I'd been up to lately. I mouthed off something about being busy at work and getting ready for an annual festival the crew was involved in. She told me she liked her job, but I didn't believe her. Not that I voiced it, but based on the way she tried extra hard to sound chipper about it, I knew she hated it.

And yet, I still didn't ask her to quit, never asked her to come back to me.

I still didn't tell her I fucking missed her so much, I couldn't wake up or fall asleep without thinking about her. That I still hadn't stepped foot inside her café because the thought of her not being there, crouched with her arms around a customer's dog, filled my chest with fire. That even the sight of sprinkles on ice cream or doughnuts made me sick. That any sweatshirt with something funny written on it reminded me of her.

Everything reminded me of her and yet, I still didn't tell her.

I wasn't trying to be a martyr or doing her some big favor; I just didn't want to be the reason she left something she wanted to do. And even if I didn't believe she loved her job, her pretending she did kept me from asking her to come back.

Maybe she wouldn't want to come back because she'd found someone else. Her boss, who bought her those flowers, perhaps? Maybe it was the same guy whose car she got into all those months ago.

I sat in my car and stared at her empty apartment for an hour. I'd originally driven there to tell her how I felt, convinced she'd see things the same way—that we had something. *That we had everything.* But the longer I sat there, the more I realized what a foolish plan that was. Because if she was really happy, if she'd indeed moved on to someone else so quickly after the night we shared, then maybe I didn't need to add more complication to her life.

Maybe she really meant it when she asked me to forget what happened between us because that's what she'd done. Forgotten.

Maybe it was better for me to pull away, even if it hurt like hell doing it.

So, aside from the minimal texts here and there—more so in our group chat than privately—I've done just that, pulled away and thrown myself into work. I've taken on more extra shifts over the course of the past few months than I ever have since I became a firefighter. It's the only thing that's kept me sane.

I run my hand through my shorter hair, staring at the concrete floor when my phone vibrates with a text and my pulse increases as I read it.

Sprinkles: I miss you.

I swallow, rereading those three simple words. I need to tell her . . .

My eyes blur and I don't read the name on my phone when it buzzes in my hand. "Come back. Fucking come back to me."

Fuck, the sob that's been building all day releases and I hear the same sound echo back to me through the line.

"Dean?"

I blink rapidly, pulling the phone off my ear to check the name and make sure I heard right. "Mom?"

Her voice is strangled and throaty, like she's been crying. "Honey, it's Grams . . ."

My grandma's face, lit with her ever-present smile and

kind, knowing eyes, flashes across my eyes. The pang inside my chest worsens as if announcing what it's been trying to tell me all damn morning—that something is wrong.

Because something is very wrong.

Blood rushes past my ears but I suck in a shaky breath. "What is it? What about Grams?"

"W-we're in the hospital with her," Mom sputters, barely understandable. "We found her unconscious on her bathroom floor this morning after Douglas and I came back from our walk."

I zone out, disregarding her sobs or the sirens ringing inside my head. I'm not a newbie to this kind of thing, and aside from being a firefighter, I'm also a paramedic. My tone is more business than I feel inside. "Was she breathing when you found her? What are the doctors saying now?"

Douglas, my stepdad, takes over the phone. I'm assuming Mom's in no state to talk anymore. "Hey, son. She had a shallow pulse when we found her. The doctors said she was in some sort of respiratory distress where her lungs weren't removing enough CO_2 from her body. Hyper-something."

"Hypercapnia." She was having another one of her coughing fits when I spoke to her a few days ago. It was at the tip of my tongue to ask her if she'd gotten another checkup, but based on the tongue-lashing I got from her the previous time I asked, I kept my mouth sealed.

Douglas curses under his breath. "There's one more thing . . ."

I run a hand through my shorter hair, clutching it at the roots before letting it go. "They need to intubate her."

Douglas is quiet on the other end for a moment. "Yeah . . . but—"

"Fuck. Don't tell me she has a DNI."

Knowing Grams, I'm not surprised that she wouldn't want to be intubated, even if it meant saving her life. I can hear her now. *"I will not be picked and prodded like a lab rat. If my body says it's time to go, well then, it's time to go."*

Douglas puffs out a heavy breath. "We had no idea she'd signed the *Do Not Intubate* order, but they found it in her files."

Of course they didn't know. Neither did I. Grams isn't the type to ask for permission or look for approval being the stubborn mule she is, and she knew we wouldn't have given it, either.

I'm already rushing back out of the bunk when Douglas speaks. "Son, I know it doesn't need to be said, but I think you need to get here as soon as possible."

With my heart crawling up my throat, I respond, "I'm on my way."

MY EYES STAY AFFIXED to the doorknob to her hospital room. I haven't moved from this spot since the doctor came out to tell us the news. The somber, apologetic look on his face telegraphing his impending words before he spoke them. That she was gone.

Gone.

Like a dream you can never recreate, no matter how long you try. A flash in the sky right before the most beautiful storm. A dandelion in a gust of wind.

Just gone.

Mom sobs inside Douglas' arms; my own feel useless, numb.

I watch Garrett through the window as he takes her hand in his. His thumb slides over her knuckles and he whispers something into her ear as if she can still hear him. Maybe she can. Who the fuck knows.

Knowing her, she'll be listening to everything, even from

beyond the grave. She always did have a way of hearing things—*knowing* things—when you least expected it.

"Bye, Dean!" The brunette, with the hair that went all the way to her ass, waved at me as she got into the car with her friend—the brunette with the short bob. Both of them gave me sultry grins that indicated they were still thinking about last night.

For the life of me, I couldn't remember their names. Lara and Sophie? Or was it Lana and Shelby? I know they gave their names to me somewhere between when I saw them at the bar and when I got back to Grams' lake house with one under each arm.

"You have an adorable lake house, Grams!" the brunette with the bob chimed. She gave Grams her most innocent smile, but only I knew not to buy it, given all the not-so-innocent things she was capable of. "Dean told us how much he loves it here."

Behind me, Grams' voice resounded. "Ah! Did my grandson give you a whole tour of the house, or just his bedroom?"

I slapped my palm over my face, cursing under my breath. The woman reserved her comments and thinly-veiled sarcasm for no one.

Fuck. I just needed these women to leave.

Both the girls chirped out awkward laughs, finally leaving with another wave and a flying kiss in my direction. "Let's do that again sometime, Dean."

I winced, finally turning around to face Grams, convinced I'd be met with one of her reprimanding looks. Instead, what I saw was one laced with concern.

I sighed. "Let's hear it. I know you have plenty to say."

Grams took a sip from the cup in her hands before she looked toward the lake. "Grief does funny things to us, dear boy."

I swallowed, knowing she was speaking about Zander.

I'd just lost him not even three months ago, and my life was in a tailspin. Some days, I'd wake up with a thought in my head that I couldn't wait to tell Zander. I knew I'd hear his loud guffaw as soon as I got to the station. But then tentacles of the present would slowly ensnare me, and I'd remember that talking to him again was never going to be a possibility.

Last night was just an outcome of those tentacles having entangled me too tight.

"We all process loss in our own ways," Grams continued. "Some of us turn inward, more quiet and distant. Others throw themselves into work, or friends, or nights of fun to help us cope and to make us forget."

She gave me a knowing look. "But from having lived through a fair amount of loss in my life, I've come to realize that, for most of us, grief starts off as a catastrophic thunderstorm. It wipes away everything in its path; it floods every part of us like internal bleeding. But with time, it recedes. What once was a thunderstorm becomes a heavy rain, and then a steady sprinkle, to what eventually becomes a light mist."

I looked from the wet porch under our feet to the darkened sky and realized why she'd been sitting out here in the first place. It had just rained, and she was looking for one of her damn rainbows. The woman was obsessed with them.

A frown pulled down my mouth. "Does the light mist eventually go away, too?"

"No." She smiled sorrowfully at the cup in her hands. "You just get used to walking around with wet clothes."

Garrett sits down next to me with his elbows on his knees and his face in his palms. I squeeze his shoulder before laying my head back against the wall.

I stay like that until Mom and Douglas come back out of Grams' hospital room.

"Do you want to see her?" Mom asks me, wiping the tears under her eyes. "I know how much she would want you to visit with her."

Reluctantly, I get up, even though there's no part of me that wants to go into her room. But Mom is right. Grams would be pissed if I came all the way over here and didn't see her.

My throat closes, but somehow, I manage to open her door and walk inside.

She's laying on the hospital bed with a few machines surrounding her. Her skin is paler than she'd ever allow it to be, her eyes sunken in. But even in death, even as she lay there motionless and lifeless, she looks beautiful.

I find her hand and grasp it in mine, feeling it's cold pressure against my skin. It's as soft as it always was, but it's completely different, too.

I think about where she might be. Definitely heaven, if there is such a thing. I wouldn't be surprised if she was delivered to its pearly gates on a rainbow or maybe she flew up on a cloud.

"Hey, Grams," I start and clear my throat. "I'll try not to talk your ear off like I'm sure Garrett did. But . . ." I swallow through the thick building inside my throat. "Fuck, I'm going to miss you. And yeah, you're probably pursing your lips at me for cursing, but I'm not apologizing for it."

My vision blurs and my hand shakes under hers. "I'm going to miss you, Grams."

I wipe my eyes with my thumb. "I didn't say it enough, but I hope you know you meant the world to me. You set the bar so high, no one even comes close." I pause, chuckling mirthlessly. "Well, there's someone but . . . I think I fucked that up. And now she's gone, too."

My chin wobbles as I think of all the chats we had, all the summers I spent with her, and everything she taught me, from knotting a tie to baking a cake. "Who's going to tell me to get my head out of my ass now, Grams? Who's going to make me laugh and say the things I need to hear, even if I don't want to? Who's going to listen to all my nonsense?"

I shake my head. "No one, because no one can take your place, and no one ever will." A tear lands on her hand when I bend down to press a kiss to the back of it. "I love you, beautiful. From one end of the rainbow to another. Immeasurably."

Sniffling, I get up and wipe my eyes again before taking one more look at her. I'm just stepping out of her room when I follow Garrett's gaze to the end of the hall, and my heart stalls.

Mala's puffy red eyes stare back at me and before I even know what I'm doing, I'm rushing over to her.

Is she really fucking here?

She runs to meet me halfway, wrapping her arms around my neck and, for the first time all day, I allow myself to break down. I'd been holding it all in, keeping everything bottled inside like a fucking carbonated drink, ready to burst.

I didn't know how much I needed to see her.

Her.

Only her arms. Only her soft skin.

Only her whispered words.

Just her.

There's not another person in the world I want more.

My shoulders shake and my legs feel weak as I sob into her neck. I pull her flush with my body and she arches her back, holding me the way I'm holding her.

Her fingers tangle in my hair. "I'm so sorry, Dean. I'm so sorry." Her breath grazes the shell of my ear, and her hoarse voice has me tightening my arms around her. "I know how much she meant to you. She knew it, too. She loved you so much."

I mumble against her neck. "She's fucking gone, Mala. Just gone."

Mala's lips brush over the side of my face. "I know. I'm so sorry you didn't get to say goodbye."

My sobs finally quell but my chest still heaves. I pull back from her even though my body protests, and finally take her in. She's wearing that same dark skirt and black fishnet pantyhose from the day I saw her get into the car at her apartment. She's paired them with heeled shoes and a silvery gray blouse. And instead of the bun I'm used to at the top of her head, her hair flows down in a shiny curtain over her shoulders.

I love it and fucking hate it.

I clear my throat. "How did you . . .?"

"You told the chief, and he told Rohan . . ." She touches the burn mark on her wrist, and I notice she's still wearing her leather strap. When she looks back at me, there's vulnerability in her eyes, like she suddenly doesn't know if she should be here. "I didn't really think. I just took the first flight. I can stay at a hotel—"

"Why?" My nostrils flare and I hate how every one of my emotions feels jumbled. "Your boyfriend not okay with you staying with me?

Pain shines through her eyes, and I know she wants to snap back at me, but then she looks over my shoulder to where Grams' room is and her shoulders sink. "No, Dean. I just didn't think you'd want me close."

"Why?" I grit out, knowing damn well I'm hedging for a fight. I just don't know why. "Why wouldn't you think I'd want you near me?"

She raises her arms and slams them at her side, looking at me like I've lost my mind. "Um, I don't know, Dean. Maybe because you haven't talked to me in *months*. Maybe because everything feels different between us now."

I step in closer to her, towering over her. "Everything *is* fucking different between us—"

"You know what, Dean?" She huffs out a breath. "This isn't what I came here to do. I'm here because of you. *For* you. I knew you were hurting, and I wanted to be here."

"Then fucking *be here*, Mala!" I almost boom but end up

gritting it out, remembering we're in a hospital corridor. "Don't tell me you're here, only to give yourself an out by staying at a hotel!"

Her watery eyes bounce between mine. "I wasn't giving myself an out."

My eyes stay on her. "You sure fooled me. Because the way I see it, it's all you've been doing lately."

Her face falls, her chin hitting her collarbone before she nods and looks back up at me. Her eyes pleading, apologetic. She must see the crack in my facade, because she takes a step forward and wraps her arms around me again, putting her head on my chest. "Well, I'm here now."

Part Three

THE PRESENT

Theme Song: "Drive" by Incubus

Chapter Twenty-Eight

MALA

Present Day

FLAMES DANCE TO THE BEAT OF THE COOL BREEZE, MOCKING the somber mood all around them. I stare into the scintillating pyre, lost in thoughts of the past few days.

Since Mom and Dad's death, I'd been lucky enough to not have had to attend another funeral. There are times I feel guilty about it, but I don't really remember it. Like I was mentally missing during their last rites and cremation. It's unclear if the lack of those memories is a good or bad thing.

I remember the urns we received with their ashes better than the room I was standing inside. Better than the people who attended. Better than their condolences.

They were a happy teal color with gold edging for Dad, and an eggshell color with silver designs for Mom. I remember wondering what we'd do with them once their ashes were scattered in Lake Tahoe. Would we keep them on our mantel? Would we use them as vases? Would we pack them away so we could erase the memory of the day as much as possible?

In the end, I believe Rohan did the latter because I never saw those urns again.

Dean leans down to pick up his beer bottle wedged in the sand and takes a long swig. His eyes meet mine briefly before he plucks at the strings of his guitar and plays *Storms* by Fleetwood Mac.

He and Garrett exchange a few childhood memories of Grams, laughing softly, but my mind wanders again. Despite the reason I've been here over the past four days, it's been emotionally exhausting.

I've been *physically* close to Dean—sharing the same bed with him—but other than embracing him well into the morning while he sobbed into my chest that first night, forcing him to eat because he'd get so caught up in planning everything from the funeral to writing the obituary to planning a wake that he'd forget to eat, to holding his hand through the funeral, we haven't really spoken.

Not for the lack of me trying, though.

The bed dipped beside me and the familiar scent of sandalwood wafted into the surrounding air. I didn't know what time it was, but Dean and his mom were still talking well after I excused myself to retreat into our shared bedroom. I'd fallen asleep to their muffled voices and the tiny wet spot of tears on my pillow.

It didn't seem like he noticed when I left, anyway.

No matter how close we were physically or how our bodies wrapped around each other at night, all was erased in the morning, like two other people had performed the act.

He'd gotten upset when I told him I'd stay at a hotel, but he didn't seem to want me here, either. I knew he was hurting. He'd had to bear a loss almost as great as the loss of a parent, and I understood that all too well, so I wanted to give him that space. After all, I was here for him. To support him. To shoulder some of his pain.

But that didn't mean I didn't want to poke a little deeper.

Time was running out for us too, in a way.

In only a couple of days, I'd be heading to L.A., and we'd be going back to the way things had been before I came here.

Infrequent texts, occasional conversation, nonexistent bouts of laughter.

Dean laid on his back, his palms behind his head. Even though it was dark, I saw him blink up at the ceiling.

Instinctively, my hand moved to his chest and for a second, he tensed under it before he relaxed.

I was losing him. That much, I was sure.

It didn't mean I was coming to terms with it any more than I had over the past few months.

I blinked back the haze forming at the realization. "I miss you." I'd texted him the same thing, on the same day we both flew out here, before the news about Grams. "We . . . we need to talk, Dean."

He turned his head toward me. "Then talk."

"I . . ." My mouth opened and closed, words suddenly stalling inside my head. "I want us back. I want things to be the same as they were before . . . before . . ."

My chin wobbled. It was a night I'd never ever forget for as long as I lived, but a night I hadn't realized would cost us so much. A night that left me empty-handed with nothing but memories to replay in my head for the year to come.

Dean laughed softly, but the sound seemed to echo off the walls. "That's what you don't understand. Things can never be the same as before."

And with that, he turned to give me his back while I stared at it until my eyes closed again.

Dean's voice brings me back to the present. "She was the ultimate believer when it came to us." He stops strumming to take another sip of his beer. "Fuck, I'm going to miss her."

Darian leans back on his Adirondack chair and takes Rani's hand in his. She gazes at him softly, like he literally lights up the sky. Between her and Darian's incredible love, and Bella snuggled in Garrett's lap, the air feels even chillier where I'm sitting.

I'm so incredibly happy for them and wish them nothing but a lifetime of togetherness, but . . .

I look up at the spangled sky—twinkling like diamond dust scattered over the heavens—questioning my fate. My future. Is a happily-ever-after even written somewhere in the stars for me?

"I still remember when I spent part of a summer here when I was eight or nine. Every single night, your grandparents would watch WWE religiously," Darian says, staring into the bonfire.

Garrett chuckles softly, likely recalling their shared memory.

"She was a kooky little thing." Dean's choked rasp, his watery eyes visible only from my seat next to him, has my hand reaching out for his.

I grasp it in mine to tell him what I can't with words. What I want to say but feel too selfish to at this second. That I love him. That I always will.

He stares at it—my hand inside his—as if examining some sort of experiment. As if trying to figure out if he's happy with the results or not, before pulling it from my grasp.

And while my hand is left cold in his wake, that's not what kills me inside. It's the wake of *him*. The distance between us.

Dean starts strumming again and only three or four notes in, I realize it's our song. *Drive*. The one that had meaning for me for other reasons until he came along and changed it entirely. He became the reason behind the song. The only face I'd see whenever I heard it.

My heart throbs as I eye his profile. Is he trying to lodge the stake so deep, we can never remove it? Why play this song *now*? What gives him the right to dangle my feelings in front of me like a dead man on a noose? Does he get some sort of sick satisfaction from it?

Rani's yawn intermingles with the cracking of the embers

from the fire, and a few seconds later, both her and Darian retreat back into Grams' lake house. It's where we've all been staying the past couple of days.

The chilly breeze from the lake hits my bare legs, and I pull the sleeve of my sweatshirt over my palms, wrapping my arms around my chest before rising to my feet. "I think I'm going to take a little stroll around the beach."

I can't sit here for another minute. Not when he doesn't want me here, though he says he does. Not when his actions don't align with his words.

It's fine. I've done what I came here to do. Now I'm just drained, depleted like I've never felt before.

And it's not just him. It's everything. My life in LA, my job . . . my boss.

After the last time Jason asked me to a "celebratory" dinner—on my three-month job anniversary—and I refused, I can't say it's been the dream job I always thought it would be. Not quite a nightmare, either, but not one I spring out of bed for in the morning to get to.

I told him I didn't want him to get the wrong impression, and that I had "someone back home." So, I might have embellished a little, and while Dean wasn't my *someone back home* officially, he *was* the only one I thought about in that way.

Needless to say, Jason was put off and his promises to support me in managing a team of the size I was dwindled. It's not to say I'm doing a terrible job without his support—because I'm not, and it shows in our financial numbers—but it also doesn't make for the best work environment when your boss generally avoids you. It was disappointing that my rejection of his ulterior motives for a personal relationship and his attitude about that made going to work so painful.

I chuckle as my sneakers lightly dig into the pebbled sand, leaving the strum of Dean's guitar behind me.

Promises.

They're made only for one purpose, aren't they?

To be broken.

A few yards down the beach, I turn toward the lake, admiring the way the stars reflect and glitter across it.

I take a seat on a grassy patch, pulling my feet in front of me and hugging my knees. Everything aches, as if my body is nothing but a vessel for pain.

I know I have a lot to be thankful for, like my brother, his wife, and my adorable nephew. My friends, like Malcolm and Betty, who I still talk to often. But no one balms the loneliness inside my bones.

No one but him.

And it pisses me off that I put so much of myself into cultivating that friendship, that love and affection, only to have him strip it away in one night.

One night that he promised wouldn't change us, only to tell me—*show* me—that it had.

I turn my head, catching him strolling toward me. A gust of wind has a wisp of my hair snapping over my lips, and I drag it behind my ear, turning my head back toward the lake.

Why is he here now when all he seems to have wanted is to keep me away? I almost chuckle. Maybe he thought I'd get lost, taken by a wayward wave.

He's always been a caretaker, a protector.

Clearly, he couldn't take care of my heart.

A vision of him bashing Warren's face with his fist flashes behind my lids.

But if he doesn't want to be in my life, then what's the purpose of trying to protect me now? Is it so I don't disappear under his watch?

His voice startles me, despite knowing he's close. "You promised you wouldn't run away."

I almost throw my head back and laugh. I promised? *I*

promised? The man has fought one too many fires and clearly melted his brain cells.

After a pause, he clears his throat and starts again, "You promised to–"

Oh, hell no. He wants to throw blame? Well, he'd better be ready for me to toss some back his way.

"No, Dean." I shake my head and stagger onto my feet. "*You* fucking promised." I jab the breeze between us. "You promised nothing would change. You promised that night wouldn't affect us. Remember that? But it did, didn't it? It changed *everything*! And all the years prior to that, when you told me you couldn't, *wouldn't*, mess up what we have . . . or should I say, what we *had*? What happened to that promise, huh?" Anger, betrayal, and so much fucking sadness blends like a bitter cocktail inside my chest. "I waited for you. Eight fucking years, I stood on the sidelines, waiting for you . . ."

"Yeah?" he bellows. "As if I fucking *didn't*? You think you're the only one who had front-row seats to watch a show you never wanted to see?"

My hands fist at my sides and a current that's been building up slowly over the course of the past few months, maybe even years, canters through me. "So why didn't you say anything when you had the chance? Why wait until I was moving on?"

"Moving on?" His nostrils flare. "Is that what you call it, *sprinkles*? Because the way I see it, you weren't moving on; you were *running*."

I narrow my eyes. "Yeah, fine. I *was* running. But have you taken even one moment to consider why? Or is that too hard for you to do, given your brick of a brain?" I grit my teeth. "I was running because I was fucking tired. Tired of waiting, tired of wanting and wishing–"

"Wishing for what?" His gaze sears me, the frame of his broad chest carving itself against the dim light.

I shake my head, realizing my cheeks are wet, my tears pricking slightly under the chill. "It doesn't matter." I laugh hoarsely, like I've gone insane. Maybe I have. What else would anyone call the last nine years? "Why does it matter? I'm not the one who can make it matter. I never have been."

My eyes open only when his hands are wrapped around my biceps. I didn't realize I'd closed them. The determination in his features, the warmth of his hands and his closeness has my breath stalling. "Wishing for what, Mala? *Say it*."

My chin wobbles like the idiot I am. Crying about someone who will never be mine. But I'm tired of holding it all in. If we're going to torch this friendship anyway, then let's light the damn thing on fire and get on with our lives.

I sniffle, whispering, "For it to be me."

His eyes narrow and at first, I think he's going to shove away from me, as if he's been burned, but then I see it. The tears he's been holding back. Not tears because of this weekend or for the loss he just experienced, but tears caused by my words.

"Don't you fucking get it?" His palms cup my face and his warm breath fights with the cold against my lips, my cheeks. "It's *always* been you. From the moment you blazed into my life, it's been you. You were the reason I woke up, so I could see your face. You were the reason I slept, so I could dream about you. You were the reason I smiled, because you smiled back. And you were the reason I lived, because you made it impossible not to. You were the reason, *sprinkles*. You've always been *my* reason."

My breath stutters on an exhale, tears streaming down my face competing with the waves in the lake.

His hand tightens on my face. "I love you beyond words, beyond measure, beyond distance. I love you so fucking much, that when you left, I lived for an entire year as half of myself. Because you'd cruelly taken the other half with you and expected me to forget about it. You hadn't just made me promise not to let that night affect our friendship, you'd asked for more of the impossible–to forget it happened entirely. And while I was willing to pluck the moon from the goddamn sky for you, *that* was something I couldn't do. Forget you? Forget that night?" He shakes his head. "Never."

A sob emits from my throat unbidden. "So, what took you this long to tell me, you idiot?"

Before he even has a chance to answer, my mouth collides with his, crashing and melding in resignation. Not an ounce of fight is left inside me. I snake my hands behind his neck and pull him closer, arching my back so he can feel my breasts against his chest.

A low moan travels up through his throat, floating into the wind, but he never lets go. Everything between us connects so tightly, not even the air could get through. Our tongues clasp around each other just like our hearts have, and Dean reaches under my thighs, pulling me up so I'm wrapped around his waist. His erection prods my center, making it pulse with need.

Sincerity shines in his eyes. "I'm sorry, Mala."

I nod, cupping his jaw, while my heart thunders inside my chest. "You love me?"

He chuckles. "You just now heard that part?"

"No," I shake my head, pulling him in to kiss me again, "I just wanted to hear it again."

"I love you." He kisses down my neck and I arch so he can get more access. "I've always loved you."

He lowers to his knees, lying me on the sandy shore and placing his palm under my head. With his other hand, he searches for the buttons of my shorts, unfastening them and pulling down the zipper. He looks to my eyes for permission, and I give it to him wholeheartedly before he yanks my shorts off my legs completely. Neither of us can wait a second longer.

In record time, he unfastens his jeans, shoving them down his thighs and has his thick length springing out. He strokes it, hovering over me, but never unpins his eyes from mine.

"You're mine?" he croaks.

"Always have been. Always will be."

He lowers his head to kiss me. "I want you."

"I love you, Dean."

His breath stalls at my admission, his eyes softening just a touch as he lines up at my entrance. I feel the exquisite press of his piercing inside my folds, making me mewl in need. He runs the head of his erection through my wetness, and I notice that delectable flare of his nostrils again.

Inch by inch, he pushes until he's seated fully inside me, with his mouth at my shoulder. We both moan loudly, mine reaching the starry night and Dean's vibrating against the side of my neck.

Opening up my legs, I reach for his bare ass, pulling him further, deeper inside me before he starts to drive into me in rhythmic bursts. He pummels me into the sand with his palm still under my head while our mouths stay clasped.

I moan at the feel of him. His thrusts, and that jewelry at the end of his length knocks at my G-spot, creating an intense current zipping down my spine.

"You were made for me." His hips drive into me, his balls hitting my skin in a way I can't even describe.

I feel breathless and unsteady, almost at the cusp of collapse. And when I do, it'll be like a supernova. One the stars will watch while I watch them.

I wrap my legs around his waist and my arms around his neck. God, I love this man.

I'm seconds from shattering, like porcelain dropped on concrete.

I *was* made for him; I was born for him.

I've lived for him, and I'll die for him.

"Dean . . ." I can't get a breath in. "I'm . . . oh, God. I'm so . . . so . . . Please, don't stop."

Dean seems to understand my garbled speech. "Come for me, sweetheart. Come right now, or I'm pulling out and eating you out until you do."

Jesus. His filthy mouth. It does the trick though, because before he's even finished speaking, I'm fracturing from the inside out. My body tenses as my climax takes over. I can feel my skin ignite, my ears ringing, and my eyes shutting to take on the onslaught of Dean's continued thrusts.

"Fuck, yeah." He hammers into me. "God, you're so beautiful. So fucking beautiful and all for me."

I'm just coming down from my high, my wet center sensitive and still pulsing, when I feel Dean stiffen, followed by the familiar whoosh of his release coating my insides.

As his ragged breaths waft against my own and he tugs me closer into him, I look up at the sparkling sky, accepting this as their blessing. This dream, that feels so close to fulfillment, within a fingertip's reach.

Dean's fingers drag wisps of my hair off my face and his stare pierces mine. "Either you're moving back home or I'm moving to LA, but I'm not spending another goddamn second without you."

I smile as my fingers dig into the coarse hair around his jaw. I love the feel of his scruff over my skin. "I thought you'd never ask."

MALA

"You cut your hair. I like it." I run my hands through his still-longish locks, tucking them behind his ear.

I'm straddled around his hip, my knees on the mattress. His back is against the headboard in the room we're sharing at Grams' house and his hands cup my ass.

We took a shower together as soon as we walked back into the room—making out like teenagers. Moments after he'd rinsed the shampoo out of my hair, Dean was inside me again, taking me up against the wall.

And now, not even ten minutes after we've gotten into bed, his erection is straining under the panties he protested me wearing.

"And they say men don't notice things." He smirks, those beautiful creases forming around his mouth. But was there anything about this man I didn't find beautiful, enticing? "I lost a bet to Darian, and the bastard asked for my hair! I'm surprised you just noticed."

I smile, but it withers quickly. I hate that I didn't know the reason until now. "I noticed earlier, too. The day Grams died, when I was on a video call with Rohan and I saw you behind him." My chin drops, remembering how I'd felt when I saw him through the camera after months of not seeing or talking to him. "I just . . . we hadn't talked."

Dean lifts my chin with his fingers, his eyes tender. "Hey. Don't do that. We're all good now."

I nod, feeling that same knot in my throat. "I hate that we missed talking to each other all that time—an entire year where things felt off. I hate that I had to see your new hair—something you've *never* changed in all the time I've known you—through a call with my brother instead of you calling me to tell me about it or sending me a picture."

He leans in to press his lips to mine, his hands sliding up and down my back. "I love you, and I'm sorry I broke the promise I made you. I swear to you, I will never cut you out like that again."

"I hated every moment of it, Dean. I hated not being around you . . . *with you.*"

"You think it was easier for me?"

I shrug, knowing it'll annoy him, but still wanting more of that honesty and vulnerability he gave me earlier on the beach. "It didn't seem like you were struggling hard."

Dean stares at me, his eyes flaring slightly. I know he's trying to veil the hurt from his expression, but it's all too obvious. "Want to know how hard I struggled? Want to know how much I died every day without you?"

Yes. Call me selfish, call me a glutton; I don't care. But, yes, I want to know. I want to know because it's taken too long to get to this point, and all I want are his words. His truth.

I swallow, keeping my eyes on him.

"The night you told me you were moving—the night I came over to your place late and saw the boxes in your apartment—I was going to tell you I was in love with you. That I'd always been in love with you but had finally grown the balls to tell you."

I gasp softly. "But Jessie said—"

"Jessie didn't know shit." He pauses. "I even told Rohan."

"You talked to my brother?" I knit my brows, placing my hand on his bare chest, feeling his warm, taut skin and the light smattering of his hair under my fingers.

My brother knew?

"I'd spoken with him a couple of days before that. Told him exactly how I felt about you."

I think back to all the moments I've chatted with Rohan since then. We talked almost every single day. "He never said anything to me . . ."

Dean's hand envelops mine. "I made him promise not to, and even up until the day you were leaving, he begged me to tell you . . . but I couldn't." His blue irises swim with regret. "I couldn't hold you back like that, not when you'd finally gotten what you always wanted."

My eyes fill on their own accord and my hands wrap around his jaw. "*You're* what I always wanted, Dean. *You.* I just didn't . . . I didn't think you wanted me back. Plus, you told me it could never happen between us all those years ago . . ."

Dean sighs. "I was denying something my heart knew the second I met you. I've always wanted you, sweetheart. I just thought I was protecting you by staying away from you."

"Protecting me? From what?"

He shrugs, letting his shoulders fall. "From me." At my questioning gaze, he continues, "My job, my life . . . they're unpredictable. It would take one wrong move, one wrong decision, and I could lose it all." He brings my hand up to his lips, brushing them over it. "I didn't want someone I loved, someone who loved me back, to go through heartbreak like that, so I kept you at a distance."

I run the pad of my thumb across his jaw, loving the feel of his stubble under it. "So what changed?"

His eyes connect with mine, but I can tell he's somewhere else. "Someone once told me that life is short either way you slice it. It's our last chance to live, our last chance to love." He blinks as the haze clears and he pulls my face in his hands. "I didn't want to waste my last chance without you."

My face blooms with a smile and my hands follow a trail around his neck, tangling inside the hair at his nape. "I'm glad you came to your senses . . . even if you took the long way getting there."

Dean smiles, his plush lips impossibly beautiful against the hard lines of his jaw.

I clear my throat. "It was that day when Jessie came to the café to tell me she'd heard you speaking to someone on the phone at the grocery store about your feelings for a woman . . ." I gnaw at my bottom lip, feeling slightly nervous all of a sudden. "It was that day I knew I couldn't watch you start dating someone else again."

Dean lets out a breath, the warmth of it hitting my lips. "That woman was you, *sprinkles*. I was talking to Grams about you. She was the only one who knew before Rohan."

Dean leans his head back on the headboard as exhaustion settles in his eyes. It's been an emotionally draining few days, and I know this conversation isn't helping. Still, it needs to happen. There are too many years of missing communication and opportunities that need to be brought to light.

"Is that what made you decide to take that job?" His pained eyes rove over my face, his fingers trailing under my tank top. Despite the somber mood between us, the feel of them on my skin has my nipples pebbling and goosebumps sprinkling over my skin.

"It sounds stupid now that I think about it—that I made a

decision based on what Jessie said—but at the time, I truly believed you couldn't have been talking about me."

"I'm an idiot for not telling you sooner."

We stare at each other for a moment, our admissions both monumental and sad. Monumental for the fact that they're finally out in the open, but sad for the time it took for us to get here.

His voice is raspy when he speaks again. "I drove to LA to see you."

My fingers freeze in his hair. "When?"

He licks his lips, and it has me wanting to reach down and kiss them. I realize I can now. I can kiss him any time I want. I can kiss him without restraint.

"A month after you left." He looks to the side, avoiding my eyes as if his confession is something to be embarrassed of. "I wanted . . . I *needed* to see you, so I drove to your apartment."

"Wha—" A shocked whisper leaves my mouth. "You drove all the way back to see me?"

His gaze flicks back to me. "But then I saw you get into a car with some guy . . . and you looked happy, so I decided not to intrude."

"No, Dean." I shake my head. "The only guy whose car you could have seen me getting into is my boss's, and that's all he is to me. Nothing more, nothing less." I pause. "Why didn't you call or text me to tell me you were there?"

"I wanted to, but—" His throat bobs as he swallows. "But I didn't know where we stood. I didn't know if you'd moved on. And if you had, I didn't want to put you in a weird position to choose between me or your new job or this other person—"

"Dean." I hold his face, inching my body closer to him.

No matter how close we are, my body wants more. More of his exquisite sandalwood smell. More of the feel of his warm skin and sculpted form near mine. More of him.

"No job, no person, no dream compares to you. You're it. *You're* my person." I blink rapidly, feeling the press of tears behind my eyes. "The irritating and charming man who's made me laugh since the moment we met. The man I've been in love with longer than I can remember. It wouldn't have been a choice for me when I'd already chosen you."

Dean lets out a deflated breath. "I fucked up, *sprinkles*. I let so much time pass—"

I lean in to kiss his lips, stopping him from saying more. "We both did. But let's not do that again."

Our kiss deepens when Dean pulls me over his erection—the sweetest slide of his hard length at my center. I can feel myself getting wetter, my stomach clenching with need. My nipples feel almost painful against the fabric of my shirt and my clit throbs as he drags me back and forth over him.

"Dean." I moan into his mouth, grasping his soft hair. "I want you."

His hand travels up my stomach and over my breast, thumbing my nipple before he pulls my tank top off. Licking over my scar, as if to make sure he gives it all his attention, he finally pulls one of my nipples into his mouth. He kneads my ass, dragging me over his length again and again while he sucks and bites on my nipple.

My skin heats, a flush creeping up my body as I feel my juices drench my panties.

Letting my nipple go and moving to the other, Dean pulls my underwear aside, exposing my slick center. I raise my hip, grabbing his erection in my small hand before running the pierced head between my folds, circling my clit. I hiss at the contact, hearing a soft groan from Dean.

When I can't take it another second, I line him up at my entrance. We both watch raptly as I slide down over it.

He disappears inside me, inch by delicious inch, and Dean's breath hitches just as my own gasp fills the air between us. The way his thickness stretches and fills me, the feel of him throbbing inside me, the press of the two metal beads against my G-spot has me practically shuddering.

With my hands secured on his shoulders, I lift up again, watching him come almost all the way out—wet and veiny—before I slide all the way back down.

"Fuck, baby." Dean curses, his nostrils flaring and eyes like two black pearls. The hunger in his expression has my heart flipping inside my chest, knowing I put that look there. "Look at how good you take me."

I lift up and down on his heavy length again and again while Dean grabs my ass with one hand, guiding me over him, as his thumb circles my clit.

"Oh, Dean! Fuck, that feels good." I throw my head back, bouncing over him, taking him deeper and harder with each thrust.

His thumb rubs my center lazily as he watches me fuck him. "That's it, baby. Take my fucking cock just like that."

There's so much lust and heat in his eyes, I'm shocked it hasn't caused the walls to burn, but there's something else in them, too. Something we can finally name.

Wonder, surrender . . . love like no other.

Every emotion flashes across his face as I continue to rock over him. My breaths come out in sharp pants, and I'm just about to come—so fucking close, I'm right at the edge—when Dean flips me over on to my back.

"Wha—?" I land with a *thud* as my breath shoves out of me.

But before I can protest, Dean has my knees pulled open and his face buried inside my pussy. I moan and mewl at the feel of his tongue against my throbbing center.

A moment later, he growls in disagreement, lifting his mouth before pulling my panties off, as if they were offending him.

Once he's tossed them to the floor, he goes back to

stroking me with his tongue, and I shove my hand into his hair, arching to meet his every lash and lick. "Oh, God, Dean! Please! Please!"

Dean laps at my entrance like he'll die if he doesn't before he circles my clit. "Love the way you taste." He plunges his tongue into me, groaning, while my thighs tremble around his head. "Needed you on my tongue."

I moan, my head turning this and that way over the pillow, my orgasm on the brink of release. My hand tightens in his hair and I shamelessly grind my sex against his mouth, letting the current of my release travel down the length of my body.

I come so hard against his tongue, I can feel the vibration of his name from my lips all the way into my stomach.

Dean continues his feast over my still pulsing clit before the scrape of his scruff becomes almost too much, and I squirm under him.

He glides over me and the primal look in his eyes does nothing to settle my heart rate. I've seen that hunger in his gaze before, and damn if I don't feel sexy being on the receiving end of it.

My knees open in invitation as he hovers over me on his elbows and our eyes lock. I trail my hand down the hard ridges of his abs until I grasp his cock, rubbing my thumb over his tip, playing with his beads. I pull them lightly, making him hiss in agreement.

Fisting my hair in one hand, Dean takes my mouth against his and, before long, I'm moaning and humming into the kiss as I stroke him between us.

He pulls back, panting against me as his eyes rake over my face, my neck. His eyes flare as they roam over my chest, my mangled skin. "So fucking beautiful."

I line him up against me again, and Dean enters me in one smooth thrust. My fingernails press into his firm, muscled back as he drills me into the mattress, giving just as much with each thrust as he takes.

I feel the beginnings of another orgasm kindling in my core when Dean leans on one arm and clasps his hand around my throat.

I've noticed how much he loves this position—being able to lock his eyes with mine as he possesses me from head to toe. He looks spellbound, enraptured as he continues his tempo, thrusting in and out of me until I'm begging for release.

"Please, Dean! Oh, God!" My voice shakes with each word.

I know he's close, too; I can tell by the clench of his jaw and the slight droop in his eyes. He drives into me deeper, and I tilt my hips to meet him, thrust for thrust.

"You ready to come for me again, beautiful? You like my cock?"

Thrust, drive, pound.

Thrust, drive, pound.

I can barely catch my breath, but I mewl and mumble in response.

Dean pulls his hand off me, and the second his fingers circle over my swollen nub, my body tenses in pleasure. I clench hard around him and groan out another release.

For the quickest second, Dean's eyes flash before he buries his face into my neck. His movements become jerky before I wrap my legs around his torso, pulling him into me as far as I can. With one more final thrust, his body shudders and he rolls his hips slowly, taking every ounce of his pleasure before he stills.

A moment later, he pulls out of me before laying on his side, facing me. We both breathe harshly, staring into each other's eyes.

Dean lifts his hand to drag a strand of my hair behind my

ear. His gaze is so soft, so tender, my heart feels like it's being hugged from the inside.

"What are you thinking?" I whisper, turning my face into his hand and placing a kiss to the center of his palm.

A slow grin dances on his face. "About all the ways I want to fuck you after this. All the ways I want to fuck you for the rest of our lives."

The rest of our lives . . .

"Gosh, you really know how to woo a gal," I tease, even as my heart does a somersault.

The rest of our lives . . .

He pulls me into him, my nose against the base of his neck, his chin resting on my head, and my arms wrapped around him. I press soft kisses over his collarbone, dragging my nose over his skin, and feel his arms tighten around me.

I'd always figured he'd be a cuddler, and I'm totally fine with it. In fact, it might be my most favorite thing. Well, besides his smile, his blue-as-a-summer-sky eyes, and his luscious hair—whether long or short.

"I was actually thinking about next steps," he murmurs after a long silent moment passes between us.

I look up at him, kissing the bottom of his jaw. "Hold that thought. I need to get cleaned up."

I rush out of bed, all naked and not very lady-like, feeling Dean's eyes on my ass. Once in the bathroom, I quickly clean up and walk back, grabbing my panties from the ground and putting them back on while Dean grumbles in protest.

Once I'm back in bed, he pulls me in—his big spoon to my little—wrapping his arm around me and stretching his hand out possessively on my stomach.

"Now, tell me what you were thinking about next steps." I look over my shoulder and he brushes his lips on my cheek, my temple, my shoulder.

"I looked into an open position at the fire department near your apartment."

I take in a soft breath. "You–"

"Well, it's actually closer to your work, but I think that would be okay. I don't know what kind of shifts I'd have–maybe two days on, two days off–but we could commute together if it worked out."

I can't not look at him. Turning around in his arms, I grasp his face and kiss his lips. He pulls me closer and I trail my tongue into his mouth, tightening my hands over his jaw.

Of all the things I'd expected in terms of next steps–the first being that he'd ask me to move back–I hadn't expected that he'd already have looked into moving near me. And it's clear he has no idea how deeply that sweet gesture affects me.

I pull out of our kiss, trying to get air into my lungs. "You would move to L.A. for me?"

"Sweetheart, I don't care if it's Antarctica, Timbuktu, or Mars. I'd move anywhere for you." He sees my wobbly smile and adds, "Because if you're there, I'd be home."

I speak around that damn knot in my throat. "I love you, Dean Emerson Meyer. I don't want to live another second without you."

He runs his nose along mine, leaving a kiss on my lips. "Good, because you don't have to."

"But," I say, finding his eyes again, "you don't have to leave your job in Tahoe. I'm actually putting in my resignation as soon as I get back and returning to the bakery."

His eyebrows lift. "What? Are you sure? It's been your dream to work there. Why would you quit?"

I shake my head. "It was a dream after I graduated college, yes. But it isn't what I want to do now. I miss running my bakery. I miss what I had for all those years in Tahoe."

"Are you sure you really want to come back?"

I nod. "One hundred percent. Betty and Samantha are

doing great running it on their own, but Betty's getting older. She hasn't been in the same health as before." I smile. "Both her and Samantha will be happy to know I'm coming back."

Dean's smile lifts before it drops completely and his eyes narrow, like he just remembered something he didn't want to. A vein pulses in his temple. "And what about your *boss*?" he grinds out. "What will he have to say?"

I grin, pinching his nipple and hoping to make him flinch, but he doesn't move even slightly. "Sparky, do you think I'd let you be inside of me for the past, oh," I look over at the clock on the wall, "three hours, if anyone else was even a consideration in my life?"

That seems to stop his caveman nostril-flaring before his eyes turn dark again. "Turn around and get on your knees. With all those dog names you're always calling me, at least let me live up to them for the next three."

Chapter Thirty

MALA

Two Months Later

Isn't it funny how a certain sound or smell can take you back in time or soothe you the same way a bowl of chicken soup can when you're sick or a warm blanket does when you're cold?

It's the way I feel when I'm enveloped in the freshly baked scent of bread or the sweet perfume of vanilla icing wafting through the bakery. It's the same way I feel when the bell chimes over the café door.

At home. At peace.

Like I belong.

I belong *here*.

It wasn't easy putting in my resignation with Jason all those weeks ago. Despite us barely talking much over the last year–after I declined his offer for dinner multiple times–he made it seem like it came as a complete shock.

"You're resigning?" His suited form filled the entrance of my office while his blue eyes studied me sorrowfully.

I was in the middle of putting away a few files. I'd need to clear my desk in the upcoming week, too. "Yes." I glanced at him, then went back to what I was doing. As far as I was concerned, he hadn't come through on his end of the bargain to support me every step of the way, so I didn't owe him much more than that glance.

I'd learned almost everything on my own, and while I wasn't one to be dependent on anyone, I certainly wasn't a fan of the concept of "trial by fire," either.

I'd come out the other end of a *real-life* trial by fire with all my body parts still intact and considered it to be enough of a victory.

"Why?" I felt the intensity of his eyes on me.

I stopped what I was doing and stared back at him, trying to put on my sincerest smile. "Thank you for the opportunity to be a part of this team, Jason. I've learned a lot in my short time here, but it's not really what I want to do."

"It's not really what you want to do?" he repeated, scoffing. "So what do you really want to do? Run your little bakery in your little town with your little customer base?"

I sat back in my chair, not giving him the satisfaction of showing that his condescension affected me. Because, in all honesty, it didn't. "Yes."

He huffed. "You're making a mistake, Mala. You're walking away from an opportunity of a lifetime; a chance most people would throw everything they had away for."

"I don't believe in throwing everything away for a chance, Jason." I smiled. "But I will throw everything away for a sure thing. And what I have in Tahoe . . . he's a sure thing."

The double doors open to the back of the bakery, and Samantha's wide smile peeks out behind a bouquet of flowers. She's holding a little gift bag with tissue paper sticking out of it, too.

If there ever was a list of criteria written for what makes someone the perfect sister-in-law, she checks them all. She's supportive, sweet, and hands-off. Not hands-off in a way where she doesn't care, but more like she trusts my decisions. *Ahem, completely opposite to my big brother, of course.* He still calls me ten minutes after sending me a text if I haven't responded to it by then.

"There's a special delivery for a 'Mala Sharma.' Know anyone by that name around here?"

I roll my eyes, wiping my hand on my apron. I close the distance between me and my flowers before grabbing the giant bouquet from Samantha's hands. She puts the gift bag on a nearby counter.

"Do you need any help for tomorrow night?" she asks, lingering at the door, watching me bury my nose in the unique bouquet of flowers.

I shake my head, my chest feeling warm, my senses enveloped with a sweet perfume. "No, Dean and I have it covered. I'm making pizza from scratch, and Dean's making his secret orange velvet pound cake. I'm also making sangria."

"Ooh!" My sister-in-law gleams. "Fancy. What movie are we watching?"

I giggle, thinking about my conversation—or argument, rather—with Malcolm the other day when I told him what movie we'd be watching. "*Ghost* with Patrick Swayze and Demi Moore."

The number of times Malcolm repeated, "Oh, hell nah!" has my smile stretching uncontrollably. God, I missed him and our *movie madness* nights. I missed the entire group.

Samantha snorts. "Oh, I'm sure Malcolm and Rohan are going to *love* that."

I laugh, finally putting the large vase on the counter. "You know, half the reason I pick the movie is so I can watch them as they watch it. The torture on their faces is pure gold."

She laughs with me, turning back toward the double doors. "God, you're evil, but I love you for it." She winks over her shoulder. "I'll leave you to tend to your flowers in peace."

I whisper my thanks to her before turning around to inspect my bouquet.

A confused smile plays on my lips when I regard it closely. Not a single flower looks like another. There's a yellow rose, a stem of a blue hydrangea, a blush-colored dahlia, a carnation, a tulip, a stargazer lily, and more I don't know the names of.

I pluck out the little note stuck inside it. It's not signed, but it doesn't need to be.

> I didn't know what your favorite flower was, so I got you one of each kind.
>
> P.S. Since you refuse to get that tattoo we talked about, I got the garments inside the bag personalized. I suppose I'll settle for seeing you in those.

I huff out a laugh, not understanding what the heck he's talking about, before reaching for the gift bag. I take out the tissue paper and pull out one of the seven, very silky and very expensive-looking, panties.

Holding it in front of me, I throw back my head and laugh after I read his name and declaration on the backs of each one, and remember the conversation I had with him last week after he gave me not one, but eight orgasms in the span of a few hours.

After the last one, he placed his head on my lower back while I laid on my stomach with my head turned to the side, resting on the backs of my hands. Dean made little circles at the base of my spine with the tip of his finger that elicited little shivers from me now and again.

"You should get a tattoo," he murmured, as if he was helping me decide on an outfit to wear, like, 'You should wear this purple dress.'

I snorted. "You're right. It's exactly what's been missing from my life all these years."

He bit my bare ass gently and I squirmed, giggling. "But seriously, you should," he repeated.

"Uh-huh. And what, pray tell, should I get a tattoo of?" I bit my bottom lip, closing my eyes and taking in the moment. It was one of many moments I'd enjoyed with him over the course of the past couple of months. And each moment contributed to my colossal, earth-shattering love for him.

"Right here." He made a circle on the center of each of my ass cheeks and my stomach clenched. Only he was capable of bringing about a full-body tremble with just the slightest of touches. "You should get the words, 'Property of Dean Emerson Meyer' written on each one of these cheeks."

"Hmm," I hummed, pretending to consider his preposterous idea. I swallowed an oncoming laugh, knowing I was about to piss him off. Preparing myself for his flared nostrils and caveman chest-thumping. Not like the idea of inking myself with his name and ownership wasn't caveman enough. "That seems reasonable enough, except . . ."

He tensed. "Except?"

"Except, what will I tell all the other boyfriends that come after you?"

Before I could even prepare for his reaction, I was turned around with Dean hovering over me. How he'd crawled up my body and had his flared nostrils and clenched jaw in my face so fast, I'll never know. His heavy erection settled between my legs, and I relished under his solid weight.

"Just for that, I'm going to need you to tattoo your forehead, too."

I giggled, but then my smile washed off as I laid there, looking from his clear blue eyes, framed by those dark lashes and thick eyebrows, to his plush pink lips. "Is it not enough that you're tattooed on my soul? It's been yours from the moment we met."

He shook his head. "Soul, heart, mind, skin. I want it all."

I lifted to brush my lips to his before I felt him nudge my entrance open with the pierced tip of his erection. "You have it all."

~

I DRAG my nose through Sage's warm head, his dark and soft curls tickling my skin. He takes a deep inhale, settling further into my arms, and I watch his little eyelids flutter. His lips twitch in his sleep, and I almost wonder if he's about to smile.

He's a hot sleeper. I can see the beads of sweat forming on his forehead, but apparently, this is just a normal thing for him. No matter how low the A/C is running, the boy sweats like he's running a marathon in his dreams.

I lay a kiss on his cheek before placing one on his closed fist. When I look up, I feel a set of lips on my temple.

I've been sitting between Dean's legs on the ground, while holding my sleeping nephew in my arms, while Rohan and Samantha cuddle on one couch and Malcolm and his girlfriend, Denise, take the other.

I tilt my head up and Dean answers with a kiss before moving his mouth to my ear. "I can't wait."

A crease forms between my eyes and I whisper back, "What?"

His gaze falls to my nephew's head on my chest before it comes back to meet mine. We're locked in a silent exchange when the music to *Unchained Melody* by the Righteous Brothers starts, and I faintly recall we're in the middle of the movie.

My eyes drag to the scene on the screen, my breaths heavy for an entirely different reason.

I watch as Molly, played by Demi Moore, sways with the ghost of her boyfriend, Sam, played by Patrick Swayze. And even though I've seen this movie before, the moment is so heartbreaking between them, it's hard not to feel that constriction in my throat, the longing for them to somehow be together again.

But maybe some stories are destined for tragedy. Maybe some stories are more beautiful *because* of their tragedy.

It's a scene that has Rohan shifting in his seat, and right when the tightness in my throat seems almost unpalatable, I hear Malcolm's sniffles.

At first, I don't think I'll be able to hold back my impending sob, but the way he shakes his head in his hands has my mouth lifting upward.

My gaze flies to Samantha's, who is pinching her lips in between her teeth, before it finds Denise. I'm not sure that she's been in Malcolm's life long enough, which is why her expression is a mixture of both panic and discomfort at the sight of him breaking down.

I should feel like an asshole, but I can't help the muffled chuckle that escapes my lips, only to transform into an all-out laugh. I try not to let my shoulders shake so as to not awaken Sage, but my smile stretches almost painfully.

Malcolm pinches the bridge of his nose after wiping the bottoms of his eyes. "Man, fuck this shit." He sniffles, peeking through his hands at the TV, like he can't help himself, before shutting his eyes and shaking his head again.

He finally opens his eyes and turns with a finger pointing toward me. "You."

I cackle softly, hoping not to wake up Sage.

"You're never *ever* allowed to pick movies. Always picking the worst shit. I can't sleep for days after—"

I laugh harder and feel the rumble of Dean's laugh against my back.

"You're sick in the head. Watching all this sad shit. What's wrong with you?" He quickly turns to his girlfriend as if just realizing she's there. "Baby, you know I'm not like this. I'm fucking hard—tough as nails. Stony interior *and* exterior, you feel me?" He shrugs. "Just had a tough week, that's all. It all caught up with me, and this movie got me in the feels."

Denise rubs his back. "I understand. Need a tissue, sweetie?"

Malcolm nods with a frown. "Yeah. Just give me the whole box." He brings his accusatory glare to me while I put my hand on my mouth to hold back more of my laugh.

In all the time I've been back, I haven't thought of LA once, not even for half a second.

Why would I when everything I've ever wanted is here, in this room?

"So, you're telling me dogs and humans can eat these?" Bella stabs a corner of the mini peanut butter cake with her fork and hums around the bite. "This is fucking delicious, Mala."

I nod over my crossed arms atop the bone-shaped bistro table at the café, feeling pleased with our new concoction. "We're coming up with new recipes every day."

"I could probably even get Darian to eat one of these." Rani wipes the corner of her mouth with a napkin. "I swear, the man has no appreciation for stress-eating or dessert in general. He eats rabbit food all day."

I nod at her empty plate. "Well, it does have carrots and apples in it, so *technically*, it could be considered rabbit food."

Bella came into town a couple of nights ago with Garrett. She and Rani are actually cousins and have an incredible bond—one much like sisters would—though they have very different personalities, with Bella being more cautious and guarded and Rani more lackadaisical and bubbly.

Either way, they've always been really warm and friendly with me. I can't recall when I first met both of them—some Meyer family event, perhaps—but it wasn't until Grams' funeral that I got to know them better. We even chatted about the Meyer brothers and their . . . unique personalities and antics. Despite the occasion and the weird tension between me and Dean at the time, I actually laughed quite a lot in their company.

And when Dean and I broke the news to all of them about us working things out and becoming a couple, both Rani and Bella had similar reactions, saying something like, "Well, it's about damn time!"

So now, whenever Bella visits Tahoe—or on the rare occasions I've driven to the East Bay—the three of us make it a point to hang out and catch up.

Like today, when they both decided to come see me at the café.

I'm just about to tell Rani that I'll pack a box of the mini cakes for her to take home so Darian and Arman can try them, when the doorbell chimes and I hear a Southern drawl I haven't heard in quite some time.

"Well, hey there stranger! How have you been, Betty? Didn't realize you still worked here. Usually Samantha's the one at the counter."

I turn over my shoulder to see Jessie greeting Betty. Same red hair with the bangs just a bit too long over her eyes. But . . . she looks different, too.

Betty gives her a polite smile. "Good to see you, Jessie. Samantha's in the back baking. What can I get you to drink?"

Betty chances a glance in my direction, and Jessie's head snaps to follow her gaze. Her eyes widen when she sees me.

"Well, I'll be! If it isn't my old boss, Mala Sharma, at her old stompin' grounds!" Jessie eyes the two ladies sitting by me as she walks up to our table, dismissing a waiting Betty. "I heard you were back in town, so I thought I'd come by and see for myself."

I excuse myself from the table and get up to give Jessie a hug. "Good to see you, Jessie." I smile down at her obviously pregnant belly under the long maxi dress. "I see congratulations are in order. How have you been?"

She runs her palm over her stomach. "Oh, well, I've been busier than a moth in a mitten, as you can see. Been seein' this guy named Todd for a while now, and," she looks down and smiles at her swollen belly, "we're havin' a baby boy. He's due in about three months."

"That's great, Jess. I'm so happy for you!"

She straightens as if just realizing she got carried away with her emotions and blows at her bangs. "Well, I suppose I should be saying the same thing to you?"

My brows fold. "What do you mean?"

She tilts her head as if waiting for me to figure it out, but when I don't respond, she adds, "You and Dean? Mala, this is a small town and I'm not one to gossip, but I won't play deaf, either. Now, don't pee on my leg and tell me it's rainin'. I'd love nothin' more than just the truth."

Her mouth turns downward and, despite the fact we're not close, my heart still tugs for her. I know how much she cared about Dean.

"Was it *you* he was talkin' about that day when I heard him on the phone at the grocery store? Has he always had feelins' for ya?"

I grasp her hand. "Jess, who he was talking about when you heard him, is something you'll have to ask him yourself. I won't lie to you . . . mine and Dean's relationship has been complicated from the start, but if there's one thing I can reassure you of, it's that he never cheated on you. He cared about you deeply, and I believe he always will."

She seems somewhat satisfied by my answer, processing it for a moment. "And now you're together? As in . . . you're seein' him?"

I nod. "Yes."

She swallows. "Well, I appreciate you bein' honest. I

suppose I shouldn't be *that* surprised. Though I am surprised it didn't happen sooner."

I huff out a laugh because . . . well, that's *literally* the story of mine and Dean's life. "I guess we just took the long scenic route to get to each other."

"Well, I'm happy for you, hon, but here's a little cautionary advice from someone who was on the Dean Meyer roller coaster for longer than I shoulda been. The man is plagued by his own demons, and you might could think all your love will save him from 'em, but they won't. Not until he decides that there is somethin' bigger living for than his fears. Will that be you?" She shrugs. "Maybe, maybe not."

I lift my head, feigning confidence I don't quite feel all of a sudden. "Thank you for the warning, Jessie."

She pulls me in for another hug. "I know things didn't end well for me and Dean, but tell him I said hi, will ya? It took a while, but I did move forward and I'm . . ." She takes a breath as if overwhelmed with emotion again. "I'm really happy now. And I'm happy Dean is, too."

"I promise I'll tell him you said hello."

"I'll talk to you later then, Mala. It was good seeing you."

She heads to the door and for reasons I can't quite pinpoint, I stare after her well past when she's gone.

Chapter Thirty-One

DEAN

LIFE FEELS LIKE A DREAM.

A fantasy I can't fathom waking up from now that I've seen how beautiful it truly is.

This is what I was missing all these years. The woman I love in my arms, like the goddamn vision she is. Her hair splayed out on the pillow, her sweet lemon scent floating over me, inside me.

Her eyes flutter open before she blinks a couple of times, a smile pulling up the corners of her mouth. She lets me look at her, hold her, breathe her in.

Her groggy voice has me smirking. "How's my creeper doing this morning?"

My fingers trail down her stomach, under the waistband of her panties. Why she refuses to sleep in the nude is beyond me—it'd make my life so much easier. "Considering I haven't seen you in forty-eight hours . . . hungry."

It's been almost three months since Mala moved back to Tahoe. Almost three months that we've been living together, and three months where I've had her in my arms on all the nights I spend at home.

But if there's one thing I now hate about my job, it's the overnight shifts. Never in my entire life have I ever had an issue with spending more time at the station, until now.

She latches her palm around my wrist, stopping it from diving further. "Aunt Flo is visiting, so you probably don't want to do that."

I drop my head to her neck, kissing and licking her skin down to her scar, continuing the downward journey to her slick center with my fingers. "I don't give a fuck which of your family members is visiting; no one is going to stop me from making you come."

She whimpers as I circle her clit with my middle finger before I trail my tongue down to the top of her breast. I peel down the top of her tank top with my teeth, and Mala shifts so her gorgeous tits peek out.

I take a nipple in my mouth, sucking it, before playing with it on my tongue. My eyes fall to the other nipple. "Pinch the other one for me."

She's panting and squirming under my touch as I press two fingers inside her, but she does what I ask. "Dean . . ."

Fuck, I love the way she says my name, the way her eyes shut tight, and the way she shoves her head back into the pillow, sucking in soft gulps of air.

I continue to lick and play with her nipple, loving the feel of her pebbled bud over my tongue, while my fingers dive in and out of her.

Mala digs her teeth into her bottom lip, her tan chest and neck flushing slightly. "Oh, God."

I press my thumb over her clit while I pull my mouth off one nipple and place it over the other, sucking and teasing it just the same. She buries her hand in my hair as she lifts her hips in time with my fingers, taking from them what she needs.

"That's it. Fuck my fingers," I say, listening to her groan and mewl under my touch.

A few moments later, I feel her clench around me, her breathing ragged as she comes over my fingers with a low groan.

I find her mouth with mine, swiping my tongue against hers. I'll never tire of this.

Pressing another kiss to her mouth, I lift my brow. "Stay right here. I'm just going to clean up."

She groans, squeezing her eyes shut. "God, so embarrassing."

My brows pinch. "That was, by far, the hottest thing I've ever seen. Why would it be embarrassing? Don't believe me?" I get out of bed to show her exactly what I mean, looking down at my cock bobbing against my stomach. "Case in point. There's not a single thing about you my dick doesn't find appealing."

She giggles as I shuffle off to the bathroom.

I come back to bed, pulling her to me the way I love—with her face tucked under my neck and her arms around me, my nose on her hairline.

It's early, right past five, and I know she has to meet Samantha at the bakery, but all I want is to hold her for a few more minutes, breathing in her scent and feeling the delicious weight of her in my arms, her much smaller frame against my larger one.

"Dean?"

Her soft whisper against my skin has me drawing her even closer. I stroll my hand over her back, making her shudder in my arms. I love that the smallest of movements from me gets that kind of reaction. "Yeah?"

She looks up at me, a mix of mischief and vulnerability in her eyes. This is new. I've seen both those looks separately, but never entangled the way they are now.

"Remember that day all those years ago when I told you I thought you were good looking?"

I run the tip of my nose over hers, trying to hold back a grin but failing. "I believe your exact word was 'gorgeous.' Or wait . . . I think it was 'god-like' or 'magnificent.' It's all a little blurry, so you might want to remind me. Feel free to add more adjectives."

She snorts. "Pretty sure I used *none* of those words, and I refuse to placate you fishing for compliments."

I sigh. "After that earth-shattering orgasm I gave you, it's the least you could do."

She giggles. "Fine. I said you were hot." She kisses my jaw. "And you are. So fucking hot."

"Now you're just fishing for another orgasm."

"Unfortunately, I need to figure out a way to untangle myself from your steel grip and get to work."

I tighten my arms around her. "What were you going to ask me when you asked about that day?"

She pauses, seemingly thinking about her question. "Why were you so upset when I said that?"

I try to recall my reaction from that day, but I remember the other thing she told me. Not being able to control the irritation that surges inside me at the thought of that fucking piece of shit who had the gall to lay a hand on her, I grind my molars. "Probably because it was the same day you told me you were going to move in with that asshole ex-boyfriend of yours."

Mala shifts in my arms, placing her hands around my jaw. "Firstly, stop your molar grinding and nose flaring. As sexy as it is, I'm seriously afraid you're going to need dental surgery." Her smile drops when she sees I'm not laughing. "He's gone, Dean. You made sure of it, and I'm grateful for having you there to be by my side during that time in my life."

"It fucking killed me, Mala. I hated the thought of you

with anyone, but it killed me to see you with him. I would have strangled him—" I take in a shaky breath as memories flood my brain.

The tears pooled in her eyes, the bruise on her shoulder, the way she hid it from me. I should have known he was going to hurt her. I should have protected her better. I should have—

"Dean." Mala's voice has me focusing back on her face, and I notice her eyes shimmer from behind a wall of tears. "You *did* protect me. You've always protected me."

I realize I must have said some of my thoughts out loud.

"I should have broken his goddamn arm," I grit out.

She presses her lips to mine. "I didn't bring any of this up to stir up bad memories." She nips my lip with a smile, and I know she's trying to take me out of the funk I'm in. "So back to what I originally asked. I told you I thought you were attractive—"

"Hot."

She giggles. "Right. *Hot.* I told you I thought you were *hot* before I told you about moving in with Warren. But . . . you seemed pissed, and I never understood that. Then you ran off to Colorado."

I huff out a breath and a soft laugh. "I wasn't angry at you. I was pissed at myself. Pissed at the situation, knowing you were with him and I couldn't do anything about it. I'd finally admitted to myself I wanted you . . . but I couldn't have you. I couldn't kiss you when that was the only thing I wanted to do."

"So . . ." She clears her throat. "What about after that? After Warren and I broke up, and the times you and Jessie were broken up, too? Was the reason you didn't say anything about your feelings for me then related to what you told me after Grams' funeral? Because you were trying to protect me from you?"

My voice is raspy. "Yeah. I was an idiot."

She nods, not disagreeing, but I wonder what's fueled her thoughts. "And now? Are you no longer afraid of those same things now?"

I gaze into her chocolaty eyes. "If I was scared before, I'm terrified now, sweetheart. Now I know exactly what I'd lose; I know exactly what's at stake." I swallow. "But I also refuse to lose my last chance to love."

SHE'S STANDING in the backyard of her bakery, looking out through the wire fence at seemingly nothing. A couple of dogs play off-leash behind her while their owners converse with cups in hand.

Her hips swing from one side to the other, her toned legs long under her shorts and sneakers. Even from where I stand inside the café, I can see her biting her thumbnail, deep in thought.

She doesn't wear those bulky sweatshirts during the warmer days anymore—opting for T-shirts and tank tops—and I'm so fucking proud of her. Not because I cared what she ever wore—because, let's be honest, she'd look gorgeous in a garbage bag if that's what she chose to wear—but because I am so proud of how far she's come.

She's always been witty and strong—*so damn strong*—but now her confidence shines through. She no longer hides behind bulky clothing, hoping no one asks her about her past. Now she displays that past like a prized possession, an accolade of her survival. In fact, I don't recall even seeing her touch the smaller scar on the inside of her wrist in all the time she's been back.

My beautiful, incredible girl.

I couldn't survive without her. How did I survive this long without being able to call her mine?

And with everything we'd shared with each other over the past three months, I know exactly what I mean to her, too.

I know exactly what it would do to her if something happened to me . . .

I shove the thought aside, walking toward the back door to get to her, even as another thought springs up unbidden.

You're being selfish and reckless. Willing to hurt the one person who looks at you like you hang the moon and stars in the sky every night. The one person who's already been through so much.

But it's not like every firefighter dies in the act of duty. So many are happily married, living their best lives and growing old with their spouses. Taking their *last chance to love.*

It'll be the same for me and Mala, too.

I have to believe that. It's not that easy to stow away a fear that's been a part of me for so many years, as if it's a simple carry-on inside the overhead compartment of an airplane. It's a daily reminder, a mantra I have to believe in, for both mine and her sakes.

I lean down to place a kiss on the space between her neck and shoulder, making her jump in surprise. "What are the most kissable flowers in the world?"

She turns to face me with a smile stretched over her lips, her perfectly white teeth gleaming between them. "Tulips, of course."

I bring my arm from behind my back, watching her expression morph from happy to elated. "Am I ever going to stump you?"

She takes the red tulip bouquet from my hand, burying her nose directly in them with a smile. "No. Not if you give me the world's easiest riddles. Also," she looks up at me, "*these* are my favorite flowers."

Closing the distance between us, I lean down to brush my

lips over hers. "You'd think I'd know everything about you after all these years."

Her eyes crinkle at the ends as her smile brightens. "Nope. You'll have to endure many more years with me to know everything."

"How many? Give me a number," I murmur, still close to her.

"Hmm." She twists her lips, pretending to calculate something. "Approximately eighty-two years, ten months, and thirty-nine days."

I lift my hand and tuck a strand of her hair behind her ear. "I think I can manage that."

She giggles, clutching her bouquet closer. "Thank you for the flowers. Though, the huge bouquet you had delivered a few days ago still looks perfectly beautiful on the counter inside. You didn't have to get me another one."

I reach for the bouquet in her hands. "Well, in that case, let me return them."

She draws the flowers away from my reach. "No way! Take your hands off my boyfriend's flowers."

The dogs that were playing yip and pant in the background, but we ignore them as I pull her into me again with my hands at her hips. "This boyfriend seems like a lucky guy."

"The luckiest," she whispers, closing her eyes, giving me a cue to put my lips on hers.

I do just that, but pull back when I start to feel myself harden inside my jeans and she giggles again, knowingly.

"Still thinking about the dog party idea?" I nod toward the area behind the wire fence.

She's been talking about something she saw at the company she worked for in LA. Apparently, they owned a few open areas where they'd set up birthday parties and adoption events for dogs. They had obstacle courses and more space for dogs to run around in. She figured it would be a great way to expand her business, since the bakery would provide all the catering for the parties.

She turns over her shoulder, following my gaze before looking back at me with a forlorn look. "Yeah, but I don't think it's possible anymore."

"Why not?"

I place my hands on her shoulders, my thumbs running up the warm skin of her neck and watch the way her lips move as she speaks. "I called the number on the *For Sale* sign that was there a few weeks ago, but the person who answered said someone took ownership of it already."

"So, it's gone?"

She shrugs. "It looks like it."

My frown mimics hers. "I'm sorry. Maybe something else will open up nearby."

She sighs. "It's fine. Probably for the best for now, anyway. This way I don't blow through my savings and can focus on more sales at the bakery and getting more catering orders in."

I rub up and down her bicep, and I am about to say something when my phone vibrates with a text at the same time as it rings.

I pull it out of my pocket to see a call coming in from our fire chief. Both mine and Mala's brows pinch. She's likely thinking the same thing I am—the chief wouldn't call me on my two days off unless it was important. I pick up the call. "Chief?"

"Meyer." Chief's voice has its usual thunderous rumble, but there's an urgency in the way he says my name that has my spine straightening on its own accord. "You been keeping up with the situation in San Diego?"

My heart drums and I flick my gaze from a tree swaying behind the wire fence to Mala's concerned expression. "Of course. The whole station's been keeping up with the news. We've been texting back and forth as more information comes in. The two major fire clusters seemed to be about seventy percent contained last I checked a few hours ago."

"Well, not anymore. The fire's spreading farther toward rural areas, with the wind gusts now up to twelve miles-per-hour. Everyone's been asked to evacuate, but the blaze has destroyed close to two-hundred square miles and about a hundred and fifty homes already with no end in sight. The crew on the ground is getting exhausted, and Cal Fire is calling for reinforcements. We need all available fire engines on the scene." He pauses only a second to let his words sink in. "I need you and most of the crew to head over there to help."

I swallow as a weight plummets to the bottom of my stomach. "Yes, sir. I'll be right there."

Chapter Thirty-Two

DEAN

"ALRIGHT, LISTEN UP!" McADAMS YELLS OVER THE DIN OF helicopters above us and the faint sounds of feet on dried grass. The silver in his mustache contrasts with the dark smoke behind him. "I need a man every three hundred feet. We've got the wet line around the fire, but the blaze has jumped in several areas. We gotta fight this thing decisively and aggressively, hear me?"

McAdams is the deputy chief in charge of our crew, and though he's a shorter, stockier man than most of us here, the authority in his voice makes it clear he doesn't put up with any sort of insubordination. Rumor has it, he's fought more wildfires than house fires, so if there's anyone who knows what they're doing, it's him.

The lot of us standing around him take stock of each other before surveying the brush fires around us. While a decent number of us have fought wildfires before, I doubt any of us have been around long enough to have fought one of this caliber. So, it's not surprising that the same anxious energy is coursing through all of us.

We're all thinking the same thing—the fire's continuing to

push against the control lines and the weather isn't on our side. One misstep, one wrong decision, could be the difference between life and death.

Hell, even the right decisions—the ones made after evaluating all the data at hand—could still have the same outcome, with us fighting for our lives.

I tug on the necklace around my neck and give the pendant a kiss. Mala gave it to me before I left, and just having it on my skin reminds me what I have to get home to. A smile pulls at my lips as I eye the infinity sign with the dog bone inside it. Perhaps no one else would understand the reason why it's special to our friendship—our love—but no one else needs to.

A few guys shift on their feet nervously, but I take in a few shallow breaths of smoky air, tasting the ash at the back of my throat and hoping for it to distract me from my thoughts.

Fear is only going to hold me back, keep me from the task at hand. So, as much as the memories of once being in almost this exact position years ago—looking at a similar raging inferno of trees, feeling the same dread trying to creep in—threaten to cloud my brain, I fist my hands at my sides, shoving them off.

Right now, at this very moment, I have no other choice but to believe things will end better than they did last time. They have to.

Because now I have so much to lose.

Now I have *everything* to lose.

Just like he did.

"Let's fight this thing and get the fuck outta here, yeah?" he'd said, looking over his shoulder at me while I helped him carry the hose toward a large burning redwood tree on our first day. "Cuz, I got a girl whose bed I don't like being away from for too long."

I'd snorted. "And this is only day-one, ladies and gentlemen. How are you gonna deal if we're stuck here for a week or longer?"

Zander's eyes darkened, and I wished I could take back my words. "That's the thing. I'm not, brother. I won't be able to deal with it well if it's too much longer." He saw the skepticism in my expression, perhaps, because he added, "You'll get it one day, Dean. I swear to you, you'll get it."

And he was right.

I do.

McAdams' voice has me blinking back from the past. He goes on to remind us all of the basic protocols, like maybe we'd forgotten them over the past hundred times he's repeated himself today. "Stay informed on weather conditions, know what the fire is doing at all times, identify escape routes, communicate often and clearly, hear me?"

We all shout our affirmations as my eyes drift beyond his shoulders to the crew scattered across all parts of the visible terrain. Some are fighting active fires while others are digging trenches to stop them from advancing.

"Remember, fight decisively and aggressively. There's no room for mistakes," he repeats. "First and foremost is your safety."

"Yes, sir," we all respond collectively.

Malcolm, Rohan, and I have been here for four days, fighting on the ground throughout the day, resting for a mere two to three hours in the encampments set up for us nearby before heading back to do it all over again.

It's hard to tell how long we'll be here, given how unpredictable the fire has been—due in large part to the weather, wind, and the dry conditions—but if it continues like this for even a couple more days, I'm not sure how many of us will make it through the exhaustion alone.

It doesn't help that we've barely seen the sun with how deep we are in the woods and the amount of ash floating over us, veiling the sky like black plume.

Today, Malcolm and I are split off from Rohan, who is

taking on a larger fire even deeper in the woods, while Malcolm and I are assigned to the cluster fires at the edges. I try not to think about the fact that I don't have eyes on him, reassuring myself that we're all supposed to stay close together, and that if, God forbid, anything happens, he'll have help near him fast.

But, fuck, if something happens to him . . .

A couple of guys cough behind me, and I take my hard hat off, shoving the sweat at my hairline back into my hair before putting it back on, the warm breeze doing nothing to cool my skin.

"You boys," McAdams points to me, Malcolm, and the guys standing next to him, "head west toward the spot fires starting up over the hills. There are a bunch of evacuated structures and homes there, so carry another hose line up."

We do as he asks, jumping into action to climb the hill while carrying the hose with us. It's not an easy feat, given the rough terrain, the heated wind blowing almost toward us, and the fact that we're carrying all our own equipment and pulling the hose toward the blazes.

"Fuck!" Malcolm grumbles, almost losing his footing on the ashy soil behind me. He rights himself, but his voice grates like sandpaper from all the smoke he's inhaled over the course of the past few days. "This is insane. Never seen a fire this bad."

"Just think," I venture, hoping the change in topic will keep us optimistic, "by this time next week, we'll be home. Maybe even watching a movie at one of our houses."

Malcolm huffs. "Yeah, *my house*, so I get to choose the movie. Fuck if I'll watch some sappy shit your girl seems to love to pick."

My lips twitch as I shove a low-hanging branch, working my way past it. "I think she just likes to see you cry like a little girl."

"Shut up, jackass. Pretty sure I saw you tearing up too when Sam had to go into the light. That entire movie was totally unnecessary. Shit like that doesn't happen in real life–people speaking from beyond the grave. Ridiculous."

I look over my shoulder with a smile, seeing the rest of the guys behind us. "So ridiculous it had you weeping."

Malcolm gives me the middle finger, making me chuckle harder.

With my breathing heavy–the scent of charred wood and burning soil flooding my senses–and my muscles straining, I focus on getting over the last part of the hill, seeing what McAdams was referring to. Fires burn the various structures–homes and small shops–at the edge of the wooded areas, threatening to ignite the trees behind them, if they haven't already.

Malcolm wheezes behind me, and I study him with concern. "You okay, brother?"

He lifts his chin. "Never better. Let's get this shit over with."

His response might sound sarcastic, but I know it's as much to ward me off my concerns as it is to keep us moving forward. We're all tired, all ready to get home to our loved ones and our own beds, but our number one concern is saving lives and smothering this motherfucking fire, and none of us are ready to throw in the towel yet.

I point toward the guys behind Malcolm. "You three head toward the shopping structure over there. Malcolm and I will put out the fire in these two houses."

The guys nod in understanding before shuffling toward the shopping structure fire.

I look over my shoulder as an air tanker releases red fire retardant over the trees, my thoughts going back to Rohan. I know I shouldn't be thinking about what it would do to Mala if something were to happen to him, but I am.

Just the thought of seeing her lose anything more . . . I can't even fucking bear it.

I've only had a chance to talk to her for a minute here or there since the signal is so shitty up here, but hearing her voice for those mere few seconds is enough to keep me going.

She's been so fucking strong and positive. Telling me to focus on being safe and coming home to her in one piece. Reminding me how much she loves me . . .

And fuck if that isn't a bittersweet pill to swallow. Fuck if that doesn't make my anxiety spike.

What if this ends badly?

Swallowing the anxiety emboldening in my chest, I rush toward the burning home in front of us, with Malcolm at my tail. Even in what should be broad daylight, the smoke and fire around the structures are so thick, it's like we're under the curtain of night.

We start by hosing down the roaring fire around the fence, sending billows of black smoke into the sky before we douse out the outside of the front-facing wall. Once we have a path cleared, I tell Malcolm to head toward the entrance before I follow him in. I switch positions with Malcolm, leading the charge as we drench the entryway and walls, then make our way up the stairs as fast as we can.

Between the two of us, we work fast to snuff the fire, checking each of the rooms before we head to the next house.

I call in through the radio, letting the others know that Malcolm and I are heading to the next house, but just looking at it from here, I can tell the fire is going to be worse than it was in the first house.

Dousing out the fire in both its front and back yards, we finally make our way into the second house. The walls hiss as the water collides with them, sending up rivets of smoke and soot, but we keep charging inside.

The house roars as beams above us groan and creak, tongues of flames encircling them like fiery claws. Working quickly, I pull on the hose, flooding the second-story walls. The floor creaks and whines below me, letting me know the fire's been burning for quite some time here.

I look over my shoulder for Malcolm, but with the low visibility, I'm not able to spot his yellow gear anywhere.

"Malcolm!" I bellow through my mask. "This floor is gonna collapse. We need to get out!"

When I don't see or hear him in my periphery, I snap my head this way and that, trying to find him through the haze of smoke. My heart feels like it's in my throat. "Malcolm?"

I hear him groan from my right, and make my way as fast as I can toward him, drenching out the fires nearby in the process.

My stomach plummets when I see him curled over on the top of the stairs, holding onto the railing. He has a facemask on, but with the levels of fumes and carbon monoxide in the air, it's likely he's inhaled enough that he's going into respiratory distress.

Fuck! The voices and screams of the past threaten to ensnare me as I run toward him. *No.* Fuck no! I will not let this happen again under my watch. One major loss is all I can handle, and even that almost completely broke me.

Crouching next to him, I pull Malcolm's arm over my shoulder. "I got you! Let's get downstairs now!"

He uses part of his weight to steady himself while the rest of him lies on my shoulder. From the way he's wheezing and coughing, I know my hunch is right. He's going to need a medic, but my hope is that it's not too late.

I won't lose him.

I won't fucking lose him.

Using my available strength the best I can, I hoist him

toward the bottom of the stairs, seeing that he's having a hard time keeping his head steady.

"Malcolm." I tap his face, trying to get his attention. "Stay with me, buddy. Fucking stay with me. We're almost outside."

I'm almost at the entrance when I see a couple of guys from the crew outside. I yell to them, not quite sure what I'm even saying except for, "Help him," "Fucking get a medic," and, "I can't lose him, too."

The guys jump into action, rushing over to pull Malcolm and me out of the house.

I'm right behind Malcolm, making my way out, but as I do, I decide to douse the fire to my left, thinking it'll spread fast if I don't, and completely miss the loud groan from a weight-bearing wall behind me.

My body locks for a split-second when I recognize the rumble of the wall collapsing. Every instinct combined with all the adrenaline in me has me gearing up to run.

I'm rushing to get away when a beam falls right in front of me on the grass, thankfully missing the others still standing nearby. I only barely register their shouts as the wall behind me comes crashing down and the house starts to give way.

I feel the heat of the wall at my back, the jerk of my neck as my body collides with the ground, right on top of the hot beam.

I don't register the ash inside my nostrils, the scent of searing flesh—is that *my* flesh?—the boom of what feels like an explosion inside my head and my chest.

And then . . .

Her lips are brushing over mine, soft feather-like caresses against my skin. Her mouth curves into a smile before she giggles. Her eyes crinkling at the corners, her nose wrinkling like it does when she's happy.

"You suck at riddles, Fido." Her voice sounds far away, like a wind chime in a desert. A sound I'm desperate to find.

I smile back at her, raising my hand to feel the strands of her silky hair slip through my fingers, almost like it's happening in slow motion.

"But I love you, anyway," she murmurs near my ear before placing a kiss on my temple. "I love you more every day."

"*Sprinkles*," I breathe out before everything goes dark.

"Try this one, it's flatter." He flips the rock between his fingers before handing it to me.

I use his technique, flicking my hand, keeping my elbow steady while my wrist does all the work, and the rock skims the surface of the lake. It glides across the lake's rippling expanse, as if intentional in its course—four, five, six times before it sinks with an almost inaudible *plop*.

Zander gives me a proud smile, as if I've just accomplished the world's most difficult task under his guidance.

He's dressed in a white linen button-down, the sleeves rolled up casually, over khaki shorts. His light brown eyes reflect the vast lake in front of us, and he places his hands in his pockets, leaning back on his heels, as if taking it all in.

My brows furrow, and a thought I can't shake floats to the surface. "What are you doing here? How . . . how are you *here*?"

Zander gives me a sidelong glance before turning to the lake again. "Been here the whole time, buddy."

I look down at my toes in the sand before I scan the ground, the lake, the sky. I lift my hands in front of me, like I'm seeing them for the first time, before I examine his profile next to me. He's about as tall as I am, but perhaps a little broader.

"Fuck," I gasp, feeling like my throat is closing up, my chest caving in on itself. "Did I fucking *die*?"

Zander chuckles softly. "Nah, brother, you're alright. Well . . ." He pauses. "You will be."

An incessant beeping chimes from his pocket and his hand pulls out a two-way radio—the same kind we use as firefighters to communicate during emergencies. *Strange.* The pockets of his shorts didn't seem big enough to hold it, but somehow it doesn't register as completely odd to me, either. Probably because a part of me recognizes my mind is justifying the details that don't make sense.

In this dream, they do. In this dream, it all makes sense.

"So, why are you here?"

Zander makes no attempt to stop the beeping, shifting to face me. "Two reasons. One, to thank you."

I shake my head, frowning. "I don't deserve it. I couldn't even keep my word," I remind him, recalling the promise he asked of me, to not let Jane lose her spark. "It wasn't until Jane found Owen that she smiled again."

"You were there for her from day one. She knows that, and so do I." He raises his dark brows. "You don't think I know it was *you* who cleaned her driveway right after the big snowstorms before she'd even wake up? That *you* made an anonymous donation to the college fund Jane opened for Catherine? A donation that'll pay for a huge chunk of her tuition.

"You don't think I know that you kept in touch with her—visited her—even when she wouldn't text you back? Even when you rang the doorbell and she wouldn't answer. You don't think I know that you kept going back?" He glares at me incredulously, almost like he's accusing me of doing the things he claims. "You know why you did all those things, brother?"

I don't answer, though I suspect I wouldn't be able to even if I wanted to. My throat feels too dry to attempt.

"Not because of that promise, Dean. It had nothing to do with that promise, because what you did—*what you kept doing*—

was so far beyond a mere promise." He squeezes my shoulder. "It's why I wanted to thank you."

I swallow, trying to coat my dry throat.

The beeping continues from his radio, and I open my mouth to ask him to turn it off, but Zander speaks before I can. "The other reason I'm here is to tell you to wake up."

Strangely, his voice morphs into something familiar, but higher-pitched. "Wake up, baby. Please, Dean."

I stare at him in confusion. Why the hell is Zander calling me *baby,* and what just happened to his voice? And why won't he turn off that stupid beeping radio?

"Dean. I love you."

A gust of wind carries droplets of water toward me and one lands on my forehead, trickling down the side of my head.

A sniffle registers in my ear, and as if my eyes are being pried open, I blink up at the harsh lights above me. My heart races as my gaze takes in the light blue walls around me. The various machines beeping and clicking. A woman with blonde hair, similar to mine, sits with her head resting against the wall behind her, her eyes closed. I realize after a few seconds that it's my mother.

But it's the shift of soft hair at my shoulder and the scent of lemons that has me closing my eyes again.

And though the tentacles of sleep pull me back and I'm wavering at the threshold of consciousness, I register the ache inside my heart. The tears drenching my skin. The soft whispers and sobs right at the shell of my ears. Heartbreak and fear curled around each syllable.

If this is the pain I've given her from surviving, then what would it do to her if I didn't? What would it do to her next time?

She doesn't deserve this. No one does.

Chapter Thirty-Three

MALA

"DEAN."

His name feels like a prayer, a plea on my lips.

Though he's been in and out of consciousness over the past four days, the doctors have lowered his meds and are hopeful he'll awake fully on his own soon.

I see him stirring and pick up his hand, leaning over to lay a kiss on his forehead. His skin is paler than normal, and in vast contrast with the dark circles under his eyes. Still, he's doing better each day.

His hand tightens over mine ever so gently, as if he recognizes my touch, and I quickly blink away the tears threatening to emerge again. I don't want him to see my tears when he wakes up; I only want him to see my smile, my reassurance that everything will be okay. That everything *is* okay.

There hasn't been a single moment over the past week—eight days since the guys found out they'd be going to help fight the fire—that I haven't prayed. I've begged God to keep them safe, *reminded Him*, in case He overlooked it, that they were risking their lives to save *His* other children. That they deserved just a little more of His benevolence for the work they were doing. I also promised Him I'd be a better person—more devoted, more generous, just *more*—if He brought them home safely.

Yeah, so maybe I was pulling out some feeble negotiating tactics with the Almighty, but I wouldn't be the first person in history to do so, nor am I ashamed I did.

Aside from Dean getting hurt and Malcolm having to stay at the hospital overnight on account of his respiratory issues and dehydration, He came through for me.

I got them all back safe and sound, with the exception of the third-degree burn on Dean's chest, for which he had to be airlifted to the hospital when he fell unconscious.

Dean's lips twitch, his eyes fluttering, before he opens them and a collective gasp between me, his mom, his dad, and stepmom Karine, resounds inside the room. Karine clasps her hands, looking up at the ceiling before thanking the Big Guy in Armenian.

My smile wobbles with a mixture of relief and restlessness. A part of me wants to weep grateful tears that he's awake—that he'll be alright—while the rest of me wants to crawl against him and hold him until the end of time.

Dean wearily regards the faces around him before his eyes find mine. A glimmer of hope and longing passes through them and then, as if a switch has been turned off, it morphs into something else entirely.

I cup the side of his face in confusion. "Dean, what's wrong? Are you in pain? Do you—"

"Let me call the nurse," Karine says, jumping into action.

"No, I'm—" Dean's voice is a coarse rasp. He takes a fatigued breath, trying to stop her from leaving, but is too late. She's already out the door. "I'm okay. I just . . . need water."

His mom, Jolene, reaches for the straw cup near her, handing it to him while Dean's dad, Marvin, helps him sit up in bed. Dean takes a tentative few sips and hands the cup back to his mom.

"You know," I venture with another shaky smile a moment later, "I get that you're somewhat of an attention-seeker, but this was over-the-top, even for you."

Regardless of the lighthearted humor I was going for, my voice cracks and I practically sob out the end of my sentence.

Marvin pulls me into a side hug while I quickly dab at the damn tear that escapes from the corner of my eye. So much for showing him only my smiles and reassurance.

Dean's eyes bounce against mine as he takes in a shaky breath. His chest heaves a little before he squeezes his eyes shut, like he's physically warding off his pain.

"Dean?" I whisper as a pang rises through my chest. *Is he in pain?* Why won't he say anything?

"How are you feeling, sweetheart?" Jolene asks softly, clasping a hand over his forearm. From the way her brows furrow, I know that even she can tell something isn't right with him. "Do you need anything?"

He shakes his head and then, as if remembering something, he looks around the room, the strain in his voice only eclipsed by the concern in his eyes. "Malcolm?"

"He's fine," I answer hoarsely. "The doctors sent him home to rest for a few days, but he's going to be alright. From what we found out, you saved him."

Dean pinches the bridge of his nose, grimacing. "I shouldn't have even asked him to follow me into that house. He was wheezing—"

I take his hand in mine again. "You couldn't have known, Dean."

He sighs, as if not wanting to argue with me, and slowly slips his hand from mine. "How's Rohan?"

I swallow, trying not to glean too much from his lack of . .

. enthusiasm after seeing me. Is it selfish of me to have expected a warmer reaction from him?

I quickly shake off the voice inside my head telling me something feels off . . .

I must be seeing this all wrong. The man's just been through a horrific experience—one he's gone through before and lost a dear friend in. And while that, thankfully, isn't the case this time, he *did* just wake up in a strange hospital bed with most of his family lurking over him.

Of course, things are going to feel off.

I force another smile. "He's fine. He came back a little dehydrated and with a residual cough, but he's back to being the pain in the ass he always was."

Nothing.

While Jolene huffs out a small laugh, I get nothing from Dean besides the slightest sag of his shoulder, letting me know he's relieved. Other than that, not even a minuscule smile.

Something unwelcome stirs inside me. Something that has me wondering if he even heard me, if he's even noticed I'm here. Does he even *care* that I'm here?

But it's also a ridiculous and selfish thought. How can I expect him to be jovial and like his old self so quickly?

His gaze travels to the middle of his chest, and he lifts the cover to examine the bandage around his torso.

The nurses enter as Marvin starts to answer Dean's silent questions. "I don't know how much you remember, son, but you were in a burning building when the structure toppled over behind you and you landed chest-first over a blazing beam."

Marvin pauses as the nurses ask Dean a few questions and start their tests and scans. "You were airlifted here and treated for your burns." Dean's dad tilts his head toward Dean's chest. "You've got a rather large third-degree burn on your chest, but the doctors are saying you should heal nicely over the next few weeks." He pauses. "But you're going to have a nasty scar to show for it, though."

Dean's eyes flick to mine at the mention of the scar, a flash of affection swimming through them before it disappears, transforming into something that looks a lot like . . . anguish.

"I remember most of it." He nods toward the TV, which has been on with the volume muted. Currently, the news is being reported on screen. "And the fire?"

Dean's mom scrubs her hand over his arm. "They've contained it to a small area and things are looking much better—"

Just then, Dean takes an audible intake of breath as his gaze pins on the latest headline. *"Deputy Chief Leonard McAdams Dies During One of California's Deadliest Wildfires."*

"He . . ." Dean's eyes glaze. "He was leading my crew."

My hand immediately finds his, my chest feeling tight.

"Oh, honey," Jolene consoles. "I'm so sorry."

Dean's quiet, his eyes still trained on the TV, but aside from the twitch in his bottom lip—the one that gives away how hard he's trying to keep it together as the news of the deputy chief's death hits him like a sledgehammer—he stays stoic.

A few minutes later, the doctor comes inside to ask Dean about his pain levels and talks to him about when his bandages can come off. Based on his assessments, Dean should be able to go home in the next couple of days, but he is required to stay at home for the next couple of weeks until his wounds heal more.

When the doctor leaves, Jolene makes her way back to Dean's side. I haven't left my spot next to his other side ever since he woke up.

"I think we're going to run downstairs to find something

to eat," she states, looking over at Marvin and Karine. "I also need to call your brothers to let them know how you are. They've been messaging me incessantly." She turns her gaze at me. "Sweetheart, you haven't eaten a decent thing in the past four days. Can I get you something other than hospital food?"

I shake my head. "No, but thank you, though. I'm not very hungry."

Jolene's palm wraps around my wrist before she brings it closer to her, looking at me with that same motherly affection she gives Dean. "The way you've been here for Dean . . ." Her chin wobbles, her watery eyes turning to Dean. "The minute she heard about you being taken to the hospital, she booked a flight here. She hasn't left your side for even a minute, sweetheart. I don't think she's even slept—"

"I wouldn't want to be anywhere but here," I cut her off, feeling my cheeks heat. Yes, I took the first flight here and have been spending the nights in Dean's room here, but I've done it as much for him as I have for myself. I couldn't eat, couldn't sleep, couldn't even breathe right without being near him.

Jolene nods in understanding before heading to the door, where both Marvin and Karine are waiting for her, leaving me and Dean alone for the first time since he woke up.

I turn toward him and release a breath when he finally lets his eyes linger on mine. But the smile that was forming on my lips quickly falls when I see that same torment in them again. Like he's trying to form words he hasn't found sounds for. Like he's trying to say something he doesn't have the courage to.

My heart aches inside my chest, a sense of foreboding filling its cavity. I lift my fingers to his hairline. Maybe I'm just reading this all wrong. He's just going through a lot.

My fingertips flutter over his skin, and I'm just about to

ask him what's wrong again when he turns his head to the side, letting my fingers fall.

I watch his chest rise and fall, his lips twitch the same way they did when he saw the news about the deputy chief who died. His hand forms a fist at his side.

"Dean?" For reasons unbeknownst to me, reasons I can't quite make sense of, my voice cracks, like I already know what he's thinking. Like he's created this huge, cavernous hole between us and my hand isn't able to reach his on the other side. "What's—"

He shuts his eyes tight, like even my voice isn't something he can bear. "You should go join them downstairs, Mala. I need to rest."

A sharp pain shoots through my chest at his dismissal, like I've been stabbed, and I take in a shaky breath.

I get that he's just been through something most people can't even imagine. That the loss of the deputy chief, along with waking up, not knowing if something happened to his friends, likely catapulted him into that same place he was in when Zander died. That he's tired and recovering and needs to rest.

I get all that. Really, I do.

But something about the way he's turned himself away from me—the way he hasn't been able to meet my gaze without his own filling with agony—doesn't sit well with me.

And while I *should* give him the space he's clearly asking for and not push the subject right this second, I can't help but think that walking out of the door right now will only strengthen his belief that he's doing the right thing for us.

Which he's not. He's absolutely fucking not.

And if he thinks I'll allow him to create an even bigger cavernous pit between us and keep us apart even a day longer—after I've spent the last nine fucking years without being able to call him mine—he must not know me very well.

Wrapping my palms over his stubbled jaw—his scruff longer than usual and in need of a trim—I turn his face back to me. "Dean, look at me."

I wait for his eyes to meet mine and when they do, I see the same misery from earlier intensify inside them. But I also see something like desperation and self-torture, like he just needs someone to save him from himself.

And God, that gives me hope. That gives me so much hope.

"I know you. I know you better than anyone else. I know the depth of your love and the strength of your fears. I know your overwhelming need to protect me and everyone else around you and the lengths you will go—the *years* you will abstain—to torture yourself because you think you're doing the right thing." I slide a thumb over his cheekbone. "But right now, the only person you need to protect is yourself from letting that fear take over."

His voice is strangled, as if every word weighs heavily on his tongue. "I wish I could. I'm just . . ." He drops his head back into the pillow with an agonizing sigh. "Fuck!"

"Talk to me, Dean. Let me in. Tell me what you're scared of."

He squeezes his eyes shut for a moment, but when he opens them again, they're hazy. Tormented.

"This. *Us,* here in this hospital. Your worry and pain." He takes a trembling breath. "This wasn't the first time I've been caught in something that could have ended my life, Mala. And it won't be the last, either. Who knows if I'll make it out alive the next time . . ."

His mouth curves into a downward half-moon. "It's not fair for you to have to suffer because of my decisions. It's not fair for you to be in a state of constant stress, even when I might be on a routine call, thinking I might not come back. You deserve more—"

"No, Dean." My watery gaze bounces between his. My incredible, big-hearted, beautiful man. How can I convince him how much I love him? "I deserve *you*. I've waited my whole life for *you*. Don't you see that?" I take a calming breath, trying to string my words together. "It doesn't matter to me if we get one more day, one more month, or one more year together, because, in every moment I have with you, I plan to live out a lifetime."

"Mala—"

"Listen to me, Dean, and listen to me good." I bring my face closer to his so he can see the resolve in my eyes. "Fire has taken a lot away from me, too. I know *exactly* what it's capable of, and yet, I've been forged from it, stronger because of it. Will I worry about you, my brother, and my friends? Yes, I'll always worry. But I'll be damned if I let my fear taint another moment we spend together."

I press my lips to his, feeling the tension in his shoulders release under me, and he sighs into my mouth, his hands running up the sides of my torso.

Lifting up, I look at him again. "There's not a single person on this planet that could replace you, Dean. So whether you choose to walk away from me today or you're taken from me tomorrow, you'll leave me in pieces either way."

My nose tingles as a tear breaks over my bottom lid and I whisper, "Because *you*, Dean Emerson Meyer, have owned every one of my heartbeats from the day you walked into my life, eating a burned, penis-shaped dog biscuit, and that will never change. *Never*."

His hand tightens behind my head and his eyes burn with an intensity that leaves me breathless. He pulls me down to his lips again and his tongue sweeps over the seam, urging my mouth open to let him in. A shiver runs down my spine as our kiss deepens, our mouths exploring each other again. My hands travel up his biceps, and I carefully avoid putting weight on his chest, even though my own feels like it's going to burst.

The moment is so palpable and all-encompassing that I release a sobbing moan into his mouth, hoping to express exactly how I feel about him through my kiss alone.

"I love you, Mala. I love you so goddamn much," he murmurs against my lips. "I'm so fucking sorry I made you feel like I could walk away from this. I thought I'd be doing it for you. So that you could find someone you could rely on to be there day in and day out. But the truth is . . ." his voice shudders before he reins in his emotions with a clench of his jaw, "the truth is that I'd die every moment apart from you. I couldn't bear the sight of you with anyone else. Because the only one I belong to—the only one I've *ever* belonged to—is you."

Chapter Thirty-Four

DEAN

ALL I WANT TO DO IS HOLD HER.

With my arms wrapped around her, my hand splayed on her bare stomach, under my T-shirt she's claimed for herself, I hold her against me. My nose is where it loves to be, at the curve of her shoulder and neck, drawing in puffs of her lemon scent, and my lips are pressed against her silken skin.

This. This right here is what life is about.

Being alive isn't something I've ever taken for granted. It's a luxury, a blessing, and a bounty you fight for each day in my world. But there's a difference between being alive and *actually* living, and that difference is her.

This woman in my arms. The little blaze that burns so bright, it wields the power to annihilate the darkness that threatens to loom at my periphery.

She's my reason for living—for more than just having a pulse, more than just existing. My best friend and the love of my life.

"You were talking in your sleep." I lay a kiss on her skin as my hand travels upward, my thumb grazing over the underside of her breast.

She wiggles her ass against my groin, making my already hardened bulge swell and press into her. I don't need to see her face to know she's smiling with the sigh she just released. Her voice is a rumpled whisper, sleepy and sexy. "Yeah? What was I saying?"

My hand climbs upward, and Mala's ass makes another circle over my erection.

We've always had this palpable need for each other, a chemistry we've never felt with anyone else, but it's been supercharged ever since we came back from the hospital a week ago. And though the burn on my chest is still tender, I can barely even feel it when I'm near her.

In an ironic twist of events, now I have a scar very much like the one she does on her chest, and for reasons that seem simple enough to figure out at this point, I feel closer to her because of it.

Lately, we've been insatiable—ravenous and frenzied in our need for each other. Like we're fighting for our lives with each touch and every kiss. Like nothing else matters but the need to deepen this connection, to find each other's souls and stay there for eternity.

"Something about how hot I am. How you can't stop thinking about me and want to have eight of my babies."

A laugh tied around a moan slips from her lips when I pinch her nipple and she pulls her bottom lip in between her teeth. "All of that definitely sounds like something I'd say . . . if I was having a nightmare."

My smile is immediate, like it always is with this sassy, witty beauty I've loved for so long.

I turn her around, nipping her lips and making her yelp, before I move down the length of her body. I pull up her shirt, laying kisses against her stomach and making her squirm. She's ticklish, and the more she giggles and squirms, the harder my dick strains to delve inside her.

I grasp the side of her panties—the ones she refuses to sleep without even though they get taken off in the middle of the night at least twice, if not more—and pull them off her legs. Leaning down, I lay open-mouthed kisses over the sides of her thighs, watching as her stomach contracts in anticipation and her breaths come out as pants.

And then I bury my face between her legs, licking and sucking her swollen little nub. Mala tangles her hand into my hair as she mewls and whispers, murmurs and chants, undulating under me.

"Dean . . . Oh, God, Dean."

She arches up, shoving her needy center into my mouth, and I devour her with the ferocity of an untamed animal, slurping at her folds and lapping her entrance.

My hand travels up her body, grasping her nipple and pinching her once again the way she likes, while my other hand finds her wet entrance below my mouth. I press two fingers inside her, curling them to make her go crazy.

I pump my fingers as my mouth stays latched on her clit, and Mala's thighs clamp around my face. Her short breaths and the way she tugs my hair even harder tells me she's close.

I increase the pressure inside her, licking and relishing her, before I feel her let go against my tongue. I lap at her juices, lingering between her thighs until her heaving chest slows and her fists loosen from my hair.

I crawl back up her body and Mala quickly pulls my lips to hers, tasting herself with a moan. "I want you inside me."

I don't waste a single second, pressing her knee down on the mattress so her legs open wider for me and sliding inside her in one go. My strokes are hard and deliberate, punishing and unrelenting, as I pump and drive inside her, like I can get deeper with each thrust. Like I can embed myself in every cell in her body.

My forehead rests against hers, our breaths intermingling while our hips collide. The necklace she gave me hangs between us—my good luck charm—the pendant resting on her skin. Like me, she's seconds from breaking and when we do, we shatter with the force of a thousand suns—groaning and panting, a sweaty entanglement of limbs and lips.

I roll off her to the side and pull her to me, not wanting to be away from her for even that one moment. Our hearts continue to thump against each other, trying to settle into their normal rhythm.

I kiss her languidly, like she's the only thing worth cherishing. "I love you, sweetheart. I'll love you until . . ."

She clasps her hands around my head as our eyes cling to one another. "Until we're nothing but ash."

"WHERE ARE YOU TAKING ME?" Mala touches the blindfold over her eyes for the fifty-seventh time in the past five minutes, wiggling in her seat. "You know I hate surprises."

I snort, turning the steering wheel to take a left onto the main road. "That's a lie if I've ever heard one." I turn my head to look at her even though she can't see me and slide my hand over her thigh, squeezing it gently. "You certainly didn't mind the surprise I woke you up with this morning when my tongue was inside your—"

"Yeah, okay." She grabs my palm and entangles our fingers. It's hilarious to me that even after all the ways I've had her, she still manages to blush. "So maybe I like *some* surprises. But this . . . this is making my stomach go all loopty-loop."

I bring the back of her hand to my lips. "Patience, young kung-fu panda. I know you're waiting on tender hooks, but we'll be there soon."

"*Tenterhooks.*"

My brows bunch together. "The fuck are tenterhooks? It's *tender hooks*," I assert.

She shakes her head, her lips pressing against each other and though I can't see her eyes, I know she's closed them in that way when she worries I'm a card short of a full deck. "Dean, when has a hook ever been tender?"

I turn onto the rocky driveway and put my truck into park before turning toward her. I place my index finger under her chin, turning her face to mine. "See? I'm *hooking* your chin, *tenderly*."

Mala's mouth stretches into a smile before she gives up and giggles. And God, I'll act like the biggest idiot in the world for the rest of my life if that's the reaction I get from her. "You are such a cheeseball."

I lean over the console to press my lips to hers before I drop my voice. "You ready for your surprise, beautiful?"

It's been a month since I came back from San Diego, but this plan's been in motion for weeks before that.

"Yeah," she replies, and I can see her eyes move behind the dark blindfold, hoping to get an early glimpse.

"Sit tight," I tell her.

I make my way out of my driver's side and around the front of her truck to her side. I take in a deep inhale of the beautiful summer breeze, urging my pulse to steady before I open the door and help her out.

I wrap my arm around her waist, pulling her short frame to me as I guide her to the entrance.

Mala reaches out her hands, trying to feel what's in front of her. They land on the metal bar of the fence and linger there, as if she's trying to figure out what she's just touched. "What . . . Dean, what is this?"

I pull the key out of my pocket and twist it into the lock before pulling the chain and dropping the entire thing to the ground. Unlatching the metal arm, I swing the door open, making it creak.

Mala's mouth drops open, her head turning this way and that to try to glean the answer from the sounds and smells. "Wait . . ." She sniffs the air, tilting her head up. "Do I smell . . . vanilla and . . . and pumpkin? Are we . . .? Are we near the bakery?"

With my hand at the base of her spine, I urge her forward, closing the gate behind us. I keep her steady as we walk toward the little pergola. With exact timing, I tell her to step up and help her into the structure.

Before she can ask any more questions, I turn her toward me and cup her face with my hands. Mala tilts her head up, her luscious lips glistening with the pink gloss she rubbed over them earlier.

I lean down to speak into her ear and revel in the way she shivers in my arms. "Think you can solve every riddle, *sprinkles*? Well, I have one more for you to solve."

I lay a kiss on her lips when I hear her take an audible breath and linger there a moment with my heart beating wildly inside my chest. "Some have long ones, some have short–"

"Dean," she warns.

I chuckle, knowing exactly where her mind went. "Madonna and Prince don't have one at all . . . but I'd love if you took mine. What is it?"

Her mouth opens and closes, and I know her mind is working a mile a minute. She repeats the riddle in a whispered mumble to herself before she shakes her head. "I . . . I don't know."

"You give up?"

She nods. "Yes, I give up. Now, tell me, Rufus! The suspense is killing me!"

I laugh again, pulling her so close, not even the breeze can get between us. I place my mouth on hers and murmur, "A last name."

"A last . . ." Her breath catches before her hands lift, pulling off the blindfold from her eyes. She blinks, adjusting to the sunlight before her head tilts down, realizing I've gotten on my knee. She sees me holding the box open in front of her, and her fingers immediately find her mouth. "Dean . . ." she gasps.

"Mala, you're my best friend, my every reason. You've taken my mind, body, and soul. Will you marry me, and do me the honor of taking my last name, too?"

Her eyes fill, a sob emerging from her lips before she gets down on her knees in front of me. She throws her arms around me and sobs into my neck, and I hold her to me, pressing my nose into her hair. "Fuck, baby. I'm really hoping those are happy tears. You've got me on *tender hooks*."

Her sobs turn to laughs as her chest shakes against mine. She pulls away, cupping my cheeks before kissing me. "Yes." Her voice cracks. "Yes, I'll take your last name, and yes–*fuck yes!*–I'll marry you."

She gives me her hand, and I wiggle the small diamond ring over her finger before we both rise and I pick her up, kissing her as I spin her around, holding her against me. "I love you."

"I love–" she gasps, looking around as if seeing where she is for the first time. Her smile wobbles in confusion and she steps off the pergola to stand on the overgrown grass. Her eyes lock on her bakery on the other side of the fence. "Dean?"

I come up behind her, wrapping my arms over her and pulling her to me. "Yes, beautiful."

Her brows pinch in bemusement. "How did you . . .?" She gasps again, as if not believing what she's strung together before spinning around to face me. "What is this? How are we standing on this land? It was sold!"

I nuzzle my nose with hers. "It was, yes."

Her eyes become saucers. "You . . . you're the one who bought it!?" At my affirming smile, she shakes her head in disbelief. "For my dog party idea? But how? When?" She looks around again. "How did you–"

I shut her up with another kiss. "It doesn't matter how or when. All that matters is that you're in this with me."

She climbs into my arms, and I lift her again before she wraps her legs around my torso. "Until we're nothing but ash."

EPILOGUE 1

Dean - Two Years Later

For years I lived in fear.

Fear of action, fear of inaction.

Fear of gain, fear of loss.

Fear of living, fear of dying.

Until *she* came along and made me realize that the only fear I could have room for in my life was the fear of regret.

Like the regret of missing the day two years ago, when I got down on one knee and asked her to marry me. Or the day a little less than a year ago, when I scooped her up and crossed the threshold to my house again with her as my wife.

Or today, when our lives are about to change once more.

"The exam room is right this way, Mr. and Mrs. Meyer. Please follow me."

The woman with a curly black bob and thick lenses, wearing a white lab coat, leads Mala and me down a short corridor, to the door marked as *Exam Room 4* on our right.

I place a hand at the bottom of my wife's spine as we enter and she looks up at me, giving me the same reassuring smile she's given me so many times before. The smile that says, *we've got this, you and me.*

I train my gaze on her, hoping I don't blink and miss even a second of her. Mala curls her arm around her back and grabs my hand, pulling me further into the room. She knows how hard my heart is beating—I'm sure she can hear it. It hasn't found a steady pace ever since she told me the news last week.

I'd come home late after a shift at the fire station and found her curled up on our couch—a book resting atop the blanket on her chest. I knew she'd had a long day at work—there were two dog parties back-to-back that she and Samantha had to get DoggLandia ready for—so I'd texted her to tell her not to wait up for me.

Putting the book on the coffee table—one of her beloved romance books with the cover of some shirtless asshole—I lifted her into my arms and carried her to our bed. I had just put the blanket back on her when she stirred awake.

"Hi." She'd tightened her arms around my neck, not letting me lift up.

I placed a kiss on her lips. "Hi."

"I have a riddle for you." Her sleepy voice rasped against my ear.

I grazed my scruff against her cheek, knowing it would cause the little shiver it did in her. "At twelve-thirty in the morning, you have a riddle for me?"

She nodded. "When does one plus one equal three?"

My brain was already fried from the long shift, but I couldn't miss the opportunity to make her smile. "When someone's shit at math."

She giggled like I'd hoped. "No, my silly husband. One plus one equals three when your wife is pregnant."

I'd just blinked at her. I'd heard what she'd said, but I hadn't quite processed it. I mean, it's not that we were trying . . . but it's not that we weren't not trying, either.

A laugh bubbled out of me. "Holy shit!" I cupped her face. "Holy shit. Are you serious?"

"As serious as you are when I make a fresh batch of dog biscuits."

I'd gotten right on top of her and kissed her like she was my life-line. Because she was.

"Alright, now if you can get onto the exam table for me and lift up your shirt," the ultrasound technician addresses Mala with a smile, "we can get started."

I help Mala onto the cushioned stretcher and pull up a chair next to her. She entangles our fingers together, and I pull them toward me to graze the back of hers with my lips. "I love you," I whisper against them.

She leans over while the ultrasound technician sets up, wrapping her hand over the base of my neck and pulling me closer. "I love you, Dean. You're my world."

The exam starts a few minutes later as the ultrasound tech glides the transducer over the lower part of Mala's stomach. The echo of a pulsing sound resounds through the room while both mine and Mala's mouths drop as we take in the black-and-white picture coming into view in front of us on the monitor.

The technician hums, moving the wand this way and that, but when her humming stops and her eyes narrow on the screen, it has Mala shifting uncomfortably on the table.

Even the echoes—heartbeats—sound louder than they did a few seconds ago. *Or maybe that's just my pulse inside my ears.*

"Is . . . is everything alright?" Mala asks guardedly. Her usually dry hand feels clammier inside mine.

The technician turns around, eyes finding mine before she turns them toward Mala. "Well, I don't know if you were expecting this news . . ."

MALA HANDS MY ONE-YEAR-OLD NIECE, Rayne, back to Bella after nuzzling her nose into her soft, dark curls once more. Between my other niece, Darian's daughter Avya, and Rayne,

Mala's been holding one or the other all evening, and I'm a little worried she's going to tire herself out.

We invited her and my brothers, their wives, and their children to the house to give them the news of what we learned a couple of days ago. We also invited Hudson, since he was in Tahoe for work this week. Needless to say, we're going to need all their support, though they have their hands full, too.

Rani gives my nephew Arman, Darian's son, a kiss on the cheek before reminding him he's already had four of Aunty Mala's cookies and that he's going to ruin his appetite for dinner. He grimaces, but not for long, because Bella's daughter, Meera, pulls him away to go play outside in our backyard.

Rani curls her legs under her on the couch while Darian rocks Avya in his arms. She's been fussy today but seems to do better being held by someone—no thanks to Aunty Mala spoiling her.

"Where's her pacifier, Rani?" Darian asks over Avya's soft whines. He seems to be mindlessly scrounging around in the diaper bag they brought with them.

"Look in the front pocket." Rani eyes her daughter with a frown. "She's so addicted to that thing, I have a feeling she'll want it even when she's on her way to high school."

Darian's mouth twitches with a barely-there smile. It takes an act of God to make my brother smile outright like Garrett and me. "Fine by me. It'll do the job of warding off boys."

Rani rolls her eyes, sighing exhaustedly to Mala and Bella as if to say, *do you see what I have to deal with?*

Garrett hands me and Hudson beer bottles before finding a seat next to Bella, placing a kiss on her temple.

Hudson promptly takes a swig, settling back into the couch. The man is seriously a machine with the amount he works, but he's always made my brothers and me a priority in his life. Now, if we could all see him get settled . . .

He might deny he wants to be in a relationship until his voice is hoarse, but we all know he's only lying to himself. Both my brothers and I have seen the way he looks at the woman who just started working for him. The way his gaze squares in on her, the intensity in his expression . . . it's only a matter of time before he figures out what we all have.

"So," Rohan's brow lifts at me and then Mala, "what's this news you guys wanted to share with us?"

Mala turns a smile in my direction and my eyes roam her face affectionately. I pull her hand in mine and place a kiss on her lips. Fuck, I can't get enough of this woman. "You want to tell them or should I?"

She chews on her lips but turns back to our awaiting family. "Dean and I are pregnant."

Bella gasps, jolting Rayne awake in her arms momentarily before the baby makes an annoyed noise and goes back to sleep. "That's amazing! Congratulations, you guys!"

Everyone else starts congratulating us as well, but my eyes connect with my twin's across the room and his gaze narrows at me. He knows something is up. He always does.

"With triplets.," I add, creating a pin-drop silence inside the room.

"Say what?" Rohan's face mimics the others, who all seem like they're in a state of shock.

"Holy shit," Hudson whispers. He's not a newbie to raising kids either, so I'm sure he's only imagining what it'll be like to raise three at the same time.

I run a hand over my face, but my smile is in full-force when my hand drops back down. "Yup, three unique heart-beats." I pull Mala closer to me, placing my palm on her stomach. "Three little *baby Deans*, or what I like to refer to as *beans*."

I thought I was pretty clever when I came up with beans. "Baby Deans! 'Beans!'" I'd repeated.

To which Mala just responded with a shake of her head. "No."

"Lord, help me." Mala exhales, making a *pfft* sound before her shoulders slump dramatically, feigning exhaustion and surrender. The truth is, she's just as excited as I am since we got the news.

Sure, I was completely taken off-guard when the technician told us we were having triplets—who wouldn't be?—but the woman had to leave the room because a moment later, I was hovering on top of my wife on the exam table, kissing the bejeezus out of her.

This incredible, unsurpassable, irreplaceable girl of mine. She was carrying my babies—three out of the eight I wanted, which I still haven't been quite successful in convincing her about, though I feel I'm getting closer day by day.

It's going to be a rough pregnancy, I have no doubts about it based on the aches and pains she's already feeling only a couple of months in, but if there is one woman who has the strength, optimism, and fortitude to take on whatever life throws at her, it's her.

And I'm the lucky bastard who gets to call her my best friend and my wife.

EPILOGUE 2

Mala - The Triplets Turn Five

THIS PLACE HAS BECOME A ZOO.

I don't mean that metaphorically or in a manner of speaking. I mean, this place really has become a zoo.

Not only because our triplets, Ignatius, Fintan, and Enya—all named for the element that marks both Dean and I emotionally and physically, fire—are currently in varying states of overexcitement or that our dog, Tulip, is running around an enclosed chicken pen, but because I had the brilliant idea of hosting their fifth birthday party at *DoggLandia,* my dog party business, with one of those traveling zoos.

"Momma!" Fintan, the quieter, more responsible one of my brood, rushes toward me at full-speed, pulling on the hem of my shorts. His face is flushed, his blond hair—very much like his dad's—is a mess, like it hasn't seen a comb in years, though I'd straightened it myself this morning. "Momma! You have to come with me! Ignatius opened up the animal pen and let all the animals out!"

"What?" I gasp, looking toward where the temporary pig pen has been set up, but can't get a good visual of my first-born from here. Though, I definitely see there's some commotion in the area with kids squealing and running around.

"Oh, gosh." Bella quickly takes over for me at the cake table where I was handing out slices to our guests. "Go, go! I've got you covered here."

I grab Fintan's hand as he leads me to what I'm sure is a crime scene if Ignatius is involved. I swear, that kid was born to test me.

"Where's your dad?" I ask as we approach, but I get my answer before Fintan can even respond.

With Enya on his back, her little arms squeezing her dad's neck, Dean is chasing the animals—a couple of ducks, a pig, and the bunny—right behind Ignatius. The glee and mischief on his face is identical to his son's, and in that moment, I get a clear vision of what he must have been like as a kid.

I make a mental note to deliver flowers and a spa gift certificate to my mother-in-law.

Fintan pulls on my hand. "I told them not to do it, Momma. I really did. They wouldn't listen."

I crouch to place a kiss on his head and tell him not to worry. Then, as has become usual in our household, I place both hands on my hips and march closer to where my husband and my two wildlings are still running after the animals, while the travel zookeepers try to wrangle them back into the pen.

Enya places her hands on both sides of Dean's head, turning it toward me. "I think we're in trouble, Daddy."

I press my lips together, holding back my smile and narrowing my eyes at Dean, who freezes in place. "Are you serious right now? You're *encouraging* this?"

He has enough courtesy to at least look apologetic, though I know he's faking it. He slides a glance at Ignatius, who is still running after a duck. "He started it."

I shake my head, my mouth open. "You're unbelievable." I

turn toward Ignatius, yelling out his name. "I'm giving you til the count of three, mister, and you better leave all the little animals alone. One . . . two . . ."

I don't even have to say the last number before he's charging toward me. He wraps his arms around my legs and looks up with a feigned innocence, much like his dad's. "I'm sorry, Momma."

I bend down to him, scrubbing some dirt off his shirt and cheek. Of the three of my children, he's the only one who got my dark eyes and hair. "What have we talked about, Ignatius? When you don't follow the rules, then your brother and sister won't want to follow the rules, either. You're the oldest, and you have to set a good example."

He's only older than the other two by a few minutes, but he's always acted like the big brother, especially when it comes to protecting his sister, much like my own brother, so I try to lean into that when I discipline him.

He glances at his dad, who is now taking Enya off his back, laying a kiss on her forehead. I swear, the girl has all the men in our house wrapped around her pinky. "Well, Daddy said that he played by the rules for too long and it didn't 'mount to nothin.' He said breaking the rules was how he got you."

I lift a brow, turning my head to look at my dear husband, who now has a sheepish grin on his face. "Oh, did he now?"

"Hey, squirt!" Dean nods toward where Fintan is now playing with his cousins. "Why don't you take your sister and join the rest of the heathens over there? You've gotten me in enough hot water with your mom for today."

Ignatius does as he's asked, grasping Enya's hand in his before running off with her, and I apologize to the zookeeper for the trouble.

This is life with my Meyer clan.

A new adventure and a reason to laugh every single day.

For years, it was Dean who brought a smile to my face, and now, it's not just him. It's also the three little crazypants we brought into the world. Three beautiful, incredible, and fiery little people who light up our lives brighter than the sun itself could.

And though my husband can be even more unruly and charmingly mischievous than our kids, that grin on his face—the one he directs at me every time I look at him, the one he's directing at me *now*—makes even the most tiresome of days worth it.

He pulls me to his side, his fingers pressed into my waist, and leans down to murmur in my ear, "Fuck, I love pushing your buttons."

His raspy voice alone has me forgetting the reason I was angry in the first place. Add that to the way his large palm presses into my side, and the heat of his body next to me, and I'm basically a puddle on the floor.

Still, I try to maintain my composure, pretending to be unaffected, though he knows exactly what he does to me. "I hadn't noticed."

His tongue peeks out, running over the shell of my ear and making my knees weak. His hand tightens over my hip and the rumble of his laugh settles into my stomach. "But you know what I'd like to do instead?"

I swallow, my eyelids feeling heavy. "What?"

"I'd like to *unfasten* those buttons, instead. Then, I'd like to take those shorts off your legs and worship the spot between them with my tongue, my fingers, and my—"

"Dean," I cut him off, feeling my cheeks heat. I look around and thankfully, no one is standing within hearing distance.

And despite not having moved from this spot next to him, I feel winded, breathless.

He chuckles, turning me to face him with both his hands

on my waist. He lowers his forehead to mine. "So, how about we cut and run from this thing and go make another one of those eight babies we talked about?"

I snort. "Firstly, we can't *cut and run* from our own children's party–"

"Sure we can! They have all their aunts, uncles, and grandparents here. Even Jane and Owen are here. Any of them would happily babysit for fifteen minutes, tops."

I place my hands over his, brushing my thumb over the leather strap around his wrist that matches mine. "When have you ever taken fifteen minutes?"

"We've had quickies before." He wiggles his brows.

I roll my eyes. "Our last quickie was in a women's changing room at the mall, and from what I recall, I got dirty looks from several women in line because we were in there for well over a half hour." He starts to speak, but I place an index finger on his lips, which he promptly pulls into his mouth and I tug back out, knowing we're in public. "And secondly, what do you mean *the eight babies we talked about*? You talked about eight, and I told you that you were out of your mind. That's how I recall that conversation."

His eyes blaze. "Alright, then how about one more?"

I dart my gaze toward our children. Ignatius is running after Darian's daughter, Avya, trying to put his muddy hand on her dress. Enya is licking the frosting off two cupcakes, one in each hand. I squint and notice she has one tucked under her armpit, too. And Fintan is collecting worms and bugs off the ground, showing them to Meera.

I laugh, shaking my head before I turn back to face my husband, who seems completely unfazed by our wild bunch. But it's what I love about him, too.

The guy who couldn't fathom the idea of marriage, of having his own family, because he was so fearful of a future where he'd leave them, is now the guy who can't fathom the idea of not having this exact life.

A life of playing in the sprinklers under the summer sun and roasting marshmallows over a winter campfire.

A life where not missing his children's evening routine takes precedence over being able to raise his feet and relax after a long day.

A life where he no longer looks backward, recounting all he's lost; instead, he keeps his gaze forward, welcoming everything that comes his way with open arms.

"Okay," I breathe, relenting. "One mo–"

I haven't even finished speaking before Dean has me over his shoulder, carrying me like a sack of rice.

"Dean!" I squeal.

He hollers at both his brothers and their wives, while they look at us in puzzlement, "Watch my kids for fifteen minutes, will you? We're going to see about making another set of triplets."

Lord, help me. This man . . .

The End

ABOUT THE AUTHOR

Swati M.H. prefers to call herself a storyteller rather than an author. She lives in the Bay Area with her incredibly patient husband, two beautiful daughters, and her pitbull, Sadie Sapphire. Her days start with caffeine and sometimes end with a glass (or three) of wine.

Swati's goal as a storyteller is to distract her readers from their daily grind with stories about everyday couples finding and fighting for incredible love with the help of a little luck.

Swati loves staying in touch with her readers. Find her at www.swatimh.com or through Facebook and Instagram. Be sure to join her Sweeties reader group for daily fun.

ACKNOWLEDGMENTS

If you've come this far, then you've managed not to throw this book against the wall, and I commend you and thank you for it. Or maybe you did throw it against the wall but decided you still needed to read the acknowledgments and I respect that, and commend you for it anyway.

Thank you for reading the angstiest romance I've ever written and I hope you loved Dean and Mala as much as I did, despite the fact that you wanted to shake them sometimes.

This book could not have been written without the never-ending support of my husband and family. Thank you for promptly going into your hiding places when I came out of my room in a huff after having slammed my laptop closed because there were days Dean and Mala made me lose my shit. I know I was a mess and I so appreciate you still sticking by me.

Thank you to my PA, Stephanie Rash for always finding a way to crack me up and tell me to get out of my own way. I am so thankful for your support and friendship.

My incredible and patient editor, Silvia Curry. At this point, you already know all the dang red-lining you'll be doing in my books and yet you haven't thrown in the towel. For that, I'm so very grateful.

An ENORMOUS thank you to my alpha-readers: Rachael Poxon, Rachel Childers, and Michelle Mastandrea. Thank you so much for pulling me back from going off the cliff so many times. There were so many times I didn't believe in myself during this book and your belief and support in me, helped me get to that last page. Thank you for your personal chats, voice memos, and your enthusiasm for jumping into the doc as soon as I needed you. Your friendship and support is invaluable to me.

Another huge thank you to my beta readers: Ramishah Ahmad, Marla Knobb, and Melissa Schmidt. Your insight, support, and attention to detail was astounding! This book is better because of you and I am so lucky to have you on my team.

Thank you also to my girl and sub-in beta reader, Jenni Bara. If it's not approved by you, it's not getting published. That's how much I believe in your instincts and support.

A huge hug and thank you to my incredible author friends, Brittanee Nicole, Daphne Elliot, Emily Silver, Rin Sher, Monica Arya, and Garry Michael, who support me daily with giggles, chats, and phone calls. They've even put down what they're doing to get on a zoom call with me to walk me through how to create special editions (ahem, Emily Silver!) because I was too scared I'd mess something up on my own! I couldn't make it without you guys so thank you for everything.

And lastly, thank you to firefighters everywhere for keeping us safe, risking your lives everyday, and always managing to look so hella attractive.